THE ASTRAL'S BONDED

KIMBERLY M. RINGER

KIMBERLY M. RINGER

Contact Information: www.kimberlymringer.com

ISBN Paperback:978-1-957447-05-6

ISBN E-Book: 978-1-957447-06-3

First Edition: 2022

Content Warnings

This book contains situations of physical violence, explicit adult situations, and instances of murder and child death.

To K. Elle Morrison and my Hype Girls, Elisabeth Garner and T.S. Tappin. Thank you all for keeping me sane through everything that has lambasted me this year. When life got to be too much, you were there for me and helped make sure that I didn't fall into my own pit of darkness.

This book and series wouldn't exist if it were not for one specific Elisabeth Garner. So, thank you. When I sat there trying to write a contemporary romance, and it wasn't working, you guided me along a path that took off like a rocket.

CONTENTS

Ashstrike Sanctorum

The Overseeing Primals

Minstrel
Always an Astral & Seer
One Other to be determined

Astral Primal   Exorci Prima

Astrals and Exorci's

Species Primals

Species Heads

Kismot	Therugi
Werewolf	Immortals
Bacri	Seers
Aamanti	Phrenic
Changling	Ovexa
Iamu	Angels
Puroklets	Witches
Kir	Vampires
Calassei	Fae

CHAPTER 1

JADE

I had been driving for what felt like forever. Yeah, okay, I was being dramatic. I left the house this morning before the sun was up, and seven hours later I still had another forty minutes up a windy redwood lined road after I got off the 101. Not to mention that the book I had been listening to, just ended on a horrible cliffhanger. Cursing the author, I pulled into a little gas station and pulled in to top off the truck.

There were only two pumps at the station, and I backed in next to the unoccupied pump. I smiled a wordless greeting at the little old lady who had just put the nozzle back in across from me. Stretching a bit as I got to the pump, my back popped, release instantly flowed through my hips and down my legs. When I slid the card in, the card reader failed and I groaned. Why did it always work fine when I was at home, but any time I traveled, it decided to act up? I looked over the bed of the truck to see a woman no more than twenty filing her nails and smacking her gum at the register inside.

"How stereotypical." I muttered and went inside. I stood there for a moment, while she continued filing her nails, and finally said, "Excuse me. The card reader isn't working. Can I get fifty on pump two please?"

Her eyes scanned me. "You ain't from around here?"

"No shit." I said matching her snarky tone, but felt that little tang of energy in the air, telling me she was one of the supernatural living in the area. "Now are you going to give me my fifty on two or are you too busy giving those claws a manicure?"

There was a distant spark of recognition at the business name on the credit card I handed her, but she ignored it and said, "I like you ma'am. Sorry the readers don't work. Owners haven't been the best at updating things around here. Where you headed?"

"The name on the card didn't give you that answer, pup?" She blinked, and I raised an eyebrow at her and said, "Doing some work at the Porter Ranch for a bit." I said, narrowing my eyes at her.

She froze for a minute before she looked at the card again. "You are who they sent?"

I nodded, then rolled my eyes. "Nice of you to catch up."

"I can let Alpha know you've arrived." Her voice was low as the bell at the door rang.

"You do that." I didn't let any ounce of compassion or decency come through in my voice. Astrals weren't exactly known for asking questions first. "It will be a few days before I can meet up with him. Understood?"

"Yes ma'am." Her smile turned bright as she finished the transaction, and then asked, "Do you know Kolton Webster?"

I narrowed my gaze at her and crunched my nose. "I do."

"He is something to look at, for a human, ain't he?" She leaned back and sighed dramatically. "He says I'm too young for him, but age is just a number. Damn, the things I would let him do to me in my grandpa's barn."

"For a human?" I looked around, noting the one other person in the store. Stupid pup running her mouth.

"Don't worry about Chuck. He's one of the pack." She said, smiling brightly at the man who had walked in. What was with this pup? "So, Kolton. You gonna make a go at him?"

"He's not all that. Bit of an arrogant ass, actually." Gods knew that I had spent enough time on video calls with him on this project to come to that conclusion.

"Who cares. As long he could..."

I cut her off, and let a little of that Astral show in my eyes before saying, "Yeah. Keep that to yourself. Not really the discussion to be having with an Astral is it?" The man, Chuck, froze a few steps from me, and I saw the color drain from him. I nodded at him before turning back to the girl behind the counter. "Now, do I have fifty on two?"

"Prude." She said under her breath, and I giggled. If she only knew. "Yeah, it's set. Tell Kolton that Candy says hi. Oh, and if you have to pee, you probably should, it's a half hour to the Porter Ranch from here, and next stop isn't until you hit Brookings in Oregon."

"I'm good." I turned and hurried out to fill up the truck. I had bought it used, in cash, six months after getting this job, but it only had about fifteen thousand miles on it at the time, and had been in really good condition. I huffed a laugh as I put the nozzle in the tank and set it to fill. She'd gotten beat up on the job sites I've been on. I've put ninety thousand miles on her since then, and not all easy miles. Hell, the shocks had been replaced twice now, and even though the body looked good, she was a wreck under the hood. I was sure there was some serious engine work coming.

My phone rang and I answered it without looking, "This is Jade."

"Hi, Jade, it's Rose Porter."

"Hi, Rose. I just got into town. Any trouble today?"

"Nope. Been quiet since the rumor was that the Agency was bringing someone up."

"Of course, it has been." I sighed. "Topping off the truck quickly before I check in at the B&B."

Rose chuckled and said, "I'm assuming you met little Candy?"

"I did." I rolled my eyes and looked at the girl through the window.

"Let me guess, she grilled you about Kolton?"

"She mentioned him." I was not going to repeat any of it.

"The whole state knows how hard of a crush she has on him. He's turned her down on more than a few occasions, but you know how crushes go. He used to date her sister, so she won't let it go." Rose said and muttered something about thanking the Gods that was over. "So, by the time you stop at the B&B, you will be about an hour?"

"If what Candy tells me is true, then yes. I should be up there in about an hour."

"Great. I'll meet you at the office." Rose said as I heard Kolton call for her through the phone. "When you get to the gate on BeeLine, about 500 yards up will be the gate. You'll need to punch in 5233 to get in. You can use that any time you want to come onto the property."

"5233. Got it." I said finding a scrap sheet of paper and grabbing a pen from the center console.

"It's your name Jade. Just punch in your name on the keypad and it will go in." Rose said giggling. "I forget that some of the younger generations don't remember when people would use words for codes."

"Thanks, Rose. See you soon." I said hanging up and looking at the time. It was only one. I could be on the property by two -thirty. The click of the nozzle brought me out of my thoughts and I put it back in place and closed up the gas tank.

I checked text messages again, knowing that signal was only going to get worse from here on out, and addressed a couple of random things for projects being handled at the office, before putting some Jason Aldean on and heading out.

Rows of redwoods lined both sides of BeeLine Road, and I couldn't help but relax a bit as the tree canopy created of a tunnel effect over the road. I may have driven a little slower than was necessary just to enjoy it before getting to the turn off. When I reached the black iron gates, I slowed, punched the code that Rose had given me, and waited. The black iron gates crunched the gravel as they rolled out of the way, and I headed up the road.

It was another mile up the gravel road before I saw the main building. It was a two-story worn wood building with a walkway along the top level which looked to be the breezeway to rooms upstairs. Employee housing if I remember correctly. Downstairs had large open windows and doors to see into the main room downstairs.

Driving up to the main office, Rose Porter was talking to someone with their back turned. Male, probably around six – five, and as my eyes ran the length of him, he looked to be 220 pounds of pure muscle. While the blue jeans were not tight, they hugged in all the right places, ensuring that I knew that man did not miss leg day. That ass, though. I wanted to bounce quarters off that thing and itched to take the patch on the back pocket off with my teeth. Oh, how I wanted to get my hands on it.

"Get a grip, girl. You are on the clock. Pull your mind out of the gutter for just one damn moment." I muttered to myself as I took a long drink of my water that had long since turned warm on the long drive up here.

Rose lifted her hand to greet me. I waived back as I reached for my bag in the back seat of the truck. As I did, the man turned and I groaned. Of course, Mr. Muscles was none-other than Kolton Webster. All those video conferences had done nothing to show his height and what a beautiful body he had.

My cell rang in my hand, and when I looked down, I signaled to Rose I would be with her in just a minute. She nodded, and answered, "This is Jade."

"Hey, Jade. You're breaking up a bit, can you hear me okay?" Paul said.

I looked down at the phone screen and noticed the signal bounced between one and two bars, "Yes, I can hear you, but the signal is really bad out here. Just got to the Porter property. What do you need, Paul?"

"The Jackson project. The County came back and said that they need some changes to the electrical plans. Who is your contact at Zeus? Have you been talking to Bennie or Frey?"

"Frey. Bennie is in Barstow overseeing a project there. They will be able to get the changes made. I trust them more than Bennie at this point."

"What did Bennie do?" Paul said giggling.

"Nothing specifically, he's just swamped. Frey can take care of it. They've always answered our calls. I think Manuel has a project with them too. Their direct line should be in the file, but if you can't find it, Manuel can get it to you."

"Thanks Jade." There was a pause, then, "You -- video -- arrow?"

"You're breaking up. I'll be on the video call tomorrow morning. I have wifi at the B&B, so I should be able to go over anything you need. Thanks for the extra hands."

"No problem. Watch for horse shit." Paul said with a laugh.

"I'm on a horse rehab center. Horse shit just comes with the territory. I'll see ya'll tomorrow." I hung up and slipped my phone into my back pocket.

I had just reached in to grab my bag with the files for this project, when *Never Gonna Get It* started playing out of my back pocket. I pulled the phone out and just put it on speaker, so I could grab all my shit from the back seat. "I'm just getting to a property. Can I call you tonight?"

"Fine, Hooker, but you are up there for a month. If you are this grouchy now, I don't want you coming home. You need to find yourself someone to take care of you." Ryan said seriously.

"I can take care of myself sir."

"Please tell me you brought the entire 'go bag'?" Ryan teased. He had been my best friend since my second year at Fresno State. If Ryan were not strictly against taking females to bed, many thought we would have been married by now. "I'm serious. I don't want to deal with you if you come home after starting the trip this frustrated."

"Rye, you know me way too well." My eyes caught Rose and Kolton making their way toward the truck. Kolton took his ball cap off, and when he ran his fingers through his just too long wavy blonde hair, it made the muscles in his arms and shoulders move in ways that had me thinking about what was in that go bag.

"JADE!" Ryan screamed into the phone.

"I umm... what? Sorry I was distracted." I said as they stopped at the hood of the car. I quickly switched off the speakerphone, and said, "Seriously, I'll call you tonight."

"You sound a bit flustered. See some eye candy? Ohhh, tell me all about him."

"You have no shame, which is why I love you. I'll call you tonight. I have to work."

"Okay. Tonight, I want all the details. Don't you hold out on me Jade. I will make the drive up and beat your ass, if you leave so much as one tiny detail out."

"Bye!" I hung up on him and pulled my things out of the truck. I locked it, and when I turned around, Kolton stood there with his arms over that muscular chest. I swallowed and had to consciously look away to keep from having my mind wander.

"Glad to see you made it okay, Jade." Rose reached her hand out and I shook it firmly.

"Of course. I'm a visual person. Easier to see what I'm working with if I see for myself." My eyes flicked to Kolton, next to Rose, just as his gaze rose from looking me over before they met mine. There was something glinting in his eye, with his mouth just slightly hung open. If this hadn't been a work visit, I would have asked him if he wanted a drool bucket. He certainly looked like he needed one.

I blinked, looked back to Rose and said, "Do you want to walk the property with me? I can get a better idea on where things should be. I received the geographical reports the other day, but I haven't had a chance to look over them."

"I have a video meeting in about five minutes, but Kolton can walk you through. He knows where every branch and rock are on the property."

Great. All alone with Mr. Muscles who has the attitude to match. When I looked back at Kolton, his eyes were still on my face as he said, "It's no problem, Ms. Rose. It will give me a chance to show her where we would like to make some changes from the initial consultation and sketches."

His voice was different in person. Lower, more… sultry. A string of inappropriate thoughts went through my mind, and I could not help the ragged breath that I took before I said, "No problem at all, Ms. Porter. I would love to see what you and Kolton have in mind."

"Please, call me Rose. Mrs. Porter makes me sound like an old dirty grandma at one of my husband's social meetings." She grimaced.

"Yes, Rose." I smiled at her, and while we had had a great rapport on the video calls and phone conversations, respect and professionalism were something I usually kept pretty close to the front lines of any project. Not to mention, the long discussion about the wolves creating havoc on her property.

"You have your earpiece in case I need to reach you?" Rose had said to Kolton, who confirmed he did and tapped his ear. She smiled warmly at him before patting his arm. I could have sworn that she whispered for him to behave.

Behave indeed. I smirked before I said, "After you."

CHAPTER 2

KOLTON

"**F**uck me." I muttered as I watched Jade Romero step out of the Blue Ford Ranger. Fucking city truck. At least it was a 4x4.

"Kolton?" Ms. Rose said.

"Sorry." I said meekly. Jade turned to get something out of the back seat, and I didn't realize I had groaned until Ms. Rose put her hand on my forearm, stopping me before she studied the look on my face.

"I thought you said you two didn't really get along in those meetings?" Her eyebrows rose in question, "Or is it just that she can push your buttons, and now that you see her, you want her?"

"Ms. Rose." I groaned. "I don't want Jade Romero."

"Kolton Kash Webster." Upon seeing the look on my face, she chuckled and said, "I have known you your entire life. I can see it. You want her."

When I didn't say anything, she gave me the ever-famous Rose eye that meant that I had to start spewing the truth, or there was going to be a lot of trouble or embarrassment coming.

"Alright, I'll admit she's pretty. Gorgeous even, but she's demanding, controlling, and she thinks she is better than me. All I am is the hired help."

"You know that isn't true. Do you think I would have signed everything over to you when I die if that were the case?"

"Ms. Rose, that isn't what I mean."

"I know it's not." Rose looked back to where Jade was, whose cell phone rang and she held up a finger toward us as she answered it. Ms. Rose put her hand on my forearm, squeezed and said, "You are kind, sweet, and one of the hardest working men that I know. If I were 30 years younger, I'd make a buy for you."

I huffed a laugh. "Only Mr. Paul would probably have a say in that."

Ms. Rose studied me a moment, and her hair shifted in the breeze, making the silver under her dark brown hair shimmer. When her eyes narrowed, I asked, "Are you getting one of those Rose feelings again?"

"Something like that." Her eyes flicked over to where Jade was, and then back to me before she smiled brightly, and said, "She's the best at ranch conversions. Be nice, and if you get laid, just don't let it fuck up the project, okay?"

My eyes flew open, and I would have said something, but Ms. Jade Romero had turned back around and gave me a spectacular view of her well-defined ass.

I ran my hand over my face, trying to will it into something that gave off some sort of professional appearance. "Ms. Rose, I will be the pillar of professionality. I promise."

"You have no shame, which is why I love you. I'll call you tonight. I have to work." Jade rolled her eyes, and then there was a dramatic "Bye!" before she hung up the phone. Slinging her bag over her shoulder, she met us at the hood of her truck. Professionality be damned, I couldn't help but let my eyes roam from her boots, up her fitted jeans that clung to well-muscled thighs, full hips, and up her sides. My gaze hung for a moment on the bend of her throat as I pictured all kinds of non-professional things I would like to do to that body. I took a deep breath and crossed my arms across my chest to stop the thoughts, when I felt her eyes on me.

My eyes snapped to hers, and I wondered how I had not noticed the shine of wicked intelligence in her dark green eyes. Her long lashes fluttered as she blinked repeatedly before looking back to Ms. Rose. "Do you want to walk the property with me? We can get an idea on where things should be? I received the geographical reports the other day, but I haven't had a chance to look over them."

"I have a video meeting in about five minutes, but Kolton will walk you through. He knows where every branch and rock are on the property." Ms. Rose said.

It took everything I had not to whip my head around and not call her on the bullshit. She didn't have that meeting until tomorrow. I felt my shoulders tense though. I took a quick breath to let it go and held Jade's stare. It took effort to keep the heat out of my voice. "It's no problem, Ms. Rose. It will give me a chance to show her where we would like to make some changes since the initial consultation and sketches."

I swore her breath was ragged, and I let the side of my lip raise slightly as she said, "No problem at all, Ms. Porter. I would love to see what you and Kolton have in mind."

"You have your earpiece in case I need to reach you?"

"Yes, ma'am." I tapped my ear and Ms. Rose smiled before she patted my arm and under breath she said, "Behave, Kolton."

Jade matched the smirk on my lips and said, "After you."

"Where do you want to start?" I asked her.

Jade pulled the survey maps out, laying them out flat on the hood of her truck. The plans showed the existing house behind the office, and the lodging stables behind and to the right of the main house.

"Quick recap of new building locations?" I asked, and she nodded, pulling a pen out of her bag, and looking at me.

Those eyes were bright and thoughtful, and when I didn't say anything, "You are free to talk, Kolton."

I blinked and I saw her do the same and bite her lip before turning her gaze back to the plans. "Give me the overview layout. Then we can figure out where we want to start."

Damn if her biting her lip didn't make my pants tighter. I was so royally screwed. Why was this happening? Jade was arrogant, smart mouthed, and demanding. I took a deep breath and looked back to the maps, pointing the locations out as I said, "The plan was to build a new main house a little farther back on the property and have guest houses near the front stables."

She made a few extra notes, and studied them a long moment before she pointed to the back left corner of the property, her nails tapping on the paper. It didn't escape my notice that the thumb nail and skin looked to be a bit beat up. "Is this where the new critical care vet building will be?"

"Yes." I ran my finger along the back property line and added, "Only, we've rethought it and want to have a full vet clinic back there. While it will house the most critical of patients, it needs to be a fully stocked, self-serving, location. We were thinking of adding a whole line of stables along here, that are protected from the elements, with temperature controls, and make sure that there is housing for the on-site vet."

She studied the map more. "The Winchuck River runs along the back property. Getting the riparian exemption might be tough considering the flood plain, and we could run into some environmental issues." Her fingers cradled her chin and tapped her nose for a minute, but said, "If we move it back 100 yards, we should be alright. Elevation rises, and it gets us out of that floodplain. This area is all designated for open pasture anyway, right?"

"It is."

"There we go." She pulled out a pen and made a few notes on the plans, before turning to me. Jade came alive while working. It was so strange to see the shift from the all business girl in the video conferences to the enchanting woman before me. A bright smile crossed her face and was so bright that I couldn't help but blink. "Do you still want a clinic up here at the front of the property? In case there are any animals that need help and can't be moved to the back of the property?"

"Yeah." I took my ball cap off and ran my hand through my hair again. "Ms. Rose really wants Philip in the back of the property to concentrate on the most injured horses."

"Philip Montegue?" Her head snapped up and she looked around.

"Yeah. Know him?" I focused on the crunch of her eyes as she asked, then blinked, as she was surprised by the casualness in which I spoke about him. I wondered how she would even know him.

"Of him." She took a deep breath, and rubbed a tattoo on her wrist. It was a miniature knife. Well, it looked more like a throwing dagger. As she rubbed it, that color seemed to deepen, but she said, "What about for the livestock at the front of the property. Will Philip be overseeing those too?"

"Rose thought she might decide to hire another vet for a standard clinic up front. Open it up for locals. Generate a little more income for the center. Can a studio or small home be put up front, too?"

"I don't see why not. We have the room to move buildings around." She chewed on that same thumb that was beat up, and the section between her eyebrows bunched as she thought through it. "I would suggest moving the front stables and guest suites out toward the Johnson property line, and new residence back to this area, here. It's already pretty flat and it will help cut some expenses. Those funds will have to be redirected to the second vet residence."

I nodded. "I'm not the financing guy. I can tell you where we want things, and the practicalities of running the place, but when it comes to money, that's going to be your job, Jade."

"I'll talk to Rose about it, and we can crunch some numbers. Do you have a preferred construction company? Are we going to have to bring someone else in from Eureka, Bay Area or even Sacramento?"

"We haven't talked about it. There are some guys up here, but I don't think there is anyone who will have the manpower to do this size of job up here. Brookings would, but then you are talking about a different set of licensing requirements, and a whole new set of insurance and building code issues."

"Yeah. We need to keep with a California licensed contractor." She looked up at me, and my eyes settled on her chewing on the end of her pen. Then the way she bit that lower lip, when she removed it to make notes... Someone was playing a sick joke on me. I leaned against the grill of the truck, because the urge to do something wholly inappropriate was getting harder to resist.

"I talked to the guys. We were thinking of having the staff housing over near the river." I pointed to the outlook on the map, noticing a coffee stain on it. I chuckled.

"The river is still an issue. Have time to take me out there so I can take a look at it?"

"What can't the plans tell you?" I said teasing her, "Or is the coffee stain an issue."

She narrowed her eyes at me, put her hand on that very distracting hip, and said, "I can just go by the maps, but there can be differences. I like to see things for myself. Things like exactly where the trees are. Or do you want a large window that is meant to see the river, just be blocked by a row of trees, that no county is going to allow you to remove because they are good and healthy? So, it's those things I need to see. Otherwise, I wouldn't have come all the way up here. So, again, are you available to take me out there?"

"I'm teasing you, Jade. I can take you out there."

"You driving, or me?" She asked with a gleam in her eye that dared a smart-ass comment. Ask and you shall receive.

"I'll drive. Don't think your city truck can handle the road out."

"My... city truck?" She said looking at the pick-up she drove. I just nodded and I could see the irritation on her face as she said, "Fine. Let's see what this road looks like then."

CHAPTER 3

JADE

When I arrived the next morning, Kolton met me at the office and gave me an overview of the specialized communication system they have installed on the property.

"Have this in your ear while you are on site. Click the button and it will make the mic live." Kolton said, handing it to me. I noticed he was careful not to touch me as he tipped the small earpiece into the palm of my outstretched hand.

"Thank you." He had been much nicer and not so... controlling or defensive yesterday while we scouted the site out by the river. The location really was a great place for staff housing. It was close enough to the front of the property, and there was already a perimeter road that would allow them quick access at night to the back clinic if needed.

He blinked at me, and sat up straighter.

"What?"

"I never thought I would hear Jade Romero thank me for something." He looked honestly shocked.

"I'm not a royal bitch, Kolton." I said teasing him, but it still hurt a little. The longer I looked at him, the more I realized just how serious he was. "Did you seriously think I was a raging controlling bitch? Someone who wasn't capable of common decency?"

"No. Well, Jade, you have always been direct, to the point, and over the top professional on each one of those video calls." He said, then took a deep breath, and looked a little sheepish. It wasn't fair, because it was completely adorable. "So, yes. Controlling. Arrogant. Those words may have passed my lips."

My eyes couldn't help but go to those damn lips for a few seconds too long before they started to lift on one side. "I have to try to keep those meetings on track and get the most direct information so that I can make sure that I can make the property what the client wants. If we are telling truths this morning, I pretty much thought the same thing about you."

My eyes lifted to meet his, and he smiled. "Well, I may have just been mirroring you. I tend to turn into a bit of an asshole when people don't listen to me, or try to control me."

"So, since I'm here for the next month, let's start over." I said after studying him for a long moment. His eyes looked me up and down, stopping a moment too long on my neck, before settling on mine again. Something in me pulled toward him, but I couldn't figure out what it was. I reached my hand out, "I'm Jade Romero. Lead Designer and Architect for the Porter Ranch project. You are Kolton Webster, Foreman of Porter Ranch. Nice to meet you."

He took my hand, squeezed and I swear there was a glint in those brown eyes, "Nice to meet you, Jade."

"So, now that we have become decent human beings again, will you be joining me on the property walk today?" My eyes looked back down to our hands, and there was a tingling warmth that spread up from where they met. He hadn't let go of my hand, but he did rub his thumb across my knuckles twice, squeezed again, and then let go.

"Jade, I do have a job to do." He said with a small blush to his cheeks. "If you need anything or have questions though, you can reach me on comms. Where you headed?"

"Northeast side of the property. Out near the leach fields. Need to look at the sewer system."

His eyes rose. "You sure?"

"Why wouldn't I be?"

"Wouldn't you be worried of getting..." His eyes met mine and I saw the contemplation in his eyes and I smiled.

"You think because I'm from the Bay Area, that I don't know that sewer systems and leach fields are filled with biohazardous materials?"

"That isn't exactly..."

"Kolton, I'm used to this. I tromp around in a number of different property set ups. This won't be the first sewer system or leach field I've been in. I can be walking anywhere on this project and get shit on my boots." I raised an eyebrow at him, and he just tipped his head to the side as to say, that's fair. I took the earpiece and put it in my ear and rose to leave. "I'm going to head out. If I get too deep in shit, I'll call for you to help."

I quickly turned on my heels and heard his chuckle behind me, and when the door started to close behind me, it turned into downright laughter.

Just as I pulled up to the sewer station, I received a text message from my best friend, Ryan. Kolton had explained that there were some sections of the property where the cell towers would just randomly catch a signal, but warned me not to rely on it. Opening the message, I laughed.

Rye:
Spend time with Mr. Muscles this morning?

NO SHAME, FUCKER.
Of course. I told you I would last night.

> **Nothing is going to happen.**
> **Do you hear me?**

Rye:
No one has to know, babes.

> **I have a job to do here.**
> **Both for appearances and for the Agency.**
> **You know how it is. The two can't mix.**

Rye:
Just make sure the wolves don't get a hold of him.
Keep him out of the crossfire.

> **He's the foreman of the property, Rye.**
> **Not going to be an easy thing to do.**
> **Besides, you know I wear everything on my sleeve.**

Rye:
He could wear you like a sleeve.

> **RYAN FREDRICK HARRISON!**

I couldn't help but laugh, because well, he wasn't wrong, but it was so inappropriate. I looked down to yell at him some more, but noticed I lost the bar of service I had. I huffed a laugh, threw my phone in the truck, grabbed the earbud for the comms, and heard one of the guys giving Kolton a bad time.

A Hispanic accent mixed with a little southern twang said, "Come on Kolton. You're an ass man.

There is no way you missed that ass as she bent over in that city truck yesterday."

Kolton's voice came through, "Will ya'll just shut the fuck up?"

A new voice fed through the com. "When she left the office an hour ago, he had to go splash water on his face. He noticed."

Rose's laugh flitted through the comms. "Don't you boys have work to do?"

"Good morning, Ms. Rose." The two strange voices said.

The second person said, "Kolton add posts on the purchase order. Section JR10 has some that needs pounding."

Kolton's voice came through and said, "James. I swear your innuendo is pathetic." It was easy to tell Kolton was quickly getting tired of the bullshit, but I couldn't help but chuckle. It was such a boys' club. If that was James, then the accented voice belonged to Fernando.

"We just want you happy, man." Fernando said genuinely.

"Who says that's with Ms. Romero?" Kolton said grunting as I heard something land with a solid thud in the background.

"Who says it ain't? We just sayin'. She's got a good-looking ass. Just admit you noticed." Fernando's voice almost sounded fatherly when he said it.

Kolton sighed before saying, "Y'all know I gave her an earpiece earlier, right?"

I reached up and clicked the mic on. "Good morning, boys." I couldn't help but laugh as I said it.

Multiple voices came through at once. "Oh, fuck!"

Apologies came through from Fernando and James, and I just shook my head half smiling, "You are only sorry because you got caught. It's a boys' club. No shame."

Silence

Not willing to let it go, I said, "Besides, I know I have a nice ass. Thanks to everyone who was smart enough to notice."

It was Kolton's voice that came through next, sounding annoyed, yet meek, "Did you make it out there alright?"

"Yup. I'll let you know if I get too deep into shit, Kolton."

A light throaty chuckle, one that made me hot and wet in all the right places, came through as he said, "You mentioned that."

Then I clicked off the comms and noticed how the voices that came through were softer when I didn't have the mic on. I clicked it on again, and Kolton came through a bit louder, chastising the others. I knew this was the way it was, and while he would likely apologize to me later about it, he hadn't killed the chatter. He allowed it. Rose did, too. I sighed heavily, muttering to myself, and got my tablet out to make some notes.

I snagged some pictures of the manufacturing specs, and a few of the area. The little green light at the top panel lit up, and digital letters scrolled across the screen.

REPORTS GENERATED.

FORWARDING REPORTS.

REPORTS DELIVERED 12:22:44PM.

I blinked and looked down at my watch. It was after noon. Having that video call this morning, really had eaten up the morning. I sighed and went over to the latch and lifted it. Taking my flashlight, I looked down the tank, and noticed it was about two-thirds full.

"Is that..." I groaned. "Really?"

"Really what?" Kolton said through the earpiece.

"Shit. Sorry Kolton. I thought I had the mic off."

"It's all right, it was interesting to listen to you mumble to yourself, but now I'm wondering what you found out there."

"We will talk later."

"No, that sounded like you found something wrong." Kolton pressed.

"It's a pet peeve of mine." I grumbled. Stupid shits.

"What?" His voice was hard and one that I'm sure he used often with everyone on staff when he was not really asking, but rather demanding an answer.

"You all know that flushable wipes or wet wipes are NOT supposed to be flushed down the line, right?" I said through my teeth. Total silence met me. "Do you guys seriously not know what kind of damage those stupid things do to your sewer systems?"

"They are flushable though, Ms. Romero." James said. "Says so right on the package."

"And legos go down the drain, too. That doesn't mean that they degrade in the lines or tanks. Just because something can go down the line, doesn't mean it isn't going to cause you a shit-ton of repairs later. The fibers get caught, then more get caught, and so on, until you have a massive tight ball, causing a backup and other issues."

"The grinders—" James started to say, but I interrupted him, "Are just going to get clogged with these things. They don't grind up the wipes into little pieces. Are you seriously telling me you've never had to pull the pumps and unthread them from the grinders trying to remove these things?"

"We have, but there was rope and other things, too." Fernando said softly. "Sorry, Ms. Romero."

"Don't apologize to me. Apologize to Ms. Rose." I let out a long breath.

"Is there damage now?" Kolton said carefully.

"Not on a cursory look, but there are a bunch hanging from your screens. You aren't filtering properly. When do you pump next?" I asked, looking at the screens and the intake.

"It's scheduled for in four months." Kolton said, and I could almost see him either rubbing the back of his neck or rubbing his face. "I'm assuming you would recommend we have that done sooner to prevent any issues."

"Oh, look, he does have some brains under that thick skull." I teased as laughter came through. "Your intake looks like you are starting to get some build up. Maybe a hydro-flush to get them all in one spot to be pumped. Otherwise, this is going to be an issue again in six months. I will say, I'm impressed with your fire clearance, though."

"Ahh, thank you for noticing." Kolton said sarcastically.

"Oh, does Kolton want a gold star?" I teased and rolled my eyes. There was silence again on the coms, and I had to wonder what they were all thinking. "I'm heading to the leach field to the north of here."

There was still silence for a long while before Fernando said, "Kolton, I swear on my mother, if you don't make a move, one of us will."

"Shut up. You know she can still hear you, right?" Kolton said.

"I know." Fernando said. "Don't make it any less true."

"Boys club indeed." I muttered. When I got the info off the equipment I needed, I double checked to make sure the location was right on the maps, and then headed back to the truck.

Two hours after trudging through the leach field I reminded myself that I needed to sanitize my boots before going back into any of the buildings. I usually kept a second pair in the truck, and when I got there, a folded sheet of paper was under the wiper.

I looked around and thought I saw movement at the tree line. "You could just talk to me." I shouted, but whoever it was, just bounded off into the trees. There was more movement off to my right, and then off to my left. A small smile crossed my lips as I wondered just how many he had surrounding the leach field.

Lifting the note out from under the windshield wiper and unfolding it, I sighed. I set my tablet and back into the back seat, turned the comms off, set the ear piece in the center console, and shut the door. Leaning against the truck, I looked at the note. It was wrapped tightly with twine, and I rolled my eyes. I tapped on my wrist, and one of the shuriken's sprung from the tattoo inked there. I used it to cut through the twine and put it between my teeth as I finished opening the letter.

ASTRAL,

ALPHA IS NOT PLEASED WITH WAITING.

EXPECT HIM TO MAKE HIS MOVE SOON.

HE WILL TAKE IT BY FORCE.

-G

"The Alpha can wait. He will do and say what I command." I grumbled. I expected him to make contact any time now that I was onsite, regardless of the fact I told the pup at the station it would be next week. I heard rustling behind me, and smiled as I turned around and saw him standing there.

"Yet, here I am." A voice that tried to promise death said.

My eyes flicked up to meet Alpha Devon's. "Did you think I didn't expect you here?"

Alpha Devon was shorter than I expected. Only about an inch taller than I, and with short black hair, I watched his hazel eyes scan me from head to toe. "Only because the Agency is trying to keep things away from the humans."

I tucked the note into my pocket, and crossed my arms. "The Agency denied your request."

A growl came up his throat. "My pack needs the land."

"Again, you should have thought of that before growing too big for your britches."

"Astral…"

"What?" I said, my daggers instantly in my hands. "We can discuss other avenues for you. Sign off on use of the National Forest?"

"We already utilize all of Klamath." He said, taking a breath to calm himself.

"Apparently without Agency authorization. You must be behind on your paperwork." I saw him blink, before I said, "I can discuss usage of Rogue River – Siskiyou, but only as far north as Cave Junction. Any further north and there will be territory disputes with the Kismots." The mountain lion shifters would already be pissed at me giving them any of that area, but I could work it out with their King.

There was a huff of disgust from Alpha Devon, and I stared him down, raising an eyebrow. "That is the only offer on the table. Either you deal with your current allotment of territory, or you take the southern portion in Oregon."

"I want the wild Porter property."

"And you won't have it."

"We will see about that." Devon said as he turned on his heels and strode off.

"I didn't dismiss you." I threw my hand out, and he froze as my power wrapped around him. His head swiveled in that animalistic way, and I smirked. "Don't forget who I am, Devon. I am higher on the food chain than you. Don't forget that I speak for the Agency. I am who you will be dealing with here. It's best you don't piss me off."

As I released him, he growled and shifted. "You have my offer. Speak with your pack council. Let me know your decision."

There was a small nod of his head, and just as he bounded into the forest, a man stood at the tree line staring at me. I tapped the note in my back pocket and he nodded. Well, I know who left it then.

When I was sure they had all left, I got back into the truck, and put the comms back in my ear. I sat back and leaned my head against the headrest for a few minutes, before a crackling filled in my ear.

"Jade, you there?" His voice came through carefully. I sighed. Did I really want to answer and deal with Kolton right now? I looked over at the daggers and knives on the passenger side seat, and with a wave of my hand, the weapons were gone.

"Jade?"

Fuck it. Why not? "Yeah, Kolton. What's up?"

"Take your earpiece out and turn the nob two clicks." He hesitated for a moment and said with a heavy breath, "Please?"

"Hold on a second." I took it out, rotated it two clicks, and pushed the mic down. I took a deep breath before I said, "Done."

"It's just us on the line now."

"Okay." I blinked. "What's wrong?"

"I wanted to apologize for the banter earlier." He said, his voice low.

"Kolton, I know it's a boys' club. I get it."

"Doesn't mean it was okay. We all have the utmost respect for you."

"Utmost respect?" I said laughing. "You hated me, and we just started over this morning, Kolton."

"I didn't hate you." He said defensively. "I just thought you were controlling and arrogant. That doesn't equal hate."

"You didn't stop it, earlier." I let a little of the hurt I felt come through. "I won't be treated as a sex symbol here, Kolton. Put your guys straight. I've worked too hard to earn the amount of respect I have in a very male dominated profession. Put your guys straight." I emphasized every word of the last sentence.

"I will, Jade." He said, and then a moment later, said, "I promise you that."

"Alright. I'm heading back." I said starting the truck and turning around. "You staying on the line here, or do I need to get back on the main one?"

"Stay here. I don't want to listen to them right now."

"Can't take the teasing?"

"It's not that." There was something in his voice that I couldn't read. I hit the straightaway of the road and pushed the pedal down.

"What is it, then?" I asked, and I would be lying if I didn't want to know what he thought of my ass. I spent too many leg days to get my ass looking as good as it did.

There was a long silence before he finally said, "Nothing."

I let it go, because well, this truce was a tentative thing. My mind wandered for a long moment, and then was a blur rolled across my hood. The next thing I knew, I was sitting sideways, and Kolton was yelling in my ear, "Jade!"

"Yeah." I said but blinked, mildly dazed.

"What is that thrashing noise?" He asked. I looked over to see part of a deer rack poking through the windshield. Just as my windshield cracked, it got loose and took off.

Then there was silence, when clarity hit me like a mack truck.

"Fuck! I hit a fucking deer." I undid the seatbelt, and climbed over the console and forced the passenger door open.

"Jade. What's going on? Are you okay? Where are you?" Kolton sounded frantic. I heard a bunch of rustling, and then a truck started. "Where are you, Jade?"

"I'm fine, Kolton. I'm standing on the road, staring at my city truck. That is now ready for the fucking pick n' pull."

A burst of laughter came through. "Finally admitting to the city truck huh?"

"Fuck off, Kolton. I don't... nevermind. Not the point right now. Come and get it out of the ditch so we can see just how much damage there is."

"Pull it out of the ditch?" He said carefully. I could hear the truck he was driving on the other end crawl to a stop. "Did I hear you right?"

I walked around to the front of the truck and the front left corner was completely bashed in against a boulder. "You heard me right. I need pulled from a ditch."

"Alright." He said carefully. "I'll make a stop and get the wench."

"Fuck!" I said, noting the angle of the tire. I kicked at a rock and sent it sailing through the air where it hit a tree, bark spraying in every direction. Oops. "I'm not gonna be able to drive it back. Do you guys have a flat bed?"

"Not driveable?" He said, seemingly calmer.

"Nope. Wheel is bent, I think. Won't know more until we get it out."

"Alright. Give me a few."

He drove up about thirty minutes later, and I was just sitting on the ground leaning against the bent tire, playing with the dagger from my thigh. Just before he could see it, I waved my hand, and it disintegrated. He leaned out of the window and said, "Need some help there, pretty lady?"

"Asshole." I muttered under my breath, getting up and brushing my hands off. When I stood, I rolled my shoulders, and when I looked back at him, he put the truck in park, and got out.

"Jade, you're bleeding." He said turning me to face him.

"I'm fine." I tried to push him off, but he held tight, and hauled me back to the truck. He reached in and pulled a first aid kit out, rummaged around, and then he was standing just in front of me again. "I'm fine."

"Shut up." He went to clean my face up, and I couldn't help but notice how gentle he was about it. I looked at him, and his sparkling eyes met mine. "City girl."

I rolled my eyes. "Yeah because, it's my fault a fucking deer decided to play chicken with my truck."

He huffed a laugh, and the musky mint smell of him made my eyes go back to his. He was staring at me, and I honestly didn't know what I felt in that moment. Attraction, frustration, anger. It was all there. All I knew was that feeling I had yesterday, the one pulling me toward him, was still there. His thumb ran back and forth on my cheek after he stopped, and then there was someone else talking in my ear.

"Kolton? Jade?" James' voice fed through.

"Yeah. We are here." Kolton said, without taking his eyes from mine.

"Oh, good. We wondered where you ran off to. Is everything okay?" James actually sounded a little worried. "You took off in the flat bed like someone was dying."

My eyes crunched in confusion. Why would he have been that worried? I told him I was fine, but there was that tug in my chest again.

"Yeah. Jade's truck is in a ditch. I grabbed the flatbed so I could bring it back and we can see how much damage there really is." Kolton said, but his voice was soft and heated. That alone made me want to squeeze my legs together, because damn if it didn't heat all the places that my go-bag was used for.

"Shit! Jade, you okay?"

"I'm... I'm fine. Deer decided to play chicken without warning me." I said, but was only half paying attention. Why couldn't I pull my gaze from Kolton? I forced myself to take a deep breath as I heard someone say something, but I didn't comprehend it at all.

"Fernando can handle it. I'll see you in a couple hours." He reached up, and clicked the mic off, and when I didn't move, he reached up and turned mine off for me, too. With a too-gentle touch to my jaw, he backed away, and said, "Go ahead and sit in the cab, Jade. I'll get your truck loaded."

I blinked, and then he was pulling out what he needed. I climbed up into the passenger seat of the truck, laid the seat back, and threw my arm over my eyes. Nothing was going right. Nothing was going as planned. Devon was supposed to take the deal. I was just supposed to be here to make sure it went smoothly. Most of these 'negotiations' were just that, a little back and forth, but ultimately it was pretty diplomatic. Only, the look in Devon's eye, and the way he growled at me, it was pure violence. This was going to get ugly. I just knew it.

I looked back at the truck and groaned. My shoulder hurt, and I knew I would hurt more in the morning, but all I could think about was how soft Kolton's eyes were, the way he had been looking at me, the way I had been looking at him. That pulsing between my legs was not helping, either. I was in so, so much trouble. I needed to keep myself together, but damn.

Kolton got in the cab and started the truck, but paused, before asking, "You, okay?"

"Yeah. Fine for someone who just totaled her truck and now has to figure out how to buy a new one."

"You don't know it is totaled." He was trying to comfort me, which, in itself, was sweet.

"Kolton, that truck has over a hundred thousand miles on it, and was already on the brink of having major engine work done. I've replaced the shocks, twice, because I'm not easy on my city truck." I lifted my arm to look at him, and he blinked, looked back to my truck, and then back at me.

"It will all work out, Jade." He said, his voice mixed with something I couldn't place. "It always does. Now, let's get it out of the ditch and to the shop. Fernando is a wizard. You are welcome to stay on the property tonight, though the guest rooms are more storerooms right now, or I can take you back to the B&B."

I was shocked at the offer. "All my stuff is at the B&B. Can someone bring me back in the morning?"

A small lifting of the right side of his mouth had my toes curling as he said, "I'm sure we can make arrangements for you. If the truck is totaled, you borrow one of ours until you get something sorted out."

"Thank you, Kolton." I said, meeting his eyes so he knew how sincere I was about it. "Thank you for coming to my rescue today, and for helping out."

"Shit. Two thank you's from Jade Romero in a day." He shook his head, "Now I know I'm gonna wake up and realize this is all a dream."

I just huffed a laugh as he hauled my truck out of the ditch.

CHAPTER 4

JADE

It had been three days since I started using Kolton's truck and as I pulled off the fire road, I had to admit the fact that it had GPS was extraordinarily helpful. There was one thing that bothered me, though. It smelled like him. The whole damn cab was a distraction and had me thinking about how close he was to me after my truck ended up in the ditch. That, and how I couldn't pull my eyes from him.

When I reached the two-mile marker off the deer trail, I stopped, got out of the truck, and leaned against the bed. I had given Devon a rough location on where to meet me. He could use those infamous tracking skills of his to find me. It took maybe five minutes for Devon and two of his goons to show up, one of which I recognized from the pack's file.

Devon shifted from his pitch-black wolf form and crossed his arms. He was roughly six-five, with a set of muscles and body that most of my romance authors would love to have him model for the cover of their books. He had a scruff of a beard, but it wasn't neat and clean. I wondered if that was due to stress, or if he was trying to actually grow it out.

"Oh, look you brought your Beta, and…" I tilted my head, and looked the third male up and down. "Who is this? I don't recognize him."

"They are both my Beta's." Devon said and I raised an eyebrow at him.

"Can't keep your pack together on your own, so that you have two betas?"

"We have tripled in size. So, yes, I need two betas to help keep order and structure within the pack."

I shrugged. "You know the procedures with the Agency. Make sure you follow them, Devon."

"That is Alpha Devon to you, Astral." The new beta ground out.

"He is whatever I want to call him. If I want to call him Omega, I will." I smirked, and the growl that came through both of Devon's betas brought me so much satisfaction. "However, I do know that he runs the pack, so I at least address him by his name."

A low growl emanated from him, and I moved. One second, he was standing, head low, growling at me like the mutt he was, the next he was flat on his back, my dagger at his throat, and the heel to my boot on his dick. I pressed the tip of the dagger into his skin, just enough so that I didn't break skin, and said, "Now, you don't seem to know your place. I believe you are to be seen and not heard. Probably supposed to be here as an intimidation tactic. Considering your current position, obviously, isn't working too well for you."

"Enough." Devon growled.

"Agreed." I stood, but let my heel grind into his crotch a bit, and smiled as he winced. When he stood and dusted himself off, his eyes flicked to Devon, who shook his head the smallest bit. I flicked the dagger up in the air, and caught it by the point. "Now, what has the pack council decided? Do you want me to negotiate for more space north?"

"No. You will provide us full access to the Porter wildland."

"And, I told you, you can't have it."

"Astral."

"No."

Devon's hands ball into fists. "Reconsider your stance, Astral."

"No." I stood my ground. "No is a complete sentence. There will be no bullying me into accepting your proposition. You know who Rose Porter is, and the full extent of why that land won't be provided to you. Don't press the matter, *Alpha*."

I smiled at the growling at my back. I felt them come closer, and when they were within a couple feet, I moved my head slightly, looking over my shoulder. In the span of one second, there was an imperceptible move of Devon's head, the next the two betas were reaching for my shoulders. Whirling around, and pulling two daggers from my thighs, I ducked under their arms and between them, and pressed the daggers against their throats while standing behind them.

"While it is abundantly clear you have no respect for Ms. Porter or the Agency, I suggest that you start showing a little respect for the fact that I am an Astral." I said with as much calm as I could muster.

"We've taken Astral before." The new addition said through his teeth, but he didn't dare move for fear I would rip open the carotid artery with my dagger.

I raised an eyebrow at Devon, and he said, "His previous pack. It's one reason we were able to absorb them. No alpha." He stood straighter. "They needed guidance."

"Well, is *now* a good time to mention that I'm not just any Astral, but a Primal?" I felt him tense even more at that, and I pushed some of my power out toward them and shoved them toward Devon.

Devon growled deep in his throat, turned to leave, but popped his claws out and punctured the front tire. "We are done here. Have fun getting back."

Before he could move much further, I pulled a dagger on him, forcing him to stop the shift he started.

"Fuck, Astral. You almost killed me."

"You trashed the tire."

"You pissed me off."

"Aww, poor pup didn't get his way and the little girl out maneuvered his big bad puppies, so he damages someone's property?"

"Bitch." The new beta said, causing my hand to twitch, and a small drop of blood to run down Devon's neck.

"You drew an Alpha's blood. You know that is a call for war." Beta One said. I believed his name was Darrell.

"To be fair, it was an accident. Though, I'm not really sorry." I shrugged. "Devon, you need to show a little respect to those higher on the food chain."

"I would be careful threatening me, Astral. I saw how that Porter foreman looked and touched you. Like he'd like to take you to bed and—"

"Leave the humans out of this. Don't make me wipe out your entire pack, Devon."

"Little protective, Astral?" Devon asked and I pressed on that spot on his neck that brought him to his knees. "You drew Alpha blood. War is coming for you, Astral. The Agency won't be able to protect you now."

I pressed the tip of the dagger in more, a larger bead of blood welled at the tip, before slowly running down his throat. Taking a breath through my nose, I smiled as he hissed. "Leave the humans out of this. I am one of the few people on this planet that can draw an Alpha's blood. So, claim it all you fucking want, *Alpha*, but I can cut your head off, and your Betas can't do fucking shit to me."

I met each of the beta's eyes and they felt the power I had put into those words. I pushed Devon away from me, who caught himself before face planting, and quickly stood up, backing away from me.

The betas shifted into their wolf forms, and growled at me. I flipped the daggers in my hands, raising my eyebrows at them. "I'm a fucking Astral Primal. You have no claim or call to make against me. You are beneath me. I don't give two shits if there is an ounce of respect, but you *will* do what I say. Back the fuck off. You don't get the Porter Ranch. You want to grow your pack? Have at it, but you need to gain land through other means than brute force. You've been given options, Devon."

"You will address me as Alpha and you will give me what I want or suffer the consequences."

"I will do no such thing. Rose Porter is protected. She and everything she owns is off limits. That includes her staff. Do. I. Make. Myself. Clear?"

"Astral." Devon said, resisting a half second before shifting and bringing his head lower just a fraction. His lackeys growled and repeated the motion, but I felt Devon's words, *"This isn't over."* Before they lunged into the forest.

I listened carefully to make sure they had indeed left, before waving the daggers to dust and taking a deep breath. "FUCK!" I shouted and kicked a small branch on the ground that went flinging into the brush. There was a quick scattering of whatever it was that was taking cover, and I groaned. I hated having to tip my hand so much this early in negotiations. Usually we were much further along when I had to pull the Primal card, or even draw blood on anyone.

"This is going to be a complete shit show by the time we are done." I muttered and put my hands on my hips, before looking over at the tire now completely flat on the truck. "Kolton's gonna be pissed." I went and looked under the bed of the truck for the spare. After removing it, I bounced it, and... flat.

"Really? You have to be fucking kidding me. Fuck." I leaned against the truck and hit the button at my ear. Tired and frustrated, I ground out, "Kolton."

"Jade? Everything alright?" His voice came through huffy and then he grunted. I heard what sounded like a hay bale being tossed, and then a *thunk, thunk.*

"I'm fine, but ahh..." I hesitated. How was I going to explain a claw to the tire? "A stick, well more like a branch."

"What did you do to my truck?" Kolton said, more than a little frustrated.

"It wasn't my fault... entirely. It's not my fault that your truck couldn't handle a little four wheeling." I looked around and giggled. Yeah. Let's go with that story.

"Are you in a ditch again?"

"No, but your spare is flat as a fucking pancake, and you have a flat."

"I've been meaning to take care of that." He muttered, but then groaned. "Where are you? I'll send someone out there to get ya."

"North-east quad, about two miles off the deer trail." There was a long silence, and when there still wasn't anything, I said, "Kolton?"

"Yeah. Sorry. You are where?"

"North-east quad, about two miles off the deer trail."

"When you said you took my truck four wheeling, you meant it." He said, but then there was anger and confusion, "Why in the hell you out that far? Why are you in the wild land?"

Well, if that wasn't a damn good question. There was absolutely no construction occurring out this way, and Kolton had been there when Rose had said she wanted to keep this area wild. "I was checking the groundwater levels out here. That way we could plan for an extra well if needed." There. Let him have that.

"We got six different... You know what. I'm not gonna tell you how do your fucking job, but I need to do mine." There was the slamming of a truck door, and then he said, "Give me a few minutes. I'll pick up a spare, and get out of there."

"Thanks."

I took a deep breath, and pulled the sat phone out of the bottom of my bag.

I pushed the button for it to connect and a moment later a deep rumbling voice, "Hello dear, Jade."

"Carlos."

"I take it you just met with Devon?"

"I did." I chuckled. "He didn't take it well. Says his pack is growing and he needs the hunting grounds. Oh, and he's already utilizing Klamath, *and* he has two betas. I may have reminded him that he needs to file his paperwork."

"What does he really want out of all of this?"

"He wants all the wild area of the Porter Ranch."

"Sucks for him, doesn't it? If he wants to grow his pack, he needs to rightfully address the landscape issue." Carlos said, chuckling through the phone.

"Pretty much what I told him." I was quiet for a moment before I let out a long breath and said, "Carlos. Two things. First, heads up. I drew Alpha blood. Second."

I didn't know how to say it, but after talking to Rose this morning, I knew, just knew she had seen something having to do with me. "Rose has seen something she isn't telling me about. Has she told you about it?"

"Rose and I have spoken."

"Are you going to tell me? Or are you going to keep me in the dark and jeopardize this whole thing?" I rolled my eyes and I heard Carlos chuckle.

"Jade, me keeping it from you won't jeopardize what you are doing with the pack." I heard him heave a heavy sigh before he said, "As for you drawing blood on an Alpha, your position protects you. It won't be a problem."

"I don't think my position as an Astral with Ashstrike Sanctorum means two shits to him. I did it in front of his betas. He is going to take it as a personal insult. He used his fucking claws and popped the tire on the truck I'm having to borrow. Kolton, I think, is a bit pissed he has to come out and rescue me, again. And before you say anything, you know I know how to change a fucking tire. The spare is flat."

"Kolton Webster?"

"Is there another Kolton I should know about around here, Carlos?" An amused chuckle rang through the phone, but he didn't say anything. "Carlos. What aren't you telling me?"

"He is going to get pretty entangled in this."

My heart stopped. "He's human, Carlos. He won't survive a fight with the pack."

"If what Rose is telling me comes true, it's more complicated than that."

"If Rose told you something, you know it will. It's just a matter of how and when. She's the best Seer on the Pacific. Fuck, maybe the whole North American continent. Only Bet in Belize has a better record than Rose Porter."

"I know, which means you need to make Kolton aware." His voice was pained, as if each word hurt to say it.

I didn't move a muscle. Carlos had never told an Astral to tell a human of what was happening. "Why does that scare the hell out of me, Carlos?"

"I..." Carlos said, but it was if the words were stuck in his throat. "Jade, you are family. I want you happy, okay? Please just trust me on this. I shouldn't be giving you this order, but for you, I'm going to."

"What in the fuck does that even mean?" I bit back. I looked at my watch. "Explain. I got maybe five minutes before Kolton shows up with the tire and I need to put the sat phone away."

"Astral, I am ordering you to tell Kolton Webster of our world and ensure he stays safe."

"Carlos..." I gulped. "I'll carry out the orders, but I have to tell you something else." I heard a truck off in the distance, so had to make this fast.

"You already know you have feelings for Kolton, don't you?"

"I think there is something going on. There is something, pulling me to him, and I don't know what it is. It scares me, Carlos. You know I haven't allowed myself to be close with anyone for a very long time because of this job. The last time it did, it cost me his life, and almost mine. I can't lose anyone important again."

"I know. It will all work out. I promise. *Te amo, mija.* Be safe."

"Love you too, Carlos." There was a click on the other end, and my heart was racing at all that was just said, at the memories flooding around me. Sliding the phone into the bottom of the bag, I crumpled to the ground as it all crashed down on me. I put my head down on my knees and watched everything that had happened four years ago go through my head again.

I can't go through that again, but I... I felt my chest shudder. I put my head down between my arms again, tried to shut off all those feelings, and shove all those images of Daniel getting slaughtered by the Selki in Indonesia.

We had worked together for years, and because of his unwillingness to listen to reason, he dove straight down into the depths of the Selki's lair. Just as I had reached where they were holding him, they shredded him apart. The waters had turned red with his blood.

They left nothing of him to bury. I had nearly lost my left arm in that fight to get out. Every emotion that I had felt that day came rushing back over me.

A hand was on the side of my knee as a voice that felt like velvet said, "Jade?" My head snapped up, and Kolton's face filled my view. "Oh my god. What's wrong? Are you hurt?"

I just threw my arms around his neck and held him, trying to remember how to breathe. I had to get myself back under control. I had to shove it all away again. His arms wrapped around my waist and he held me close.

"Are you hurt?" He asked again, and I shook my head. "Okay." He lifted me, popped the tailgate to the truck, and sat me down on it. I hadn't unwrapped my arms from around his neck, and had to admit I was surprised by his ability to lift and move me so effortlessly. I was by no means small and dainty. I liked to eat. I had muscle on me, and just being an Astral insured I was hefty. We had to be in order to hold our own in a fight.

When the tears finally subsided, I pulled back, and I reached up to wipe my face, but he caught my hands in his. He took a cloth out of his pocket and wiped my face as he said, "Your hands are filthy. Don't want to smudge mud all over that beautiful face."

My heart leapt, and there was a small smile on his face. "Now, do you want to tell me what is wrong?"

I shook my head. "Just sitting idle left me too much time to think about some things in my past that hurt."

"I'm here if you need to talk." He said carefully. "No that doesn't mean now. I realize you may not want to right now, and just want to stuff all those feelings away, but when or if you want to talk. Come find me."

"You were so mad earlier when I told you I broke your truck, though." My voice sounded so small.

"Well, because I'm out here fixing my truck instead of working on the million other things that need to get done. James is a bit pissed he now has to unload all the hay on his own." A small smile crossed his face, and I returned it. He kissed my forehead quickly, and I froze as he said, "Now, let's get this tire changed."

CHAPTER 5

KOLTON

When she called me and told me she needed rescuing again, I seethed the entire way to the point on the map where the GPS said she was. All of our trucks were equipped with them. She had given me a good idea of where she was, and wasn't actually too far off. I was impressed, but damn if this wasn't going to put me so behind schedule today. I couldn't afford to be rescuing Jade all the time.

When I saw her crumpled up next to the truck, crying, every protective instinct I had pulled me toward her. I would be lying if something hadn't been pulling me toward her the last few days. It was stupid and reckless, but here I was holding her, wiping her tears and offering to be a shoulder for her to cry on any time.

Then I kissed her damn forehead like it was the most natural thing in the world. I didn't miss how she had frozen at the gesture, but I just turned and got the jack to fix the truck.

What was wrong with me? Hell, the other day, I couldn't take my eyes off her. With each crank of the jack, I let any frustration flow into it and fuel my muscles. She stood there watching, and holding the good tire between those two long beautiful legs of hers. I suppressed a groan, and cranked the jack one more time.

"Need any help?" She asked, knowing there wasn't anything she could do, but it was nice she asked anyway.

I shook my head, unable to make myself say anything looking up at her, and finished taking the old tire off. She rolled the new one over, and while I got it secured, she threw the old one into the bed of the truck like she had been tossing tires her whole life. When the truck was set and ready to go, I turned to her and asked, "You okay to drive back?"

"Yeah." She took a deep breath, and when she looked at me there were a million words in those eyes. "Kolton?"

I raised my eyebrows in question.

"Nevermind." She turned and opened the door to the truck. "Thanks for the tire change."

I ran around to the driver's door and kept her from closing it. "Jade. What is it?"

Tears lined her eyes again, and I honestly didn't know what could be going through her mind.

"Not today, okay?" She said, reaching up and putting her hand on my cheek. "Not today, but soon. We need to talk."

I blinked. There was so much in that gaze that I didn't know where to start. She was also touching me like... like I was someone important. I craved that touch, and I leaned into it. I wanted to turn my head and kiss her palm, but instead I just reached up and laid my hand over hers. It was only then I realized she didn't say she wanted to talk, but that we needed to talk.

"Whenever you are ready." My heart was thudding so hard and fast, and I noticed that her eyes fixated on my chest before widening and meeting mine again.

"I'm calling it for the day. Can you follow me back? I'll ask Rose to take me back to the B&B." Her voice was shaky, and I struggled against the need to ask yet again if she was okay. She wasn't, but ...

I nodded, and she started the truck. Stepping back and heading back to my own, shaking my head. There was something about Jade that I couldn't deny. I don't know what happened just now, but I wanted answers. Fuck that, I wanted to do anything to have her keep looking at me like that. No one had ever looked at me with that much depth.

The entire way back, I struggled with what to say and do next. When she asked Rose to give her a ride back, Rose gave me a mischievous look and asked, "Kolton can give you a ride back."

"Rose, I would appreciate it if you could." Her voice was so drained. "I have some questions for you."

Rose looked at me again, and I gave her the out she wanted. "I have some things that still need to be done. One of which is getting that tire fixed so that Jade can have a functioning truck tomorrow."

"I'll be working near the front of the property. I don't need a truck tomorrow. It's fine. No rush." She was chewing on her thumb again and looking at the ground.

"Okay. We will see you at eight." She just nodded an acknowledgment and headed for Rose's car.

CHAPTER 6

KOLTON

Fernando had been working on fixing Jade's truck over the last few days, and promised to have it up and running in just a few more. Jade had been lucky. The axel was fine, and there wasn't much under the hood damage. The front end had some extensive damage from the bolder she rolled into, and the deer had fucked the grill and windshield, but it was technically drivable. It was mostly cosmetic, and Fernando said he and James could get it cleaned up enough. I ordered the windshield this morning and it was set to arrive by the end of next week. Until then, she could continue to have my truck for getting around the property.

When I picked her up this morning, she was a bit surprised to see it was me. Rose had picked her up the last couple of days, and James had begged to do it this morning. Over my dead body was I allowing him alone with her.

"I half expected Rose, or for you to send one of the guys." She said opening the door.

I just shrugged. "No big deal."

Yes, I was lying through my teeth. I couldn't get her out of my head last night. All I could see were those green eyes and full hips. Then it was the thought of how her skin felt under mine, the way she had held my face in the palm of her hand, and the panic I had felt when she went silent on comms, before she said the truck was in a ditch.

Then, she called me yesterday saying that she broke my truck again. Sure, I was frustrated I was behind schedule and had to work late to get things done, but when she groaned my name across the comms... God, I feared she had seriously hurt herself and she thought I was mad at her. She's been here for a week and she's already getting under my skin.

She'll be out doing her thing today, and I'll be working on rebuilding that damn fence out on the north side. I could get her out of my head. I had to get her out of my head.

"Kolton?" Her hand was resting on my forearm resting on the center console. I blinked. Had she been talking?

"I'm sorry. What did you say?" I felt a bit dumbstruck, and I hadn't even noticed she had climbed up into the truck. I looked into the backseat and her bag sat there too. I really had been out of it. As I turned my sights back to her, her long brown hair was sticking out of a ballcap of her own. I looked at the front of it, and chuckled, but couldn't help but reach up and flick the bill. "What does the saying mean to you exactly?"

"It's a quote from one of my favorite books, and it resonated with me. Reminds me to never give up. Don't yield to the hard stuff. Fight through it all. Saw the hat online, and bought it from a small shop maker who does all her own embroidery work." She shrugged as if it meant nothing, but I tipped my head a little while studying her.

"What?"

"Just trying to figure you out." I put the truck in drive, and when I got back to BeeLine, I asked, "Need coffee, tea, or other caffeine?"

"Coffee would be great, but I can get something up at the property."

"No rush to head up the hill. It's only a mile down to town. My treat." I turned right on BeeLine and headed straight for Ashton's shop. "Besides, the owner is one of my best friends."

In no time at all, we were pulling up, and when I parked, she turned to get something out of her bag. I hurried around, and opened the door for her, just as she reached for the handle. There was a questioning look of annoyance, but I just said, "Don't get all high and mighty on me. Ms. Rose would kick my ass if I didn't open the door for you."

"Oh, so you do it because Rose would whoop your fine ass, and not because it's just nice and considerate?" She slid out of the cab, and put a hand on her hip waiting for my response.

"So, you think my ass is fine?"

"Pig." She said, dismissing my comment, but I couldn't help but notice the blush in her cheeks.

"That I might be, but I am still going to open the car door for you." I chuckled, and at the look on her face, I turned and headed for the door, holding it open for her, too. When she didn't move, I raised an eyebrow at her, and she shook her head. I could make it a daily goal to see that color in her cheeks every damn day.

"Kolton!" Ashton said as we walked in.

"Hey, man. How ya doing?" I put my hand on Jade's back to move her forward and to the counter so we could get what we actually came for.

"Good. Good. Who is this?" There was a glint in his eye, one I didn't appreciate, and that alone brought me up short.

"This is Jade Romero. She's the lead planner for the redesign of the property."

"Nice to meet you, Ms. Romero. I hope that Kolton is behaving himself." He winked at me, and I looked at the ceiling, praying for patience or for the ground to swallow him alive.

"He is today." She said with a bit of playfulness as she leaned forward. "But the day is young."

"Only today? Well, it's a start. Wouldn't want him to get his ass kicked." He smiled at me, and I shook my head not believing him. "Now what can I get you?"

"Just a large Colombian coffee, please." She said, answering after she scanned the chalkboard, then turned to look at me.

"Same." Knowing that he wasn't looking at me for that reason, but more along the lines of *'Damn, boy, you hitting that yet?'* Ashton would just have to wait to talk to me later. No doubt he'd call me tonight to find out exactly what the story was between us. Not that I really had an answer for him.

"Do you need room for cream, Ms. Romero?" Ashton says.

"Just a splash, please."

I paid for them, and we turned to wait off to the side. Jade was leaning against the bar, and I couldn't help but look down the length of her right down to those steel toed boots she wore. On the way back up, I felt my heart race as I got to her perfectly formed ass, and up to her neck, that was tilted off to the side, exposing the curve of it. I really needed to get myself together, but what I wanted more was to run my hands over her ass, and wrap a hand around the back end of her throat to bring her close to me. Her lips wrapped around her thumb as she thought, and I wanted to see what they would look like wrapped around my... Damn it, Kolton. Get your shit together. This was so wholly inappropriate.

"What are you thinking about, Jade?"

She shook her head and I asked again, before she looked at me, her eyes narrowing slightly, before she shook her head again, and sighed, "Just trying to work out the layout for the staff housing. The bluff is beautiful, but I want to try and make sure that each unit has their own private area overlooking the river without it feeling like it's a townhouse row. I want to use the natural landscape so each staff member can have privacy. Y'all work together so much, that I don't want you to feel like you have to then live with each other. Leave room for potential families... If I can space it all out... Maybe cover more space... Don't want to have to remove trees..."

"Jade, you are speaking in tongues and half sentences." I chuckled.

"Like I said, just thinking it through. I want to have concept drawings to Rose in the next couple weeks, but I'm going to need more time on the land to get it right." She stretched and let out a yawn, but I noticed the circles under her eyes.

"Did you sleep last night?"

"Couple hours." She muttered the words, just as Ashton said, "Kolton, Ms. Romero."

Her head popped up, and she all but ran to the counter, put two yellow packets in her coffee, stirred it, cradling it in two hands, before taking a sip. Her shoulders sagged, and there was nothing but bliss on her face. "Perfect. Thank you."

"You need your morning IV drip?" I teased, tipping my head toward the door so we could get moving.

"That I do, and I am all out at the B&B. Running out of caffeine at 1am when you are staring down a ton of sketches, and modifications, not a good thing." She took a long sip of her coffee, and sighed. "It's not like I can just walk across the street to the convenience store to get more." When she climbed back into the cab, she took another sip and sighed as she said, "Ashton, while making you turn all shades of red in there, can make a damn good coffee."

I smiled and turned down the main road to head up to the property.

About a mile up the road, her voice was low as she said, "Thank you again for yesterday."

"Did you think I was going to leave you up there?" I smiled at her, but her face was too serious.

"And I'm sorry you found me in such a state." Her eyes met mine, then flicked away again, as she took another sip.

"We all have a history, Jade." Some more severe than others. "I was serious, you know. If you just want to talk, I'm here for you."

"Do we know each other well enough to do that? I mean we are only on what day seven, eight, of being nice to each other?" There was a teasing note to her voice, and that alone released a knot in my chest.

"That's fair." I drove in silence, before she heaved out a long breath just as I pulled up to the main gate. I punched in the code, and looked at her.

"You serious? About talking that is. It's pretty personal." Her eyes were questioning, soft, hesitant.

"I am." I wanted to know more about this girl. I needed to know more about her.

"No judgment?"

"None." I smiled softly, "As long as you don't judge me for anything that may be in my past."

She looked at me for a long moment, as I drove through the gate. I could almost see all the thoughts flying around in that head of hers. She wouldn't have been able to verbalize them if she tried. Then she nodded.

"A few years ago, I was in a pretty serious relationship." She said, and I blinked. That was one way to start a conversation. Well, if that was the direction this morning was going, I was not going to go straight up to the office, where anyone and everyone could hear us. I turned down the first left and then she asked, "Where are we going?"

"You want to talk, let's talk, but I'm going off the beaten path so we aren't bothered." I said and looked over at her. "And this sounds like we are going to be unloading some baggage."

"I'm sorry. We don't—"

"No. I said I was here to talk, Jade." I said cutting her off. "If you want to unload your baggage, then let's do it." I pulled into the tree line, and turned off the truck. Turning in my seat, I faced her, and took a sip of my coffee. "You were saying?"

She blinked at me. "Just like that. I say one sentence, and you put off everything you have to do today, to sit here and unload the baggage cart?"

"If you don't want to talk, I'm not gonna make you, Jade. It sounded like you wanted this conversation. I offered to sit and talk, so here we sit. I'm making the time for it." What was with her? Of course, I was going to make the time. Okay, so it wasn't just like that. There was something desperately flinging me toward Jade Romero and I was on a crash course. At least with this conversation, I would know what I was falling into.

She sipped her coffee and studied me again, before she said, "Okay then."

I waited for her to start, and when she didn't, I said smiling, "Are we just going to sit here and stare at each other?"

"Look this isn't the kind of discussion you have with someone after just a few days of niceties." She shook her head, taking another sip, "But there is something about you, and I don't know what it is."

Her cheeks reddened and when her eyes met mine, they warmed and her shoulders relaxed. "See! That right there is what I mean."

"What?"

"I look at you, and I relax. How do you have such a calming effect on me, Kolton Webster?"

"You expect me to be able to answer that honestly? I could give you about a million different snarky comments, but I really don't know how to respond to that."

She tipped her head to the side and shrugged, agreeing. Then she took a deep breath and said, "As I said, a few years ago, I was in a relationship. A good relationship. We were happy. I think we would have gotten married at some point even."

It took every ounce of control not to reach out and take her hand. I gripped my coffee tighter and sipped before I said as calmly as possible, "What happened?"

"We were... working together, and he died." Her throat tightened up, as the words came out, "It broke me, Kolton. I wasn't myself for a very long time. I'm still not that girl."

"After going through something like that, you aren't going to be that same person. You emerge from the flames different." The shock on her face was entertaining. "Did you not think I would understand that?"

She shook her head, and said, "You know the burn of those flames."

I took a shuddering breath. "I do. Differently, but I do." I looked out the front window, and said, "Want to go for a walk?"

"Okay." She said it slowly, but turned to get out of the truck. I took a deep breath again, and watched her walk around to the front of the truck, and I was once again struck dumb by that which was Jade Romero.

Getting out of the truck, I reached back behind the seat and grabbed my hand gun. There were all manner of creatures out here, and I wasn't taking the chance there might be the lone mountain lion prowling around. I was just putting the holster on my belt, when Jade walked around and smirked.

"Do you even know how to use that?" The teasing tone on those lips did things to me.

I couldn't help but say in a voice way too husky for the situation, "You have no idea what I can do, Jade."

Those cheeks of hers reddened and I swear she clenched her legs closed just the smallest bit. I couldn't really blame her, there was no hiding how tight my pants were now getting. Her eyes flicked down and she indeed noticed, because that smile got a little wider and her eyebrows flicked up.

"Guess we will just have to see about that." Then she drained the rest of her coffee, and tossed the cup into the truck, before turning for the forest.

I finished securing the gun and covering it with my jacket, before draining the rest of my coffee. I shook the nerves out, and followed Jade into the forest.

When I reached her, her eyes were flicking around through the trees, and asked, "The southwest end doesn't abut the National Forest right?"

"No. That's the Johnson's property."

Her eyes narrowed off in the distance, and she was muttering something, as her arms slacked to her sides. I focused on where she was looking and just barely saw the outline of a large wolf.

CHAPTER 7

JADE

Without thinking, he drew the gun and pulled me behind him. My muscles were tense, and I just kept muttering low enough that he couldn't understand me but Devon's Beta would. "Threats won't be tolerated. Stand down. Leave the humans out of this."

"Shh. It's staring straight at us." Kolton muttered. "Back up slowly to the truck."

The wolf let out a loud huff, felt him say, "*and Devon won't let it go, Astral.*" I swear he rolled its eyes, and then took off north. "It's fine. It left."

"They don't usually leave that easily, and where there is one, there is more." His eyes scanned the area, and I put my hand on his arm, lowering the gun.

"Kolton, it's gone. I have really good hearing and don't hear anything."

Slowly he re-holstered the weapon, and turned to me, eyes scanning me from head to toe. "You okay?"

If he only knew. I couldn't help but smile. "I'm fine." I took his hand and then led him over to a fallen tree, straddled it, and said, "So, what were we discussing before the wolf?"

"You really aren't rattled?"

"Not really." I wouldn't let him know that it was his safety that I was worried about. Too much of what Devon and Carlos had said was still running through my head. "You said something about having come through the flames differently than I did? Do you want to talk about it? Or not yet? I understand if you don't."

He watched me for a moment, shook his head, and then let out a breath as he looked up through the tree canopy. "Ashley wasn't a girlfriend. She was more like a sister to me. Rose's daughter, actually. She died of a brain aneurysm." He sat down on the log next to me and then threw a leg over to face me. "It wrecked me then, and it still hurts to think about. Rose is the only one I've talked about that pain with. I know I'm a stronger, better person since dealing with it, but doesn't make it hurt less."

I picked at the bark, and a big chunky part came off in my hand. I continued picking at it before saying, "It doesn't matter who they were to us. Whether it was my Daniel or your Ashley. It's that they were that important to us, that we can't be the person we used to be after their death. Death of someone who means that much to us, it changes you. Sometimes for the better, sometimes for the worse."

I felt Kolton studying me, but I couldn't look at him. "I know dealing with that death helped me grow up in a way I needed to. I don't want to go through that kind of pain again, but I needed it to grow up. I was immature and stupid back then."

That lump was back in my throat again, and took a shaky breath, seeing the Sekli tear Daniel to shreds again, when Kolton's voice whispered through me. "Which was it for you?"

"I... I don't know." I swallowed around the lump in my throat and fought against the tears burning in my eyes. He was quiet for a long moment, and I looked at him, there was a solid understanding there.

"Okay." There was a finality to it, and I tilted my head to the side and narrowed my eyes. "What? If you don't know, you don't know. That is okay. You don't have to have an answer for everything, Jade."

"My job kind of requires that I do." I said knowing he would take it to mean the property design and not being an Astral. Gods, did Carlos seriously mean I have to tell Kolton about that and everything else?

"Kolton." I said, but froze. It was so ingrained in me to keep that part of my life quiet if you weren't one of the supernatural, that as I met Kolton's gaze, every word fled.

"It's okay, Jade. I know how hard it is to talk about. So, let's just do something easier. Tell me about him. Who was he, what was he like?"

Now I was even more puzzled. "Don't you need to get back to the ranch? I mean, I took you off site for hours to come rescue me yesterday, and now it's almost 10:30. We've been out here a lot longer than you realize."

He shrugged and smirked. "Ms. Rose. She umm, when I say something didn't get done because..." He ran a hand through his hair and it strained his t-shirt, showing off the defined muscles in his arms. It was such a contrast to the blush rising in his neck and cheeks that I was taken aback. "Because I had to rescue you or pick you up. She seems to be completely forgiving. Granted, things have to get done, and I've stayed late to get them done, but she's pretty forgiving. It's like she knows something."

That blush got a lot brighter, and I just laughed. "I have no doubt she does know something."

"You say that pretty confidently."

"I've had enough interactions with Rose Porter to know that woman knows things she shouldn't."

"So, tell me about him." He said after a long moment, as he studied me carefully. "Or do you want me to talk about Ashely first?"

I shrugged. "Daniel is a hard person to explain to someone who didn't know him." Daniel wasn't human. He was a Chalkri, technically part of the Therugi demons. That wasn't something I could tell Kolton. "He was blunt, to the point, and never apologized for anything."

"Sounds like he and Ashley would have gotten along well." He chuckled. "Ash was such a hard worker, that if she thought you were slacking off at all, then she would tell you. My work ethic is because of her. She practically beat it into me."

"Yeah, that is one way to describe him. He had a soft spot in him though that only a few people could break into. Once you were there though, he would have killed anyone and anything for you. He did once." I picked at the wood some more, and without thinking, continued, "I had... gotten into some trouble and he burst through the doors, covered in blood, picked me up, covered my eyes, and took me out of there."

Then I stiffened when I realized just what I had said. Not to mention that I had said it so casually, like it was an everyday occurrence. My heart raced as I slowly looked up to Kolton. There was a fierceness there that wasn't fear. That alone surprised me. "That... doesn't scare you?"

"No." I think that surprised him as much as it did me. "I would have done the same."

"I'm sorry. That probably wasn't the best thing to tell you." Ignoring what he had said.

"What do you mean?"

"I just told you that my ex literally killed who knows how many beings to get me out of a bad situation." The words were slow and heavy.

"You don't think you are worth having someone go through hell to get you back?" He asked.

I looked away. "Death leaves a mark on your soul, Kolton."

"And, you say that like you know that mark."

I met his gaze and didn't flinch as I said, "I do."

He blinked. Once. Twice. "Okay."

"Okay?" I said incredulously. "*That* is all you have to say? I just told you I've killed before, and all you say, okay?"

"Jade, I've learned not to judge people without knowing their stories." He said, grabbing my chin, and forcing me to not look away from him. "You just told me your ex had to kill people to get you out of a bad situation. So, no. It doesn't surprise me that you may have been put into similar situations."

"Who are you, Kolton Webster?"

"Who are *you*, Jade Romero?" He retorted. He stared at me with an intensity that burned for a too long moment, and just when I thought he was going to kiss me, he stopped and reached up and gave me an apologetic look as he clicked on the ear piece. "I swear, if the property isn't on fire right now, I might punch you, James."

His cheeks fully bloomed red this time, and said, "Jade and I are on the southwest road, we will be up in a bit... She needed to check something out for the plans on the way in... James, shut your mouth before I shut it for you."

I couldn't help the chuckle from bubbling up my throat. His lip raised slightly on the right side.

He reached up and turned off his mic. "I'm sorry, but we gotta head back."

I looked at my watch, and it was close to noon. "How does time go by so fast around you?" Without looking at him, I blinked a few times, because that didn't sound like flirting at all, did it?

"I'm not sure, but I don't mind." He said, taking my hand, as I swung my leg back over the log and stood up, brushing the dirt off my ass. He didn't let go of my hand, and held it the entire way back to the truck. When he opened the door, he said, "I enjoyed our talk, Jade."

I climbed in, and watched him carefully as he walked around and got into the driver's seat. Who was Kolton? He took all of that like it was nothing. What the actual fuck? Maybe he would take everything that was the Agency with a grain of salt.

Neither of us said anything until we reached the main office. "Need the truck today?" He asked before opening the door, but I felt him rub his thumb across my hand. I looked down at it, only then realizing he was holding it tight.

"No. I'll—" My phone went off, and when I looked down at the screen it said, Rose. I answered it, "Rose? What's wrong?"

CHAPTER 8

JADE

"What?" I asked, looking at Kolton.

"The wolves attacked the chicken coop. Come by the main house. Leave Kolton and the others." Rose's voice was hesitant and so I faked a relieved sigh of relief.

"Sure. Kolton is just dropping me off. Give me a few minutes to grab my comm piece, and I'll head up. We can talk more about the plans when I get there."

"Make sure Kolton stays there." There was a pause, before she said, "Tell him to work with the gelding some more."

"Of course." I smiled as Kolton gave me a questioning look.

"See you in a few minutes." I hung up the phone and when Kolton pulled up to the building, he parked and turned in his seat, raising an eyebrow. "Everything is fine. She wants to go over some of the plans for the main house with Paul before he takes off for the day. Mentioned wanting you to work on the gelding some more."

I hated lying to him, but I couldn't tell him anything else or he would have hit the gas and rushed me over to the house. I reached for the door handle, but Kolton grabbed my elbow, holding me there a moment.

"Jade, what aren't you telling me?"

"A lot, Kolton. We will get there. I promise." I smiled at him and when his thumb moved back and forth. It calmed me, calmed something deep within me with that little movement. "I am just meeting with Rose, to go over some things."

"Alright. If you need anything..."

"I will be on comms." I smiled and pushed the door open. He let go of my elbow, and as I jumped out of the truck, I turned and said, "We know how to find you."

He looked me up and down and I swear I saw his cheeks redden just slightly before I smiled and closed the door. Kolton shook his head before putting the truck in reverse, and when the driver's side was next to me, he rolled down the window and said, "Don't think for a minute I don't realize you and Rose are hiding something."

"Go tame your horse, Mr. Foreman." I teased. I watched him as he drove off, and hurried into the office. I grabbed the comms, and when I got out of the building, I rushed up to the main house. When I saw Paul Porter, he jerked his head around to the back of the house.

I nodded and when I walked around the corner, I took in the sight before me. Blood, feathers, and bones littered the entire pen. I inhaled and smelled the mix of iron, chicken shit, and... wolf.

"Jade." Rose stuck her head out of the hen house, and jerked her head for me to come inside.

Sighing, I looked around quickly, and leaped across the forty by fifty-foot pen to the red painted hen house. I walked up the wood ramp that creaked under my weight. The smell of rotting chicken hit me and I wrinkled my nose.

Rose stood with her back to one of the walls lined with two rows of built-in hen nests. Each one looking much like the outside. As my gaze trailed across two other walls looking much the same, I groaned.

"Jade, what are you thinking?"

"That everything looks like you had your pillows explode with red paint." I let the corner of my lips raise and she huffed a small laugh.

"I know it was the wolves, but this is what I wanted you to see." She pointed to the wall my back was to. I turned, my feet easily spun on the feathers that coated the floor.

"*Tell the Astral to back off.*" Was written in chicken blood that had dripped slightly before drying. The wall had also been shredded by claws, with one set standing out above them all.

"Dramatic much?" I sighed and rolled my eyes.

"Jade." Rose chastised.

"What? It isn't the first threat I've received." I crossed my arms and stared at it a moment, before looking around the coop again.

"What are you thinking, Astral?"

"What's the point? Why kill off your hens? So you don't have fresh eggs for a while, until you can get a new flock in? So what? What is the point of all this though? It's not like they killed them to use. Apparently, they didn't want chicken for dinner. So, what is the point of all of this?"

My earpiece clicked, and James was asking, "Ms. Jade, is Ms. Rose with you?"

I reached up and clicked the mic on. "She is. What you need me to tell her?"

"Nothing really. No worries. We just hadn't seen or heard from her this morning and wanted to make sure she was okay." James' voice relaxed with a long sigh I could hear through the earpiece.

"James, I told you she was fine and meeting with Jade about the house." Kolton sounded annoyed.

"What is wrong, Kolton?" Rose's face scrunched up in concern.

"Nothing."

"Kolton..." I sighed.

"I'll see you later." His voice was more relaxed now. "Actually, can you come up to the office for a moment? I have some questions about the front vet office locations."

"Yeah. I'll be back up in a few."

I poked my head out of the coop, and only then noticed the claw marks in the ground amongst the debris. I stepped down, and went to the far side toward the open pasture. There was a section of the fence broken. Running my fingers over it, and shook my head.

I was staring off into the pasture to the tree line, when Rose came to stand next to me. "Go ahead and head back up there."

"I'll find out what he wants then come and help with the cleanup."

"Nah. Paul and I got it. Once the coop wall is cleared, I'll ask the guys to come and get the carnage." She paused for a moment and I opened my mouth a couple of times to say something, but stopped. "You feel something for him don't you?"

Nodding, I didn't say anything. I didn't know what to say. There had been flings, short bursts of enjoyment after Daniel, but that was it. Kolton felt different.

When I looked back at Rose, she muttered, "Go. Paul and I got this."

CHAPTER 9

KOLTON

The next few days were rough. Every morning I would pick her up, we would talk about nothing or about the planning of the property, but we didn't bring up what was shared that morning.

I wanted to go back to that morning in the woods. There was so much I wanted to ask her. How was her ex able to kill so many people? How was she able to tell that story, like it was nothing? How did she feel about someone, literally killing others to save her? Did she really feel like she wasn't worth that sort of love and dedication? Who did she kill? What were the circumstances? I had so many damn questions. None of which I could ask though. Even while we quietly sat in the truck every morning, I just couldn't bring myself to ask.

During the day, there was always someone around, and today wasn't any easier, but for completely different reasons. She pretty much used the hood of my truck as a desk all damn day. Occasionally, as if someone was pulling a rope, I'd turn to look at her, only to find her staring at me. Her face would heat, and turn back down to the paperwork she was on.

Once when I looked at her, she was standing on a bale of hay she had brought over, and was bent over the hood scribbling, and drawing feverishly. My eyes had trailed over her and may have rested a bit longer on her ass. When she adjusted her stance, and she cocked a hip out, I had literally turned, put my fist in my mouth, and bit down to keep from saying or doing anything I shouldn't have. There was no denying I desperately wanted to explore every inch of her body.

This afternoon, I had been so distracted that when I was working on halter training one of the abused mares, I lost my focus when she looked up at me, worry on her face, and then a second later, the mare nailed me in the leg. I cussed a bit, assured Jade I was okay, but it was almost as if she knew it was going to happen.

I was just finishing up shoveling the horse shit into the composter out in the barn when she popped her head around the corner and said "I need to talk to

Rose before I head back to the B&B. Are you taking me back or should I ask Rose, or one of the other guys?"

"I'll take you back. I'm just going to jump in the shower first, if that's alright. Just come get me when you are ready to head out."

Jade smiled softly, and said, "Thanks." Before heading to the main office.

When I turned back around, James and Fernando were standing there, arms crossed and eyebrows raised.

"What?"

"That was smooth as hell man." James said.

"What?"

"You are going to shower before you take her back?" Fernando said carefully.

"I reek of horse shit. I don't want the smell in my truck either. I didn't hear either of you offer to take her back."

As if someone had smacked them both upside the head at the same time, their eyes popped out of their sockets in shock.

"Like either of us would dare!" Fernando said carefully.

I pinched my eyebrows at them, and it was James who chimed in next, "You have staked a claim on that woman. We wouldn't touch her even if you threatened us with a cow prod."

"Whatever." I turned to head to my room.

"Stand there, Kolton, and tell us that you haven't fallen for that woman harder than you did for Nicole, or any other girl in your life. The way you both look at each other is a huge hands off sign to any other male on the whole Pacific Coast."

I couldn't tell them that, because I *was* falling for her, and hard. Sure, I had found her attractive from the moment she stepped out of that city truck of hers, but this was something more. Jade touched something deeper than just the physical attraction.

"I'm getting in the shower." I said turning on my heels. When I got to the door though, I kicked my boots off, because they were covered in horse shit and I didn't want to track it throughout the apartment. I carefully tiptoed to the bathroom so that I could get undressed without too much of it falling onto the floor. The place wasn't big, but it suited me fine.

There was a tiled entrance that fed into the dining room and small kitchen. The living room just had a big fluffy couch and bookshelves, because a tv was useless here. It was separated by a small hall where the two bedrooms and bathroom were.

I jumped into the shower and cleaned up, but leaned my forehead on the tile, letting the hot water run on my back, and desperately trying not to think about Jade too much.

I failed miserably, because each time I closed my eyes, I saw her looking at me over the hood of the truck. Then there was the way she was bent over it, and damn if I didn't get hard. Reaching down I stroked myself as I pictured her lips wrapped tight around them. Every time she chewed on her thumb, I imagined it was my cock. I could easily imagine her swallowing me bit by bit, and I bit back a moan as I gripped the head in short small strokes. Gods, would she be my little slut, or my little good girl?

Long deep strokes as I saw her taking me down her throat. The feel of hitting the back of her throat, and eagerly taking each and every inch. Those beautiful green eyes looking up at me, begging for more.

"Shit." In a blink, it was nothing to picture how that ass would look bent over the hood of my truck and being balls deep within her. The feel of her gripping my cock, the mewling and writhing of her under me.

I stroked faster as I saw myself grab her neck and pull her up against me and pound into her, her moans filling my head. Moments later I came with a force I hadn't in a very long time. My knees felt weak, and I slid down the side of the shower, and just sat for a moment.

I rinsed my hands, and rested my arms on my knees as I leaned back. I sat there for another minute trying to get my wits about me, when I heard knocking on the door.

"Fuck." I cursed. How long had I been in here? I reached over turned the water off, and cussed again, because there was no towel in the fucking bathroom, except for a small little pink hand towel.

I grabbed it, slipped on the floor, and covered myself, just as I poked my head around the door and told her, "I'll be just another minute."

Her gaze looked me up and down, and she bit her lip. When her eyes met mine, they were filled with so much heat, that it was with a concentrated effort I wasn't instantly hard for her all over again. I took a shuddering breath and said slowly, with a heated smile, "Jade. I do need to get dressed to drive you back."

She blinked, looked down again, and smirked. "Like the towel, Kolton." Then she bit that lip again, and I couldn't help but reach over and remove it from her teeth, because FUCK that was so Gods damned sexy! Each time she did that it was so hard not to pull her to me and kiss her senseless.

"You can come in, but do your best to keep your eyes to yourself." I teased, but tried to move so that she wouldn't see every inch of me. I was trying so hard to keep my hands off her right now, and her eyes sparkled as I turned my bare ass to her.

Jade smirked at me and said, "Do I need to leave you alone for a minute so you can rub one out?" Her eyes trailed down the length of me again, and then back up. Gods, if she only knew.

"If you keep looking at me like that…" I muttered and hurried to the bedroom, grabbing a towel from the linen closet. I toweled off the best I could, threw on some clothes, and took half a minute just to compose myself.

When I turned the corner to the living room, I found her crouched down, studying my bookshelves.

"See anything you like?" I asked. She didn't even jump, and I had tried to be quiet coming down the hall. She just continued to run her finger over the spines of some of the books that I had there.

"A lot of paranormal stories here. Mythology books, too." She looked over her shoulder at me, and I could see her mind was running a million miles a minute. She turned back, "You even have multiple books on the origins of many of the paranormal and supernatural mythologies."

"It's fascinating. Why do some mythological history's stand the test of time, while others don't? The myth of vampires, werewolves and witches stand the test, but the mythologies of any pantheon that isn't Greek, Norse or Egyptian don't? Sure, Sumarian, Chinese, and other Mythologies are still discussed, but aren't believed in to the extent the others are. Why not? There has to be room for it all to be there. Is some of it just wild imagination, sure, but there has to be more to life than just humans occupying Earth. Occupying space."

She stood up, and when she turned around, she had a small Ironman figure in her hand. "And this?" she teased.

I smiled, "It was the last thing my father bought me before he died."

She nodded, and gently set it down back where it had been on the shelf. When she turned toward me, she covered her mouth and yawned.

"Ready to head back?" I asked.

"Yeah." But there was something else in her voice when she looked at me again. She looked at her watch and groaned. "I have a video call with the boss man in an hour."

We headed down to the truck, and once we got to it, I heard her stomach growl. I looked at the clock and sighed. "Jade, when was the last time you ate? You've missed dinner at the B&B."

"I had a protein bar around one." She said, stretching, and I thought I heard her back pop as a moaned wave of satisfaction went through her. "It's fine. I have lunch meat, cheese, and crackers back at the room. There's a small mini-fridge."

"You need a real meal. Can I take you to dinner first?" I asked, surprised by the butterflies in my stomach at the question. I rubbed my leg. That damn mare had nailed me good earlier, but it was my fault. I hadn't read her signs.

Her answering smile was dazzling, and it didn't do anything for those butterflies, but she said, "Any other night, I would say yes, but I really need to talk to Carlos about the plans."

"And they can't wait?" I said, a little disappointed. "Reschedule for even just a little later?"

She rubbed her face, and leaned her head back as we pulled out onto the main road. "Unfortunately, not. He likes to have constant communication, and with this property so remote, he doesn't have his usual control." Her head stayed leaning back, exposing her throat, but she turned to me. "Seriously. Rain check? Tomorrow night? I'll even tell Carlos that we have dinner plans, so I won't have to check in with him when I get back to the room."

I smiled hesitantly. "So, you're not blowing me off. You legit have a video call."

Her head came up and looked at me seriously. "I wouldn't blow you off, Kolton. I'm not that type of person." A blush filled her cheeks, and she said, "I really would like to have dinner with you tonight, but I have a video call with Carlos."

"Tomorrow then. It's a date." I said, my palms now definitely sweaty, and a whole new set of nerves raced to the forefront.

"It's a date." My eyes flicked to hers, and they were bright, with a wide smile to match.

CHAPTER 10

JADE

"I'll meet you here at seven." Kolton pulled into the B&B's parking lot, slowly, almost as if he was pained to do so. "I need to meet with some folks first thing."

"You better have my coffee if you are picking me up that early tomorrow." I teased.

"I'll be here with coffee." He promised.

"Goodnight, Kolton."

"Night, Jade." Then he was driving off.

I stood there, watching him turn back onto the main road, and just stared at where his tail lights faded out into the trees. What was I doing? He was basically a client. I'm going on a date with a client. This was so beyond unprofessional. Not to mention he was human, and there was the situation with the wolves. This was so stupid.

But Kolton made me feel things that I hadn't, even with Daniel. This was something so much more than just butterflies in my stomach. Then there was the fact that Carlos had ordered me to tell him about my life. About the wolves. About everything. Carlos never did that.

I looked up to where my room was, took a deep breath, and walked in. When I got there, my laptop was still sitting just as I had left it this morning. I unlocked it, checked my email quickly, and switched to the video call program that was still open from the office meeting this morning. I looked at the time; I only had a few minutes before Carlos would call.

I pulled out my phone and opened the text messages window.

Why am I such an idiot?

Rye:
Well good evening to you bitch.
Why are you an idiot?

The foreman asked me out on a date.

Rye:
Get some girl!

Rye. He is the foreman of the property I am doing a
project on.
I'm basically agreeing to go on a date with my client.

Rye:
What really has you worried? If you really like him,
then test the waters.
Is it because of Daniel? Carlos? Ashstrike?

All of the above.

Rye:
I'm calling you.

Can't talk. I'm supposed to be on a video call with
Carlos any minute.

Rye:
So tell Carlos to fuck off for a few minutes

Can't. Hell I blew off the dinner date with Kolton
because of this stupid meeting with Carlos.

Rye:
I'm more important than both of them. You know
that.

I do, but not the point asshole.

Rye:
Do you really like this guy J?

I do. That is what scares me.
There is something pulling me to him.

Rye:
Then ride it out. Figuratively and literally.

I love you. <3

Rye:
Love you too. Seriously though, test the waters. If it is meant to be, it will be.

I had just pulled the meat and cheese from the minifridge when the call came in from Carlos. Groaning, I reached over, accepted it, but turned my laptop toward where I was preparing my so-called dinner. "You are early."

"You haven't eaten yet?" His eyes went off screen and I had no doubt he was looking at his mother's clock. I could hear his grandkids playing outside, and I couldn't help but smile.

"No. It was a long day, I just got back to the B&B." I told him. The exhaustion in my voice surprised even me. "You are taking the call from home?"

"I am. The grandkids are in town and I wanna spend time with them." Then he shook his head, "*Mija*, are you just having lunch meat and cheese for dinner?

Good thing *abuela* isn't here to see this. She'd be overnighting you some tamales."

I flipped him off over my shoulder, and heard him laugh at me. "I wouldn't say no to some tamales, though."

When I finished throwing it on a plate, I turned and said, "Well, I had a much better offer, but my fucking cousin is a bit of a control freak so I had to take a video call with him."

"A better offer?" He raised his eyebrows. "Please tell me it was with a certain foreman of the Porter Ranch?"

I sighed. "First, it's none of your fucking business. I will date or *not* date whomever I wish. If I decide to have a date with that foreman, it will be because I want to, and not because the Agency tells me I should."

"Jade Cecilia Araceli Romero." He said pointing at me, his onyx eyes stared me down.

"Don't you fucking full name me on this. Who I want to date and fuck is my own business. The Agency will have no say in it."

"That isn't what I mean. *Fuck*, Jade. The Gods know that after what happened to Daniel, ain't no one telling you how to live your personal life." He took a deep breath and said, much calmer this time, "I'm asking as family. You seem to have a connection with Kolton. I told you, I want you happy."

I studied him for a long moment and took a bite of the meat and cheese roll up I put together. "You tell me that we are connected somehow, order me to tell him about the Agency, about me, and then you sit there and tell me that you are asking as family and you just want me happy? Sometimes it's hard to tell when you ask as my cousin or when you are asking as the Pacific Representative of Ashstrike."

He chuckled and his eyes softened. "I know. I have to blur those lines way too often with you, and I'm really sorry for that, Jade. Now, as your cousin, is that date with Kolton?"

I nodded, "Yeah."

"You are blushing, *mija*."

"*Cabron*." I smiled brightly at him. "As family, I'm having this discussion. I will deny it under every torture you give me as Ashstrike. Sí?"

"Sí."

I bent down and pulled a beer from the fridge, twisted the cap, and took a sip. It was one step above piss water, but it's what they had the other day when I went by the store. I took a deep breath before saying, "There is something about Kolton. I can't place it, but there is a thread there. I can almost see it, but its faint. I also know Rose knows about it, and I think you do, too." I looked at him and pointed my beer bottle at him, "I also know that the pinch in your lips means I am right, but you won't tell me, and *that* pisses me off."

Carlos had the good sense to just nod.

"Will you at least just confirm whether whatever it is that binds Kolton and I together, has been seen by Rose?"

"*Mija*." He said hesitantly. "You are asking me to blur that line."

"No. I am not asking you to blur it. I am flat demanding you break that line. Give me some sort of heads up. Please. I can't have my heart broken like it was with Daniel." I stared at him through that computer screen. "Carlos, the only thing saving you from having a dagger at your throat right now is that there are over five hundred miles between us." I took a long drink of my beer, and sighed. "Carlos. Please."

"You've told him about Daniel." He said more as a realization, than a question. When I nodded he said, "Oh, shit."

"Pieces." I said softly. "Nothing about Ashstrike or what he was, but I did kind of tell him that Daniel slaughtered a bunch of people to save me."

There was a long silence. "And he still asked you on a date."

"Well, dinner, that I had to decline tonight to talk to my riddle-filled cousin. I'm going with him tomorrow." I drained the last of my beer, and got a new one out of the fridge.

"Yes, Rose has seen it." He said taking a deep breath, but he studied me a lot harder. "I hate video chats. I can't read your aura right now."

I smiled. "Good, because it would be all kinds of fucked up. I've talked of Daniel to a man who does things to me, Carlos. I can't explain it. Even Daniel couldn't turn me on like Kolton has with just a look. Maybe it was the history, maybe it's the unknown, but I know I turned him on too."

"Well, you are a beautiful woman, Jade. Deadly, too." He smirked. "I'm proud of the being you have become."

"Thank you for making sure I lived to be someone you can be proud of." I said genuinely. Warmth filled his eyes, and I felt it all the way into my chest. There wasn't anyone on this Gods forsaken planet I loved more than Carlos. He had literally saved my life.

"Was there Agency business you wanted to discuss?" I took a sip of beer, and put another bite of the meat and cheese roll up in my mouth.

"There is. You spoke to Devon and things didn't go well."

"Nope, and the other day, his Beta decided to try to scare us on the south side of the Porter property." My eyes snapped to his as I said, "Kolton pulled a gun on him. All kinds could have gone wrong in that moment. I would have had to reveal myself, because I will protect Kolton." Every ounce of my protective instinct went into that statement, and then I paused, because I realized what I just said. More importantly, *how* I just ... and... fuck, so did Carlos.

"It's begun." He muttered just loud enough the mic picked it up.

"Carlos." My stomach flipped. "That is what Rose saw isn't it. He's the other half?" He nodded. "That's the thread I've been feeling. That's why Daniel and I... I never wanted... I... I..."

"*Mija.* You have to be careful. I'll keep it out of the books for as long as I can, but it will come to light. You know the Kindrel will feel that thread and it will be recorded. It will... Alpha Devon will find out. Take care of the situation before he does. *Te amo, mija.*" Then he did the one thing that he had never done with me. He reached over and hung up on me.

I slid down to the floor and just stared into space.

Kolton Webster was my other half. Every Astral had one. I thought Daniel and I were... but we could never get that bond to set into place. We tried. We loved each other wholly, but that bond would never snap into place.

With Kolton, from the first moment I laid physical eyes on him, I had been drawn to him. At first, I thought, maybe it was just a physical thing, that if I decided to throw it all to the wind, that I could literally fuck him out of my system, and move on.

Only, there was that cord, a thread that pulled me toward him. Was it the fates that had caused that deer to play chicken, making it so that I needed a ride up and back each day? I had heard his heartbeat. In all the years I was with Daniel, I couldn't hear his, not the way I had heard Koltons. Was that why ...

My mind shifted, and... oh Gods. I had seen him hard and ready with only a washcloth barely covering him. I do mean barely. That spot between my legs thumped and I looked down. "Shut up, pussy. I'm sort of freaking out over here."

The signs had been there, the knowledge of where he was, even before I should be able to know he was there. I knew his truck was close even before he had gotten there when I put the truck in the ditch. Sure, my hearing picked it up, even though he had been further than what my hearing should have caught, even as an Astral. I just didn't realize it. There was the way I already knew something wasn't right when I watched him earlier trying to halter train the abused horse today. I knew that something was going wrong, and he got kicked in the leg. Sure, he wasn't seriously injured, but it had hurt the rest of the day. I couldn't not be aware of his every move when he was near.

I thought through every single thing that had happened since I saw him in person. Everything lined up. The Fates were a bunch of bitches.

Each time I'd find myself getting angry, I'd see him stand there with that little pink towel, water drops running down each muscle on his chest, his abs, down that happy trail.

"Fuck this." I got up, went to the go bag, found my favorite vibrator, and grabbed one of the dildos.

I stripped and laid on the bed, spreading my legs. Running the dildo up and down my slit, before slowly sliding it in, I imagined it being Kolton's cock... that damn cocked covered in a pink washcloth. My head tilted back, Kolton's heated stare the only thing I could see. I had the vibrator on my clit a moment later.

My moan filled the room, and all I could think about was pushing Kolton down on the couch, removing that fucking excuse of a towel and letting him deep throat fuck me. I pumped the dildo in and out of me a few times, and flicked my clit with the vibrator. I could almost taste the saltiness of him on my lips, and moaned as a wave of heat spread through me.

That heated look he gave me when he opened the door, even though he had nothing on but that... Gods, I pumped that dildo, in and out of me and circled my clit again and again at the thought of Kolton standing there in nothing but a washrag before me. How did I resist not just taking him right there on that couch? Riding him, letting him take control and fucking me until I didn't know my name anymore. The thought of him pounding into me, holding me against him, dominating every movement. That thought was all it took as an orgasm rocketed through me. My mind completely blank as wave after wave rolled through me.

I never came that fast. I sat up, my vibrator hitting that spot again, sending me over the edge again, as the dildo pressed in further.

"Fuck." I moaned. Kolton's face was all I could see, and that in itself was intoxicating. I didn't move, letting the feeling flow through me.

I twitched and flopped down, panting and spent.

CHAPTER 11

KOLTON

It was 6:50am and when I pulled up to the B&B, the truck had hardly stopped before she had the door open and climbed in.

"Jade?" I asked, concerned. She looked like she hadn't slept at all. She just put her seatbelt on, grunted, reached for the coffee, took a sip and leaned her head back with a sigh.

"Morning?" I said, trying to get her to say anything.

"Humm." The small sound came out of her as she just kept her eyes closed, her head back on the headrest.

Putting the truck in park, I turned to her and pulled her face toward mine. "Jesus, Jade. Did you even sleep last night?"

"You can still see the bags under my eyes?"

I nodded as I looked at the concealer she had used. I reached up and rubbed a couple of the blotchy parts smooth. "You tried to cover them, but I ask again. Did you even sleep last night?"

"For an hour, after..." Her face flushed and she looked away from me. I let her, because I had a pretty good idea, and it was likely the same thing I did half a mile down the road after dropping her off, and then again before I could finally sleep last night.

I gave her a heated knowing look and she scoffed. "It's going to be a long day."

"You sure you don't just want to go back upstairs?" I asked. Would anything she did today be worth a damn if she didn't get any sleep?

She turned to me, looked me up and down, and then huffed a laugh. "Only if you were going with me."

"Jade, as much as I would love to take you up on that offer, that isn't exactly what I meant." Last night broke through a line we had been teetering, making the comment roll off my tongue easily. I studied her for a moment, and she just yawned.

"I know, Kolton. I'm mostly teasing." She was trying to stifle another yawn. "Let's head up."

"You sure?" She looked so incredibly exhausted.

"Yeah. I have a few things to do near the front house, but after lunch I need to go up to the northern property line." Her eyes slid over to me. "That is if you trust me with your truck."

I outright laughed at that, put the truck in drive, and headed out. "Let's talk at lunch. Did you get breakfast?"

Nodding, she said, "Had a bacon, egg and cheese bagel about 4:30."

"Jade." I shook my head. "I'll get you something when we get back."

She didn't say anything. She just took another sip of her coffee. Before turning onto the main road, I looked at her. Really looked at her. I wanted to ask her what we were doing. Was she still serious about me taking her to dinner tonight? All those words got stuck in my throat, when I opened my mouth to ask, but I turned back to the road, and asked, "Why couldn't you sleep?"

Out of the corner of my eye, I saw her look at me, and then down to her lap, where she started playing with her fingers. "Many reasons." Then she was chewing on her thumb. Something I noticed she did when she was deep in thought.

"Don't go away on me. Talk to me. Why couldn't you sleep?" I turned onto BeeLine, and when she didn't answer, I asked again, "Jade, whatever this is, I need you to talk to me. Please don't shut me out. Please, answer why you couldn't sleep?"

"Like I said, lots of reasons." Her voice was light, and she leaned her head back again, rolling it toward me. She studied me a long moment before she said, "Honestly?"

"That would be preferred over lies."

"I had a conversation with my cousin last night. He gave me a lot to think about. Some of it having to do with you. Our date tonight." There was a small curve of her lips.

"Would you like to put it off so you can get some sleep?" My stomach flipped, and I wished I had something with my coffee, but I was already so nervous about picking her up this morning. "I understand if you need to turn in early. Don't want you falling asleep during dinner."

She reached over and squeezed my forearm. "That's really sweet, Kolton, but no, I don't want to reschedule dinner." My eyes flicked over to her, and there was a contentment to her face that I felt pool in my chest. Her eyes closed, and then she just fell asleep. She looked so peaceful. Her hand was still on my forearm, and I didn't want to move it. It felt like a hot brand that flowed into and through each of my veins.

I had to take a deep breath as I turned into the ranch driveway. I punched in the code, and tried not to have the truck jostle too much as we made our way up.

She was still asleep when we got to the office. I parked, and slowly slid my arm out from under her hand. It was enough movement that it woke her up, and she looked at me. "Sorry. I was going to just let you sleep in the truck for a bit. Come back and wake you in an hour or two."

"There is too much to do." She yawned herself awake. "I need to have drawings to Carlos by the end of the week, and I haven't even started on them yet." She took her coffee from the center console as I walked around the truck and opened the door for her. She grabbed her bag and coffee, and as she slid from the truck, she kissed my cheek quickly and whispered, "I appreciate it."

I blinked, and I was sure I was red as a tomato. I looked across the bed of the truck to see Rose standing there with a knowing smile. I narrowed my eyes at her, and she jerked her head toward the office.

"I'll see you around lunch then?" I asked Jade.

"Yeah. I'll meet you back here." She looked to Rose, who gave her a little nod as well, and I thought I saw fire in Jade's eyes, before she strode straight for her.

"You..." she spat, before her eyes flicked to me.

"Kolton, wait in my office please. I believe Jade and I need to have a quick chat." Rose had that knowing, quirky look on her face again, one that meant that she knew exactly what Jade was so upset about. She was going to enjoy the conversation. I had been on the receiving end of it before, and it never turned out the way I wanted it to.

"Yes, Ms. Rose." I looked at Jade, and wanted to warn her, but, again, I knew better.

Just as I closed the door, I heard Ms. Rose say, "You spoke to Carlos."

"No shit, Rose." Then the door closed, and I strode into the office and waited.

Five minutes later, Rose came in, chuckling.

"Conversation go that well?" I said.

"Well, I knew it was coming."

"You always do."

"It's what I do, Kolton. I know things." She said, waving her hand. "Just like I know that you finally stepped up and asked her to dinner last night."

I blinked. "How do you know that? Did Jade tell you?"

"No. Like I said. I know things." Her eyes burned and for a moment, I thought I saw the silver in her hair swirl and shimmer, before she shook her head and said, "Just as I know that you will be working with the Bethzald gelding today. I need him broken."

"He takes the saddle well, and will sometimes let me sit on him, but he gets a bit jumpy. Likes to crow hop." I said rubbing the back of my neck. "I'll work with him for a couple hours this morning. Jade needs to go to the north river edge this afternoon. Was thinking I'd drive her out so she doesn't break my truck."

Rose laughed, "Is that the only reason why?"

"Hey, she put hers in a ditch, Fernando won't have it fixed for a few more days, the windshield will still be awhile, and the last time she took mine, she got a flat. That's in a week, Ms. Rose."

"Which she would have been able to handle on her own, if you hadn't left the spare flat as paper." She retorted, but there was no bite to it.

"Not the point. She still broke my truck."

"Fine. Fine. Work the gelding this morning, then take her to the river."

"Ms. Rose?" I said, staring at my feet. "I know it's crossing a lot of professional boundaries to take her out tonight."

"Kolton, there is more going on here than you two having a crush on each other." I looked off to the side, and wondered why that didn't sit right with me. "Look at me, Kolton."

When I did, she continued. "I haven't seen your eyes light up like this in a long time. This is more than just a crush for you. It is for her, too. Feel it out, but be careful, okay."

"No other boss would be this understanding."

"Well, I'm not just your boss."

"No ma'am. You ain't." I smiled at the woman who had taken me in, given me a job, and had given me a life I was proud of.

"Also, Paul and I were driving the perimeter over morning coffee." Ms. Rose's voice was tentative for a long moment before she said, "Some wild animals tore up a long stretch of fence along the wildland. Get the guys to fix it today, please. Can't afford for the horses that are at pasture to get loose out there."

"You sure you don't want me to handle it?"

Ms. Rose smiled at me and teased, "I thought you wanted to make sure Jade didn't break your truck."

Heat flashed across my face, and I knew I had been had. "Right." I sighed.

"No, I already told you that you will be working on the Bethzald gelding. Put it on the list for the guys. This afternoon you can take Jade out where she needs to go, and make sure your truck doesn't break."

I stood up and smiled as I walked out the door saying, "Yes, ma'am."

Reins in my hands, I stared up wide-eyed at the gelding, who pulled on them. I stood up, jerked on them, and pulled his head to me. "Why are you being such an asshole?"

A light chuckle behind me reached my ears, and I smiled. "Even Jade thinks you are being an asshole." I rubbed the gelding's stripe, down the front of his forehead to his muzzle.

"Or I could be laughing at the fact that this is the third time this morning he has thrown your ass to the ground." Jade chuckled again behind me.

I scratched the gelding's forehead some more and ran my hand down his neck to settle him back down, before I said, "You saw that, huh?"

She shrugged and came to stand before the gelding. She laid her palm out flat, giving him a small carrot, and smirked at me.

"Horses who throw their riders don't get treats."

"Well, too bad for you, I don't listen." She said and stuck her tongue out at me. I bit my lip, because there were so many retorts I wanted to give her right now. Her eyes lit up, and I felt my cheeks heat. Gods, she was making me blush at my own thoughts.

"You about ready to head up to the river?" She asked.

"Give me a few minutes to stuff some lunch down my throat, and I'll meet you back at the truck."

"Sounds good. I got a couple quick questions for Rose."

I handed the gelding off to James and hurried upstairs to my place for a sandwich, and when I came out, I heard Rose say, "Carlos would agree."

"I know that Carlos would agree. We talked about it, well, I figured it out before he fucking hung up on me." Jade was pacing and ran her fingers through her hair, and I chuckled when her hands got caught in it, and she had to redo her ponytail.

"You know there are things Carlos can't tell even you." Rose said. I didn't know why I listened, but I couldn't help it.

"You didn't even give me a heads up about him, though, Rose. We've known each other since Daniel, and..." there was pain in her voice, and I wanted to go over there and wash it all away. "You didn't tell me about Kolton."

About me? What about me? I looked at Rose and I thought I saw her eyes flick in my direction and then focused back to Jade.

"You know I couldn't." She said, then muttered something so low I couldn't understand, then louder continued, "Doesn't change anything. It's not a bad thing."

"It's binding. What if something happens to him, Rose? I can't go through that again."

"I know you are scared. He is too. Whether he wants to admit it or not, he is too. That boy cares for you. Just trust it. You know the bond won't do you wrong."

She pulled her into a hug, and I gathered myself before walking out, and waiting for Rose to let her go.

"I'm more worried about it fully binding without him knowing what it means." Jade said as I walked up, and while Jade waited for an answer from Rose, Rose instead met my eyes and said, "Please take care of her."

I could only nod. Jade froze at Rose's words.

I cleared my throat, and Jade pulled back, but only stared at Rose. After a long moment, she looked at me and her eyes swam with sadness and warmth, but it was the fear that I felt in my heart.

"Ready, Jade?"

"Not in the least bit." She said, but stepped away from Rose.

"Would you rather go lay down? You can sleep at my place if you want." A smile crossed her lips, and that spark in her eyes lit up again. "No. Like seriously sleep. You are working on what an hour, maybe two? It's okay to sleep."

"You only got an hour of sleep, Jade Cecilia Araceli Romero?" Ms. Rose said. My eyes widened, as I looked to Rose. She was definitely getting the double stare down. I couldn't believe that Ms. Rose had just full named Jade. Wait, how did Ms. Rose *know* Jade's full name?

Jade blinked, raised a finger and said, "I will tell you the same thing I told Carlos. Don't you fucking full name me."

"You slept an hour, and you are standing right now?" Rose took her hand and pulled her to the office. Turning back toward me she said, "Come on, Kolton."

I followed Rose as she half dragged Jade to her office. "Rose, I swear I don't need anything. Don't make me call Carlos to order..." She caught herself and looked back at me.

"Well, ain't it obvious that the two of you know each other much more than just what is going on. Yes, we will discuss that." I said, unable to put anything other than amusement in my voice because frankly, watching Ms. Rose haul Jade down to her office like she had each and every one of us on this ranch, was satisfying as hell.

When we got to the office, she put Jade in the chair, and went to the area behind her desk and started mixing things together.

"Let me guess, turmeric, cinnamon, chai, lion's mane, and that little extra that is all Rose?" Jade crossed her arms. I looked at her eyes wide. Jade looked up at me and smiled. "Surprised I know what Rose is putting in the energy boost that she has probably given ya'll a million times?"

"We have been trying to sort it out for years!" I plopped down in the chair next to her, shaking my head.

"You will never make it right though. Rose... Rose has her ways of making it actually work though."

"Alright Jade Romero. How do you know Rose Porter?" I had had enough.

"You are not ready for that answer, Kolton." Jade's voice was soft, careful, and tentative. She turned toward me and she held my gaze for a long, long moment before she sighed. "I don't know how to tell you everything yet, Kolton."

"Will Carlos let you tell him everything?" Rose muttered.

"He's kind of ordered me too." Jade said with a heavy sigh.

Now I was thoroughly confused, not only that but a part of me was... guarded. Gods, if everything since she was here was a lie, I'm... I can't... "Jade."

"Kolton, first, I know what you are thinking. Whatever this is. Whatever is going on between us, it's real, okay? I don't fully understand it, but it's real." She was holding my hand and squeezing it tight. Her eyes flicked across my face.

My shoulders relaxed, and I looked to Ms. Rose, who smiled softly as she looked at me and nodded. She mouthed the same to me, and I took a deep breath. "Real. Okay. Not that we have really talked about any of that, and we probably should. After you've slept, and when Ms. Rose isn't here to overhear all of it, because while I have no doubt she knows something, this is a discussion we should be having without overhearing ears."

"She knows more than us... about us." She shook her head and looked at Ms. Rose, who looked at her for a moment. I swear the way the light hit her hair again, made her hair swirled. I loved when her highlights made it do that. It was just one of those things that made her Ms. Rose.

Jade's head cocked to the side, and when Ms. Rose looked at her again, she nodded. Jade turned to me, and said carefully, "Rose and I have worked together in the past. She... she has also worked with my boss, who happens to also be my cousin, Carlos Medina."

"You said worked with, but you said you would have Carlos order her..."

"Yeah, it's a whole lot more complicated than that." She said smiling as she took the tea from Ms. Rose. Jade took a long sip of it, and leaned back. "I'm sorry I'm keeping more details from you, but it's mostly because I don't know how to tell you. I'm trying to sort out *how* to tell you everything, but I want to figure out some other things first, because... well, damn this sounds cryptic as hell, and I'm really sorry Kolton." She was rambling, and I blinked at her as she took another sip, and took a deep breath.

"I'm sorry. What did you just try to tell me?"

"There are things I need to tell you, but I don't know how to explain any of it to you."

"I don't like secrets, Jade. If we are going to explore whatever this *real* thing is between us, there can't be life altering secrets."

"I know." She took another drink, and heaved another long breath. "I know, but I need to make sure that what we have or are going to have, or might have, is going to stay before I tell you. Which isn't fair, because if we are..."

"You are doing that not complete sentences thing again."

Her eyes burned into mine, and I could see the fear and heartache in them. "My life is not easy. It is extremely complicated, and not normal in any way. Not normal by any stretch of a human's imagination."

I studied her. While it made my head spin, I could see the logic. Hell, we hadn't even kissed. We hadn't even gone on a date yet, and I was practically telling her to bear everything to me. That wasn't fair. I certainly hadn't told her every tiny detail of my life.

"I have a lot of questions, Jade. The first of a long list is, what is so complicated about living a life as a project manager?"

"Those answers are coming, Kolton. I promise you, but can you please be patient while I work some of the other bizarre things out first?"

"Yes. I can be patient, but if I need to know, you'll tell me, right?" I answered her.

"Yes. There are things you should know now, but I just can't, well, I don't know *how* to explain it to you, without having to explain everything." She reached over and took my hand again, and it was warm, and it felt like a lifeline.

"Now that Rose has given me enough energy to run a marathon, ready to head up to the river?" She said looking up through her lashes.

"I don't know what just happened in this room." I muttered. "But why do I feel like I just got steamrolled?"

"Because you did." Rose smiled brightly at me, "But she's not wrong Kolton. What is between you is not a figment of your imagination. There is a lot we will tell you, but one step at a time okay?"

I nodded. "You owe me shots, Ms. Rose."

"Deal."

Standing, I pulled on Jade's hand and said, "I'm driving. I know how it feels to have the brew Ms. Rose gave you, and I'm sure you will be jittery as hell for the next twenty minutes."

I practically dragged her to the truck, because I would be lying if I didn't feel a little betrayed from everything that Ms. Rose had said. Why couldn't they have said from the beginning that they knew each other. I mean, it isn't that they really hid there was more than a professional relationship. Jade would be extremely frank with her, in a way no one had ever spoken to Ms. Rose before, let alone gotten away with.

I got Jade settled in the truck, and when I reached my door, I took one last deep breath before opening it and getting in.

"Kolton." She said hesitantly.

"Jade." I said carefully, "I am going to stick my foot in my mouth, and you need to tell me the truth. I... I can't."

"Kolton. What I said in front of Rose is the truth. It's real."

"Jade, I really like you, but I can't go down a road of lies."

"I know it will sound like splitting hairs, but I'm not lying. I feel something for you, and it is real. Realer than I have ever felt before. It's different and feels more settled within me than it did with Daniel, kind of real." I looked at her, and there was nothing but sincerity on her face. I reached over and ran my thumb across her cheek.

"Not all in my head?"

"Not in the slightest." Her smile was bright and her eyes sparkled. Mine flicked to her lips, and I wanted to kiss her. When I looked up at her eyes, again, I leaned in, but then someone was thumping on the hood. We jumped, but I refused to look at who it was.

"I swear for all that is holy." She said gritting her teeth. "Can I kill him?"

My eyes widened, and I couldn't help but laugh. "Maybe tomorrow."

"Kill joy."

I took her hand, kissed it, and then slowly turned to the asshole at the hood of my truck. I climbed out, and when James' eyes met mine, they were wide.

"Fuck. I'm sorry, Kole."

"Ya should be, but my personal life aside, what do you need?"

"There's a broken fence out near the dam."

"I'm aware. Ms. Rose, told me about it. It is on the worklist for the day."

"Must have missed it." James rubbed the back of his neck and looking down at the ground. He kicked a small stick on the ground with his boot before looking up at me again.

"Take Fernando with you and get it fixed." I hissed the words through my teeth to keep from screaming at him. I took a visible deep breath at his wide-eyed stare at me.

"I'm sorry, man. I would have just told you over comms, but since your truck was here, I figured I'd just tell you, but I didn't realize you were with Ms. Romero. I'll get the fence fixed, and leave you two alone."

"I'll be on comms."

I went back into the truck, and took off, before I had the urge to drive over him. Jade reached over, and squeezed my thigh, when she noticed how I was white knuckling it. That squeeze was doing more than just calm me, and when I shifted in my seat, she giggled.

"Jade." I warned.

"Not my fault you're easy to fluster." She teased. Her hand stayed there the rest of the way up to the river, but at some point, she had gone dead silent, and started chewing on her thumb again.

We pulled up and she reached down and looked in her bag. "Where did my hat go?"

I shrugged getting out of the truck and walking around to her side, where she actually let me open the door. "Must have left it in Ms. Rose's office."

Jade pulled her bag out of the seat, and pulled some plans out, spreading them on the hood of the truck. She went to studying them, looked up, made notes, and repeated the movements for a long time. I just leaned against the truck and watched her. It was fascinating.

"I need to see the ravine." She said, rolling the plans back up and stuffing them into her bag before stomping off toward the ledge. I headed for the ravine, as she secured her belongings, and jumped down. When I looked up at her, I felt every nerve within me go taught. She had taken the jacket, thrown it on top of the hood of the truck, and was pulling her hair back into a messy bun.

"What?" she said, freezing mid-way through securing her hair.

"I... nevermind." I reached out my hand to help her down the hill and the disbelief on her face shocked me.

"Kolton. I'm not going to break. I quite literally have to be able to climb down embankments, over hills, and through brush for my job." Her hands were on her hips, and my eyes fixed to them. I wanted to know what they felt like under my hands, under my lips...

CHAPTER 12

JADE

"Kolton. I'm not going to break. I do this for a living. I have to be able to climb down embankments, over hills, and through brush."

His eyes stopped at my hips for a long moment, before his eyebrows raised and he looked up at me. "I realize that, but it's a tight space, and I was merely trying to be helpful." His hand was still outstretched, and after a moment I took it.

I took a step down the small embankment, and the ground gave way under my foot. His hands were instantly on my waist, holding my weight, as he set me down right next to him. I took a deep breath, my chest grazing the lower part of his, and when I looked up at him, there was something warm and needy in his brown eyes. His thumbs rubbed slowly against the curve of my hip, and I felt my heart stutter slightly, that thread between us going taught.

I blinked, and he slowly stepped back. My hand rested on top of his on my right hip, and as he moved to take it away, I pressed on it, rubbing my thumb against his knuckles. He turned to look at me, opened his mouth to say something, but turned to face me. His eyes hadn't left mine, but we were once again standing so close together that the deep breaths we took had our chests brushing against each other.

"Kolton?" I breathed his name.

"Jade." His other hand lifted, and my heart raced.

"What are you thinking right now?" He said, his hand hovering over my cheek. There was a hesitation in his voice, and I didn't know what to say. "There isn't anyone around for miles. You can say—"

"Kolton. Shut up." My voice was husky, even to my own ears. He blinked. "Just shut up and kiss me like you wanted to in the truck."

There was a split second of shock before his lips hovered over mine, and he whispered, "Jade?" His hand threaded through my hair and I could feel the restraint in the grip he had there and at my hip. "There is no going back after this."

"I know." I wanted this. Gods, there were so many reasons not to. He tightened his fingers in my hair a little more, pulling on the roots enough that it sent a bolt of shock straight between my legs, and I pressed my chest against him. "Real." I whispered.

His lips were soft and tentative at first, but the second my hands threaded through his hair, he deepened the kiss, picked me up and leaned me against the bank. Then there was that cord that became a real and tangible thing.

When he pulled back, I was breathless. He was bracing himself so that he wasn't laying on top of me, but I felt the muscles in his shoulder clench in restraint. "Kolton."

"Yes, Jade?"

"I..." His eyes were warm, and full of everything I knew I was feeling. Hell, my whole body wanted to be against him.

His forehead rested on mine. "Can you feel that?"

I couldn't say anything. There were so many things going through my head all at once. The Kindrel were going to know. The wolves would know soon. My eyes met his, and I said, "Yes, but what does it feel like to you?"

"Like you are mine. Like there is a rope that binds us together." He closed his eyes and took a deep breath. "I'm not gonna lie, Jade, saying that scares me."

"Kolton, I know this probably isn't the right time, but if you are not in this for the long haul right now, you have to say so now, before that feeling becomes stronger and unbreakable." Each word hurt and burned as I said the words.

I met his eyes as he said, "Are you serious? I haven't wanted something more in my life. Jade, you are something I don't think I could walk away from even if I tried. I want this. I want whatever this is between us. I need you."

"Are you one hundred percent sure?" I pressed the words through the knot of tears that were in my throat. Sending him away with this thread between us now would cripple me. More so than when Daniel died. I blinked. That was the first time I had ever thought about Daniel where it didn't hurt. I blinked twice again in quick succession, and looked at Kolton. "You want this?"

"Every inch of it. Not just physically, but I need *you*, Jade Romero."

I reached up, and kissed him again. Every nerve in my body lit up. I could feel that Astral strength and power feeding into that thread, that bond, making it stronger, setting it in stone.

When he pulled back, he smiled and said, "I have never felt more settled in my life."

I don't remember even thinking the words, but I whispered, strong and fiercely, "No Alpha, beast or being will take you from me, Kolton Webster. I will protect you with my life."

"What?" He said, but then his face changed and softened, "I know we have to be careful, Jade. There is a lot at risk." His voice was restrained and it almost sounded like he was trying to convince himself.

"We do have to be careful." I said and brought my hand to rest on his cheek.

Something passed through his eyes, and he asked, as if he was pained to do so, "Do you have someone back home? I won't be some work trip fling."

"No, Kolton. There isn't anyone back home. I would have told you that already." All the images of rejection over the years flooded back. "I'm not exactly someone's first choice anyway."

His eyebrows came together, "Why?"

"Are you serious?"

"Yes. I'm dead serious."

"Kolton. I'm not exactly a model. I eat too much, and no amount of exercise is going to keep all the cake off my hips."

His hand ran down the side of me, and over my stomach, until he curled the tips of his fingers into the waistband of my jeans. Each movement sent a spark through me. His touch, while exploratory, was gentle, kind, and I could feel the way his hands trembled against me.

"Jade, you are beautiful. You hid yourself during those video calls. When you stepped out of that city truck of yours—"

"Don't you diss my truck, mister." I said as his hand curled around my leg and wrapped it around his hip and slid back down to hold my ass.

"I will, because it is a city truck." He kissed me quickly, then said, "I was struck dumb by what I saw. Ms. Rose had to tell me to behave. Do you know how hard it has been for me to behave around you?"

I narrowed my eyes at him, but willed my heart to slow because I wasn't so sure that he couldn't feel it.

His was beating a thousand times a minute, but he raised his eyebrow at me.

"Kolton. I don't know what goes through your head. For months we have talked and done nothing but butt heads. Then I get here, and then this..." I bit my lower lip and I swore I felt him harden against me. Why was I suddenly getting shy and reserved?

"You are beautiful. I want you in every way you will allow me to have you." He kissed me quickly and when I scoffed, he pressed against me, effectively stopping all thoughts. Yeah, that imposing length against my stomach, pressing against my core made my toes curl. My eyes heated as I melted against him.

"Jade." His voice had gotten low and demanded my attention. "When I am buried deep inside of you, you will never second guess that."

"When?" I breathed, not sure I heard him right.

"When." Then his whole body stiffened, and he reached up to his left ear and said, "I'm here." His eyes met mine again, before he said, "We aren't far. ... Out by the beaver dam. ... Okay. Give us ten minutes." He reached back up and hit the button on the earpiece before lowering his head, and kissed me again, making every thought completely vanish out of my head.

He pulled back. "As much as I want to bury and lose myself in you right now..." His voice was rough and needy. He took a very deep shuddering breath and said, "Rogue horse. We gotta go get him."

CHAPTER 13

KOLTON

Jade climbed up into the truck, and when she went to put her seatbelt on, I watched her as she readjusted it across her chest.

"What?" She said, her lips swollen from what we did in the ditch, and I reached up and cradled her face, running my thumb along that bottom lip.

"Are you sure about this?" While that thread between us felt like it would hurt like hell to sever, I had to make sure. "I'm serious. We can't go any further, if..."

Her hand rested on mine, and when I paused, swiping my thumb across her bottom lip, she moved and grabbed it between her lips. My breath caught as she sucked gently and ran her tongue along it. There was no doubt what she wanted.

"Sweet baby Jesus, woman."

"Does that give you an appropriate answer?"

"It does, but I need to hear you say it, Jade."

Her head cocked to the side, before she asked, "Do you have someone else, Kolton? If so, we should discuss that now."

"No. I haven't been in any relationship for a few years. It... It didn't end well." I said pushing down the memory, but then the way she had said... "What do you mean, we should discuss that now?"

"Exactly what it sounds like. I know there are people out there who don't wish to be monogamous. I've been in those relationships. I don't mind them, but I need clear communication and boundary setting before anything else happens if that is the case."

I blinked. Whatever I thought she was going to say, *that* certainly was not it.

"So, no. There is no one else for me. No one else for you?" She said carefully.

"Nope. Just you Jade. If we do this? It's just you." I leaned over the center console, and kissed her. When I pulled away, I asked, "Deal?"

"Deal. Now are we going to go get this horse, or are we going to fuck?" A smirk crossed her lips and I growled deeply as I leaned back and started the truck.

"Fuck, woman." She knew exactly what she was doing. "You make it very hard to be responsible."

Throwing the truck into reverse and heading down the river, her smirk didn't leave her lips until we saw the chestnut gelding galloping across the river line. I reached up and hit the button on my earpiece.

"I have sights on him." I told Ms. Rose.

"Noted. I'll have Philip waiting at the stables when you return."

He was running along the fence line and something had definitely startled him.

"That's him?" Jade asked and turned to look in the back seat.

"Yeah. Looks pretty spooked." I scanned the fence line and noticed three very large wolves on the opposite side of the fence. "Shit."

Jade's head whipped around to look where I pointed. Her eyes went out further, and said, "There are at least four more in the grass." She scanned the rest of the area and I thought I heard her mutter something about the whole pack, but I couldn't be sure.

Before I could ask her about it, her seatbelt was off, and she was half climbing into the back seat. Her ass was right next to me, and in any other situation, I would have bitten it. I knew we had some bumps coming up so I just reached around and secured her, as I drove through the dips in the pasture.

"Got it." Was all I got before I released her. Jade came back up to the front with a bridle and two leads.

"What are you..." I looked at her, then back at the gelding and wolves.

"Just floor it. Those wolves are out for a meal." She reached down into her bag, and pulled out a long buck knife out of her pack and clipped it to her belt. Looking at me for a moment, Jade shook her head as if trying to convince herself of something.

"Where did you..." I said, but then she was lowering the window.

"Get me as close to the gelding as you can."

"Jade!"

"Kolton, trust me, okay?"

"Do I really have a choice right now?" I said through my teeth. "Just please don't get yourself killed. I don't want to have to explain it to Ms. Rose."

"I'll try." She said climbing out the window, out on top of the roof. With an ease and grace that meant she had done it numerous times before, she crawled up into the bed of the truck.

I reached up and clicked the button on my earpiece. "We have wolves. Large wolves. Minimum of eight. Likely more. Gelding spooked. Jade and I are on it."

"Kole. What do you mean you two are on it?" Ms. Rose said.

"Well, umm... Jade is in the back of the truck and I'm trying to get her close to the gelding."

"Kolton!" I heard Ms. Rose say before I clicked my end off, so she wouldn't hear whatever in the hell was going to happen now. When I didn't answer, all I heard was, "Stay out of Jade's way. She knows what she's doing."

Whatever the fuck that meant. I thumped on the top of the truck and Jade answered back.

Barreling through the pasture, I swerved just in time to miss two very large wolves lying in the grass. Shit they were huge and everywhere. This wasn't a normal hunting pack. There had to be thirty of them out there. Where did they all come from? I'd never seen wolves this big before.

The gelding took off down the fence line, and I lined the truck up against him, looked in the side mirror to see Jade... Jade had another rope lasso'd and ready to go.

"What the fuck?!" I blinked and the rope was around the geldings neck. She thumped on the roof and I slowed, as she pulled the gelding close. She slid the halter on, clipping it faster than I would have thought. I shook my head when I realized she had clipped both leads to be a makeshift bridle. How did she know...

"There is so much you aren't telling us, Jade Romero." I said smiling, but it faded, when I heard the howls ring through.

Jade's head swung around toward the sound and then back at the side mirror where our eyes met. I vaguely heard her scream to floor it as she jumped from the bed of the truck onto the gelding, putting her heels to his sides. They took off past the truck at a full gallop.

"Oh, yes, you have so much to explain, you fucking beautiful beast."

I followed them in the truck, but then I saw the trap that the wolves had set. Off to the left, six of them bolted from the grass. Jade saw it too and had that knife in her hand a moment later.

She pushed the gelding harder, and I could see the foam building at his haunches and the sweat building on his chest. The stables were still a way up, and I floored it. I passed her and she gave me a nod before leaning into the gelding.

When I reached the stables, I called for Philip who came out with his rifle. I brought mine out from behind the seat and loaded it.

"Shit. How many are there?" Philip shouted, loading a couple rounds and climbing into the bed of the truck.

I laid on top of the roof, and looked through the scope. "Six? At least on her tail. There are a lot more in the grass, though."

One of the wolves broke away from the pack and lunged for Jade but fell mid-air.

"Did she just?" I heard Philip say next to me. I looked over at him and blinked. Something registered on his face, and his lips thinned as he muttered, "Oh Ms. Rose you have some answering to do."

"I thought she was just some city girl, but damn, that was hot." I mumbled, looking back through the scope, and lining up the shot.

I had to be careful, one wrong move, and this would go so horribly wrong. I took a long deep breath, lined up the shot, then as I slowly let the breath out, I squeezed the trigger. The shot rang out, and one fell.

Philip did the same. One after another, until there was just one left. Philip cursed, when he misfired, and the remaining wolf's claws scraped along the back flank of the gelding. "Jade, careful who you kill." I heard Philip mumble under his breath.

I narrowed my eyes at him, but then turned back to look through the scope on my rifle. Bareback and without her knife there was nothing that Jade could do but put her heels to his sides again as the gelding tripped and stumbled. Two other wolves joined just as the other lunged, but again fell mid-air. Just as it fell, the other lunged, and it followed suit with a loud yip.

"She only had a buck knife. I'm sure of it." I said and looked to Philip who sighed and looked through the scope on his rifle after clearing it. The last wolf was on the wrong side, and I realized, "I can't get a clear shot."

I kept my sight on her and watched as she rubbed the gelding's neck, trying to sooth him as they attempted to outrun the wolf.

The wolf lunged for her, and Jade kicked out. There was a yip and a scream that echoed through the air, but when the wolf landed it changed directions. Jade matched the wolf, and it was then I saw what she had done. She left me the shot. Without thinking, I took it. The wolf went down and everything went silent before howls erupted, loud and sorrowful.

Time slowed as she neared the stables. Once she was within a hundred yards, I ran to her, Philip right behind me. She handed Philip the lead, and there was a shared look between them, but Philip kept his mouth shut when she said, "His back haunch." He nodded, turning to take care of the gelding.

Once Philip was around the corner, I pulled her to me and kissed her. "You have so much explaining to do."

"I'm sure I do." She chuckled. "But first, can we get my leg and arm cleaned up?"

That cleared my head, and I looked at her. Blood. A lot of blood flowed down her jeans, and there was a gash on her arm. Training took over, and I swept her into my arms and carried her inside.

CHAPTER 14

JADE

My left leg really hurt. When I jumped down off the gelding, I felt something fundamental fail in it. Pride wanted me to walk into the stables, but when Kolton pulled me into his arms, I didn't have the energy to fight it.

I looked off into the field we had left, and saw Alpha Devon launch himself over the fence, and when he turned to face me, I felt him say, *"I know who he is, Astral. This isn't over. Retribution for today will be had."*

There was another painful howl that filled the air, and I curled into Kolton's chest.

He was practically running with me in his arms. I stilled and closed my eyes at the sound of the wolves' howls echoing through the wilderness. I hated to kill creatures. They belonged to families, and I wondered who I had known that may have died today. There were at least eight.

I knew some of the lesser members of this particular pack. Alpha Devon's brother, Brandon, was one I had the utmost respect for. He always came to the council meetings and was consistently a voice of reason. There had been so many there today, though. Had Alpha Devon really sent out the entire pack after one horse?

I vaguely felt Kolton set me on a table, but I just laid there. My chest tightened at how I wasn't going to be able to keep everything from him anymore. He agreed to us earlier, but would he now? I was about to ask but... fingers prodded my leg, and I hissed and groaned.

"Jade. Look at me." My eyes flung open, and when my eyes met his, they were hard and serious. So much different than they had been in the ditch. "Jade, can you feel this?" I winced and nodded.

"How about here?"

Poke.

"Yes. Can you please just stitch me up, give me some aspirin and then you can check on the gelding. His back haunch got sliced up pretty bad."

"Philip is attending to the gelding." His hand went to his ear. "Can someone get me the med kit? Jade's hurt bad."

"I'm fine, it's just gonna hurt for a few days." I said through gritted teeth as he continued to clean out the wounds.

I looked down and saw the slice go right through the handle and bottom tip of the dagger tattooed on my thigh. That was going to be a problem. I'll need to get that fixed immediately. I lifted my arm and breathed a sigh of relief as I noticed the slice on my arm didn't go through the small throwing dagger tattoo at my wrist.

"Not gonna happen Jade." His voice was hard.

"What's wrong with you? Don't be a dick."

"I'm not being a dick. You are hurt and I'm trying to fix you. So, shut up and let me take care of you." His voice softened as he said the last part.

I turned my head to the only door. It was shut, but I still kept my voice down. "I take care of myself."

His hands paused, and then started again. "That is something we will have to discuss later, because now you have me to help take care of you, and I won't be taking no for an answer. Now, hold still, this is going to hurt."

"There is nothing to ta..." I grit my teeth and screamed through them. When he let up, I heaved deep breaths.

Rubbing small comforting circles with his thumb, he watched me for a moment. "I need to do below the knee. There's a bit of dirt in there, and I need to see what kind of damage we are dealing with, darling."

My heart skipped a beat, when he poured whatever it was he was cleaning my leg out with and it stung like a son of a bitch. "You did that on purpose, you ass." I finally hissed when he was done.

His head lifted and tilted to the side. "I'm trying to be as careful as I can be. I warned you it was going to hurt."

Still hissing through my teeth as he worked on getting the wound cleaned up. "You called me *'darling'* to distract me."

He huffed a laugh as his cheeks reddened, "If that's what you want to believe."

"What is that supposed to mean?" I said before he hit an especially painful spot right next to my knee, causing me to jerk.

"On a scale of one to ten, how painful was that?" His voice was methodical and professional as he peered down at the knee.

"About a seven." I said, looking down the length of myself at him.

He raised an eyebrow. "Only a seven?"

I nodded and he moved his hand up my thigh and asked, "And here?"

"About a four?" He pressed harder against it, and I said, "Okay, a five."

He mumbled a few things under his breath. Something about me being a stubborn ass woman.

"I'm not being stubborn. I just have a high pain threshold. It's part of who and what I am. None of this feels like I would take more than a couple aspirin. I'm tired, and yes, it hurts, but I can handle it."

He looked up at me, pursed his lips, and just when I thought he was going to say something, someone came in. His eyes shifted to the new arrival, and when I looked up, I saw Rose.

"Hi, Rose." I smiled brightly at her, and her eyes widened.

"How is she doing, Kolton?"

"She needs stitches, and I need that kit, please." He reached out for it, and she handed the bag to him.

"Pulled it from the bus, along with some other supplies, so you'll have to restock." She said looking at the leg. Her eyes narrowed on my dagger tattoo. "The wolf did that?"

"Yeah." He dug around in the pack and pulled the things he needed out. He got up and washed his hands off again in the sink. Rose came over and slipped a piece of paper in my hand and I slid it in my pocket.

"Was given to me when I got the pack out of the bus." Rose murmured so I could only hear.

I mouthed, "Wolves" and she nodded. I sighed and she raised her eyebrows. "I have to tell him everything now."

"I wouldn't wait too long. That howling sounded personal."

"Devon all but said as much. Do we know who died today?" I asked and eyed Kolton who was reaching into the bag again. Rose shook her head just as Kolton turned and I saw him draw some liquid into a syringe, I half sat up and asked, "What do you think you are doing?"

"Giving you a rabies shot, then I'm going to give you some standard antibiotics to stave off any potential infection." He looked over at me and gave me a droll look before saying, "And you aren't going to fight this. You are going to do as I say right now."

"Are you even allowed to dish out those kinds of things?"

"Legally? No, but I'm the only one within a hundred miles that can and will." He said a glint in his eye.

Rose stood there and smiled for a hot minute, before asking, "You don't know what he does in his time off do you?"

"He doesn't have time off. He's here 24/7."

"True, but he can and does leave on a regular basis for emergencies. Don't fight him."

"I'm a licensed paramedic. Now, as I said, I'm going to give you these shots, and then you are going to hold still and let me sew that up and dress it. I'll have to clean it every few hours, though." He came over and stood before me blocking his hand from Rose's view.

He rubbed his hand against mine, smirked and I felt him stick me twice. I shook my head and stuck my tongue out at him.

"Shots aren't a problem for me, Kolton."

"Please tell me you two are done flirting over there, so she can take this." Rose said a giggle in her voice. She handed over a small bottle.

"Healing potion?" I asked, and she nodded. I didn't even hesitate and downed it as Kolton turned to look at Rose with his jaw wide open.

She looked at us carefully, her silver hair shimmering slightly before saying, "It snapped in?"

I nodded. "Earlier today."

"What?" Kolton asked and I took his hand, kissed it, and said, "She knows we are moving forward, Kolton."

Kolton just said, "We've already talked about this, Ms. Rose."

"Rose, what is your relationship to Kolton?" The question came out before I even realized I had thought it, let alone think it through.

This time Kolton turned and blinked at me. "I don't even know what is going on in this room right now." Then he shook his head and went back to working on my leg. There was the bite of the needle and the tug on my skin. I winced, but it was fine.

"I have known Kolton and his family for a very long time. I had a daughter once." Her eyes flicked to Kolton.

"Ashley. I remember. Kolton also told me about her. Said they were close. Not like together close, but close."

Kolton froze and looked at my leg and said, "What was in that tea you gave her?"

"Just some healing herbs." Rose said carefully.

"I swear there was some torn muscle here, but it seems I was wrong." He muttered and continued to stich me up. I looked at Rose who was smiling warmly at him.

Rose turned back to me. "Kolton is like a son to me, Jade. I know him better than probably anyone else on this planet. Better than he knows himself. He hates it, really."

There was a long, drawn-out silence as Kolton worked on my leg. Just as he was finishing up, his eyes rose to meet mine, and he smiled softly.

"Like a son to the owner, and for the last three months, you have been only the foreman?" I whispered. "Didn't think to correct me even in the last few days either, huh?"

He took a deep breath, looked at Rose, then took my hand. "Ms. Rose took me in as a teen when my parents died. A drunk ran them off the road. Car was found in the ravine off BeeLine Rd. About a mile or two up from here. Her daughter, Ashley, was like a sister to me. I told you that in the woods."

"You did."

"I've worked on the property every day of my life since I arrived. Until she insisted I get an education, so I went to school and got my license. It was something that could be practically used here. My entire life is this ranch."

Rose's gaze met mine again. "Jade, I only want what is best for the ranch and for Kolton. But, Philip and some of the hands are already taking bets on when they find you two in the hay loft together."

"Seriously? I swear. I will make them shovel shit for a week." Kolton said, smirking. "Besides the hay loft is way too cliche."

"I already threatened them with a month of stable duty." Rose said, and I couldn't help but laugh.

Kolton finished putting the wrap on my leg and said, "The cut is mostly superficial, but there is some light muscle damage in the thigh. No walking on it for at least a week, two, if we can manage it. Then if, and that is an if, things are healing decently, we will get you in a steel knee brace to help with the weight distribution. You'll need to be in that for two to three weeks. I'll order one once we are done here."

"Kolton." I groaned. "I need to walk this property. I need to see it, walk it. The ravines and the ditches."

He chuckled, and when my eyes met his, there was once again that adorable blush on his face. I raised an eyebrow at him, and the corner of his mouth twitched up.

"Seriously. I do have work to do." I sighed.

"Well, if you hadn't gone all impressive on us out there..."

"Your gelding would be dead. Wolf food." I bit back.

"Not the point." I said pointedly and tried to sit up. Kolton was there instantly and helped move the leg as I scooted to lean against the wall.

"Would you like to explain how you know how to lasso a moving horse, have, well, had a buck knife..."

"Oh shit. Can one of the hands go out and get it?" I blurted.

"We can." He drawled. "But again, not to mention that you know how to use it, and ride bareback, very well I might add."

I bit my lip.

"Don't do that." He whispered. I cocked my head to the side in question, and he just reached over and released my lip. "Unless you want something else to happen."

My eyes widened in understanding, flicked to Rose who just said, "I don't think you would medically clear anyone else for that particular activity, Kolton. Don't give yourself special treatment."

He looked at her and smirked, "And who is going to overrule me."

"Stop thinking with the wrong head, Kolton."

"Yes, ma'am." He turned to me and shrugged.

I looked to Rose. "I need Carlos on a call as soon as possible."

"You need to get that tattoo fixed right away, too."

"Not until her leg heals." Kolton said. His hand rested on my calf, and it was a solid reminder not to fully state everything.

"I heal fast." I said then turned back to Rose, "How soon can you have someone out here?"

"It's only a tattoo, Jade." Kolton said, looking between us.

I looked at Kolton and closed my eyes and took a deep breath. "Remember how I said, I can't tell you everything, yet?"

He pinched the bridge of his nose before he said, "This is part of that? Having a non-damaged tattoo is part of all that?" He looked at me and I nodded and then to Rose who nodded and shrugged like it wasn't a big deal. He looked back at me, and said, "It's a good thing you are cute."

"Oh, so I've downgraded from beautiful to cute." I said, smirking at him. I felt his chuckle more than heard it, and I froze. He did too. His eyes widened as he realized I felt it as well, and when his mouth opened, I interrupted, "Not now, Kolton."

"Philip can fix it." Rose said. I blinked.

"Your vet?" I said just as Kolton said, "Philip?"

"He can fix your daggers when your skin has healed." She said. "How are the knives on your arm?"

"Not damaged. He really is *that* Philip Montegue?" I asked.

"He is." Rose stood proudly.

"Shit. Never saw a picture of him at the Agency, so I didn't realize it was the same person. But shit. Rose. How did you collect Philip fucking Montegue?"

Rose chuckled and I looked to Kolton, who was looking between Rose and I with confusion. "I'm sorry hun. I promise answers are coming."

"I know darling. What I'm still reeling about is the fact that Ms. Rose has a personal artist?" Kolton said, his eyes wide. "And it's Philip?"

"You may be like my son Kolton, but there are things even *you* don't know." She said, and her eyes flicked to mine. "I suspect you want to talk to Carlos about more than just the tattoos." I nodded.

"Devon knows about Kolton."

"Well, shit. I'll talk to him. He will likely send back up."

"I know, but I'm too tired right now to deal with it." I said, leaning my head against the wall. "Can I just take a nap for a bit? Haven't had a whole lot of sleep, and the adrenaline crash is hitting pretty hard."

"Ms. Rose, I'll move her to my place. I want her staying with me so I can oversee her healing."

"Agreed." Rose said, as Kolton lifted me and carried me out of the room.

I was so damn tired as I snuggled into his strong chest. I vaguely heard Rose give Kolton some instructions, and help with opening the door of his apartment and was drifting off to sleep when he laid me in a soft bed.

"Sleep darling." Kolton said, but I distinctly remembered the burning of his lips on my skin as he kissed my forehead and walked away.

CHAPTER 15

KOLTON

"Kolton. I really do need to work." Jade said as I set some food in front of her. She had slept for a few hours, and when she woke up, I redressed the leg, which was already healing. I wanted to talk to Rose about what was in that drink she gave Jade, but I knew she would just say it was Rose magic.

"You aren't going to be up and moving around much, at least for the next couple weeks, darling."

"There you go with the darling, again." She gave me a look of hesitation. "What are you buttering me up for?"

I smirked at her, and brushed her hair behind her ear, and said, "Have your previous boyfriends ever had pet names for you before?"

She hesitated for a moment before saying, "Yes, but not ones that were ever used outside of the bedroom."

Determination and understanding hit me and I asked, "Praise or degradation?"

She bit her lip again, and looked up at me through her lashes. And I cleared my throat, because damn if that alone didn't have me ready for her.

"I prefer praise, but have had both."

Without realizing it, I growled, "Mmm. A good girl then?"

"If you earn it." She said with a twinkle in her eye. Oh, she was going to be fun. "But I'm not medically cleared for sex right now, Kolton. Plus, we have had a wild day. A lot has happened. My leg needs to heal, and... while I want to have the sexual preferences discussion with you, we only really started things a few hours ago."

"I know, darlin'." I reached over and rubbed her cheek. It was so natural to be with her. I wanted to set those guidelines. Those boundaries. I wanted to take her right to the edge of her limits and see just what sounds I could pull from those lips of hers.

I took a deep breath, reeled my thoughts in, and said, "So, pulling back. How do you know how to use that buck knife, ride bareback, and lasso a freaking horse?"

"I kind of avoided that earlier, didn't I?" She said looking up at me again under those fucking lashes.

"You did." There was way too much heat and seduction in that look. "Jade, you are laying it on thick to avoid the conversation. You are not medically cleared for sex, and trust me, anything that we did right now would only set you back."

"You have amazing self-control. You know that?"

"I am trying, but you are not helping the situation at all." I grabbed her chin and kissed her. Her kiss was a shock to my system every time. Nothing made sense when it came to this woman. How could she turn me so completely into a pile of mush so quickly?

"Now tell me." I said kissing along her jaw. There was a gasp, and I felt her hand slide behind my neck and her nails dig in. I moaned into her neck, and forced myself to sit back. "Tell me."

"My dad used to run a ranch in Mexico. There was a group that came through, wiped out all the livestock and killed him and everyone else onsite." Her voice was hushed and pained.

"I'm so sorry."

"My brother and I were at Carlos' house in Fresno when it happened. A distant relative contacted us and told us not to bother coming home. There was nothing left but ash. We were lucky my cousin was able to take us in. He busted ass through the immigration system to get us our paperwork, and got our citizenship." She looked down and played with her fingers for a moment, and I could tell she was contemplating what to tell me and what not to.

"The only thing that Carlos demanded of us was that we got an education. He didn't care if we got a certificate or a masters. All he wanted was for us to get some sort of education that allowed us to get a decent paying job. Something that would allow us a roof over our head and food on the table. I went to school and got my Masters, and my brother became an RN."

"Where is he now?" Her voice had so much pride in it when she spoke of her brother.

She looked at me, and there were tears running down her face. "He... he died last August. Was working in the ER and they turned the corner to find him just lying on the floor. Brain aneurysm. So, I know that pain that you and Rose spoke of about Ashley."

I stared at her. *'I take care of myself.'* She had said. This woman had no one, but was strong and determined. "I know you don't want to hear this..."

"Then don't say it." She said, crossing her arms.

"I need to change the dressing on your leg every few hours, that includes the middle of the night, and you are going to need help getting around for a bit. You are going to stay here for the rest of your stay. Cancel your room, and let them know I'll be by to pick up your things." I said carefully.

"Kolton." She was wary.

"What? Don't want me seeing your dildo collection in your hotel room?"

"Oh, no you're more than welcome to see the dildo collection." A bright smile crossed her face and the wickedness in it was a band around my heart.

"Then what's the problem?"

"I don't want to be a burden." She said just above a whisper. "I take care of myself. My leg is sore, but like I said, give me some aspirin and I'll be fine."

I reached over and pulled her chin around with a single finger to make her look at me. "You are no burden. Medically speaking, you need the help. Personally, I want to be the one to take care of you. It will give me an excuse to be here and spend time alone with you. I'm not even going to hide that little perk."

She studied me for a very long time before she said, "Get my buck knife back out of that wolf, and I'll let you collect my sex toys."

That offer was not one I was going to take lightly. "Yes, my darling."

CHAPTER 16

KOLTON

Pulling up to the bed & breakfast with her room key in hand, I checked in with the front desk and they showed me to the room she was staying in. Like hell she was going to stay here. Her room was on the second floor, and the steps were steep. No way she was going to be able to make it up these things, no matter how stubborn she was. When I walked in, I chuckled.

The bed was unmade, but her clothes were meticulously hung in the closet and shoes were lined up perfectly at the base of the bed. I found her suitcase, and threw it on the bed to load up her things from the bathroom, and not surprisingly everything was laid out carefully on the shelf above the sink. Right down to her own personal cup for her toothbrush and flosser.

After double checking the shower and grabbing her other toiletries, I opened a cosmetic bag with angry little cactus all over it. "Alright then." I chuckled when I looked inside. At least I would know which bag to grab for her if her cycle came in the next two weeks. I opened the purple sparkly one, and cursed as glitter dusted the front of my shirt. "Fucking devil's dust."

I sighed and just muttered, "It's a really good thing you are cute, darling." I got her cosmetics and other toiletries, stuffed them all back in their bag, and threw them onto the bed. When I opened the suitcase, there was a medium sized black duffle bag inside, which hadn't been closed all the way, and allowed an eight-inch purple dildo to roll out. It hit the edge of the suitcase just right and turned on. I reached out and turned it off as I burst out in a fit of laughter. I pulled out my cell phone and called her immediately.

"Ya know, Jade." I sputtered, trying to control my laughter.

"What is that Kolton?" She tried to ask all innocent and sweet. "Find something that made you uncomfortable?"

"Oh no, your cycle bag with the angry cactus is downright adorable. It's the fact you were not, in fact, joking about me collecting your extensive sex toy collection. Key word being extensive, darling. I like what's here, though." I smiled as I put the dildo back in, noticing a few other fun toys. Oh yes, I would be having lots of fun with these. "I especially like the vibrating anal plug. I can think of all kinds of ways to make you squirm."

"What made you think that I was joking about my sex toys? I don't joke about sex, Kolton. I'm a woman who needs her daily orgasm."

I felt myself harden at the thought of having her every day. "Every day, huh?"

Her voice dragged through the phone, "Every day, Kolton." Then she hung up.

Well, fuck me. I ran my hand through my hair and shook my head. One day at a time, Kolton. One day at a fucking time. Let's get her healthy, see where things go, and... pack her shit, Kolton.

I was almost done packing her belongings when my cell rang. Looking at the number, I answered it with a "Talk to me."

"We've gone out to collect the wolves and Jade's knife." Fernando said, but there was something in his voice that put me on edge.

"Did you get Jade's knife?" I said zipping up the suitcase.

"We did. There were a few throwing daggers too, so we grabbed those. You can give those back to Jade as well."

"Throwing daggers?" I must have missed when she put those in her pocket. "Have you processed the wolves?"

"They weren't there to collect. Don't ask, man. I don't know. Maybe other predators hauled them off for food, but by the time we got there, they were gone." He paused for a moment before saying, "Where are you, Kolton?"

"Packing up Jade's room at the B&B. She's going to be staying with me while she heals."

"Only while she heals? Is that so you can keep an eye on her? Orrrr..." I could hear the teasing in his voice, and I smiled.

"Hope you didn't bet on us being in the hay loft too soon, Fernando. Jade was hurt pretty bad in the attack and she's going to need some help getting around for a bit, and the leg dressing will need to be changed out pretty regularly."

"Whatever you have to tell yourself, man." His chuckle through the phone made me smile. The guys knew me well, but damn. "Kolton, you ain't seriously looked at a woman since Nicole. We are just hassling you. We have concerns, but we all love you like a brother man and just want you happy."

"Thanks. I'm gonna miss game night, obviously."

"We already talked. We'll do it tomorrow night. Bring Jade. I'm sure she'll be ready to get out of that apartment of yours by then."

"We'll see. I'll be back on property soon. Then you can get me on comms."

CHAPTER 17

JADE

I had been regulated to computer work. Carlos had been very understanding of the situation, and said he would rather I stay there to oversee the agents being sent to help protect the property.

When I told Rose that the guest quarters needed to be ready for two more Astral, she groaned. She didn't move from her spot, she looked at me, "How are things with Kolton?"

I looked down, the wind blowing strands across my face as I played with my fingers. "We are talking."

"Jade. He is your bonded."

"And I'm trying to take it slow. The thought of him being that to me... scares the hell out of me. I... I've been through a heart shattering already. I can't do it again. Only, this time, I wouldn't live through it."

"And you don't just tell him why?"

I scoffed. "He's a human, bonded to a supernatural. That would go as well as oil in a glass of water."

"Carlos... he told you to tell him, right?"

I looked down at my hands and dropped them. "Yeah, and I will. But I need to get to know him before telling him he is stuck with me forever. Whether that be a romantic relationship, a friendship, or an unbreakable connection, I want to get to know him, because..." I looked up and hadn't realized that tears had filled my eyes, until I blinked and one fell down my cheek. "I don't hurt at the thought of Daniel when I'm with him. He calms me instantly with the smallest of touches, and he listens... really listens"

"That was one of Ashley's favorite things about him. He had an even head, an open ear, with a comforting shoulder to cry on." She gave me that Rose Porter smile and said, "And completely smitten with you."

"You are just saying that because he is my..." I swallowed before saying, "Bonded. You know how weird that is to say?"

"No stranger than it feels to have a man who I consider my son, who is human, to be bonded and smitten to an Astral. An Astral Primal at that." She raised an eyebrow before asking, "How much God blood do you have in you, anyway?"

I shrugged. "I'm not sure. Mom would never elaborate, but..." It had been a long discussion, and Dad would always look at her sideways when the question was posed.

"Which God, if I may ask?"

"It is recorded that I'm descended from Huitzilopochtli." I breathed.

"The God of Sun and War." She blew out a whistle, and then asked, "And you don't know how much of his blood you have in him?

"I don't. I'm sure the Agency could tell me. There was rumor that my lineage crossed with a descendant with one of the descendants of Xipe Totec. That may have made my line even more powerful. Likely why I'm a Primal."

"Gods of Death on two sides of the line." Rose said quietly. I smiled softly, nodded, and opened my mouth to say something, but she said, "You need to tell Kolton about all of this. He really needs to know now."

"I know. I'll talk to him, I promise. Now, about the project. Carlos said you guys talked about it, and we are still moving forward. I don't want the wolves and what is happening with Kolton to affect it. You have stated from the beginning that you were on a time table."

"And time tables can be changed for the betterment of my family. Yes, no matter what anyone says, Kolton is my family. Besides, you get to spend time with him, too." Rose winked at me as she handed me another one of her healing teas. I inhaled the earthy scent and took a sip, settling further into the pillow fort that was likely to be my home for a while on this bed in Kolton's spare bedroom.

"The project, Rose. Isn't your grant funding on a strict timeline?"

"It is, but we have some wiggle room. In the construction."

"I built in the wiggle room, because you need wiggle room with construction. Things go wrong. Supplies don't come in on time. Workers get hurt. Don't even get me started on the delays rain can cause. Gods, Rose, you know all this."

"I do, and I will get other funding if this falls through."

"You are willing to chance your entire dream. Everything you have been working for, for thirty years for Kolton and I?"

There was absolutely no hesitation in her response. "Yes."

"Rose, I've known you for too long, so I'm going to be brutal and straight. That is fucking stupid. Business and pleasure shouldn't mix. You have no idea how messed up in the head I feel right now. Yes, there is the bond with Kolton. I don't even know what to do with that. If I didn't have the pack breathing down my neck, I would take the time to ease him into everything, but I don't have that fucking luxury. You know why? Because just before Devon jumped over that fence, he told me he knew what Kolton was to me. But that is all personal, and this is business. Don't jeopardize a business deal because of it. There is too much at risk here." I said, trying to get my point across.

"You are the best Jade. I want the best on this project."

"There are other great people to work with. Or I can refer you to some other people outside of the company who would do an amazing job for you."

"No. I want you to do it." She said firmly. When my eyes met hers, she said, "I think that if you and Kolton can keep it together, that you two will turn this place into the best rehab center in the state. So, you are staying on the project."

"I will continue to work on plans where I can from here, but while here, I should be out looking at the land, committing it to memory, making adjustments, because there are differences from what was taken from the overhead maps from what should be on the onsite maps. Those need to be done with me on my feet. Me being off my feet, will slow it all down and put us behind schedule by a month if what Kolton says is true."

There was a bit of a satisfied smirk on her face, and I realized why, "You are expecting Kolton and I to stay here and run the rehab aren't you?"

Rose's smile widened and she said, "Took you long enough."

"Rose."

"Jade. You are soul bonded. You can't leave him."

"I know that, but I have work to do for the Agency. I won't be able to set roots and live a quiet life. You know the Agency doesn't work like that."

"I know."

"How am I supposed to do that to Kolton? How am I supposed to be like hey, you are stuck with me for life. Oh, but you can't travel with me because you are a liability. Oh no, I can't just stay here, either. How in the fuck is that all supposed to work?"

"We will see what we can do. I'm not having you reassigned." She stood, and studied me, "Wait, you said Devon knows who Kolton is to you?"

I nodded.

"Did you tell Carlos?"

I nodded, again. "Why do you think he is sending two Astrals?"

"One of you are deadly enough, why two?"

"Because I'm his cousin, I'm down, and he said that I could get over the special treatment."

"Well, I guess I'll have the boys clean out one of the guest rooms for them to stay in." Rose said, going to the door. "Three Astral's on a seer's property. *That's* not going to raise any eyebrows."

"Hopefully it will give Devon pause to move against any of the property for a while." I picked at the blanket. "Pause, not cause."

"When will they get here?"

"Three days. They are flying into San Diego from La Paz." I said smiling. "They were sorting out a situation with small group of demons. They will be flying up to Portland from there, and then drive down."

CHAPTER 18

JADE

"Where are we going, Kolton?" I protested as he practically forced me into some loose-fitting shorts encouraging me to get dressed.

"It's Family Game Night. We play card or board games once a week." When I gave him a questioning look, he just said, "We are family here, darlin'. This way we can spend time together without it just being work."

"Family." The word rang through me as old memories flashed through my mind. My brother and

I playing in the horse pastures in Mexico, the large wooden table with food lined up, *abuela* smacking my dad's hand as he reached for a roll...

I didn't realize I had frozen until Kolton took my jaw in his hand and made me look at him. "You okay?"

"Yeah. Sorry." I muttered but he narrowed his eyes at me in concern. "Your leg okay?"

"Yes." I sighed, and nodded my head to keep him talking. "Family."

"James and Fernando are my brothers. I would do anything for them." Nodding, he was still studying my eyes, but it was the warmth in those eyes that caused my thoughts to go in a completely different direction. I bit my lip, and his eyes immediately went to where my tooth pinched the pink flesh.

"Darlin', you gotta quit doing that to me." He said under his breath and released my jaw. The red on his cheeks was absolutely adorable, and just when I was going to ask him to repeat his words, he was lifting my leg to help me off the bed. I scooted closer to the edge and the heat in the palm of his hands certainly wasn't helping with the tightening in my stomach.

Once I was ready, Kolton helped me up and to the front door, where I leaned against the wall as he gathered his things, and when he opened the door, I shivered. He looked me up and down and whispered with a smirk, "I don't know how something so hot can be cold. Don't move, Darlin'."

"What?" Did he really just use a corny line on me?

"I should have put you in some sweatpants." He grabbed one of his sweatshirts from the little coat closet, turned toward me, but paused, going back to the living room and grabbing the fuzzy throw blanket from the couch. "Here, let's get you in my sweatshirt." He had it over my head, without me having a chance to register what he said.

My arms slid through but his hands lingered and slowly trailed down my sides, making the goosebumps on my body there for something completely other than the cold weather. When my head popped through and the hood sat firmly on my head, my senses were filled with him. He stood right against me for a moment, longer than my brain could rationally process, before he took half a step back, looked me up and down, and let out a breath through pursed lips.

"Fuck, I love the sight of you in my hoodie." I tried to control my blushing, but he just gave me a quick kiss on my forehead before handing me the blanket. His voice was low, so low I barely heard him as he said, "Let's get downstairs before I break my own rules and provide you clearance for sex."

"What?"

"Darlin', while everyone downstairs knows that I am highly attracted to you, they don't know that we..." He held my waist as he helped me through the door and turned to close it. "That we are trying. I'd like to keep it from them a little longer if possible. You've heard how much I've been razzed by them so far, and that is just when I saw what a great ass you have."

"So, James and Fernando are your brothers, but you haven't told them that you and I are involved?" I tried to hide the hurt I felt. Kolton half picked me up before we got to the stairs, and he set me next to the railing. I planted myself there, until he looked at me. "Why haven't you told them?"

"It's been two days, darlin'." He stood against me, arms on each side of me, blocking me in. He leaned in, and bent down so close I could feel his breath against my jaw as he said, "I want to make sure we are something."

"We are, Kolton Webster." I said, pulling back to meet his gaze. "Tell me you don't feel that draw, that tie that binds us."

His eyes lit up, but I had a moment of panic as I realized what I had said. No, Jade. It's okay. Carlos told you to tell him everything. This is real. Kolton is real. Carlos told you to tell him because it is real.

"Okay, Darlin'." He kissed me softly, and when he pulled back, he said, in that voice that had a wave of heat washed through and would have had me on my knees if not for this leg, "You are mine."

"Hey, fucker! Get down here." James shouted behind me, interrupting my thoughts. My fingers twitched toward my dagger on my good leg, but I smirked when I saw that Kolton's eyes showed every ounce of frustration I felt at the interruption.

"James, I swear if you value your life, you will go inside, and wait five minutes before coming back out here again."

"I drew the short straw. I tried to tell them just to let you guys figure it out, but your presence is required for Family Game Night by Ms. Rose."

I smiled at Kolton, who shook his head giggling. "We will be right down. Jade isn't exactly mobile. It takes time."

His gaze held mine. "Why is it always James that interrupts us?"

"Sounds just like a brother to me." I smiled, and there was just a half of second of hesitation before Kolton's lips slammed onto mine, and he pulled me tightly to him. His tongue ran the length of my lips, and when I opened for him, shifting and wrapping my arms around his shoulders, I felt a moan from him that sounded just as needy as I felt.

When we broke apart, he rested his forehead on mine, drawing in breath in short quick movements. "Dammit, darlin'."

I couldn't help but chuckle, and I opened my mouth to tell him there was time, but I heard the door open downstairs. Kolton sighed, pulled his head back and said, "We are coming. Just hold your horses."

A moment later the doors opened and closed. "Let's go to Family Game Night before you do have to kill James, and he seems like a nice enough guy."

Kolton reached around and wrapped an arm around the small of my back, and whispered, "Hold on tight," as he carefully slid his other arm under my knees and lifted me up. The skin pulled, and as pain ran down my leg at the movement. I winced, but tried to hide how much it hurt so I didn't worry him.

"Need something for the pain?"

"I'm fine."

"Jade." He shook his head, and asked, "Are you sure, or are you just being a tough guy right now."

"It hurt, but just when you picked me up. Once we are downstairs and I'm back in a chair, I'm sure it will be fine." I said as he carried me down the stairs.

After a bit more jostling, he carried me into the main office building and into a back room I hadn't seen yet. It was furnished much like a living room. A blue couch was against the wall with a black coffee table, but Kolton carried me over to one of the chairs that surrounded a round table already set up with a deck of cards. Fernando was right there with a stool for me to prop up my leg, and gently laid a pillow underneath so I was comfortable.

"Thank you, Fernando." I muttered and he simply nodded his head before taking his seat across from me.

"How are you feeling, Jade?" Rose asked and I looked up at her. She had that knowing smile on her face.

"Sore, but Kolton is taking care of me." Meeting her stare. Her eyebrows raised, someone coughed, and someone else tripped over their own feet behind me.

It was James who said, "Can we get you something to drink?"

"Water is fine. Thank you."

While everyone else finished setting things up, I looked around the room. There was a worn light brown leather couch across from a big screen TV mounted to the wall. The lone window was at the far end had dark blue drapes. I looked back at the couch, and could almost see one of the guys with their boots hanging over the edge of the arm as they laid there, snoring during a break.

Kolton sat next to me and scooted closer to the wood table, scraping his chair on the laminate flooring. His head popped up and looked at Rose. "Sorry, Ms. Rose."

"You scuff it, you fix it."

"Yes, ma'am."

James sat down and handed me the water, and I took a sip. "So, what are you playing?"

"We, Jade." James said with a smirk on his face, that made me want to throw a dagger at him.

"I'm sorry? Want to say that again?"

"Jade..." Rose said, and I shook my head.

"I won't kill him!" I let a smile cross my face as I looked back at James and let my gaze trail up and down him, before continuing, "Just scar him up a little bit."

"I don't want to file the paperwork. Please don't." Rose said, letting out a loud chuckle, and I swear I saw James stiffen a bit.

"Kolton, you wouldn't let her do that to me right?"

"I don't know why you think that I have control over what our Project Manager does." He shrugged, but I could almost feel his amusement through that bond between us.

"Kolton..." James' voice was a little worried.

"There are very few people who have control over my actions, and none of them are on this property." I said with a steadiness to my voice that drained the color from his cheeks.

The door opened and it was Rose who said, "It's about fucking time. We were going to start without you."

"I'm sorry, Ms. Rose. The McCarthy mare's muzzle needed to be cleaned up. She thought it would be a good idea to chew on the pen. Wasn't too happy I had to pull some splinters." Philip came in, gave her a quick hug, and sat down in the empty chair next to her.

"We are playing a variation of Truth or Dare." Fernando said, putting Philip and James out of their misery. James was still looking at me, and so I broke the tension and stuck my tongue out at him. "Technically you are supposed to drink if you fail, but instead if you fail to state the truth or complete the dare, the card goes to the middle. He or she with the most cards wins."

"How do you pick which you do?"

"You roll the D-20, and odd equals dare, evens are truth."

Rose grabbed the die after Fernando placed the two stacks of cards, blue for truth and red for dare. "Jade goes first. Whoever sits directly across from them pulls the truth or dare from the card pulled."

I looked at Kolton who just smiled at me and tipped his head toward the dice. Reaching out and taking it, I threw it a little harder onto the table than I may have needed to, onto the sunken felt portion of the table. It tipped, and I heard James beg for an odd. Phil laughed when it tipped to a 20.

Phil didn't miss a beat and grabbed the truth card and chuckled. "One of three free question cards in the deck."

I could see that there were a million questions that he wanted to ask, so I narrowed my eyes at him. "Ask. Ask what you really want to know."

His gaze flicked to Kolton and said, "Not yet, but something different." He studied me a moment and I smirked at him. I had a feeling that first question had everything to do with the man I was trying not fuck senseless every second we were alone upstairs. Instead, when his head kicked to the side and his eyes narrowed again. Rose whispered for Philip to tread carefully, and there was an imperceivable nod to me before I said, "Or do you want to know if what happened in the Indian Ocean is true?"

Philip's head whipped to Rose who shrugged. "Well, since she knows, I know. I'll ask. Is the official story of what happened to Daniel San Terenimi, true?"

"Philip…" Kolton growled next to me. I stared him down as my heart raced, then as a hand touched my thigh, it vanished.

I looked over to Kolton, and put my hand on his shoulder. "I'm fine. Though, I *am* curious how he knows Daniel's real last name. The short answer is yes, Daniel killed a number of beings to rescue me from that hell hole."

Kolton's hand tightened, causing the scab to pull. I tried to hide it, but he must have noticed, because he immediately pulled his hand back to sit on top of the table. Philip pushed back his long sleeve t-shirt, and I eyed his forearms. He waved his hand over them, an eyebrow raised at me, as the Agency's flowing symbols shimmered and vanished.

Fernando reached over, grabbed the die and rolled a 19, and looked up to Rose. The red card lifted, and she chuckled. "Oh, this is fun. *You and one other person are to do a plank until the other falls. Speaker chooses your competitor.* Kolton and Fernando. On your elbows."

"Fuck." Kolton muttered, taking his sweatshirt off, revealing the tight fitted navy-blue t-shirt. Fernando got up, and walked around the table, so that they were next to each other.

"I'm waiting, boys." Rose teased.

They both shook out their arms, and Fernando looked at Kolton before they dropped to the ground. "I'm going to make you look like a pussy before your girl, Kole."

"The fuck you are." Kolton growled as Rose shouted, "Start!"

I pulled out my phone and started the timer. When Kolton looked up at me from between his elbows, he smiled and shook his head. "I gotta see how long you can hold a plank, Kolton."

"Longer than you." His smile widened, but faded when I raised an eyebrow at him. "What's your time?"

"Two minutes, eighteen seconds." I shrugged, and the room went silent. I thought Kolton was going to drop from the shock, but when I looked at the rest of the room, they were staring at me.

"Fuck this. Come on, Kolton, we gotta beat that time. Come on. We can do this." Fernando said, but his hips were already starting to drop.

"Better get those hips off the ground then, Fernando."

"Jade, be nice to my boys." Rose chastised, and when I looked at her, the sound in her voice didn't match the look on her face. She was completely enjoying this.

I looked down at the timer, and they were now at a minute-ten. I shook my head when Fernando looked up at me, sweat beading down his face, and Kolton was starting to shake in the arms. I couldn't help but chuckle.

"Time." Kolton whimpered.

"Minute- forty."

"Fuck." He growled and started to bring himself up to his hands, and Rose, said, "You get on your hands, and you have to load hay all month by yourself."

Fernando dropped at a minute-fifty, and when Kolton looked up to me, he had the perfect view of me under the table. I smirked, and said, "You sure you want to do this Kolton. You've already won."

"Two-eighteen?" I nodded, and he groaned. "Where we at?"

"Two-five." I said, but ran my hand between my legs, and rubbed myself through my shorts, while maintaining eye contact with him. He must have registered the movement, because his gaze dropped to between my legs, and I moved my hand faster. Kolton's eyes went wide and he dropped. I pressed the button on my phone, and turned it for all to see.

"Two-ten." I watched as he rolled over onto his back, groaning. "Guess I'm better than you."

"Eight seconds, Jade." He looked up over his head to me, "When that leg is fixed, we will see who has the better plank time."

"Eight seconds is all a bull rider needs to ride, too, yet most don't make it." I said as the room erupted into laughter.

When they got back into their seats, I looked to James, who looked at me nervously, but reached for the die, and rolled it.

"Thank God. Even." James said before looking at Kolton, who lifted the card and said, "*Name your favorite body part of your significant other. If you do not have a significant other, what do you look for physically in a partner?* Well shit, that is no fun. Everyone knows James likes tits."

"Yup. Gotta fill my hands." He said holding them up. "Philip, you're up."

He reached over and rolled an eight, and sighed, "What you got for me Jade?"

Lifting the card it stated, *Free question.* "It says free question. Are you really *that* Philip Montegue?"

"I'm not sure I understand what you are asking." He said shifting in his seat. Rose gave me a look that meant to be careful, but I ignored her. Philip had gone straight to Daniel. I could go for this.

"Did a Primal contact you, buy out your contract, and hide you out here with Rose Porter?" Where you really a slave to the Therugi demons in Columbia was the real question.

His eyes held my stare and when I didn't relent, he sighed, "Yes."

"So, you can repair what's on my leg?"

"If it's ordered, yes." His eyes flicked around the table.

"Thank you." I muttered, and then looked at everyone else. "Neither Philip nor I will elaborate on the discussion we just had."

Philip let out a long breath before saying, "Everyone here knows I have a history, but you are right, we won't speak more on it. Discretion is requested on your part as well, Astral."

My lips tightened, and I didn't retort. I had pushed him. It was only fair he pushed back. I let out a long breath, and looked to Rose. "I believe it is your turn."

She glared at me for a long moment, then released it, her hair swirling, and then shook her head. "Alrighty then. Let's go." She grabbed the die and rolled an eleven. "Oh, hell."

Fernando smirked and reached for the blue stack, and chuckled and read, "*Demonstrate to the room how to put on a condom, using a banana.*"

She simply rolled her eyes, got up, went to the kitchen, and put a hand out waiting for someone to put a condom in her hand once she returned to the table. "If you don't have a condom in your wallet, you are a fucking dumbass and you will shovel shit for three months. All four of you. Now."

I don't think I had seen the four of them move so fast since I arrived. In less than a minute four condoms sat in Rose's palm. It was everything I could do not to laugh hysterically at the boys in that room. Rose had them on a tight leash, and it was amazing to watch.

She broke into one of the packages, and slipped it on, without looking. "Kolton your roll." She said throwing the condom covered banana in the center of the table.

Kolton rolled a seven, and groaned. "Shiiit."

James lifted the card, reading, "*Change your social media to "I'm a horny motherfucker, and need a cow now."*

"I only have a photo account." Sighing he met James' eye, took a photo of James smirking at him, and posted it as the caption.

It was my turn again, and we played about four more rounds, each leaving our sides hurting in laughter. I could see how they felt like they were a family. It warmed her heart, and when I felt Kolton looking at me, I blinked.

"What?"

"Ummm. James just read my card, and there was no reaction from you." Kolton came to sit closer to me. "Nose to nose with the person on your left for two minutes."

"Oh." I said, and pulled on all my professionalism to hold it together as much as I could. "Umm, can you come sit on the other side, so it will be easier without my leg up on the stool."

He came around and I moved so that he could sit between my legs. "Two minutes."

"We can't close our eyes or look away, either." He said softly, as he took a deep breath.

"Piece of cake." I breathed.

James had his phone out, and it didn't fail my notice that Fernando and Philip had theirs out as well. No doubt at least two of them were recording this. Two minutes, looking into his eyes. I could do this. There was no reason I couldn't make this time limit, being as professional as possible.

I'd battled Selki, Therugi, drug smugglers, and fought off vampires and a million other things that tore into one's nightmares. I could look into my Bonded's eyes for two minutes. Sure. Why not?

"Ready?" Kolton asked carefully. His hand moving back and forth out of everyone's sight. I nodded, and we leaned in toward each other.

"Start." James said.

Kolton's nose met mine, and those brown eyes heated like melted chocolate.

Yeah. I was so, so, so wrong. Two minutes of hell incoming.

CHAPTER 19

KOLTON

"Start." James said.

My nose met hers, and a heat went through me that seared every nerve in my body. It took me practically locking my muscles into place, not to pull her to me and kiss her.

That kiss on the breezeway had been at the forefront of my mind since I pulled away from her. I couldn't get enough of her. Two minutes of forcing myself to keep my hands to myself.

Fuck.

It was if she knew what I was thinking. She reached down and grabbed my hand, under the table, threading our fingers together. I scooted closer to her, unable to resist that pull.

"Time?" Fernando said, a chuckle to his voice.

"Twenty seconds." James voice was full of laughter. "There is no way they make two minutes."

"James. Be nice." Rose said.

"Ms. Rose, look at them. I'm with James, there is no way." Philip was right, though. If we made it to two minutes, even I would be surprised.

I couldn't think of a thing to say. I vaguely heard the guys start taking bets, but I couldn't concentrate on it. Her green eyes had me wholly captivated. There were the smallest flecks of gold in them, that seemed to shimmer back at me. There was that piece that bound us together and it felt as though someone had lit it with electricity, and started winding it together in the center, pulling us closer and closer together.

My free hand trailed up her arm, and the next thing I knew I was holding her neck, leaning into her, our lips barely separated.

I saw her pupils dilate, as she whispered, "Kolton."

My name on her lips was my complete undoing. There was no way I was going to make this dare. I needed to kiss her.

"Darlin'." I whispered back a moment before I closed that hairs distance and my lips were on hers. I wrapped myself around her, pulling her close. I felt that tie between us grow taught, and I groaned into her, needing her closer.

I felt her body twitch slightly, but her free leg wrapped around my hip, pulling me closer. I felt her moan into me. Everything about this woman settled into me, and I knew right there and then, I was ruined for anyone else on this planet. It was going to be Jade or no one.

She pulled back, her hand on my cheek. "Well, I guess keeping it from the family isn't going to work."

"Like we didn't know you two were all lovie dovie already." James said. "By the way, you didn't even make a minute before you caved, Kole."

My breathing was slightly too heavy, as I kissed her again quickly and turned to James. "You wouldn't have been able to, either."

He looked to his left to where Philip was sitting and said, "With Philip? Oh easy!"

I couldn't help but chuckle. "You know I mean with your girlfriend, you fucking assholes."

"Oh! You are admitting that Jade's your girlfriend now?" James teased.

Jade's eyes went to Philip and then to Rose, who finally said, "Jade and Kolton are allowed their secrets."

"Jade, are you..." Philip trailed off and his eyes flicked between us again. Jade looked at Philip and sighed nodding to Philip. "Well shit! I don't know whether to be concerned for all of us or break out the tequila."

I looked between them completely confused. "Philip, how do you know Jade?"

"I don't know Jade any better than you."

"You two are having a conversation that no one but the two of you understand." I gripped Jade's hand still threaded through mine tighter.

Her hand reached up and cradled my cheek, making me look at her. "Remember how I said, I need to tell you things, but I don't know how to tell you everything yet?"

"You knowing Philip and Rose is part of that?"

"You and I already discussed how I know, Rose." Her eyes flicked to Philip before returning to mine. "I know *of* Philip Montegue. Remember my truth question earlier? I asked if he was the same Philip Montegue I had heard terrible stories of. I won't divulge what I know, because those are his stories to tell if he wants to tell them, which I suspect he rightfully does not."

"Thank you." Philip's voice had dropped sorrowful, but there was clear appreciation as well.

"The only thing I will tell you, because I know you won't let this go, is this." I nodded at her. She would tell me everything in time. "I told you that Rose has worked with Carlos before. Well, Carlos asked for a favor in helping Philip. Rose agreed, and Philip came here. That is really all I know of the situation. I don't know the specifics, and those who do will not speak of it. Likely *can't* speak of it. So, I'm asking you, all of this *family*, to drop it. Not everyone's history is squeaky clean."

I studied her for a moment before kissing her, letting my lips linger, because fuck, I couldn't help it. "Alright, Jade."

"So have we ruined the mood for game night, or are we still playing?" James asked, and Fernando agreed.

I raised an eyebrow at Jade, who said, "I'm down to still play, if you can get me a couple aspirin for my leg, Kolton? When you kissed me like that, I hit my leg against the table trying to wrap my legs around you, and it hurts a bit."

"What?" I jumped up and grabbed her ankle, swinging it around, looking at her leg. One of the wrappings looked a bit red, and so I lifted it, and went for the first aid kit.

"Kolton?" She reached for my hand, and almost fell out of the chair. I caught her, and set her back upright.

"I'm just going for the first aid kit to change the dressing, and get you some pain killers, darlin'."

There was a huffed laugh and she nodded as I kissed the top of her head.

"Not a word, James!" I said over my shoulder heading into the other room.

I grabbed the first aid kit, a couple pills of aspirin from the bottle, and heard James and Fernando head toward the bathroom while we had a break. I took a deep breath and leaned on the wall. What was it about Jade that controlled my every thought? When I got the 911 call last night and had to respond, it was so damn hard to leave her in my apartment.

Shit. I had Jade living in my apartment, and in my guest room. I had to relieve myself more than ever since the wolf attack. I reached down and adjusted myself, because that kiss had made me want to bury myself deep within her. When I called her mine up on the walkway outside the apartment, I wanted to roar it to the world. Make sure everyone knew she was off the market and mine.

I pushed off the wall, and heard the hushed voices of Rose, Jade and Philip. It was Philip's who came through the loudest. "Astral. Thank you for not telling them everything."

Astral. There was that word again. Philip had used it before, but what did it mean? What in the hell is an Astral, and why is he calling Jade one?

"I can't believe I'm standing, well sitting really, before the infamous Philip Montegue." There was a pause, some muttering, and then Jade saying, "All that aside, you could fix my leg?"

"I'll ask for authorization. They own me." Philips' voice was tight, and there was so much more that we didn't know. We knew he had come here under some sort of protection, and Rose had installed the coded gate immediately after his arrival. There had been some other strange people who had come around to install some more remote security, but I never really got the rundown on that.

"That is all I can ask. Thank you." Jade said before I pushed off the wall and walked back in.

"Take good care of her, Kolt." Philip's hand was on my shoulder.

I nodded to him, "As long as she'll have me."

There was a bright laugh from Philip at that. "Oh, then I should ask when the nuptials are."

"Philip!" Rose admonished.

I rolled my eyes, and when I focused back on Jade, she grabbed my hand as soon as I put the kit on the floor. Handing the two aspirin to her, she downed them without any water, and squeezed my hand tighter.

"They are teasing, Jade."

"It's not that, Kolton." I didn't hide the smile that crossed my lips as I removed the gauze from where I could see she was bleeding, and got some peroxide to clean it before I covered it back up. "What's wrong, then? Leg hurt? Do you want to go back upstairs?"

The inner thigh of her good leg twitched, and I looked up at her raised an eyebrow, and smirked. "Not medically cleared, darlin.'"

"Well, then I guess we will just have to stay here and continue to play games." Her playfulness relaxed some of the muscles in my shoulders.

"Whenever you are ready, I'll carry you upstairs." She didn't answer for a moment. I was worried if I had looked up at her, I would say to hell with that medical clearance and haul her over my shoulder and take her to bed and show her exactly how much I wanted her.

CHAPTER 20

JADE

I t had been a few days since the attack and Kolton had duties he had to attend to around the ranch, so he wasn't in here all the time, but I sort of felt like he wanted to be. When he left this morning, he made it very clear that I was not to put all the weight on my leg until he returned with the knee brace he was getting from Crescent City. He had ordered one for me, and said that it wasn't a big deal to go to the city to pick it up because there were a bunch of other items that had come in for the property that needed to be picked up as well.

Before he left, he had helped me down to the main workspace, where I could set up a makeshift office for the time being. He even went out of his way to make sure that I had somewhere to put my leg up. It was 2:00 pm when James came in.

"Ms. Romero."

"James, I've told you a few times to call me Jade." I said, staring at the computer screen. I rubbed my eyes, and when I looked at him, I saw two very large men who looked like they should be on the front lines of just about any football team in the NFL. Both clearly had spent some time in the sun in Mexico, and I had to admit, I was a bit jealous.

"Myka, Titus." I smiled brightly.

"So, you do know these two?" James said carefully.

"I do. They are the two that will be sharing the guest quarters you cleaned out yesterday." Titus' eyebrow twitched and Myka's lip curled up. "And didn't Ms. Rose ask you to start on the other one, in case they need to stay longer than a few nights?"

"Yes, ma'am."

"Then go ahead and get back to it."

"You sure?" James asked. "Kolton would kick my ass if I left you alone with them."

"Yeah, it isn't this Kolton guy you should be concerned about." Myka said, smirking.

"Be nice, Myka." My voice came out flat and commanding.

"Yes, ma'am."

James' eyebrows shot to the ceiling. "As you can see James, I got this."

"Yes, Ms. Romero." He all but ran from the room.

"Ms. Romero?" Titus' chuckle was throaty and light.

"Did that human really think to protect you from us?" Myka said sitting in one of the chairs in front of the desk I was sitting at.

Titus took a moment to look at the leg. I had propped up. "Carlos wasn't kidding about your leg."

"Carlos is being an overprotective shithead."

"So that leg doesn't have you out of commission, Astral?"

"It does, but I'll be fine in a week." I shrugged.

Titus sat in the other chair and said, "So why did Carlos require both of us to come and help you out. He didn't exactly give us a game plan. Just said to come and protect you and the Porter Ranch."

I let out a deep sigh. "The Kiku Pack has grown too big for its britches, and despite my offers of other territory expanding options, their Alpha, Devon Wulfrunn, is demanding the wildland of the Porter Ranch. As you may, or may not be aware, the Porter Ranch is protected by the Agency."

"Yes ma'am. Rose Porter is one of the best seers in the world." Myka stretched. "I still don't understand why there needs to be three Astrals, one of which is an Astral Prime." His eyebrow raised dramatically.

"Again, because Carlos is being an overprotective ass."

"What do you need us to do, Astral Jade?" Titus finally asked.

"Get settled. I'm sorry there is only one room, but they have been used as store rooms, and it was sort of sudden notice you were coming." They both shrugged but waited for further orders. "Since I am currently immobile, I need the perimeter watched. I can't have the humans keeping an eye out on things."

"Understandably." They said in unison.

Then Titus asked, "Do we have permission to forcibly remove them from the property?"

"You do, but don't kill any of them." I leaned back and rested my head on the back of the chair, as they looked a little surprised by that order. I gestured to my leg and said, "A couple days ago, when this happened, at least eight of their pack died. A few by my hand. A few by rifle."

"Who pulled the trigger?" Myka asked.

"Kolton Webster and Philip Montegue."

"The Philip Montegue. The Agency's most secretive artist?" Myka asked, and whistled appreciatively.

"Apparently one in the same."

"And who is this Kolton? The human mentioned him, too. Seems to think he's a little protective over you." Titus asked carefully.

I stared at him for a long moment and it was Myka whose eyes went a little glossy as he said, "He's your Bonded."

"I really hate that you are half seer." I ground out. "He is, but you are under strict orders and under punishment of death to speak of anything you see, hear, feel, or come to knowledge of while on or around the property," I looked at each of them and corrected,

"While in the Pacific Northwest, not a word until your final breath. Is that understood?"

"When did you two find out?" Myka asked carefully.

"Not very long ago. Kolton doesn't know anything, yet." Their shocked faces actually brought a smile to my face. "He will be brought up to speed before too long."

"Yes, Astral." They shared a look but nodded in affirmation.

"I'm assuming he will be number one on the protection list." Titus asked with a small smile.

"He is." I whispered, and winced at putting him before Rose. Gods, if the Primals knew I gave that order... "Rose, second. The Agency would murder me if Rose was compromised. I won't chance Kolton's life like that."

Understanding was clear on both of their faces, and I appreciated that. "Now, for now, I want twelve-hour rotations. I will let you two determine who wants the night shift, whether you split it, or whatever, but I want twelve-hour rotations on the perimeter."

They stood. "Yes, Astral."

"The property has a private communication system. You might as well leave your commercial cell phones in the room. If you can hide the sat phone from the humans, take it with you, but otherwise, use the Ranch's comm system. I'll ask James to get you ear pieces, and show you how to use them. I'll see if there can be a channel designated just for the four of us. If he has questions, send him to me."

"The four of us ma'am?" Titus asked.

"As in Rose as well?"

"Yes. Rose has full control and access over the Ranch. I will let her know of everything that occurs. It is her property we are here to protect."

"Don't you out rank her?" Myka asked.

"I do, but she is sort of in her own class. We have very different job duties." I smiled, as she strolled in. "Isn't that right, Rose?"

Smiling, she said, "So these two, I take it, are the two Astrals Carlos demanded come and protect you?"

"Rose Porter, meet Myka and Titus." Both of whom bowed deeply with their fists over their chests. "Now, go and find James, and let him know that the four of us need our own channel that Kolton, he and Fernando won't be accessing."

"Nice to meet you, boys."

"You as well, Ms. Rose." They said and strode out the door.

"A half seer, half Theurgi demon and an Ovexa. Interesting choice for Astral protections."

"I'm a little worried about having two seers on the property. I've worked with Titus before, though. His strength and knowledge of the plant life here will be beneficial at some point, I'm sure." I looked out the glass wall and took a deep breath before saying, "Myka, the Ovexa, though. It could come in handy. Kind of blew the status quo out of the water when he became only the second Ovexa to also be an Astral."

"How is your leg feeling?" Rose said, bringing over an insulated mug and set it down before me. "Drink."

"If I drink any more of that healing tea you keep bringing me, I might float away."

"Do you want that leg to heal or not?" She crossed her arms and stared at me.

"Kolton is already asking how my leg is healing this quickly." I muttered.

"Kolton knows I'm doing something to help. He has always called it the Rose magic." She smiled and clicked her ear piece. "Fernando can unload the hay. James is helping Jade's assistants with getting them on comms. He will be out in a bit.... I know it's a lot of hay, but Kolton's not here, and Philip won't be back for a couple hours. He had to go to the Sanchez property to help a mare foal. ... Thanks, Fernando." She clicked it off and I chuckled.

"Never a dull day." I said.

"You'll get used to it." She had that knowing smile on her face and practically skipped out the door.

When the door clicked shut, I just sighed and went back to working on the drawings.

CHAPTER 21

JADE

It was close to 7:00pm when Kolton came in and flopped on the edge of the bed. He laid there with his arm hanging over the top over his eyes for a good five minutes while I read my book. When I finished the chapter, I stuck the bookmark in and set it on the table next to the bed.

I watched him for a moment, and just when I was about to poke him with my foot, a small smile came across his face, and he asked, "Are you enjoying the view?"

"Very much so, but I also wasn't sure if you had fallen asleep."

He rolled onto his side curling around my feet, resting his head next to my good knee. "How's your leg feeling today?"

"Alright. A bit achy, but otherwise…" I shrugged. He stared at me for a moment, and when he went to open his mouth, I said, "It's at about a two, okay? Nothing an aspirin won't fix. Last one wore off a while ago, and since I'm under strict orders not to spend time on the leg, I haven't. I spent all day in the office with my leg up while I sat in the chair. Tonight, I have done nothing but sit in this bed. Rose and Philip helped me upstairs, and Rose even made sure I ate here, in bed, with my book. I haven't even gotten up to pee. Which I really need to get up and do, or I'm going to piss myself. So, if you want to help, that would be great."

Kolton just stared up at me and smiled. "See? You are a good girl. You know how to take orders."

I threw the pillow at him. "My submission is earned, and right now you are poking a beast that is about to rip your throat out and then piss on you if you don't help me out of this bed and to the bathroom."

He threw his hands up in defeat and laughed. Sliding out of the bed, he didn't help me out of bed and to the bathroom. Instead, he scooped me up like I weighed nothing more than a can of paint.

"I am capable of hobbling on my own." I said weakly. I had tried to tell him I heal fast, but the boy didn't listen.

"You are." He said, but leaned down and kissed the top of my head. He set me down in the doorway and asked, "Need anymore help, or you good?"

"I can manage on my own, thank you."

I did in fact manage on my own, and when I got back to the door, he was there in nothing but his unbuttoned jeans, all hanging a little lower on his hips. It was just enough that I could see the top of his boxer briefs. I tried not to moan at the sign of it

"Tease." I murmured.

"Says the woman who is in nothing but a long t-shirt right now." I blushed because he wasn't wrong. After Rose helped me back into the house, I stripped and hadn't felt like keeping much else on since I would only be lying in bed. "And well, this look doesn't help matters any."

Kolton took a long deep breath, before picking me up and carrying me back to the bed. When he did, he set me on the edge of it, "Stay here. I want to try the brace on and see how much you can walk on it."

He disappeared out of the room and a few minutes later, came back with a black and metal brace in his hands. I looked him up and down and had to take a deep breath myself, because now Kolton was standing in this room in nothing but a pair of lightweight black loose fit pants, and I could clearly see the outline of him.

"Kolton." I said, my voice too full of something that couldn't be fulfilled. His eyes met mine, and those brown eyes swam with everything that we wanted to do.

"Turnabout is fair play, darlin."

"The brace, Kolton. You have something in your hands." I said redirecting his attention. Fuck that, redirecting my attention.

There was a blink as he remembered he did have a purpose other than pleasing me to no end, and then he strode over, kneeled, carefully pulled my leg up and rested the heel of my foot on his knee. Gently, he maneuvered the brace onto my knee, and tightened the Velcro straps.

His hand ran along the inner side of my thigh, while the other held my calf which was completely unfair. Each movement of his hand sent a bolt to that spot between my legs, and my gaze met his. There was nothing but the beat of my heart and the rushing of blood through my ears, and I saw more than heard my name on his lips.

"Are you just going to stare at me or are you going to kiss me, Kolton?"

"Why do you have to be so pushy?"

"Why can't you just take control?"

His eyebrow lifted, and there was that twitch at the corner of his lips, that made me reconsider my words. "Care to say that again?"

He rose, leaving his hand just between my legs, but not touching that spot. I knew he could feel the heat. Knew how much he was turning me on, but he wasn't going to give in just yet. I wiggled, and his hand clamped onto my thigh to stop the movement.

"Why can't you just take control?" I said breathier this time, my eyes not leaving his.

He bent down, and wrapped an arm around my waist, making me stand.

"Don't put any weight on the left yet. Not until I fully have your weight." He moved behind me, and slowly, brought his arm up under my nightshirt, softly teasing the skin along my ass, my hip, and my lower stomach before he held me tight. Kolton's lips grazed my neck and shoulder as his other hand wrapped around the front to my core.

"Okay, I have you now. Slowly lower your left foot onto the ground. Let me know if the pain is too much." He said against my ear, but bent down to run his lips against my throat.

My toes curled at the feel of those lips on my neck. I concentrated on lowering my foot as he kissed my neck and ran a finger through the front of me and just flicked that bundle of nerves. I jerked.

"Does your leg hurt?"

"No." He was so toying with me. I felt the curve of his smile against my shoulder, and I leaned back into him as I lowered my foot and rested it on the ground.

"Good girl."

"Kolton." I warned, even though his words sent a thrill through me that if this had been before the accident, I would have dropped to my knees right then and there.

"Yes, darlin." He whispered. "I know we haven't finished that discussion. I will try to behave myself."

I shifted, and he grazed a finger over that spot again, and down lower, dragging back some of my wetness to my clit and circling it. My other knee buckled at the wave of pleasure that I felt through me, but I didn't move. Kolton had a full grip on me.

"Try to lift yourself with some weight on the left." He whispered while nibbling my ear.

"Fuck, Kolton. You don't play fair." I said, breathlessly. "Do all your patients get this *personalized* treatment?"

"Never." He said hard in my ear and then ran his fingers up and down me again. When my knees gave out, it had nothing to do with the knee or my leg, but he pulled me against him and sat down on the bed. He used that hand to spread both my legs so they were on either side of his, allowing him full access to the center of me. "You, my darling, do something to me that I can't explain."

I turned to look at him, and he rested his forehead on mine. "Don't play with me, Kolton. Please. I can't take that." I would be lying if I said I hadn't been falling hard for him the last couple weeks. That bond or not, I had fallen for him.

His hand cupped me, and I felt his finger slide near my entrance, and just barely enter. I moved my hips, and he smiled. "Oh, Jade. I told you before I kissed you that first time that there was no going back. You are mine. I am yours."

Then two of his fingers plunged into me, and I rolled my hips against him. The hand that had been holding my hips, had moved up and cupped my breast, and as his thumb ran across the taught nipple, I moaned.

I needed this release. The release from someone else. Anyone. No, not anyone. Kolton. I needed Kolton to give me this release. In response, that bond burned bright between us.

"Jade." Kolton said, kissing across my jaw as I rode his fingers and he brought me closer to that edge. I felt him hard against my ass, and I reached around behind me, to run my fingers along the silky head of him.

"Fuck." The word came out long and throaty from him, and I continued the motion, as my ass rubbed against him. I was not the only one enjoying themselves, and there was so much I wanted to do right now, but this damn leg wouldn't let me.

I wanted to drop to my knees to taste and swallow the length that was Kolton. I wanted to push him down on this bed, straddle him and make him moan my name until he was hoarse and unable to give orders to anyone else on the property. For workers on this property to know that I was the one that took that edge off Kolton Webster.

The heel of his hand pressed against my clit, and I couldn't help the quick jerks of movement against him as my stomach tightened and I felt him twitch behind me.

"Cum for me, darling." He said, and then he fingered me faster. "I am yours." I heard him say as my orgasm hit with such a force that I wasn't so sure I hadn't blacked out for a moment.

When reality came back too, not only was I soaked, but I felt wet behind me.

Kolton, moved me to lay on my right side facing toward the door while he went to clean up himself and brought a couple of wet rags. Gently, he wiped up my back and ass with a sheepish look, and then lifted my leg to clean me. Kissing my hip, he moved my shirt back down, and threw the washcloths into the bathroom.

Kneeling before me, he asked, "You okay?"

"Why wouldn't I be?" I said, my head still a little fuzzy and in that bliss.

He looked at me carefully. "Jade." Then a lump formed in his throat as he rested his hand on my face. "I meant what I said."

I blinked, not fully comprehending what he was saying. "What?"

"Do you remember anything I just said?"

I blinked at him, and then it came back to me. "Yes." I reached out and cradled my hand around his cheek. "I meant what I said too, Kolton. Please don't hurt me."

"Darling, I am yours."

Then he leaned in and kissed me. It was possessive, and needy in a whole different way. I pulled on his shoulders, and pulled him into the bed with me.

"Stay here with me tonight." I whispered against his lips.

"I thought you would have never asked."

CHAPTER 22

KOLTON

"Rose, Devon wants retribution." Jade's voice was hushed, but loud enough it came through the thin door I was standing behind.

"Well, what was Philip supposed to do? Just let the pack take you and the gelding down?" Rose's voice was tense, and I could almost see her pacing across the room. She always did when she spoke like that.

"No, of course not. I'm on your side. You know the Agency wouldn't let the Kiku Pack take over." Jade said, paused a moment and then said, "Philip hasn't come to me since the attack or even after card night. Did he..."

"Oh, I got an earful. He came in after Kolton got you all cozied up in the apartment, and screamed at me for not telling him you were an Astral." Rose said.

"What the?" There was that title again. I opened the door, but saw two very large men standing there. One standing there like a mountain, had a raised eyebrow as he looked at me, while the other leaned back against the lateral filing cabinet with his feet crossed before him, picking at his nails with a dagger. He just turned and lifted a corner of his lips as he regarded me.

"Took you long enough, Kolton." Jade said, smiling at where I stood at the door. I looked at her, looked at Rose, and back again to Jade. I looked down at her leg, and while she had the brace that I gave her a few days ago on, her weight was way more easily distributed than it should be at this point. "I suspect you have questions."

"How are you standing on that leg that much?"

She smiled and cocked out a hip, and if I hadn't been so confused by what was going on, I would have told everyone to leave. "I have been trying to tell you, I heal fast. Plus, Rose has been giving me her healing tea, which has done wonders."

"You knew he was at the door?" Rose said, throwing her hands up. "Of course, you did."

"I do have exceptional hearing." Jade smirked, but it spread into a wide smile when her eyes met mine.

Rose turned to the two standing there, and pointed a finger at them, "And you two knew two."

Neither of them said anything but the one leaning against the cabinet just shrugged and slid the dagger into his belt.

"Jade, what is going on?" My eyes flicked to Rose, who looked a bit apologetic.

"A lot." Her gaze fell to the floor before she sighed and looked up to meet my gaze. "Myka, Titus, you can leave. Get your perimeter checks done and report back to me this afternoon."

"Oh, not on your life." Myka chuckled.

"Titus, drag him out of here."

The one who must have been Titus, tipped his head back and laughed. "Oh, call Carlos if you must, but we are flies on the wall, Astral Jade."

The fuck with that word again. "What—"

"Give Jade a minute, Kolton. She'll explain." Ms. Rose gave me a small smile that was probably to reassure me, but I felt like I was the butt end of a joke.

Jade tipped head all the way back and let out a heavy sigh. "Fine. Rose, can you bind the room and his lips please?"

"Bind my lips?" My heart started racing and Jade interrupted, by putting her hand in mine and squeezed before saying, "Not literally. It just means that you won't be able to discuss what I am about to tell you unless they are part of Ashstrike Sanctorum."

"Ashstrike Sanctorum?" I asked, but she threaded her fingers through mine, and rubbed her thumb back and forth. My shoulders relaxed, but it didn't stop my mind from racing. "Darling, you are going to need to be straight with me."

She looked back to Rose who gave her a short nod, before she pulled me to sit in the chair. "Fuck. I have to be sitting for this conversation?"

"Either you sit by your own choice, or you will be sitting on the floor by the time we are done." Standing before me, there was a wicked gleam in her eye, as she said, "You know those mythologies you have all those books about?"

"You are talking about witches, vampires, werewolves? Those kinds of legends?" Slowly she gave me a nod. "You are telling me that they are fact?"

"Every legend starts with an ounce of truth." Myka said from against the filing cabinet. Her eyes stayed focused on mine, and I blinked.

"Okay. So, are you telling me that you are one of those people? That you and Rose..." I looked over at Rose, "and Philip are those people? Which ones?"

"Gods, I am not going about this the right way. I really didn't want to have to give the textbook speech. I didn't want to sound cliche and just make it sound like it's all fairytale. And I mean Grimm Tales. The originals... Not the Disney cuddly ones."

I was now thoroughly confused. "Jade..." I said carefully.

"I am a... member of the Ashstrike Sanctorum. It's also known as the Agency. We help settle disputes between different beings across the world. That includes witches, vampires, werewolves, kismots, and any other manner of being. We step in to try to prevent war and keep them from being noticed by the humans. It's highly political, and there is way more to it all than that, but there you go."

"And how do you fall into all this? What exactly are you, Jade? Rose, Philip and those two have called you an Astral? What exactly is that?" As I watched her think through her answer, I realized the emotion running through me wasn't fear or anxiety, but morbid curiosity.

Jade double tapped her good leg, and swiped up on her thigh. I blinked. In her hand she was holding an eight-inch dagger... that she had pulled from her leg. My eyes trailed up to meet hers, and there was a small smile on her lips.

Standing and grabbing her wrist, I saw... "The throwing daggers Fernando found in the field where the wolves were supposed to be. That's where the extra daggers came from." She tapped the spot on her wrist and one instantly sat in the palm of her hand.

"I'm an Astral Primal. A born warrior. Our vision and hearing are sharper than humans, and we can move wicked fast in comparison. It's how we can usually hold our own against the speed of a vampire."

"Against the speed of a vampire?" My eyebrows shot up.

She nodded, waited, biting her lip, and the more I watched her, I could feel her panic. Not mine. Hers. I met her eyes, and it was lined there as well. I reached out and took her hand, kissed it and said, "I'm not going anywhere. Breathe darling."

Three quick blinks before her eyes flicked to Ms. Rose, then back to me.

"I told you he loves you. He ain't going anywhere." Ms. Rose said, amusement laced each word of her voice.

"I'm sorry, what did you just say?" I asked, looking at Rose. Jade had gone exceptionally still, but her eyes were only on me.

"That you love Jade." She said it like it was obvious. She looked to the two brutes who just nodded their heads in agreement, like it was the most obvious thing to everyone except for the two people involved.

I stared at Ms. Rose, and whispered, "How do you know that?"

"It's written all over you. Your body language. And you did just say you weren't going anywhere." Myka chuckled and rolled his eyes.

"Maybe that's just because if she is as fast as she claims, that she would just catch me if I did run, even with the messed up leg."

"Are you saying you don't love her?" Ms. Rose put her hands on her hips, and I rubbed my thumb along Jade's hand. It hadn't escaped my notice she hadn't moved a muscle or hardly taken a breath since this part of the discussion started.

"Ms. Rose, I don't know what I'm feeling right now." I let out a long breath.

"That is a fair response." Jade's voice was thick, and the pain in it tore me to shreds.

I turned toward Jade to find her looking at Rose. Slowly I cradled her face in my hands. "Jade, I don't know what I'm feeling, and while I *do* have very strong feelings for you? I don't know if it's love, yet. I'm still trying to figure it all out. We are still trying to figure all of this out."

She nodded, wrapped her arms around me and said, "I know."

"Now, back to this whole Ashstrike Sanctorum thing. Wait, you said you have exceptional hearing, and you knew I was on the other side of the door. Why…"

"Why did I let you overhear?" I nodded. "Because I have been too chicken shit to talk to you directly, and just because I'm an Astral doesn't mean I have permission from the Agency to tell a human." She huffed out a nervous laugh. "Okay, so like that is real fuzzy, because Carlos did tell me to, but officially speaking, I don't. It's pretty strictly enforced that humans not know about us. I need you to know right now, because it's getting too dangerous for you and the staff." Her eyes met mine, and there was a real fear there.

"Why? What is happening?"

It was Rose who answered. "We continue to see if we can work something out with the wolves, but it hasn't gone well so far."

"Work… something out… with the …" I looked between the both of them. "Work something out with the wolves. As in werewolves?" Right, because apparently, they are real. Wolves themselves were exceptionally smart, and the pack that attacked was a bit larger than I had expected. I ran my hand through my hair and let out a long breath as I sat back down and leaned my head on the wall. "Shit, you two. A little warning would have been nice."

"We are giving you that warning, now." Rose said. "I need you to keep Fernando and James on this side of the property. Bombard them with large projects. Relations between the Ranch and the Pack have escalated to a dangerous point. Any human near that back end will be considered fair fodder. Devon's pack is a bit more vicious than the usual pack. Their territory is wide and vast for a reason, and Devon is widely considered the Alpha of Alphas."

Okay. I needed that chair again. I sat down, pulling Jade into my lap as I did. I couldn't believe what I was hearing, but I locked away all the emotions I could for now. This was something to deal with later.

A wave of fear seemed to feed through that cord between Jade and I again. "Why does a badass warrior have so much fear in her?"

She gulped.

"Jade?" Her eyes searched mine, she opened her mouth, then closed it. I pressed my forehead to hers, and said, "It's okay, darling. Whatever it is, we will get through it. Together." I kissed her, and she let her lips linger on mine a moment longer. "Now tell me, darling."

"Because Devon knows what you are to me." Tears left her eyes, and I let a thumb wipe them away. "Alpha Devon wants retribution for the wolves killed on the day of the attack."

I pulled back slightly, and realized what she was saying. I stared at her in disbelief for a moment, and she didn't flinch at the intensity of it. "The wolves. The ones that attacked you and the gelding. They weren't ordinary wolves. Those were werewolves?"

She nodded, and then I remembered the day along the southern edge when she asked me if that part of the property lined the national forest. I gulped. Oh fuck... "The wolf I pulled a gun on."

"That was one of Devon's betas. I was telling him to back down and leave the situation be. They want more territory because their pack has grown too big for its designated area. They need and want more hunting grounds. They specifically want Rose's wild area, but Rose is protected by the Agency. She's one of the most powerful seers in the world, and the Agency won't allow her property to be taken. There are a million reasons for it, but we can discuss that much later."

"A Seer." I looked at her and she had a huge teasing smile on her face. "No wonder you just *know* things. Do you have any idea how annoying that is, Ms. Rose?"

"Like I said, it's what I do. I know things."

"Wait, so what about the redevelopment project? Is that a real thing happening or just a cover?" I asked.

Jade took a deep breath and took a step back from me. "Rose does want to redevelop the property, have the horse rehabilitation center, and do all the things I have been working on here. However, the main reason I'm here is to settle the problem with the wolves."

"Okay. Good to hear. I was going to be pretty disappointed if that wasn't going to really happen."

Rose looked at me warmly. "I've always wanted to have one, and when I saw your passion and love for the horses and this ranch, well it seemed like the right thing to do. The timing happened to line up."

I nodded and studied the floor for a minute. Taking my hat off and running my hand through my hair, I put my cap back on before looking at Jade. That fear was still pretty evident in whatever it was I was getting from her. "That doesn't exactly answer *why* you are so terrified."

"I received a message from Devon this morning after you left. He's seeking retribution. He believes I ordered you and Philip to kill members of his pack. He is taking this personally now and has straight up issued a threat to you, specifically. Which is really stupid on their part."

"Why me?"

Jade took those steps back to me, and put my face in her hands. I rested mine on her waist as I stared into those fear filled eyes, "Because you are my Astral Bonded."

Regardless of the thrill that burst through me, my fingers tightened on her waist as I said, "Jade, I need a translation."

"You've heard of soulmates?"

I nodded and said, "Astral Bonded are like a soulmate?"

"Yes, but they stretch the passage of time. For someone like me, it's a one-time thing." She swallowed hard and when she tried to pull away, I wrapped my arms around her and held her close to me.

"Say it, darlin'."

"Everyone lives multiple life incarnations. Only when someone is bound to an Astral, they will only have lives until the lifetime when they meet their bonded. That means that after this lifetime, we go to the Underworld. This is the last of our lives on this plane."

"Okay." I felt every eye in that room spear into me at the word, but Jade's were the only ones I met. She was blinking at me, and narrowed her eyes like she was trying to figure something out.

"Okay? I just told you that not only you have lived many lifetimes, but that this will be your last before you go to your eternity all because you met and bonded with me? And all you have to say is, okay?"

"Yeah, okay, when you say it like that." I let it sink in. A real permanent death. I had believed in the existence of multiple Gods, but hadn't really given much thought to an afterlife. Heaven, Hell, Valhalla, Elysium, reincarnation as a dung beetle... wherever and whatever. Something settled within me as I looked into the green meadows of her eyes. It was as if this woman blew through the world, and then settled next to my heart. It didn't matter as long as I had her. A life with Jade. "But if I get to live the rest of this life with you Jade, then how is that so much a bad thing?"

She pushed herself out of my grip, and I realized, just how strong she was. Anger laced her voice as she struggled to keep it in check. "Kolton. If I die, so do you. If you die, so do I. For the rest of your life, you will be used as a bargaining chip. Anyone that I happen to piss off, and that isn't a short list, could use you against me."

"So, I would just be used as a self-preservation tool?" My anger rose at that thought, and she laughed.

"Now you get angry, and at something that isn't even a major factor for me. Fuck. It's a problem, but not my main concern." She threw her hands up in the air. "Rose, he gets angry because he thinks I'm just going to use him as a way to keep myself alive."

"Kolton, you really don't get it, do you?" Ms. Rose said, and I had completely forgotten she was even in the room. She looked to the two mountains still standing in the room, who were not looking at any of us, but at each other. There was something there, but I couldn't place it. "Astrals, once they find their bonded, don't care about their own lives. Now that she has found you, she doesn't care if she dies. She's terrified to end your life early. Jade is worried about you dying before your time."

CHAPTER 23

KOLTON

My head was still spinning at all that Jade and Rose had said downstairs earlier. Bonded, for life... and afterlife... with Jade. I still had so many questions. I watched her from the edge of the bed, as she paced the bedroom. How she was even able to stand, let alone walk as well as she was, astounded me. Someone only a week out from that kind of injury should not be up and walking on that leg. Hell, she walked herself up the stairs, and proceeded to pace since we got home.

Home. I blinked, and realized that this was home. I looked forward to coming home to her. Looked forward to just having basic discussions about our day, our lives. Last night we had just sat on the couch and watched a movie. It was easy with Jade here.

She had completely taken over my guest room. It was simple enough, a double bed, pushed against two walls in the corner, and a dresser. She'd unpacked everything into the closet earlier in the week, including that sex toy bag up on the shelf. My eyes flicked to it, before looking back at her.

"How is your leg feeling?" I was trying to change my line of thinking, but it wouldn't do much good. "You should rest it. Your limp is deepening."

"I've had to hold still for days. I hate holding still."

"Okay. Can I ask some questions?"

She gave me a small smile. "I'd be surprised if you didn't have questions. You are kind of taking all of this too easy." She said coming to stand before me. I wrapped my arms around her thighs, and rested my forehead on her stomach, instantly feeling calmer.

"I get you out of all of this." I kissed her lower stomach, and she giggled. "How can a guy be upset with that?"

"Your questions, Kolton." She smiled down at me.

"Who decided to have a single agency rule? I'm assuming each subset of creatures would have their own ruling council, right?" she nodded, and I continued, "Why have someone to oversee them? Why not just let them handle themselves?"

"Well, that is somewhere to start. Not where I thought you would, but okay." She took a deep breath and let it out slowly. "About two thousand years ago there was a group of witches that found a way to make humans immortal."

"Immortal..." I said carefully.

"They killed thousands trying to convert them, only about eighty were transformed. They can only be killed if beheaded, Kolton."

A light chuckle came out of me. "I suppose just about anything dies if you remove its head." I rubbed my neck as if I could feel a sword swinging for it. Jade didn't miss the movement, and huffed a laugh.

"Anyway, while the witches eventually cleaned their own house, there was a call by some of the other... beings, that something should have been done sooner, and that these humans turned immortal should be eradicated. No being should live forever. That's when Ashstrike Sanctorum was formed."

"Wait. You mentioned vampires. Is lore right that they are immortal? But you just said that there was a call that no being should live to be immortal."

Jade gave me a soft smile and said, "No, their lifespans are longer than a humans', but they are not truly immortal. Vamps usually live a few centuries before they start to decay. In fact, most will choose to kill themselves, by walking into sunlight. It's a quick hot burn, and in less than thirty seconds they are done. It's pretty much become standard practice now. I went to one a few years back. They make it a celebration."

"Well... okay." I released my hands from around her legs, and Jade crawled up onto the bed and leaned against the headboard.

"Every myth has a kernel of truth, Kolton."

"What happened to the immortal humans?" I sat against the wall and pulled her legs over mine. She moved closer to me, and I waited for her answer. My hand ran along the scab along her leg.

"Most of them have died out. The guillotine era did in a lot of them. Wars, accidents, personal vendettas, etc. Maximus, one of the immortals, once said, 'We are near immortal, not stupid proof.' There are only about twelve of them left. They keep to themselves, run their own private businesses, and secretly hold most of the world's wealth. About a year or so ago, another was created, but what that poor girl had to go through, I wouldn't wish on my worst enemy.

"What happened?"

"It's a long-complicated story, and not really mine to tell hun. If you ever meet Kelsey, though, she might tell you parts of it." She watched me for a moment, blinked and cocked her head to the side as if she was puzzling something together.

Finally, when she didn't say anything for a long minute, I asked, "What?"

"Well, two things, actually." I raised my eyebrows waiting for her to continue, "First you are taking this very well for someone who just learned that the supernatural stuff you've been reading is real, and..." She looked away and I interrupted her.

"The world and universe are too big to think that there are just humans in this vast place. It would be ignorant to think otherwise, but what's the other thing, darling?"

She studied me, opened her mouth and closed it before finding her words and asking, "You aren't going to ask me just how long I live?"

"I'm sure that's a complicated question. If you are the bad ass warrior you claim to be, then it's likely that statistically, not many of you live to reach old age." She nodded slowly. "So, I guess the question is, statistically speaking, how old do you live to be?"

"Thirty-five. We start training at seven. That's when the speed and flexibility stick. Tests are run, and then the training starts. By the time we are teenagers, we are lethal. I finished my training, and Carlos wanted us to get an education, so while I carried out my Astral duties, I went to school. I graduated, but I think the Agency intentionally let me have that time to just be because of Carlos. I think he protected my brother and I from having to be the Agency's property. May have allowed me to live longer."

Understanding at why she was so upset, and why Ms. Rose had been so pointed about the Astral Bonded situation. I would die when she did. If someone killed Jade in our sleep, I would die with her. I swallowed the thought, and tried to stay optimistic. "So, that's still a few years away. Let's see what we can do to keep you above the average."

She just sat there blinking at me, and the pieces fell into place. "That's why you are so worried about being

Astral Bonded. That we only have a few more years together before we are beating the average?"

Her eyes filled with tears, and her voice came out small and squeaky, "We?"

"Didn't I tell you I wasn't going anywhere, darlin'?" I said, and the next moment she was straddling me and her lips were on mine.

"Kolton." Her moan undid me as she pulled back and pulled my t-shirt off, tossing it behind her.

I raised an eyebrow at her as I set my hands on her hips. My fingers gripped tight and then rolled her onto her back, kissing her. Treasuring the feel of her neck under my lips as I made my way down her neck, she moved to allow me more access, I smiled against her skin. "Mmmm. That's a good girl."

"Yes." She whispered as my whole body froze in place. I placed a small kiss just where her neck met her shoulder, and leaned back.

"I'm sorry."

"What?" She said, looking at me.

"I said I'm sorry. I slipped."

Realization shown in her eyes, "And I submitted to it."

"You did, but we haven't set that dynamic yet." I ran my hand through my hair and sat back on my heels. "I'm sorry. We have to have trust, and if you can't trust me to hold that role, then..."

"Kolton." She said sitting up and taking my face in her hands. "If you are willing to be my bedroom Dom, then I will give you my submission."

"But because of who you are, you can't submit all the time." I nodded in understanding. "Plus, I think you like the fight. I think you may be a good girl, but I think you like the control."

"I do, but my job is all about control. Maintaining it, cultivating it, and ensuring it." She released her hands from my face and let them fall into her lap. "That is why I like to give it up in the bedroom."

"Okay. I would like to make a clarification for you, though." I waited for her to meet my eyes as I said, "I'm not a strong-armed Dom. I will take care of you, give you everything you need, and take control, but I'm *not* one of those alpha doms in those romance novels you read." I jerked my head over to the current mafia romance she was reading.

"There are differences, Kolton." She smiled brightly. "While those bedroom scenes may be hot and give us ideas of things to try, there are a lot of red flag behaviors in those books. What I like in book boyfriend doms is totally different from what I will tolerate with you."

I chuckled before asking, "Are you okay with me using this agreement outside of the bedroom? Or do you want this to only be a bedroom dynamic?"

"I think it would depend. If it isn't in a way to control me, then I'm okay." She shrugged, then smiled softly and looked up at me through her eyelashes and said, "What about honorifics? Do you require them in scene?"

"You can use them or not." I honestly hadn't thought about it, but one immediately came to mind, and I grew hard just waiting to hear it fall off those lips of hers. If she wanted to use them.

"It helps provide context for the discussion." She said, and then put that lip between her teeth again. I couldn't help but let out a guttural moan that had me reaching down and running my thumb along her lip.

"Do you have any idea what that does to me?"

"What?"

"When you bite your lip like that."

"You are changing the subject." She whispered, but continued when I tilted my head in question. "Honorifics. I would like to have them for context of discussions, please."

"Okay." I looked at her and could not come up with anything else for her. "You are just my... Darlin'."

"You call me that, regardless." A small smile sat on her lips before she asked, "What do you want me to call you?"

I reached over and flatted my hand across her chest and slowly ran it up her throat. Her eyes fluttered to the back of her head, and there was a clear moan that emanated from her.

"Sir." My hand was still on her throat as she looked up at me and nodded. "Say it."

"Yes, Sir."

"Good girl." I said leaning over her, and kissing her shoulder. Then, letting my lips whisper against her skin, asked, "Now, light system or safe word?"

"Red." Darlin' said it without a second thought. Well ingrained and established.

I licked my lips as I pulled back to look at her. She was wearing one of my dress shirts, and I let a corner of my mouth lift before I said, "The next time you take one of my dress shirts, Darlin'," I ran a finger down the line of buttons and released her neck, sitting back. "Take one of the maroon ones. I want to see you in that red."

"Yes, Sir." She said, sitting on her knees before me. She wiggled, and I reached over threaded my fingers between the overlap of the shirt, and pulled it apart. Buttons flew in every direction, and the little vixen before me just pushed her chest out toward me and smiled.

Slowly I took in the sight before me. She had absolutely nothing on under that shirt. How in the fuck had I missed that? I pushed the shirt off her, tossing it off to the side.

"Like what you see?"

My eyes snapped to hers as I gripped the hair at the nape of her neck, and pulled her to me, kissing her hard. When our kiss broke, she had clasped her hands behind her back, causing her breasts to press against my chest.

"You are going to lay there and not move until I have had my fill of you. Is that understood, Darling?"

She cocked an eyebrow at me, and I said, "Lay down. I believe I need to," I ran my hand over the curves of her stomach, and a finger through the middle of her. I felt her gasp, as I said, "have an early dinner."

CHAPTER 24

JADE

I gasped as Kolton ran a finger through the wetness between my legs. When his hand released my neck he pushed me onto the bed, and when I bounced, he caught my hips and pulled me to the edge.

I giggled, but then there was a growl that ripped through the room and I looked down to Kolton, who was looking at me through those eyelashes and said, "Since the day you stepped out of that city truck of yours, bent over to get your bag, I have wanted to run my hands and lips over this."

His hands ran along my hips and then gripped my ass. It was possessive and tender, and how he made it feel like both had me sighing contently. His hands curved around and spread my legs as he kissed half-way up the inside my thigh, and my back arched in anticipation. I felt more than heard his chuckle before there was a gentle breath across me.

"Kolton." I breathed, and he ran his tongue along the outside lips before slowly wrapping his tongue around my clit and flicking it. My stomach tightened so quick, I thought I was going to cum right then, and there. "Fuck."

Then he sucked on that bundle of nerves, and my hips jerked involuntarily. I felt the smile on his lips, and his tongue explored every inch, tasting all of me. When he circled my entrance, I fisted my hands in his hair and ground against him.

One moment I was a second from cumming, the next he lifted his hand and smacked my clit twice. I whispered a groan, "Don't you fucking edge me."

"Didn't you once tell me that you required a daily orgasm, Darlin'?"

I narrowed my eyes at him, and he slowly slid a finger into me, and another into my ass. I moved, but Kolton's other hand pressed down on my hips, and I looked down at him in a daze. When he raised his eyebrow at me in question, I asked, "What?"

"I said, didn't you say you needed a daily orgasm, Darlin'?"

"You know that I do."

"Then let me please you. Now, give me another one." He slowly pressed his fingers into me. My eyes rolled back and I bit my lip, causing him to let out a guttural, "Fuck."

He pumped inside me and then lowered his head again, circling and sucking. My hands gripped his hair again, and this time he let me grind against him.

"Please let me cum, Sir."

His chuckle ripped through me as he curled those fingers within me on his way out, sending me over the edge. He didn't stop, and when his tongue replaced his fingers inside me, my stomach tightened again. His finger curled in my ass, as his tongue hit that spot, and I tightened around him. "Kolton...."

When I came down, he retreated and looked down at me. "That sound you make when you cum is going to be addictive, Darlin.'" I smiled at him as he undid his belt, and unbuttoned his jeans. My eyes trailed each inch of his chest, across his abs, and down where that trail of hair disappeared into his jeans.

"Fuck me." I whispered.

"That is the plan, Darling." His pants dropped and I was glad I was already laying down. The feel of him against me the other day as I ground against him had not done him justice.

Kolton bent down and laid open mouth kisses, occasionally swirling his tongue against my skin as he crawled up me. When I felt him against me, and slowly slide down toward my entrance, it was instinct to lift my hips.

Kolton's hand trailed up my side, across my chest, and wrapped around my neck, moving my head to the side. I leaned my head back, helping to expose that side of my neck to him, and moaned as he tightened his fingers.

He hummed against my neck as he trailed his lips from my shoulder to my jaw, before his eyes met mine and I felt him slowly press the head of him into me. There was a small chuckle from him as he kissed the side of my mouth, then down my jaw, but not moving his hips.

My fingers dragged down his side, and I smiled at his needy moan in my ear. My hands reached his hips, and when I let my fingers trail over his well-formed ass, I felt them flex as he pushed himself inside me.

"Look at me, Darlin'." He leaned back and turned my head to look at him as every inch of him filled me. The warmth, demand, and desire in those eyes was everything I needed. That cord between us burned bright, and I could finally see a future of being cherished and loved. I gasped when Kolton thrust the last inch in.

My legs instantly wrapped around him, and hooked around the ankles. I felt the skin along my thigh stretch, and in one spot near my knee split, but I didn't care.

"Fucking hell, you are amazing." Kolton said, staring into my eyes. He released my neck, when that cord burned even brighter, and rubbed at his chest. His gaze went down between us, and there was a faint blue green light that connected us just between the breast bones.

His fingers reached to touch it, and when they did, he ran them up and down it. I leaned my head back at the shivering warmth that I felt from the bond, but an extra jolt went straight between my legs. "You can feel that?"

"Yes, Sir." I said, and couldn't help but roll my hips, and grip his ass. "It's warm, but it's also like goosebumps, there is a jolt of something."

His hips rolled against mine, "And it hits right here." He bent down and kissed me softly, retreating out of me. His hand on my hip and as he slid back into me. Slowly, he wrapped his hand onto my ass and gripped it tight. "Real."

"Real, Sir." I breathed the words as I ran my nails up his back, causing him to moan. When he was seated deep within me again, his head snapped to mine, and he smirked. Leaning back, he took my legs and spread them wide, taking long slow strokes, before saying, "Put your hands under your ass."

Then he was pounding into me, and I was lost. There was only me, him, and the feel of him filling me repeatedly. I kept lifting my hips to meet him, and after a few more strokes, he moved and flipped me so I was on my knees.

"Darling, stay right there." His hands roamed over my ass cheeks, then there was a smack and nothing but pleasure flooded through me, and I bit my lip moaning.

"As I said earlier, this ass has done nothing but tempt me. There is so much I have planned for it, but not tonight."

"Sir." I moaned as he slapped the other cheek and then ran his cock up and down my slit again. When he entered me this time though, it was hard and fast. He didn't stop either. The sound of our flesh meeting over and over again combined with the sound of our pleasure.

When I felt him tighten within me, Kolton grabbed me by the neck again, pulling me up against him. His other hand reached around and cradled a breast as he tightened his grip on my neck, and kissed along that spot where my neck and shoulder met.

When his free hand slid down and flicked my clit I jerked against him, "Cum for me, Darlin'."

His finger circled my clit again, but it was when he pressed it between two fingers, and pounded into me hard and fast, that I clenched around him, leaned back, and fell into the bliss that Kolton had given me.

"Darlin'..." His voice was right at my ear, and then he grunted and stilled within me before we both collapsed wrapped in each other.

CHAPTER 25

KOLTON

ONE WEEK LATER

I took a deep breath as we pulled into the parking lot at the harbor. When I put the truck in park, I turned to face her, suddenly extraordinarily nervous.

She smiled softly, and I couldn't help but stare at her. She was radiant. There was something about her tonight that made her eyes sparkle. "Why are you so nervous, Kolton?"

"This is our first real date since I asked you out weeks ago."

"That's fair. Things haven't exactly gone the way of normal courtship, have they?" She was blushing.

Her hand reached up and cradled my cheek as she said, "No, but would it have mattered?"

"Likely not, considering the whole Astral bond thing, but I still want to have some of those normal experiences. We need to learn about each other. What we like, don't like. In *and* out of the bedroom, darling." I smiled and kissed her quickly so that she couldn't complain. "Let's go."

We had been so busy with everything going on at the ranch, that it had been extremely difficult to get away just for us. When Ms. Rose had asked if we could handle something tonight, we looked at her and both at the same time said, "No."

Ms. Rose's eyebrows disappeared into her hairline, and then she laughed.

"Ms. Rose, I promised Jade a night out. Just the two of us. With everything that has happened, we haven't had a formal date yet."

I had reached for Jade's hand, and she set it in mine before saying, "Something normal in the world of my chaos. One night, Rose. Please?"

It was that plea that softened Ms. Rose's face, and she said, "Of course. You two have been working so hard. I'm sorry."

With that, we wrapped up everything we needed to get done, and basically ran back to the apartment at the end of the day.

I walked around the truck, and when she stepped out, I couldn't help but run my hand across her ass and squeeze as I helped her out. She was in a pair of black jeans, and a low-cut flowy dress shirt with small straps. Every time she moved, I saw the swell of her breasts, and it only made my pants fit a bit tighter. She bent over slightly to get something out of the truck, and it showed a bit more of that cleavage, and I was sure in that moment, she knew exactly what it was doing to me.

When we walked in, I gave them my name. "It will be just one moment Mr. Webster."

Jade shook her head and let out a huff of a laugh. "What is it, darling?"

"Mr. Webster. Sounds weird, because you are just Kolton."

I raised an eyebrow, "Just Kolton?" I pulled her closer and kissed just below her ear before whispering, "That isn't what you called me last night."

She playfully pushed me back, "That isn't what I mean, and you know it."

Shrugging and smiling at her, "I know, darling, but it's fun to tease you. Your cheeks get this adorable shade of red, right here." I wiped her cheekbone with my thumb, and it was as if her skin knew I wanted more of that blush.

"Mr. Webster, right this way." The server led us to a table along a row of windows overlooking the harbor.

The water twinkled under the lights, and when Jade sat, I pushed the chair in, walked around and sitting myself.

"The view is beautiful, Kolton."

"I haven't been to Brookings in... three, four years. Nice to see some things don't change."

"Been here before?" Jade asked, studying me.

"Yeah. The last time was with Nicole." I sighed. "So yeah, little over three years ago."

"Tell me about that."

"Jade, you don't want to hear about my ex-girlfriend." I gave her a look, and when she raised an eyebrow, I asked, "Why? She's in the past. Ain't going back now that I have you."

"She's part of you. The guys mentioned to me a few days ago that they hadn't seen you this happy since her, so I figure she must have been pretty important for a while."

I nodded as the server came up and asked what we wanted to drink, and Jade asked, "Water and some edamame, please."

She looked back at me expectantly, and I shook my head. Jade really was asking about Nicole. "We went to high school together. You know the ways of a small town. I left, came back, we reconnected." I looked out down the river, and then back to Jade, who was still watching me. I met her gaze and there was no judgment or condemnation. Just intrigue.

"Did you love her?"

"I thought I did." I leaned back and sighed. "I hadn't seriously considered marriage, but I thought it might head that way. We had been together for a couple years, but it wasn't meant to be."

The edamame and our waters were placed on the table, and the server asked, "What can I get for you?"

I looked at Jade and she smiled in that way that had me shifting in my seat. Then like she hadn't just done so, she said, "Kani Nigiri and a Spicy Tuna roll please."

"A NegiHama roll and Mango Unagi."

"Sure thing." She collected the menus and looked at Jade for a long moment. Jade met her eye, and they narrowed slightly, I saw the smallest nod, before the server walked off.

"Know her?"

"No, but she's a Kismot." Her voice was low.

"A what?"

"Mountain lion shifter. They have a lot of territory up here, and I've been talking to their King the last few weeks about some wider spread issues." She shrugged, squeezed the lemon over the edamame, picked up a piece and bit down, splitting the pod to release the bean inside. "Oh, damn, these are good. They got the right amount of saltiness to them."

I just smiled and looked at her. "You amaze me, Jade Romero?"

"Why?

"You just casually ask me about my ex-girlfriend, jump to talking about humans who shift into mountain lions, and then the meal?"

"This particular pride are mountain lions who shift to humans. Some prefer the human form, send their cubs to school, and do human things, so they need human funds. They are a bit more temperamental because they lean into their animalistic side."

"Are all shifters that way?"

"No. There is a Kismot pride south of the Bay Area near Big Sur of humans who shift into mountain lions. They prefer to live in the Ventana Wilderness, but are humans first, where this pride is animal first."

I took a deep breath trying to comprehend and grasp all those straws. "God, I have a lot to learn."

She smiled softly. "Just because you are my bonded, Kolton, doesn't mean you have to know it all." She paused and let out a heavy sigh and said, "In fact, there will be a lot I can't tell you. Most of it, actually. I can tell you about the different creatures, and some of the politics, but I can't give you specifics. In fact, there might be times I have to go away for a bit to take care of things."

"How long can those take?"

"Depends. Can we not talk about it right now? I don't know... Let's discuss it more after the current situation settles, okay?"

I nodded, and was about to say something when she looked about the window, picking apart an emptied-out pod. "Did you and Nicole, just grow apart or did something happen?"

"Why the fascination with her? She isn't important."

"But she was. I want to know what happened. Why she isn't anymore."

I felt that pain come back, and took an edamame for myself, eating it slowly. She was right, they were delicious.

"Kolton?"

"The short version? She was cheating on me. Found out through an old high school acquaintance." Shrugging, I buried it back down, even though as I looked at her, all that pain and hurt went away. "What about Daniel? Do you think you would have married him, if he hadn't died?"

She nodded. "I loved him, Kolton. Different from what is between us, but… I did love him. I told you how I was after his death."

She had, and it made me want to take her to bed and wash away all that pain. "We love everyone differently. The way I felt for Nicole, is different than how I feel for you."

Jade stiffened in her seat. "Kolton…"

"I'm not saying that I love you, Jade. I'm also not saying that I don't. I don't know what to call this. It's intense. There is this connection, and I won't lie and say that there haven't been times those words weren't at the tip of my tongue as I held you in my arms the last couple weeks."

"I understand." Jade let out a long breath. "It is intense. It's also pretty consuming. We've jumped into the deep end with both feet. I find myself comparing my feelings for you to my feelings for Daniel, and then I realize that isn't fair to either of you."

The server came back and placed our food on the table and I just watched her. Did I love Jade? The thought both scared and settled me all in the same millisecond. I couldn't wait to see her back at the apartment every night, and I craved her every moment of my day. It was more than just that though, I wanted nothing more than to make her happy and to make every dream of hers come true.

I watched her as she mixed the wasabi and soy sauce, before pinching one of the sections of her roll with her chopsticks and dunking it into the mixture. When she put the entire piece into her mouth, she looked at me expectantly, and I giggled. She had the cutest chipmunk cheeks. To cover it up, I popped a section of my roll into my mouth.

The rest of dinner had a much lighter discussion where we just played twenty questions.

"What is your favorite color?" I asked.

"Black. It hides the blood better."

I laughed. That seemed to be right on par for her. "Other than black. If you don't have to be practical."

"Maroon. Deep maroon."

"Really leaning into the blood thing aren't you, darling?"

She shook her head, smiling. "No. Mom always said that maroon really made the color of my skin pop. After she died, whenever I needed to make myself feel better, I put on maroon. It makes me feel pretty. I know that sounds conceited, but..." She shrugged like it was what it was. I knew better than to say anything, because she was the most beautiful thing I had ever seen. I also remembered that night in bed where I told her to find one of my dark red shirts next time. I really wanted to see that.

"Favorite food?"

This time she raised an eyebrow at me. "Kolton, I'm chubby. I like all food." When I just looked at her like I was waiting, she sighed dramatically and said, "All right. *Mi abuela*'s tamales. You haven't lived until you have them. If we are talking commercialized... Italian."

"Mine too, sushi is a close second." I popped another roll section into my mouth.

"So, sushi tonight was a selfish selection?" She lifted her Nigiri and took a bite, and closed her eyes as she tasted it.

"I don't see you complaining." I teased.

"Well, no. Sushi is good, fresh sushi is pretty damn good."

On and on the questions continued, until the server came over and handed me the check. I just slid my card into it, and she walked away.

"Not even going to look at it?" Jade asked, but froze when she caught sight of something at the door.

CHAPTER 26

JADE

"What in the fuck is he doing here?" I whispered under my breath.

"Who?" Kolton asked, reaching over to grab my hand, and turn towards the door. "Who is that?"

"That is the Alpha of the wolf pack I've been dealing with." I tipped my head to the side, pulling on some of my Astral powers to enhance my hearing.

Devon strode right in and went to a table with a family of wolves sitting at a table near the front door. I ran a finger down my arm, and willed Kolton and I to stay hidden from Devon. I couldn't afford a confrontation in the middle of a crowded restaurant.

"*Wesley needs to pull his weight, too.*" *Devon said with a low growl.*

"*He is only twelve, Alpha.*" The male, who I assumed was the father, said.

"*So does Marianna. And yes, I know her age. It doesn't matter. The pack needs to pull on all resources to ensure its success. Wesley and Marianna must complete their duties. You know the price for non-compliance.*"

The man looked at his son, and his face paled. What in the fucking Gods was Devon doing with the children? Any wolf under sixteen was considered a pup, and not allowed by Lycan, nor Agency law, to be anything other than a pup. To play, learn, and have no responsibilities. The son nodded, and said, "Yes, Alpha."

"*Wesley, report at midnight for your duties. Marianna can report in the morning.*"

"Jade..." Kolton warned, noticing how I was becoming more agitated.

I watched Devon walk out, before I threw my napkin on the table and without looking at Kolton said, "Stay here. Wait five minutes, before coming outside." I kissed him quickly, and then disappeared.

I ran across the restaurant, so quickly, that anyone I passed would have thought an errant breeze had gone through the room. When I got outside, I looked right and left, before seeing Devon stop at the corner, light a cigarette, and walk around the corner.

Moving, I had him pinned against the wall, with his cigarette pointed at his eyeball. "What is this, I hear about you making pups work for the pack?"

"It's none of your concern, *Astral.*"

"It very much is my concern. I shifted, releasing a dagger from my thigh, and pointing it upwards toward his heart. "Pups are protected."

He bared his teeth, letting his canines grow, and I pushed the cigarette into his cheek and the dagger into his ribs. There was a flicker of recognition as I broke the skin, in both places, and he said, "You like drawing Alpha blood, don't you?"

"One day I will end you, Devon." I ground through my teeth. "Remember I am an Astral Primal, and there is jack shit you can do against me."

"The Agency—"

"Sent me, *me*, to deal with you, because they knew I would and will do whatever needs to be done to stop the atrocities that you are doing here."

There were a few seconds where we stood off against each other, before he leaned forward and sniffed. "You reek of human, Astral. Hope you are having fun with that." His eyes flashed and my stomach dropped. If he figured out why I smelled like one specific human, this could be very, very bad.

"This is your final warning, Devon. Leave the humans and your pups out of this."

"Give me what I require."

"You've been given an opportunity for a peaceful settlement. You push this much farther Devon, and you aren't going to like what happens. Keep the humans and pups out of this."

"The pups are mine, and I will do what I see fit."

I tilted my dagger, and pulled back, slicing through muscle. I felt wet warmth on my fingers, and he winced. There was a small groan, but he wasn't going to show that weakness toward me. Fucking Alpha machoism. "You've been given orders by the Ashstrike Sanctorum, *pup*. Follow them."

He shifted, swiping for my still healing leg, but I moved away from him. He bound off inland with a little limp, and I sighed. I took a couple calming breaths, before I walked around the corner to find the wolf family driving by and leaving.

By the time I got back to the front door of the restaurant, Kolton was there. He gave me a quick look up and down, his eyes snagging on the bloody dagger in my hand. Rushing toward me, he asked if I was okay.

"I'm fine. It's not mine." I waved my hand, and the dagger disappeared. His eyes widened just slightly before he shook his head. I gave him a quick once over before asking, "You okay?"

"Of course, I acted as though you just ran to the bathroom, then grabbed our stuff, and when I walked out, you came around the corner." He looked at my hand again. "Are you sure you are okay?"

"Yup." I went to wipe it off on my jeans, but Kolton caught my hand, and said, "I have cleaning wipes in the truck."

Kolton took my other hand and led me to the truck, opened the back seat door, and pulled out the first aid kit. He grabbed some wipes and went to work cleaning up my hands. He was meticulous and careful, but let out a long breath through his nose.

"Say it." I said a little harsher than I should have, and when he looked at me there was clear frustration in his eyes. "Sorry."

"I didn't like how you just left me in there, Jade."

"Kolton—"

"No, I need to say this."

"Okay." I let the word drag out and he let out another long breath. Was he going to say this wasn't something he could do? Couldn't be with me because of the way my life is?

"I brought you here to get away from all of our lives. Both of ours. I wanted tonight to be about us." He was disappointed, I realized. "I wanted tonight to be perfect. I wanted..."

He finished cleaning up my hand and after tossing the dirtied wipes into the trash in the back seat, he reached up and held my head in both hands. "I've never known a girl like you, Jade. And I don't mean what you do for a job, because well, that is obvious. I mean, I've never met anyone who can terrify me, calm me, and turn me on, all in the same moment. I want all of this. I want... you."

He leaned down and kissed me. It started soft and gentle, but when I wrapped my arms around his neck, he deepened it, with a need that I hadn't felt from anyone else in my life. He lit up every ounce of my soul, and that connection between us was a guiding light, and I pressed myself against him. He pulled his head back slightly, breaking the kiss, and said, "I know this is all so fast, but... fuck, Jade. I didn't like being left in there because I wanted to help. I'm not someone you are going to be able to leave on the sidelines. If this is going to be the way it is, you jumping in after the bad guys, and leaving me to the side, then that is going to be a major problem."

"I—"

"Not up for discussion." He said, kissing me again. Point made. I had to find a way to protect him but still allow him not to feel like I wasn't pushing him to the side.

"I have one final question for the night though, darling."

"What's that?" I leaned into him.

"Can we hurry back to the property so I can fix this growth you caused in my pants?" He may have asked, but he had already picked me up and placed me in the passenger seat of the truck before he finished the question.

I pushed my hand against the door, to keep him from shutting it, and he raised an eyebrow at me. I grabbed the front of his shirt and pulled him to kiss me again. "It's not my fault you can't control yourself."

We had just crossed the river, when he shifted in the driver's seat. I ran my fingers up and down his thigh in light small movements, and it didn't fail my notice that he gripped the steering wheel tighter. The corner of my lips turned up, and I chuckled.

"Darling." I turned in my seat, and smiled. "Oh, I don't know if I like this smile."

"Oh, why not?" I ran my fingers up the length of him and he groaned.

Before he could do much complaining as he made a turn around the bend, I undid his belt and pants. My hand was wrapped around his cock, and before he could do much else, I let my fingers swirl around the head of him.

"You keep that up and I'm not gonna make it home, Darlin.'"

I pulled on his pants and he lifted his hips just enough that I could fully free him. Once I had access, my head was in his lap, and I sucked on the head.

"Fuck." A hand rested on the back of my head, and I could tell he had slowed down since his concentration was now divided. When I swallowed him whole, he moaned, and the sound bounced off the walls of the cab.

My tongue ran the length of him, and when he hit the back of my mouth again, I stretched out my tongue. He jerked, then I felt the truck swerve, twice, before he threw the truck into park, and moved his hips to thrust into my mouth.

I chuckled, and a breathy, "Darlin... fuck."

When I pulled away from him, he pulled me up for a quick kiss before I went back to work on him. His hands rested back on the back of my head and when he was back down my throat, his hips moved in short, quick thrusts, moaning as he took his pleasure.

The taste and smell of him encircled me completely, and I couldn't help but squeeze my legs together. Kolton must have noticed, because he reached over and smacked my ass as he said, "Good girl."

His hips moved faster, and I sucked him harder as his cock twitched. "Swallow every drop, darlin," he said between his teeth as he thrust into me one more time, spilling himself down my throat.

Making sure he was licked thoroughly clean, I ran my tongue through the slit, smiling when he twitched at the movement. I sucked him in two quick pulses, enticing another moan from him before releasing him with a pop.

He rested his finger below my chin, as he guided me to his lips. Kolton kissed me gently, before whispering, "I wasn't expecting road head, darlin."

"Do you ever expect road head?"

"Maybe out on 99 or 5, where the road is long and straight, but here? Fuck no." I smiled at him, but he kissed me again, a little more forcefully, and threaded his hand through my hair, gripping it tight. I moaned into him, and squeezed my legs together again.

"When we get back, I'm gonna paddle that ass until you cum so hard, everything is drenched."

"Yes, Sir."

"Now back in your seat." When he had his pants back on, he grabbed my hand and threaded his fingers through mine before we got back on the road to the property.

CHAPTER 27

JADE

"Astral, it's a warning. Alpha knows. He knows that the human is your mate. He could smell him on you at the restaurant." The wolf said after shifting into his human form and striding for me. I didn't even blink at his nakedness. His light brown skin was marked with scars and showed the many fights he had been in.

"I don't have a mate." I said, rolling my eyes.

"Mate. Astral bonded. Semantics. Still natural selection. He is your chosen one."

"Not the point, Garrett." I pulled a dagger out of my thigh and sighed, when it came out broken, chipped, and warped.

He raised his eyebrows. "Haven't gotten your tattoo fixed yet, Astral?"

I flicked my wrist and there was instantly a mini shuriken in my hand and at his neck. He jerked, then froze when he realized I also had my other hand around his throat and pressing on that one little nerve that would keep him from shifting. "I am giving you everything I know, and you are standing here trying to keep me from shifting, with a knife to my throat."

I tipped my head to the side and smiled sweetly at him, "Wouldn't want you to forget who you are talking to." I winked at him, and he nodded as much as he could. "I don't need the dagger on my thigh to wipe you from existence."

"Yes, Astral."

I stepped back, and said, "And I will have that dagger back soon, so watch yourself. Now, what does your Alpha have planned?"

"He says you will personally pay for the death of the ten wolves that you killed."

I flipped the shuriken in my hand and looked at him. "I killed the three who attacked me."

"You could have *not* killed them."

"Their lives were forfeit the second they attacked an Astral. You know the laws." I said, my eyes hard. Ten? Shit. I thought there had only been eight.

"You think you are immune to shit and can just do what you want, but you also know there are going to be repercussions." He rubbed at his neck, as an example.

"I know that actions have consequences. I know that people die because of decisions that are made. Because of decisions that I make."

"I knew your Daniel." He ran his hand through his hair and looked at me. "He helped me out a few times in Kenya when I was out there for a special assignment."

I stared at him hard. I would not show any emotion here. I knew that while Garrett had given me good intel regarding Devon's movements, I would be stupid to think that Garrett couldn't be playing both sides of the coin.

He studied me a long moment. "Wow. That Astral bond is strong if you don't even flinch at his name."

"A lot of therapy helps." I waited a moment before continuing, "Now tell me, Garrett, or I will rethink this whole deal. Making a move on me is one thing, but —"

"Moving on your Astral bonded is war on the Agency. I am well aware." He huffed a hard breath and looked to the sky. "I have been trying to convince Devon of just that, but one of the wolves killed the day of the attack was his brother. His favorite brother."

"Brandon?" Garrett nodded slowly. Okay, that hurt. Brandon had been a good kid. "I'm sorry."

"You didn't do it. Your bonded did. It was a clean shot, but it is Brandon's death that has him out for your blood."

I nodded. "Who else died that day? I never got the list."

"Mostly new members hoping to gain favor with their new Alpha." His lip rose in disgust, before he said, "Brandon and Skyler were of the original pack.

"I am sorry for their deaths."

"Are you, though?"

"Just because I assisted in it, and would do it again, doesn't mean I don't value life. You and your pack trespassed beyond your territory because you wanted to bully yourselves into more territory, to take out a harmless gelding." I was pointing my finger at him, and realized I needed to make myself calm the fuck down. "Just because I protected the innocent in this, doesn't mean I don't value life."

He paced a bit, and I couldn't help appreciating the view. Wolves had no shame when it came to nudity, and while his body did nothing for me, his ass was well formed.

"See something you like Astral?"

"I can appreciate a good-looking ass." I shrugged. "It ain't gonna get me to breed with you, though. Nice try."

I knew that the thought hadn't crossed his mind, but it didn't mean that I couldn't tease him. Wolves would only breed with their mate. They would fuck each other like rabbits for pleasure, but could only knot and breed with their mate. If they dared with any other species, it was cause for immediate death. The fear in his eyes was almost hysterical.

"Now." I said, dropping my tone and hardening the look in my eyes. I flipped the knife a couple times in my hand, and said, "Again, because I am quickly losing patience, what is Devon's move toward the humans? Toward my bonded?"

"You know the drill, Jade." Philip patted the bed. It had been two days since Garrett and I had met in the wild land. He had only told me that Devon was planning something big, but didn't know any of the logistics of it. I had let him off easy, and headed back.

"Grab my book for me." I pointed to the book sitting on the nightstand. I laid down on my side, hiked the sleeping shorts I had on up, and got comfortable just as Philip turned the machine on. It was starting to get cold, so I had some tube socks on, but they didn't reach over the knee, and wouldn't cause a problem with the work he was doing.

"Are the socks really necessary?" He said, rolling his eyes at me, and I smiled at him.

"They are unless you want me to keep moving to keep my feet warm. Or we can just tuck them under your ass, and you can figure out a way to work on my thigh that way?"

"You know I can't." He sighed defeatedly.

"The socks stay then."

"Message received." Then without warning, he pushed down on my leg and put the machine to my skin. I jumped and Philip just looked up at me and smirked.

The vibration of the machine ran along my thigh, traveled up my hip, and actually released some of the tension. The bite of the needles were nothing compared to the salt that he dusted across it every couple of passes. The first few stung like a son of a bitch, especially over where the wolf had raked his claws over my leg. While it had healed, it was still tender. He smirked at me and started muttering the incantations as he worked, the soothing sounds melding into background noise as I read.

I'd wince every once in a while, and he would giggle at me. The salt was necessary for the incantation to take, but I'm not too proud to admit it hurt like hell. I just tried to concentrate on my book. The heroine was finally realizing she loved the mafia boss, and I couldn't help but smile at how many times she told him she hated him, when they both knew it meant the opposite.

"When was the last time the others were touched up?" Philip said, pulling me from my thoughts.

I blinked at him, and then I felt that cord in the world, my eyes slid to the left where Kolton was sitting reading some reports. When did he come in? His eyes lifted and when they met mine, he gave me a small smile.

"Jade."

Kolton's eyebrow rose, and I heard, "Astral!"

I jumped, and Kolton chuckled as I looked to Philip. "What?" My voice hard.

"I asked you, Astral, when was the last time your other weapons were touched up?"

My eyes fell on Kolton again, and I let out a long breath. "After Daniel died."

Philip, pulled my sock off and said, "Hold still."

"It's not needed." I said, jerking my leg back. "They work just fine."

"Astral Romero. Don't make me call Minstrel Carlos and have him order you."

"You are seriously going to call my cousin to order me to allow you to redo all my weapons? And what is with all the titles all of the sudden?" I looked at Kolton quickly, who shook his head and looked back at his paperwork, before glaring back to Philip.

"Titles, because Kolton knows what and who you are now. Titles because you are my superior in that right. Titles because it is the only way you will answer me. Now, are you going to make me call Minstrel Carlos Medina or are you going to just let me do my fucking job and help you?"

"Darling, he's here, he has the materials, and you are stretched out beautifully. Just let him."

I narrowed my eyes at Kolton and looked back to Philip. "No fair using Kolton as an ally."

"I'm not, but the fact he agrees with me is not a hindrance." He smirked and shrugged. "Now give me your ankle."

Kolton looked to the dagger now fully restored on my hip then to Philip, and asked, "Why didn't you tell me you were so talented?"

"You never asked."

"Just because I never asked, doesn't mean you couldn't have told me. I understand that you couldn't tell me about all … well this Agency stuff, but you could have told me you knew how to tattoo, and…" He stood up and looked at the shading he was touching up on my ankle knife. "What a fucking amazing artist you are. I so need you to do a piece or two for me."

Philip's eyes met mine quickly before he said, "Before you knew, I couldn't tell you. I'd have to get special permission to do any recreational pieces."

"Why?"

"I'm owned by Ashstrike." He said, but paused to mutter the incantations and rub some salt into the ink. I hissed, and my foot jerked involuntarily. When he was done, and moved onto my shurikens at my wrist, sighed and said, "I'm only allowed to do Agency approved pieces."

Philip paused, and looked at me. "Speaking of Agency approved pieces. Jesse is coming up. Will be here in a couple days. Doing a recreational piece for him."

I raised an eyebrow at him in question. "I'm the only one that can touch him without dying. Other Exorci are tough, but Jesse… Its gonna hurt like a bitch, and I'll need a couple days to recoup."

I nodded. "He's a good man, despite everything else."

"He is." Philip muttered. It was when he moved to my other wrist and I saw the throwing stars that Kolton's eyes narrowed on me. He looked at the knives that were always on display and then back at the stars before kneeling down next to me and said, "How did I not notice that one?"

I smirked at Philip whose lips twitched up.

"Any weapons on our arms are hidden. I received special permission for the throwing knife on my right wrist to show. That mumbling you hear Philip doing as he works and rubs the salt in?" I waited for Kolton to meet my eyes. When he did, I reached over and cradled his cheek in my hand. He leaned into the touch as I said, "Those are special incantations that allow us to pull the weapons from our bodies, and if they are on my arms, to stay hidden from anyone who doesn't know I'm an Astral. Someone may know that I'm from the Agency, but unless they know exactly what and who I am, they won't see them."

Kolton nodded, gave me a kiss on my forehead and went to sit back down in the chair. The entire time that Philip worked on me, Kolton went through pages of paperwork.

When Philip was done, every weapon on my body burned. He tilted his head to the side, looked at Kolton and I, and when his eyes met mine, I knew what he was going to ask. I gave him a quick shake, but ignoring me he asked, "Do you want me to do your bonding mark?"

"Our what?" Kolton asked, taking my hand in his. I hadn't even noticed him get up.

"Philip. Don't." My heart was racing, as Kolton's fingers threaded through mine and squeezed. "He doesn't know…"

"Why haven't you…"

"It's too new." I said, looking to Kolton who was looking at me with confusion. "Kolton needs time to adjust. To know what this bonding means."

"I know what it means. It means you, forever." He said softly. "It means that if I die, you die."

"It means all that yes. It's all very romantic, but what I'm concerned about is whether you want *me* and all my life entails."

"It isn't like it matters. Whether the bonding mark is applied or not, doesn't change anything. Not with you two." Philip said, looking at me curiously. "The bonding is inside. I'm sure you can both feel the pull toward each other. Always knowing where the other is, the knowledge deep inside you, that you are whole together."

"But I want him to have the mark of his own accord." I looked away.

"What makes this mark different from say, a wedding ring?" Kolton asked.

"Other than it will never come off?"

He huffed a laugh. "Other than it would never come off."

"The soul bond between you two has already taken root. I felt it while I was working on her weapons. It's in your blood, Jade, so don't give me that look." I didn't even realize I had been giving him a look.

Philip gathered more ink from his bag, and set it out as he put his machine down and cleaned up some before saying, "This would be a shared mark with each other. Like a matching tattoo. Only there are benefits. No matter where in the world they are, you can find the other."

I gave Philip a look because he knew as well as I did that there were ways to blur the exact location, or to keep an exact pinpoint on where the bonded was.

Philip ignored me, and continued, "In some bonded, there may some emotional connection, but it basically solidifies the bond after you have sex following the tattoos in romantic bondings. In platonic bondings, it's different."

"That kind of commitment Kolton, it's..." I trailed off as my eyes met his and there was nothing but warmth there. "We..."

"I love you, Jade. So, tell me why I wouldn't want this?" He leaned forward and rested his forehead to mine. I wasn't even sure I was breathing. Did he just say... ?

"Kolton." I said his name as a warning and a prayer.

"Let me repeat in case you missed it, darling. I love you. I love you so much that it hurts. Since you've been living in my apartment, I can't wait for the day to be over so that I can come back here and tell you about it. To fall asleep with you in my arms. To make you breakfast in the morning, to hear about your day. The frustrations, and joys. I want to hear how Carlos drives you crazy. I want that with you. Every damned day."

Tears fell down my cheeks and I lifted my hand to rest on his cheek. I didn't know when it happened or what was going to happen, but I whispered, "I love you, too."

Then he kissed me.

"We are getting them. Now." Kolton said against my lips. "Redwood trees."

"What if I want you to have a daisy? A hot pink daisy at that?" I whispered.

"Then I will wear that fucking hot pink daisy with pride." He pulled back and asked, "Where does it go?"

"Just under the inner elbow. On the forearm." Philip said.

I studied Kolton for a long, long moment. He raised an eyebrow at me, and I looked to his forearm. It was already covered with tattoos. "You already have full sleeves. Is there enough room to put a redwood tree?"

Philip looked at his arm, then the other. "I can put it in here. I'll have to get a little creative with the artistry though. Don't want it to look like shit or stand out from the rest of this."

He took some sketch paper out, laid it over top of Kolton's arm and traced the available space, before looking at my forearm. Kolton's eyes went wide, when Philip waved his hand over my forearm, and all the hidden protections that I had in white ink glowed.

"I thought they were the remnants of scars." Kolton whispered. "I hadn't gotten the balls to ask about them yet."

"White ink is very difficult to work with, but that is also the very reason why it is used, it isn't easily detectable, and they don't show to anyone unless they are an Agency artist." I smirked at him.

Moving the paper around, Philip found a good spot, and said he just needed some time to sketch it out to include all the runes needed. While Philip sketched out the tree, Kolton went back to finishing his paperwork.

I chewed on my thumb and when Kolton wasn't looking, I slid some additional instructions to Philip. We had a whole silent conversation, and I knew he was pushing back on me with it, but I gave him a begging look, and after a moment he sighed and nodded.

An hour later, he checked the locations again on both of us, put the stencils down, and asked Kolton, "Kole. We've known each other a long time. I have nothing but respect for you, and I'm not second guessing your choices here, but I need to ask. Are you sure this is what you want? Jade's life isn't an easy one."

I couldn't look at him as I echoed, "Seriously Kolton, there is no going back after this."

He turned me to look at him and held my chin tight as he said, "I know you want to take this slow, and that you are scared, Jade. I am yours, and you are mine. I have never been so absolutely sure about anything in my life. No one or anything is going to take you away from me." When he saw the doubt in my eyes, he said, "And to prove it, Philip, do mine first."

"Yes, sir."

Kolton's eyes never left mine as Philip lifted the machine, dipped the ink, and went to work on our bonding marks. When Philip muttered the incantations, I felt that cord glow bright, and I smiled when Kolton hissed as the salt was applied to seal it.

"Alright, I'll admit. That hurt. Worth it though." Kolton said when Philip was done.

I just held my arm out, and nodded as I kept my eyes on Kolton. It was just like with my weapons, only this made me feel hot, and there was a fierce pulsing between my legs by the time Philip had finished.

Philip packed up, and before he could give me the same speech every other artist had given me, I said, "Get out. I'm finalizing the bond, and unless you want to watch, please leave."

CHAPTER 28

JADE

I laid there for a long time just watching Kolton sleep. He had no hesitation in getting that bonding mark last night, and my fingers instantly ran over the area that Philip had inked it on his forearm.

"Jade, you keep doing that and neither of us are getting out of this bed any time soon."

"Last night wasn't enough for you?" I asked, even though my stomach tightened and I felt my nipples harden at the mere thought of having another round with Kolton. Sex was different with him. Everything was different with Kolton. I took a long breath as his eyes met mine and he said, "Never."

His eyes swirled with heat, and when I smiled at him, he rolled over and hovered above me. He studied each corner of my eyes, before he leaned down and kissed me. His lips didn't leave mine as he stripped me bare.

I reached down, pulled his pants off, and then ran my nail along the length of him. His hiss was music to my ears. He bit my lower lip, and said, "Now, now, Darlin.'"

I looked up at him, letting my finger roll around the head of him, batted my eyelashes, and licked my lips.

His eyes rolled back, as I gripped him and stroked in short tight movements, letting my hand roll over the tip. His lips trailed my jaw and down to my neck. I circled my thumb around the head of him, which rewarded me with a groaned open-mouthed kiss on my neck. When I did it again, he moved, and the next thing I knew Kolton was standing at the edge of the bed, and curling his finger toward him. "Come here, Darlin.'"

I got up and crawled toward him. When I was kneeling before him, I stretched out and ran my tongue along the length of him, before demanding, "On your knees, on the floor."

I flicked the head of him again before complying. I sat on my knees, hands resting on my thighs. I couldn't help but have my eyes flick back to his cock. The taste of him was still on my lips and I whimpered in protest.

Kolton's hand circled my throat again. "You want more?"

I looked up at him through my eyelashes as I said, "Yes, Sir." Then bit my bottom lip before looking back to where another bead of cum sat. "Please."

He grasped the base of his cock, and let out two long strokes before bringing it to my mouth. I looked up at him again, still biting my lip as he tapped the head of him against the plump part of my lips and smirked. "Open your mouth."

When I did, I let my tongue swirl around the head before slowly taking him in. When he reached the back of my throat, he allowed enough movement in my head to let me adjust to swallow him.

He pumped himself down my throat, and felt him tighten his hand around my neck just enough so that he could feel himself. He pulled out, and I let my tongue flick the head of him as he allowed me a moment to breathe. I leaned forward and when I swallowed him again, he groaned. His fingers loosened from my neck as he reached around and threaded them in my hair.

I looked up and he met my eyes, as he pulled out and then back in. There were only a few more slow strokes, before he was face fucking me. The taste of him and control over me, was pure heaven. His fingers tightened on my head, holding him deep before Kolton pulled out, but immediately did it again. His breaths were short, and his moans of desire were doing nothing but making me wetter and more needy of him.

"Damn, Darlin'." He said, his speed increasing as he slid in and out of my throat. I felt him twitching against my tongue, and looked up at him.

With a restrained groan he released me, grabbed me, raising me to face him. A small smile crossed his face as he wiped my chin with his thumb, pulled me close and kissed me. When he pulled back, he said, "Now, on the bed, I want to see that ass of yours."

I climbed on the bed, and when I looked back over my shoulder, he was in the closet. "On the bed. All four, Darlin'."

"What—"

"All four, Darlin'." He said in that tone that left no room for negotiation. I looked back to the wall and then knelt on all four, waiting for his next set of instructions. When I finally felt him smooth his hands over my ass, I sighed contently. Then he crawled up to look at me, kissed me, and slipped a blindfold over my eyes.

"I love you, Jade." He said against my ear before moving back behind me, and kissing each cheek. I wiggled toward him, right before there was a crack that sent a wave of pleasure through me.

"Don't move." He said reaching down and biting my ass hard, before there was nothing but air.

A few moments later, something metal and cold ran up the length of me, and I felt something dribble down the middle of me, before his finger massaged just around my ass. I pressed against him, wanting everything he was willing to give me, and when his finger entered me, I moaned.

There was a short huff of laughter, as he said, "My girl definitely likes her ass played with."

"She does, and if you don't fill it soon, she's going to be cranky."

"Is that so?" He said, now pumping two fingers in and out of me as he ran whatever toy he grabbed from my go bag up and down the front of me. I turned to look at him, but the blindfold stayed in place.

There was more of that cool liquid, before he was pressing the object into my ass. A long-contented moan escaped me, as he said, "I wouldn't want my darling to get cranky now, would I?"

"Fuck, Kolton." I felt every ounce of me go taught at the words as he fingered me.

"Oh, I plan on doing just that." He said, fingering my clit as his other hand ran up the spine of my back and grabbed my neck. I pushed back against him and felt his cock hard and ready.

He ran along the length of me, and then he stuck just the head of him into me, and pushed down on my neck so that I couldn't move.

"Please." I begged. I needed him to fill me. Fill every inch of me, and make me cum.

He pumped just the head of himself in and out of me, and I was helpless to do anything. Just when I was about to beg again, he slid in to the hilt. My mouth opened as pleasure filled me, and his grip on my neck tightened as he pulled me up so that his chest was to my back.

He turned my face toward him and I felt his breath on my cheek as he said. "You feel that? You feel me inside you? I will be the only one ever inside you again, Darlin'."

He moved and he hit that spot inside of me that instantly had me grinding against him. The motion adjusted the butt plug he had inserted earlier, and even he groaned in pleasure in my ear. I moved against him again, and smiled. His lips were on mine, as he met my movements.

He reached between us and he pushed a button, causing the plug to vibrate. I gasped, and I felt him freeze.

"Dear gods." I heard him say. He removed the blindfold, and when my eyes met his, they were glazed over heavily. I ground against him, and his mouth fell open.

I smiled, but didn't stop moving against him, but whispered. "Never had anyone with a vibrating anal plug, before?"

"No, but to experience it with you, like this. Holy gods."

I rotated my hips against him, and he dragged from me, but when just the head of him was within me, he smirked and pound into me.

"Fuck, Kolton. Please just fuck me." I was begging now. I didn't even care how pathetic it sounded. When he froze, I repeated, "Please, Sir. Please fuck me."

He chuckled before he started taking long powerful strokes, and at each connection, he slowed and rolled against me. The feel of his chest against my back, as he held me by the throat, gods I was so close.

"Darlin', cum for me. Scream my name." The hand that had been holding my waist slid down and with two flicks of his fingers against my clit, I was indeed screaming his name as the world spun and shattered around me.

When I had my wits about me, Kolton was half laying atop me, sliding the anal plug from within me. I heard the click of the button and it dropped to the floor.

We were both heaving long deep breaths, and my legs were twitching from the aftermath. Kolton pulled me against him, kissed the top of my head and said, "I love you, Jade."

"I love you too, Kolton."

We laid like that for a long minute, before he gently pulled away from me. A small whimper escaped me, but I heard him in the bathroom, and then he said, "On your back."

I looked over my shoulder and raised an eyebrow, but he said, "I need to clean you up, darling." I smiled and did as he instructed, and I may have spread my legs a little wider than was necessary.

"If I were not still reeling, I would dive head first into that." He said with a smirk. The towel was warm, as he wiped my legs, then up and down the center of me. Before he backed away though, he did indeed kiss my clit, and my whole body shuddered at the touch of it. There was a wicked glint in his eye as he went back to the bathroom and said, "You need to recover too."

I rolled back over onto my stomach, curled a pillow under my head and sighed. I caught a glimpse of the redwood tree now inked just below my elbow and smiled.

I had Kolton. He was really mine.

A moment later, Kolton was crawling over the top of me, his hands running along my arms to cradle me in his own hug. He kissed the top of my head. I smiled, before letting out a big sigh. I really could get used to this.

Kolton laid over the top of me for another long minute, before sliding off to the side, pulling me with him, so that we were spooning.

"We have an hour before we have to meet with Rose." He said sleepily.

"Don't you have things you should be doing right now?"

"The guys can handle it or I'll stay late to get it done." He kissed me on the back of the head again, and said, "I'm right where I'm supposed to be."

Next thing I knew, I was dozing off to sleep.

CHAPTER 29

JADE

TWO WEEKS LATER

I groaned at the banging on the door, but then my eyes popped open as I heard Philip. "Astral. Kolton. Get up. Myka's been hurt. Bad."

My eyes met Kolton's for the briefest second before I was up and running to the door. Just before I got there, Kolton grabbed my arm stopping me. I glared at him, and he looked me up and down, raising an eyebrow. "As much as I do love you like this, I don't think this is what Philip plans on seeing when he opens the door."

It was only then I realized that I was stark naked. "Shit." I muttered, as he handed me a t-shirt and sweats. For two weeks, Kolton and I had shared a bed. Both in the physical and intimate since, and there was just something about that realization that made me blink at how much I had completely accepted and brought him into my life. I shook my head to clear the thoughts. Later. I could think on that later.

Kolton at least had his boxers on, so while I threw on the t-shirt and sweats, he answered the door. "What do you mean Myka's been hurt?"

"There was an incident near the wildland. Titus is beat up, but Myka..." I turned the corner after slipping the t-shirt over my head, and the look on Philips's face paled. His eyes met mine, and he breathed, "The wolves fucked him up pretty good."

"Fuck!" I spat. "Devon or minions."

"No idea. Gonna have to get that info from Myka and Titus." His eyes moved to Kolton. "I know you just learned of the supernatural, but some stitches and general TLC from the local, off duty paramedic would be appreciated."

Kolton nodded. "Let me throw some clothes on quick and grab the pack. Where did you put him?"

"Game room. Laid Myka out on the couch. Titus is crumpled up next to him on the floor."

"Poor Titus." I muttered, and they both gave me a questioning look. I shook my head. "Let's go, Philip. Hurry up, Kolton."

Kolton gave me a quick kiss on my temple as I squeezed by him saying, "I'll be just a minute."

I vaulted over the railing, landing on the ground in a crouch, before using that Astral speed to get to the game room. When I walked through the door, I felt the incantation that they had placed against humans entering, looked to Titus to tell him to release it for Kolton, but held my tongue when I saw Myka laying on the couch covered in blood.

His face had three long claw marks starting from his right hair line, across his eye, nose, cheek to his chin, blood coating everything. His left leg looked to be broken, but I couldn't tell from where I was. Titus had wrapped it in a shirt, but the shirt was soaked with blood and pooling on the couch cushions. Myka's right arm hung limply off the side of the couch, and when I stood next to the two of them, Myka's good eye swung to me and widened.

"We will get you cleaned up." Kolton said from right next to me, and I whirled my head in his direction to face him. "You need to move, darling, so I can get to him."

"How..." I looked at the door and then back at him, as I stepped back. "Kolton..."

"Titus, I need you to go get Ms. Rose, and have her make a whole bunch of that tea she made for Jade when she got hurt." Kolton said as he gave Myka a cursory once over. "Jade, go get a comm set, and call

James to get me some lumber so we can brace this leg. Philip, get the bus for me."

"Astral..." Titus said carefully, and I raised an eyebrow at him in question.

When no one moved, he looked up and met our eyes. "What? I'm assuming supernaturals attempt to stay out of human hospitals, right?"

"Well, yeah." Philp muttered as I nodded.

"So, I'm your best bet." Kolton looked over Myka again, and said, "Actually, Titus, get his leg uncovered so I can see what is going on. Philip, can you get Ms. Rose to make a whole barrel of that tea? Myka, is going to need it. Jade, darling, get me a few buckets of water."

Kolton bent over Myka, but I didn't move.

Red. All I saw was red.

Red floating through the water, chunks of body parts floating, and when I saw the Selki tearing apart the last shreds of that being, it wasn't Daniel's face that had haunted my nightmares for years and years. It was Kolton's. It was Kolton the Selki was shredding. My heart raced, and—

"Water, Jade!" Kolton's voice broke through the haze in my head, bringing me back to where we were. What was wrong with me? I'd seen plenty of injured Astrals since that day. Seen plenty of injured beings murdered or killed since then.

I took a deep breath and ran to the kitchen, grabbing the largest bowl and filling it. Watching the water rise to the rim, I forced myself to breathe and remind myself that Kolton was whole and uninjured in the other room. The wolves had gotten to Myka and Titus, who... fuck. They were Astrals, and got the shit beat out of them. I ran my hands through my hair, causing my ponytail to fall out. Water overflowed the bowl, and I turned the faucet off before putting my hair back up.

I flung open the drawer with all the dishtowels, and grabbed as many as I could carry, before grabbing the bowl of water. I pulled on my Astral powers to move quickly and not spill the water all down the hall, when James met me in the hallway. "Hey, I can't get into the game room. Wanted to grab a couple things."

"I'm having a meeting with Titus and Myka. Can you come back later?" I was trying to keep my voice calm, but he eyed me carefully before saying, "Does this have anything to do with why I saw Philip running faster than I have ever seen him run before?"

I just stared him down, and when he gave me a look to say, '*Well?*', I sighed and nodded. "Please let it go, and come back later, James."

"Is Kolton in there?"

"Yeah, he is."

"Is he okay?" He looked genuinely concerned, as he turned back to the game room door.

"Kolton is fine. Short story; Myka got hurt and Kolton's getting him cleaned up, alright?"

James nodded. "Okay."

We were standing at the door, and I said, "I'll see you later, James. You can't see what is inside."

"That bad?" He asked, and I just nodded. "Alright. I'll come get my shit later."

When James closed the exterior door, I used my hip to open the other one and make my way inside. Kolton was picking through the wounds on Myka's face, so I set the bowl down, and dunked one of the washcloths into the water, handing it to him. He took it without looking up and started cleaning the long deep cuts on Myka's face.

After a few tense moments, he sighed, and said, "You are one lucky ass motherfucker, Myka. The claws missed your eye, and the gashes aren't deep. I'll need to put a couple stitches in on your forehead and one, here near your nose."

I huffed a laugh. "Don't forget turning into a turnip for a week from the bruising." I reached over and poked his nose, and he winced. "Oh, good, he broke your nose too. Maybe it will do something for those looks of yours."

Myka tried to laugh but winced. Kolton looked at me, and said, "Again you are a lucky bastard. You could have lost the eye." He blinked at me quickly, and put his hand on his shoulder. Myka winced and Kolton said, "Alright, now let's see what is going on with your leg." Just before he took both hands and reset his shoulder.

Myka roared in pain, and it was Titus who was up and had Kolton by the shoulders. I had a dagger at Titus' neck a split second later. "Myka is fine, and if you threaten my Bonded again, neither of you will be here by the morning. So, Titus, pull back." I ordered. When he didn't, I fed some of that Primal power into the words, "Titus, pull back. Kolton is trying to help."

Titus' eyes flashed.

"I know. Look at him. He still breathes. His heartbeat is strong." I stared at him a moment longer before saying, "Philip has already left to ask Rose to make the tea." There was such a heartbreaking look in his eye, I just repeated, "I know."

I saw Kolton's eyes pinch, but that was a question for after we got Myka stable. "Jade, get me more water. Lots more water. There are a couple of buckets in the closet just to the left of the door before you get to the kitchen. Bring them. I gotta clean this leg out to see what I'm even looking at."

Then Kolton turned back and met Myka's eye. "This is gonna hurt like fucking hell, Myka, but if you have to look at Titus' face every night, then you are used to pain." I shook my head as I turned to leave.

"Never complained before, Myk?" Titus said through a chuckle as I walked out of the room.

I found the buckets, rinsed them out, but as I started filling them buckets, I felt something through that bond. I closed my eyes and concentrated on it, and finally recognized it. Frustration and determination. When the first bucket was full, I set the second bucket in the sink, and rolled my shoulders. I stared into the water, and wondered just how Kolton had gotten into the room, if Titus had warded it from the humans, which was obvious, because James said he couldn't get in...

"Jade." Philip said behind me, and I spun around. "Kolton is facing off with Titus."

"What?" I took off down the hall, and when I returned, Kolton was indeed staring Titus down.

"Titus, I don't give two royal fucks who and what you two are to each other. I don't care how protective you are of him."

"Kolton." I warned with a snap and his eyes met mine. I shook my head.

"Look man, I'm trying to help." He sighed.

"Titus, you gotta let Kolton do this." I strode up to where they were and pushed Titus back by the shoulder, making him look at me. "Back down. Let Kolton help. He is part of this world now, and is trying to clean him up, so he can be bright and shiny new again. If you make me call Rose, that is going to do nothing but make him be in pain longer."

He took a deep breath and nodded. "Tea. That will help."

"Now, let me help get you cleaned up while he works on Myka."

I didn't think Titus was going to allow it, but Myka groaned, "Let Astral Jade clean you up."

"But—"

"Kolton will get my leg set, and when Jade is done with you, you can be a nursemaid again." Myka huffed a chuckle, but moaned against the pain it caused.

Philip came in then with the water and helped Kolton clean up Myka's leg as much as he could, while I cleaned up a couple gashes, and punctures the wolves left on Titus.

His eyes kept going back to Myka, and so I went for the distraction. "Tell me what happened."

"Myka and I were getting close to the meet point along the back property line. We had heard a few strange things on and off for the last few hours, and it put me on edge." He winced as I dug out some of the dirt and rock out.

"Kolton, toss me some tweezers." I reached back and when I felt the metal in my hand I said to Titus, "So what happened?"

"Wolves came from every direction. Alpha and the betas weren't there. I... All their auras were angry or scared. I don't know what Alpha Devon is doing to the members of that pack, but it isn't good. They were just so angry. They were more than predatory,... they were ravenous. They had stalked Myka and I, and were going for the kill." His eyes met mine and they were dark. "Jade, I thought we were dead."

I froze for a split second before I pinched out a small rock in his arm. "You're healing already. That's good."

His eyes flicked to Myka, worry lining his face. "I know, Titus, but he will be fine." I turned and Myka looked at us as he winced. "His face is healing already, too. That eye is going to be swollen shut for a day, but he's healing already. Even looking like a damn turnip for a few days, but he'll be okay. Kolton is taking care of him."

"You are just saying that because he's your Bonded." He groaned as I dug a little deeper.

"And he is yours, so you're being an overprotective shit." I whispered so no one else in the room could hear.

"Jade." Kolton's voice was hesitant, and when I turned to look at him, his eyes flicked to Titus before he said, "I need to straighten this leg out."

I took a deep breath looking back at Titus. "Do I have to tie you down?"

"No."

With my back to Kolton, I flicked my fingers to just do it, and I readied myself for Titus to jump up. Kolton took my signal and did it in a few quick movements. Myka stiffened, but only let out a groan when the burst of pain passed.

Titus, to his credit, winced, but stayed in his seat. When Myka calmed, and his breathing was just a series of deep breaths, Kolton finished cleaning and setting the leg.

"I need some supplies out of the bus. I don't have enough to stitch him up for now. That break is going to keep him off his feet for a bit." He ran his hand through his hair, and then shook his head with a small smile at me. "I could see some of the tissue start to heal as I worked on cleaning it out."

"I told you I was a fast healer."

"Yeah, that you did. Anything else you wanna tell me?" He said pulling me close.

"He needs to drink a lot of this." Rose said from the doorway, and held up a bin saying, "I grabbed this for you. Figured you wouldn't have enough gauze or thread to stitch him up from what Philip told me."

Kolton kissed my temple and went to Rose, taking the bin, but narrowed his eyes at her before turning back toward Myka to get started on stitching it up. "What is in that tea, anyways?"

Rose started to say something, but Kolton cut her off with a, "And Ms. Rose, if you say, just a few things and a dash of Rose, I swear."

"Okay, I don't have to, because you just did."

I chuckled and turned back to Titus. "You should get a couple stitches. You good with me playing nurse?"

Titus nodded, and after putting a few stitches in, I pulled a chair out to sit down. I watched as Rose made Myka sip on the tea over the next few hours while Kolton meticulously cleaned and stitched up his leg.

By the time he was done, Titus was leaning against the couch next to Myka, Philip had gone back to bed, and Rose had gone out to get the rest of the guys started on the day since Kolton was attending to Myka.

"Kolton," Titus' voice was drained, and he sounded like he could sleep for days.

"Yeah man?"

"I'm sorry I was a right dickhead." He sighed again. "I know you were only trying to help. Thank you for stepping up and getting him patched back together."

Kolton looked at me and smiled softly. "I get it. He's yours."

"How..."

"Titus, man, you were one protective asshole today. You were protecting your bonded." Kolton was keeping his voice down, and Titus nodded.

"Still, I'm sorry."

"You are welcome." He got up and stretched. "Now, I need some aspirin, and a hot shower. My shoulders are killing me."

I took his hand and said, "Come on. I'll massage the knots out."

His eyes heated and I smiled. "Only a massage. And food. You need food. You've been at this for hours. It's mid-afternoon."

"Okay, food and a massage sounds like heaven." The bliss on his face was delightful. "We need to get Myka to his bed, and out of those clothes."

"I'll ask Philip for some help." Titus said. "You've done enough. Really."

"Come on, Hero Kolton. Let's get you food and get those knots out."

CHAPTER 30

KOLTON

SIX MONTHS LATER

I was standing outside as the line of contractors drove up. Jade had been in the Bay Area working with the general contractor ensuring that they had everything ready to start the actual project. She had worked almost non-stop for almost a month after our bonding marks to ensure everything was ready for all the different approvals and submission to the County.

It had been fascinating to watch her work. The way she would chew on her lip, her thumb, then look up at me through her lashes and tell me to stop staring. She was so dedicated, and her work ethic was better than mine. There were also the constant video calls with Carlos about the project and the wolves, who had been surprisingly quiet after the incident with Myka and Titus.

Once the redevelopment plans were approved by Rose, Jade filed for all the permits with Del Norte County. When there were only small tweaks requested for the housing plans, she made them within a day and sent them back. The complete plans for the entire project were approved in only a month. The Agency must have had some pull because I'd heard of other properties in the area doing smaller projects, and it taking months for them to get signed off.

Bids came in from all over the northern part of the state, and Rose had decided to go with a contractor in the North Bay. They had another project cancel, so not only could they fit in within our timeline, they also had the resources to mobilize this far north. Jade said it was a bit of a windfall. She thought she was going to have to bring in Agency crews, but she didn't want to do that because it would only make the situation with the wolves worse.

I watched as she drove up in my truck and parked in front of the office, with the demolition and base crews pulling in right behind her. There were travel trailers, and I sighed, even a portable office. She had disregarded that request of mine.

Her truck was fine for around the Ranch, but I didn't feel comfortable with her driving all the way back to the Bay Area in hers. We had discussed it at length, and she finally gave in to taking my truck, as long as I agreed that Myka and Titus could continue to stay onsite and help with the wolf situation. I was at the hood of the truck by the time she jumped out and met me. I kissed her, and didn't even care who saw. It had been three weeks. Three weeks with her not by my side.

"Hello." She muttered against my lips.

"Hello, darling." I rested my forehead against hers and just breathed her in. "If I didn't know that you had to get all those guys set up, I would take you back to the apartment immediately."

When she looked at me, I could see the heat in her gaze. "Considering my dom hasn't let me take care of myself in a week, I'd say you have some work to do."

I smiled, kissed her forehead, and then took a step back as a man who appeared to be in his mid-forties got out of a truck bearing the Arteaga Construction logo. "You must be Kolton Webster, Foreman for the Porter Ranch."

"I am."

"I'm Benito Alcabú, but everyone calls me Boss Man or Ben." His smile was warm and open. "I've been working with Jade on the construction aspects. She had mentioned that you didn't want us to bring our own mobile office, but we can tuck it up near where the new main house will be so it will be out of your way, but still accessible to our guys."

I nodded because of course Jade had found a way to make it work for both parties. I looked at the six trailers that were lined up behind him. "We don't have sewer or water hookups anywhere for those, and the closest campground with hookups is over an hour away, but you can set up in the southern pasture. We have a water truck and can haul water out as needed to refill your tanks. The sewer is going to be a little more tricky, but we can sort it out."

"Thank you. You have someone who can show us exactly where to set up so we won't be in the way?"

I reached up and clicked on my earpiece and said, "Fernando."

"He's... not available right now Kolton. What you need?"

"Where is he, James?"

"What do you need, Kolton." He was avoiding the question, and I would have to talk to him about it later. "Can you come and show the construction crews where they can camp in the southern right pasture. They have a number of RVs that need to be set up. They are also going to be setting up a portable office next to the new home site. I have some things to go over with Jade."

James' chuckle came through before he said, "I'll be right there."

Jade was talking with Ben, and when she turned back to me, the smile on her face was dazzling. I let my eyes wander up and down her body, and I grew hard just looking at her. I felt her in the very core of me, and there was a heat in that connection. Her eyes went down to my waist and back up, and her whole expression shifted to something far more mischievous.

"As soon as we are alone Darlin', you will be wishing you didn't give me that look."

"Is that so … *Sir*?" Oh, the snark from this woman.

I took three large steps toward her, let my eyes flick around to ensure no one was looking, and wrapped my hand around her throat. She extended it, and tipped her head back, moaning. I tightened it slightly, before sliding my hand around to the back. While she was a willing partner, others may not understand our relationship at a glance. I have to control myself in public, but she made it so damn hard.

She reached up on her toes, kissed me, and said, "Play tonight." Then she sighed, and put her hand on mine at her throat. "I do need to work. So tonight, you can put me in my place."

"Are we the planner or the Astral this afternoon?"

She crunched up her nose. "I'm meeting with Garrett."

I nodded. "Be careful, please. They have been quiet while you were gone, but that in itself makes me nervous."

Jade just smiled, and raised an eyebrow that was meant to say, '*Aren't I always*', but I rolled my eyes at her. "Be careful."

"Yes, Kolton." That side of her lips rose and then she was swaying her hips at me, heading back to the truck.

"No fair, Ms. Romero!" I shouted toward her. She just climbed up into the truck and drove off without a second glance back. I felt the chuckle from her more than heard it and shook my head.

Ben came over then, and said, "She mentioned that you two were involved. You are a lucky man. That woman is wicked smart."

I wasn't sure I knew how to feel about that comment, but ran my hand through my hair and said, "Yeah, but watch out. That same woman would stick a dagger in you, in a heartbeat, if you piss her off."

"I have no doubt about that." When he picked up his walkie-talkie to answer a question from one of his crew, I heard the disruption in my ear and winced.

"Let's go inside and talk about onsite logistics. The first of which is to ensure that your guys and mine are not on the same comm frequency. That sort of hurt the ear drum."

His eyes knitted together and I pointed to my ear. "We have our own onsite comm system with ear pieces."

Laughing he said, "Sure thing. After you."

CHAPTER 31

KOLTON

"Y ou about ready to head out, darling?" I said as I slipped a jacket on. Turning toward the hallway, to see her walking into the living room, I froze, my hands on the collar of my jacket and swallowed.

"What?" Her worried look was a shock to my senses.

I looked down the length of her body, to the small black flats she wore. I let out a long breath as my eyes trailed up her bare legs, where the sundress she was wearing just barely covered the thigh tattoos on either side. It accentuated the curve of her hips, and the faux corset she wore only accentuated her breasts. Yeah. My pants definitely got a bit tighter.

"What?" she said again. "Is this okay? Do you want me to change?"

I rushed over to her, with my hands on her hips, pulled her against me, so she knew exactly what she was doing to me. I kissed her, and her arms wrapped around my shoulders. "If anything, I want you out of those clothes, and writhing under me."

She blushed. "So, it's, okay?"

"Jade, you are in a dress. I never thought I'd see the day."

"I may not wear one all the time, but I do own a few. I only brought this one back with me though."

She smirked as I stepped away from her to look her up and down again. "It's not like I've had much of an opportunity to take you out."

"You took me to Brookings." She leaned against me, resting her hands on my chest.

"I did, but since then, life has been so busy that going on a date hasn't been an option." I leaned down to kiss her forehead and as if on cue her stomach growled. I smiled against her forehead, and she groaned.

"I hate how you can always hear my stomach." I shrugged, took her hand and led her down to the truck.

We pulled up to the one and only diner in town. "It's not fancy, but their burgers are delicious." I said, opening the door as she was applying her bright red lipstick.

I groaned. How was I going to concentrate on anything other than the thought of those red lips wrapped around my cock? I took her hand and threaded my fingers through hers as we went in. Jade scanned the room quickly, and when the waitress said we could sit where ever, she led me to the back corner, and made me sit across from her with my back to the door.

"It's a thing. I can't sit with my back to the door."

I nodded in understanding, but said with a smirk, "I could sit next to you, and make sure you really enjoyed your meal."

She leaned forward doing nothing but displaying her breasts to me. She fingered the center, and pulled on it just the littlest bit, and my mouth watered at the want to taste them.

"Jade, you are not playing fair."

"Who said anything about playing fair tonight? I have you sitting exactly where I want you." She said, her eyes burning with desire. Then I felt her bare foot on the bench between my legs.

My eyes snapped to hers, "Jade."

Her only response was a crooked smile, as her foot rubbed against my already hard cock. I had to bite back a moan, as the waitress came up, and asked what we wanted to eat. I wanted to have Jade for dinner, and she knew it by that glint in her eye.

"Burger well done. Fries, please." I said trying to sound as normal as possible as Jade kept moving her foot.

The waitress must have looked at Jade, because she just said, "Same, with an ice tea. I suspect Kolton wants one as well?"

I blinked, looked to the waitress, and just nodded. I didn't trust my vocal chords to do anything but moan or growl right now.

"So, what did you want to talk about?" Jade's voice was calm, but there was a teasing smirk on those luscious red lips.

I cleared my throat, and blinked at her. "How are you so freaking calm right now?"

"I don't know what you are talking about Kolton." Her foot rubbed up and down the very prominent bulge that was between my legs.

She leaned forward, and the front of her shirt dipped low enough that I was able to see she was in fact not wearing a bra. Her toes curled along the head of my cock, and I did in fact let out a growl at that. "Oh, Jade. You came ready to fight tonight didn't you."

She smiled brightly at me, and I knew I got harder under her. My gaze went to where her shirt was gaping open, and then she looked at me through those long black lashes, and concentrated small movements against the head of my cock.

"You are hard as a rock, Kolton. I wonder why that is?"

My voice was husky and deep as I said, "Maybe because my girlfriend is being a tease." I groaned as her toes gripped the head of me, again.

"Shhh. You don't want others to hear, do you?"

I smirked at her. "You are enjoying this, aren't you."

"Oh, very much so." She said just as the waitress showed up with our burgers. Jade's eyes narrowed as she looked the waitress up and down, and scoffed.

"Can we please get..." Her foot pressed and ran the length of me again, as I tried to say, "our ice teas?"

"Anything for you, Kolton." The waitress said, but I hadn't taken my eyes off Jade. There was a fire in Jade's eyes, and after the waitress left, I asked, "What's wrong, darling?"

"That waitress."

"What about her?"

"Look at your napkin. Five bucks... no, a blow job says that her number is on it." Her eyes flicked to it.

"Don't be ridiculous." When she gave me a look that dared me to challenge her, I just said, "Darling, are you actually jealous?"

She removed her foot, as the waitress dropped off our ice teas, and reached for her burger. "I shouldn't be, but yeah, a little. I know where you sleep. I know who you are bonded to."

I reached over and took her hand just before she took hold of her burger. "Don't forget that." With another hard look at her, I said, "Thank you for being honest with me."

There was a small smile, before she nodded to our plates, "Before it gets cold."

I had just taken a bite of my burger, when her foot was back between my legs and it took all of my concentration not to choke as she worked her foot up and down me. I couldn't help the involuntary hip movements against her.

She reached for the ketchup, and I was greeted with a full view of her right nipple, and I stuck my knuckle into my mouth and bit down. Her eyes flicked to meet mine, and she smirked, taking a long drink from her ice tea. She squeezed some ketchup out of the bottle just as her toes curled around me and squeezed.

"Jade. I swear for all that is holy." I jerked against her foot, and took a deep breath to contain myself.

"You are so close to losing it, aren't you?" Her voice was low as someone sat down in the booth behind me. "You have no idea. Eat. I'll behave while you do."

After a few minutes of silence, I asked, "Jade, can I ask you something?"

She stuck a fry in her mouth and said, "Of course."

"I know this whole bond thing is new, and again, we haven't really been able to do any sort of traditional courtship thing, but even with Daniel, did you two talk about a long term future? We haven't, and I'd like to."

She took a long drink from her iced tea, and sighed. "Daniel and I were different, though, Kolton. There wasn't this." She pointed between us.

"You are right, you were with Daniel by choice. I'm biologically bonded to you."

"Don't you dare cheapen what is between us, Kolton Kane Webster." Her eyes had snapped to mine, and her voice had become lethal.

"I love you, Jade. Don't forget that." I said, but then I second guessed myself. "But is that because of the bond or because of us."

"I love you, Kolton. I am with you because I love you, because I want to be with you." Her leg lifted again between my legs and she softly ran her foot up and down the length of me. "There are those who are bonded that never have a romantic relationship. The bonding doesn't have to be romantic. It can be platonic. It happens between Asexual persons as well. I am with you because I love you, and want to be with you. If I didn't, I wouldn't be sitting in this booth wondering how I was going to wait to get you back to the apartment to have my way with you."

"But do you want a forever with me?" I asked softly. "I'm not saying let's get married. I'm asking, do you want to be with me forever? Can you see a life without me in it?"

"I've lived a life without you in it." She said, and for a split second my heart dropped into my stomach. "When I had to go back to the Bay Area without you, I hated getting back to my apartment and not having you there. I missed having you there by my side every day. I want you."

She was playing with her fingers, a nervous habit she had. "Darling." I said long and carefully, because while I felt like she was my forever, to know that she felt that as well, soothed me.

Jade looked at me, and there were tears in her eyes as she said, "You are my forever, Kolton. Please don't make me live it without you."

Reaching over and forcing her to look at me by grabbing her chin, I said, "Never. You are mine. I am yours. I just needed to know."

"This is real Kolton. I told you that before. It. Is. Real."

"Real." I whispered, as she nodded. "Okay. Then finish eating, so I can take you back and have dessert."

As her foot resumed its torture as the corners of those red lips turned up, and I felt myself twitch against her. I heard someone walking up behind us, and cleared my throat.

"Your check." The waitress said. When I grabbed it, her hand landed and lingered on mine. I looked up to her, and she winked saying, "And something extra, in case you get tired of whatever is left on your table."

I felt Jade's foot freeze under the table, and I grabbed it, and rubbed small circles on her ankle as I said, "That isn't necessary. *Only* the bill is fine. I have everything else I will ever need or want."

The waitress looked over at Jade and actually had the gall to look her up and down. "Doesn't look like she can keep up."

"Trust me, honey, you have no idea what kind of stamina I have." Jade's smile was hard and brittle.

"I know I could please Kolton a whole lot better than some *city* girl."

Jade's foot twitched again, and I latched onto it, gripping the ankle in my hand harder. I could feel the irritation flowing off her. When she finally relaxed under my touch, I released her ankle. My voice was hard as I said, "You should leave, Olivia. I will pay our tab, but you should leave before Jade gets really pissed."

"I'm not worried about her." Olivia said. I had known she had a crush on me, but she had no boundaries for relationships. She would be the side chick, and sleep just fine at night. She'd been around this town so much, we wondered who she *hadn't* been with.

"It's okay, Kolton. She has no idea how pissed I can get, or what I could do to her. How could she?" Jade's eyes were mischievous when they met mine, and I was just about to remind her to be a good girl, when her toes curled and rubbed up and down the front of my pants. I let out a guttural moan, and leaned my head back. Fuck, she knew exactly what she was doing.

"This little city girl here knows exactly how to make her man make *that* sound. If you had asked nicely, I might have even let you join us one night, but..." She trailed off, and as I realized what she just said, my cock twitched.

"Darling." My voice was a warning.

"But now, I'm considering rearranging your body parts." Jade's smile was pure brittle death. The waitress had the good sense to walk off then, and I was in half a daze as Jade slipped her shoe on and stood. I blinked to clear my head, stood, pulled out the cash to cover the bill, and just threw it on the table.

I grabbed Jade's hand and all but hauled her from the diner. I needed this woman now. Not in twenty minutes, now.

She chuckled, and even gave the waitress a flirty little wave as I pulled her out of there. When we rounded the corner to the diner, I pushed her against the wall and kissed her.

Jade melted against me, and I slid my hand up under the skirt of her sundress and moaned when my hands reached nothing but her skin as she wrapped a leg around my waist.

"Fuck, no panties either?" I slid two fingers into her, and her head fell back against the wall. "There's my good girl."

"Kolton." It was a whispered plea on her lips, and I kissed her again as my fingers thrust in and out of her. I heard someone around the corner and moved so that if anyone did see us, the shadows would make our position only look as if we were having a make out session.

"Sir." Her breathing came short and quick and I pulled my fingers from her and slapped her clit. She twitched, and her eyes flew open.

"I didn't give you permission to cum." I whispered in her ear, then pulled back so she could see as I licked my fingers clean. Gods, she tasted amazing. I took my time licking each one to get every drop. Her eyes followed the motion of my tongue, and I felt her twitch under me. "What's wrong, Darling?"

Her eyes flung to mine as she grabbed quickly undid my pants. "If you get to taste me on the backside of a building... turnabout is fair play." Before I could stop her, she was on her knees before me, the head of my cock between those gorgeous red painted lips of hers.

I pounded my fist against the brick wall, and leaned my head against my forearm. My other hand reached down and cradled her face as she took me deeper.

"Fuck, darling." I moaned watching myself disappear down her throat. "After all your affection at dinner, I'm not going to last long."

I felt the vibration of her chuckle, and that almost undid me. I watched as she slowly licked her way back up, looking at me through those long lashes of hers. She swallowed me again, licked back up, and bobbed her head a few times sucking on just the tip of my cock.

When she grabbed the base of me, and let me out with a pop, she whispered, "That waitress still wants you. She'll be out here, in a moment."

"That hearing of yours tell you that?" I said, threading my hand through her hair. Nodding, she flicked her tongue through the slit and around to the underside of me. My hips jerked, and I looked down at her, and said, "How soon?"

"Thirty seconds or so." She shrugged, stroking me. "You decide, Sir. I can finish you here where she can see, or in the truck in private."

"Let her see just how well you please me, Darlin'."

Jade's smile was bright. "So, fuck my face, and moan my name as you cum."

Her lips were around me again, and all I knew in that moment that there was no way anyone could please me more than the woman on her knees before me. I happily obliged her request, and my hips moved. Each time my cock hit the back of her throat, she swallowed me.

I felt my balls tightening, and when she grabbed ahold of them and chuckled, I thrust deep into her, spilling myself down her throat as I indeed moaned her name into the night.

Jade licked me clean, and when she stood, tucking me away in the process, her eyes were on me as she said, "I hope you enjoyed the show, bitch."

I turned my head, and smirked at the waitress that was standing at the corner. It was small, petty, and I was being a complete asshole, but I smirked and with too much amazement in my voice said, "As I said. I have everything I need and want right here." Then turned and kissed Jade with everything I had.

CHAPTER 32

JADE

SIX WEEKS LATER

"I realize that Carlos, but—"

"Jade, I'm sending more help. This is the tenth attack by the wolves since you returned from San Jose." Carlos' voice was not one anyone else in this room would have dared to combat.

"And as I said, I already have myself, Myka, and Titus." I said through my teeth.

"And it's obviously not enough. You are completely tied up in keeping the construction crews busy, and Myka and Titus need to sleep. Not to mention what would happen if they decided to get personal again. You have already been laid out and so has Myka. Titus was lucky." Carlos said, rubbing his face. "We have known that Alpha Devon has been a fierce Alpha, and that he takes brutal tactics, but shit. He and his pack almost killed Myka and Titus."

I looked up to where the two of them were standing, and had noticed how they had moved closer to each other. It wasn't a secret that they had been so gravely injured, but the scar on Myka's face was going to be a reminder of that day for both of them for the rest of their lives.

"I know you don't like it, but it's a problem, and I'm begging, *mija*, for you to stop being so fucking stubborn about this."

I narrowed my eyes at him, and I heard Myka and Titus clear their throats trying to cover a chuckle. "Fine."

"Good because they will be there tomorrow." Carlos sat up straighter, and I leaned back in my chair.

"What other bomb do you need to drop on me?" I knew that body language anywhere.

"I have a meeting with the Primals in twenty minutes."

"About the Kiku Pack? They haven't done any serious damage to the construction crews. It's just popped tires, movement of some supplies, and just stuff that is driving them a bit crazy. Most of the crew just think that someone is messing with them."

"You know Alpha Devon. He'll step up his game again."

"And we need to protect the humans. I got it, Carlos. I'm only agreeing to this because of Kolton and the guys."

"I'll talk to you tomorrow." Then he clicked off the video call and I closed my eyes, leaning back on the head rest of the chair.

Someone knocked on the door, and I just let out a long sigh. "Go ahead and let them in."

Titus opened the door, and Ben strode in looking pissed as hell.

"Good morning, Ben. What can I do for you?"

"Well, you can tell me how a bulldozer could be tipped over in the middle of a field?"

"It is too early for this shit." I muttered and Myka's eyebrow rose in a way to say, '*Still think Carlos shouldn't send help?*'

"Yeah, you are telling me. We are hauling one of the cranes out there, but Jade, this isn't just some prank, is it?" When I didn't say anything, he narrowed his eyes at me, blinked, and looked to Myka and Titus.

"You are Agency." He said, his eyes wide.

I blinked twice, the only indication that I knew what he was talking about. "I'm sorry, what agency?"

"*The* Agency. Ashstrike Sanctorum." I raised my eyebrows at him, and he shook his head. "Carlos Medina. As in Minstrel Carlos Medina. How did I *not* put that together." His eyes went wide as he said, "Oh shit. This is THE Rose Porter Ranch. As in the seer Rose Porter?" Ben started pacing and said, "So what is it exactly that is fucking with my crew?"

When I continued to just look at him, Ben turned around and crossed his arms across his chest. "What little demon blood I have in my body is telling me you are an Astral. So, *Astral Jade*, please tell me what my crews are dealing with."

"What little demon blood?" I said raising my eyebrows at him.

"I am so highly diluted, I don't show on any of your registries. My Great Great Great Grandfather was a Therugi demon. The rest of my line have all married and procreated with humans. Therefore, I am human with a drop of Therugi in me." He said, relaxing and sitting down in the chair at my desk. He sat there for a long minute before he said, "It all makes sense now."

"Why wasn't Arteaga Construction on the list?"

"Because Jorge Arteaga, the Owner, isn't on any Agency list. He's as human as they get." He paused for a moment, and said, "You should probably know that I have one crew member that is a Bacri. He gets his flights in the middle of the night, though, so he shouldn't be a problem."

"I'm aware of Donald Wilkson." I said, finally confirming everything. "Do you have any Therugi traits?"

"I'm good at math and have some of the demon strength but that's really it. Nothing that can't be passed off as human at all. Now will you please tell me what we are dealing with up here?"

"The Kiku Pack. Wolves." I said quietly.

"Why is the pack giving you trouble? I'm not really up on Agency politics. Since I'm not on the registry, I don't get the monthly emails, ya know?" He smiled at his own joke, but it helped break some of the tension. "I know there isn't much you can tell me, but if I can just have a clue, so I can at least try to anticipate how to protect the crew?"

"Basically, they want more land, the Porter wildland specifically in the north east area of the property, but it has been denied to them."

"Because Rose Porter needs it."

I nodded, "The Alpha has grown his pack too big, and is trying to bully their way into the property. I don't think they will actually cross the line of causing harm to the humans." I looked to Titus and Myka who stood there like mountains, and shook my head. "Maybe tell them there has been a lot of wildlife activity lately."

He took a deep breath and then let it out slowly. "Probably the easiest story to spin. One of the guys mentioned that they saw a wolf while having a smoke at about midnight last night."

"Probably the scout for when they tipped the bulldozer."

"I've been trying to sort out why they are even bothering the crews. You aren't even building in the wild lands."

"Do they need a reason? You are denying him what he wants. Wolves can be temperamental from what my Grandfather told me." He stood and said, "Now that there is context, I can work it out with the guys. We will be fine. Thank you for the information. If I may be excused, Astral, I would like to return to the critical care site. They've got some issues with plumbing I need to oversee."

"One more question." I waited for him to acknowledge me before continuing, "Even with the setbacks, how are we on time?"

"As long as they don't disrupt the supply chain, we are on schedule. It's a large crew, and we will be done before the rains, Astral."

"Thank you, Ben."

After he left Myka met my gaze and said, "I'm sorry, Astral Primal Jade. I felt something familiar about him, but I couldn't pinpoint it. Until I knew what it was, I didn't want to say anything."

I waved my hand off in dismissal and said, "It's fine. Probably not a bad thing that we have someone on the crew who knows what we are dealing with."

"I still apologize for not saying something earlier."

I just shrugged as Kolton walked through the door and kissed me on the top of the head and handed me another note from Garrett. When I opened it though, I found it was *not* from Garrett and froze.

Astral Jade.

I hope that you have enjoyed your time here without issue. My patience has run out. I need the Porter

Wildland. Hand it over, or things are going to get much worse.

Alpha

"Just signs his title?" Kolton said, reading over my shoulder.

"Well, he has an over inflated value of self-importance." I smirked and looked up at him. "I know someone else who is like that too.

"That's not what you said last night when I had to carry you to the shower to get cleaned up." He whispered along my jaw, and my toes curled.

"You know they can hear you, even if you whisper in my ear, right?"

Myka and Titus chuckled, and it was Titus who said, "And we heard everything last night, and the night before, and the night before that."

Myka picked up from there and said, "I think there was a twenty-four-hour break there. Yeah, the day Kolton had to go to the city. But for sure the whole week before that."

I just smiled at them, because while they were not wrong about the timing, Kolton had froze, realizing that the time frames were dead on.

"No." Kolton whispered, horrified.

"Oh, yes." Myka said, but then his eyes lit up, "It's an Astral thing. So Jade, if Carlos is sending in reinforcements, you might want to station them a *bit* further away from the apartments."

I turned to Kolton and he just sighed, "If they can hear, I suspect that James and Fernando have, too." I nodded and he smirked, "Well, at least they know I can satisfy you."

I reached up and kissed him. "That you do, Sir."

His eyes flicked to where Titus and Myka were standing and just shook his head. "So, they mentioned Carlos sending reinforcements, when do you expect them?"

"Tomorrow."

"Tomorrow?" He said plainly. "Couldn't have given me any warning?"

"I found out just before Ben walked in, who happens to have demon blood, and there is an eagle shifter on his crew, by the way." I gave him an apologetic look before continuing, "I have no idea how many he is sending. I'm hoping that they can be disguised as extra workers outside of the construction crew. I'll set up some accommodations. See if maybe Rose will allow them to sleep in the wildland on this side of the river."

"I gotta do the stables. I'll bring you some lunch, because I know otherwise you won't eat." Kolton said, giving me a kiss before striding out the door.

"Did you guys have to embarrass him like that?" I stood and stood between the two linebackers before me.

"Why not? It was great." Myka laughed.

"Do your rounds. Talk to Ben about the schedule and see if you can anticipate where they might hit next. Since Carlos is sending another group in for patrol, I want to make sure that we have protection over the supplies. I can't afford for this project to get stalled anymore."

"Yes, Astral."

CHAPTER 33

JADE

"It's been weeks of this." I said pacing the main house site. Wood was shattered and there were pieces scattered everywhere. "The critical care unit is almost completed right?"

"Yes, ma'am." Ben said.

"How long until you can replace these supplies?" I sighed.

"With the lumber shortage, I don't know. Can Carlos help at all on that front?"

"I'll call him." I turned to the three of the four patrols that were supposed to have prevented this. "What happened?"

"I'm not sure. I thought we had it covered." The shortest said.

"This didn't happen within just a few minutes. This was at least an hour of destruction. Where is your fourth?" I asked.

They each looked at each other. "We don't know. Jessica didn't report in this morning ma'am."

"Jade." Kolton's voice came in through my earpiece. It was tentative, and worrisome.

"Kolton." I said after pushing the button.

"Um, Del Norte Sheriff officers are here to speak with you." I froze.

"I'm sorry what?"

"Del Norte Sheriff officers are here to talk to you, and they said they need to speak to you *now*." His voice was strained, and I could feel the fear through that bond between us.

"I'll be down there in a few minutes." Then before I turned my mic off, I said, "Get Titus or Myka to meet me there."

"Of course."

"Any reason I should know for why the Sheriff is here to speak to me?" I asked the four people before me.

"No, ma'am." They all said in unison.

"Ben, I'll talk to Carlos about expediting the materials. Can you move some over from the staff housing units to be able to finish up the main home here?"

"Let me take inventory of what got destroyed and what we have."

"The staff can continue to stay in the apartments up front for now. If anything has to be delayed, pull from the staff housing supplies. We can order what we need, and when the dust settles, we will finish that up." Then I sighed. "If anyone needs me, I'll be talking with the Del Norte Sheriff's department."

I gave Ben an apologetic look as I climbed back into my truck. I started it, and Kolton came on the line, "Channel six dot two, Jade."

I took out my earpiece and switched over. "I just got in the truck."

"What's going on, Jade?"

"I don't know." I turned the truck onto the main road and said, "Really, Kolton. I don't, but I'm hoping it doesn't have anything to do with my missing patrol."

"Missing patrol?"

"Yeah. Are you alone?"

"Only with Del Norte's finest." There was a long pause, before he said, "I know these two. They are good guys. Myka just arrived."

I could hear Myka come through the comms, "Kolton, Ms. Jade will be here momentarily, I shall wait here with you."

"Your guys are good." Kolton whispered.

"Driving up now." I clicked off the comm and jumped out of the truck. Only then did I realize there was a note under the wiper. I grabbed it and stuck it in my back pocket.

Myka was standing at my office door, and nodded to me as I walked up. "You okay?"

I nodded, "Just a mess at the main house site. A bunch of the supplies have been destroyed."

He opened the door for me, and then followed me in. I strode around to my desk where Kolton was, and he casually put an arm around my waist, looping a thumb in the belt loop.

"Good morning, gentleman. What can I do for the Del Norte Sheriff's department?" I asked, plastering a smile on my face, but setting my shoulders back.

"Sounds like you have some trouble out on the construction site?" The taller brown-haired man said.

"Likely just some wolves or other wildlife." I shrugged.

The older red-haired, pot-bellied Sheriff opened a folder, slid it to me and as my eyes trailed it, I used every ounce of professional training I had to not let anything show. I did, however, feel Kolton's horrification through our bond. He flinched, and out of the corner of my eye, saw his eyes widen at the site. The girl in that picture had been mauled.

"Does she look familiar?" The red head said.

"Jessica Rodgers. She is... was on the night patrol. She didn't report this morning." I sighed. "And there was damage to the supplies."

"What do you know about Ms. Rodgers?"

"She's been here for a couple weeks working as a patrol for us. We had some issues with the wildlife messing with the equipment. No big deal. It's rural, it happens. We are impeding on the wildlife's land. They were here first, and our paths are going to cross. We got the patrol just to help prevent injury to our staff and the wildlife."

"Who arranged for the staff?"

"My boss, Carlos Medina. I can get him on a video call if you want to speak to him." I offered, turning to my laptop. I pushed a few buttons, turning the laptop toward the officers.

"*Mija*... I'm sorry. Who are you and why are you on her laptop?" Carlos' voice came through.

"I'm here, Carlos."

"Then please show your face, so that I know that you are okay." I chuckled and turned the laptop back toward Kolton and I. When he saw our faces, he relaxed and sat down at the desk. "What is this about, Jade?"

"One of the patrols has been found deceased." I said, and turned the camera toward the officers. "The Sheriff's department has some questions for you. I have Myka here as well."

Then Myka stood on his tip toes behind the officers, and waved to Carlos, "Hi, boss."

I huffed a laugh, because it was so child-like and so very Myka. When I looked back to the two Sheriff standing in the office though, the taller of the two gave me a hard look. Kolton's hand tightened on my waist, and I pulled on that rope between us.

"Officers. What can I help you with?" Carlos said, every bit the accommodating supervisor.

"Your staff here says her name was Jessica Rodgers." The red-head said. "We need next of kin information please."

"Jessica Rodgers." Carlos said carefully, and I heard him click away on the keyboard. "Looks like she doesn't have any listed. Correction. There is a brother, but estranged. Her power of attorney on file signs all assets, including the company life insurance policy, over to the company."

There was a shared look between the two officers. "Why would you require a power of attorney and life insurance policy?"

"Our office works to ensure a very high level of work, sometimes that entails hiring those who have sketchy backgrounds, no background, or people starting over. Sometimes people get hurt while on the job." Kolton's arm pulled me closer at the waist, and I leaned into him, attempting to hide it. "We do what we can to protect our assets, but accidents happen. Sometimes of their own doing, sometimes not. Can you tell me the cause of death?"

"Need it for your insurance paperwork?" The red-head bit out.

"I do, but even though her brother is estranged, I'm still going to give him the courtesy of letting him know that his sibling passed away." I had heard that tone in Carlos' voice a few times, and if he had been here, you would have been able to feel the wave of his power flow through the room. "Or is that going to hinder your investigation? I'm sure Jade and the rest of those employed by my company and the construction crew will be more than happy to help you with your investigation, but again, could you please tell me the cause of death."

The red-head held a photo of Jessica's body up for Carlos to see. He was quiet for a long moment, and then he said, "I hope she went quickly and that she didn't suffer through that."

"It appears to be an animal attack, but I appreciate you speaking with us, Mr. Medina." The brown-haired man said, before standing.

"Is there anything else you need from me, sir?" I asked carefully. I knew Carlos was still on the line.

"No, we will let you know when the corner has completed their assessment." Nodding and handing me his card.

"Thank you." I watched them leave, and once they were out of ear shot, I circled the desk to find Carlos pacing.

"Astral." He said finally.

"Yes, Minstrel."

He let out a heavy sigh, tipping his head back. The grey was building at his temples, and I felt bad for adding to it. This wasn't an easy job. We knew people would die, and we wanted nothing more than to keep that from happening, but what he had told the Sheriff wasn't a lie. It was carefully cultivated truths.

"Devon?"

"One of his, I'm sure. They spent some time at the supply stores where the main house is going to be." Then I realized what the other patrols said. "When they said she didn't report this morning, I should have known something was connected, and I didn't. I just assumed she had taken off to blow off steam, or drink or something. I didn't think... I'm sorry, sir."

"You couldn't have known. It's tragic, and there is nothing you could have done even if you had put those two together." He leaned down on the desk, palms flat and looked at me through the camera. "Anything more on his demands?"

I blinked and realized I had forgotten the note left on the truck. I pulled the little square out of my pocket, and unfolded it. I huffed and shook my head.

"Verification that Devon caused her death." I said waving the note.

"What does it say?"

"Get my message? It's only going to get worse for you." I looked at Carlos and he just shook his head.

"Fucking wolves sometimes. They haven't caused us problems for years, and then one of the packs goes and does something like this over petty shit?"

"It's not petty for him. When I met with Garrett last week, he told me Devon wants all of the Pacific Northwest. Not to mention, we killed Brandon." I shook my head. I felt horrible about Brandon's death, even if it had been Kolton who had apparently pulled the trigger. I wasn't going to tell Kolton that detail, though. No reason for him to feel guilty over that.

"I saw the list. Brandon will be missed. He was a good wolf. At least it was a clean death." I thought I saw Carlos' eyes flick to Kolton's, but Kolton was looking at me, and missed it.

"What do you mean it was a clean death?" Kolton asked. I tried to tell Carlos not to say more, but alas, it was futile.

"Apparently each shot to the wolves were clean and instant kills. I commend you and Philip for that. Honor in death."

"I killed people?" I felt Kolton's chest rise and then fall quickly. I turned to him and put my hands on either side of his face. His eyes were wide and I tried to feed as much calming energy through that rope as I could.

"Kolton, look at me. You were protecting me and that gelding from wolves. You knew nothing about any of this. To you, they were wolves. That is all they were. From what I understand from Fernando, you had every intention on using the carcasses around the Ranch. They would not have been wasted. You would have had meat, bones, leather, and protected us from harm."

Myka opened the door and someone else came in, but I didn't take my eyes off Kolton's. He would carry the weight, and I was not going to let him.

We stood there for a very long minute as Kolton stared me down, looking for whatever it was that he needed. "You did nothing wrong."

"But they were—"

"You. Did. Nothing. Wrong." I repeated.

"She is right." Carlos said from the computer on the desk. Kolton turned to look at Carlos, and then Myka and Titus put a hand on Kolton's shoulder, squeezed and stepped back.

It was Myka who added, "It was clean. There is no blood on your hands Kolton. Do not let it weigh on your heart."

I let one hand slide down to grasp his, and he threaded his fingers through it and gripped tight. "I've always been taught that once you pull that trigger you have to be willing to accept those consequences and be prepared with all that entails in taking that life. Animal or human. I guess that includes any being considering what I have learned since meeting Jade."

He let out a shuddering breath and then said, "I'll work through it, but what do we do now?"

"I'll continue to work with the local authorities." Carlos said.

I was still staring at Kolton when he squeezed my hand again, before turning back to Carlos. "I'm gonna need some Agency pull for materials once we get a list of the replacements needed."

He nodded and said, "When you have it put together, send it over."

"Thanks." I said and he signed off the video chat.

"I'll let the Patrol supervisor know he's going to be down one and for them all to be on high alert." Titus said and he and Myka left the room.

I turned to look at Kolton who was watching them as they strode away. "Jade..."

"Yes?"

"I trust you. Please know that. I know that I can trust you with anything." I blinked in confusion. "So why was it that Myka's words where what calmed me?"

"First, likely, because subconsciously, you thought I was just saying what I did to make you feel better, not because they were necessarily true. I *was* saying it to make you feel better, but the words also happen to be true." I said smiling at him as he gave me a droll look. "Second, because it wasn't me or Carlos. It was from a peer whom you respect and who respects you."

"Clean hands." He said heavily before adding, "As clean as they can be at least."

My stomach growled, and he chuckled. "You haven't eaten, have you?"

"And just when have I had a chance to eat yet today?"

"Come on. Let's go back to the apartment and get something to eat real quick. Then you can start in on everything else you are going to need to do."

"I don't have time. With the destroyed supplies —"

"Jade, you are going back to the apartment right now to eat. Whether you walk on your own feet, or I toss you over my shoulder and carry your sexy ass, is completely up to you."

"I'm looking forward to a vacation when this is done, honestly." I said, and he kissed my temple before picking me up and tossing me over his shoulder and carrying me up to the apartment.

Over the next three weeks, things seemed to settle down. Construction proceeded without any issue, and Arteaga had even brought extra guys over from a Grass Valley project to help out. The weather was starting to turn, and there was no doubt we could get rain at any time.

The critical care unit was completed, the new main house was completely framed, and electrical and plumbing inspections were scheduled for Monday. With any luck, the Porters could move into the house in time for Christmas.

I was inspecting and counting the bars for the stables at the front of the property and going over the interior when Ben walked up and said, "These could be done by the end of next week. I also just got word that we should have the supplies in two weeks for the staff housing."

"Where are we on the guest quarters and new vet clinic buildings? I haven't been over there yet."

"Electrical is going in today, and the plumber will be back next week." Ben said, leaning against one of the studs. "The property is gorgeous. You've done a great job integrating the surrounding landscape with it too."

"Thank you." I said lifting my head to study him. "Beyond what you told me, you haven't mentioned a family? I've heard just about everyone else talk about their significant others and kids, but nothing from you."

"I have two twin daughters." He said then smiled at the confusion on my face. "I had them when I was 19, and the mother and I are still in contact. I get to see them whenever I'm home."

"Never married?" I said, a little surprised.

"I was. After Suzanne and I decided we were better off as friends and co-parenting the girls, I realized I preferred men. I married Nick at twenty-five, and unfortunately, he died a few years ago to prostate cancer. Took him quick." There was sadness in his eyes but he stood proud.

"I'm sorry."

"Thank you, but I have two daughters I am insanely proud of, and I lived a good life with Nick. The girls loved him. Suzanne loved him. Suzanne's husband Dakota loved him. Their son loved him." He smiled brightly as he continued, "When Suzanne and Dakota's son, Rian, said he wanted to go on the trips with us and the girls, I asked everyone else. Everyone was in agreement that if he wanted to go with his sisters, who were they to hold him back. The girls wanted him to go with."

"Nick didn't mind, either?"

"God no." He chuckled. "Nick wanted nothing more than to have a big family, and we all were. I wish I could spend more time with the girls, but I video chat with them every Friday night. It's hard not seeing them on the weekends, but at least I get to see their faces."

We stood there for a moment, before he said, "Do you have kids?"

"No. Work hasn't really allowed me to settle down."

He looked at me long and hard, and said, "Do you *want* kids? I respect the choice not to have them."

"Maybe. Being an Astral doesn't really lend itself to a steady home, ya'know?" I looked back down at my paperwork. "If I have kids, they need a steady environment that will be loving and nurturing. I'm not sure my life can do that."

"Does Kolton want kids?" I looked at Ben. "He is your bonded, right?"

"He is." I couldn't help the smile that crossed my face. "I don't know, though. We haven't talked much about the future. He is my forever. There won't be anyone else after him. Again, my life doesn't really lend itself to a steady environment. Then there is the fact that I can't pull him from this place. It's in his very soul."

Ben nodded, pushed off the beam and then looked at the plans. "So, what's next?"

CHAPTER 34

JADE

"**P**ack an overnight bag. You and I are going to spend a night out camping." Kolton said as he lifted me up and swung me around.

"I'm sorry, what?" I still had the butter knife in my hand, and I tried not to hit him with it.

"Tonight, you and I are going to go out camping along the southern property line." When I raised my eyebrow at him, he continued, "I know that the wildland is too dangerous, and the place is crawling with Agency, so to get us some private date night time, where no one can bother us, we are going to camp along the southern property line."

He set me down, but held onto my waist and pressed me against him. "Kolton. I'm still not sure it's safe."

"Already cleared with Carlos. I also talked to Myka and Titus." He smiled brightly at me, and before I could say anything, "They assured me that there has been no movement at all. The pack seems to be concentrating on the construction line and the wildland."

"It's what they want. They feel like they are protecting their territory."

"It isn't like you haven't made it abundantly clear it isn't theirs to have. They know the Porter Ranch is off limits."

I sighed heavily, and rolled my neck. "And I don't know how to get them to back off."

"What would you normally do?"

"Wipe out anyone who touches the land." I said harshly, "But for obvious reasons, that isn't exactly high on my to do list."

"Your to do list..." Kolton said in a way that heated every inch of my skin.

"Not fair, Sir." I said in a breathy moan as he kissed that spot just where my neck met my shoulder and I leaned into him. "Seriously, not fucking fair."

"Can I help it if the woman I love is so fucking sexy, I can't help but want to be buried deep within her every moment of every day?" He turned me so that he was behind me, kissed up my neck and the gruffness of his voice made my knees week.

His hand slid down and undid my pants, and I didn't have the strength or will power to stop him. Slowly his hand slid in and parted my flesh. His fingers dipped into the wet pool that was forming and circled my clit.

I bit my lip and slid a hand around to palm him, but he pulled me against him, and whispered, "No touching."

I groaned as he slid my pants off, picked me up, and placed me on the kitchen table. "Kolton."

"Jade?" He said undoing his belt and sliding his pants down enough that I felt him spring free next to me.

"I thought you couldn't stop by for a long lunch. Had things to do?"

"Now, Darlin', are you complaining?"

"No, Sir." I said, and then he was rubbing himself along the length of me, and I moaned. I rocked my hips as I said, "not at all."

His lips were on my neck kissing up to that spot just below my ear, and with a small swipe of his tongue, I was tightening around him. He didn't stop pumping in and out of me, and I had to brace myself on the table to keep from falling back.

Only, Kolton grabbed my waist, and pulled me to the very edge of the table, causing me to fall back. He caught my head before it collided with the surface, but then his lips were at my collarbone, his other hand kneading my left breast. Slowly his lips trailed down and his tongue swirled around my nipple. My back arched as his teeth grazed over the tip.

"Fuck." I breathed. A chuckle was his only response as he picked up the pace, and bit down on my nipple, causing a wave of pleasure so powerful to blow through me, I thought I would have came right there. Only then he slowed, and ground against my clit. "Sir, please."

"Please what, Darlin'?" He asked as his hand reached up and wrapped around my neck, pulled out to just the head of him, and fucked me with just the head of his cock.

"Sir. Please." The words were barely a thought. My stomach was tightening, and I felt myself on the edge of that cliff.

"I'll say again, Darlin'. Please what?" He leaned back away from me, and I missed the feel of his body against mine.

"Please make me cum all over your cock."

"With pleasure." He said thrusting hard into me, one hand still around my throat, the other reaching up and tweaking a nipple. With that tweak, I was falling over that edge.

He didn't stop fucking me on that table though, and when I opened my eyes, his were on mine. "Good Girl, now again." He commanded as he reached down and flicked my clit twice, before I was screaming into the room. My whole body was on fire. Every nerve was on high alert, and I was panting as I came down from my second orgasm.

A smirk was on his face, as he moaned and said, "One more time my girl."

His fingers continued circling my oversensitive clit. Every ounce of pressure on it was a shock to my system, and my hips were moving without conscious thought. When the next orgasm hit, I only heard him moaning, "Fuck, my darling." as his release flowed over him.

He stilled, but the muscles in my thighs continued to twitch. He leaned down, kissed me, then that spot where my shoulder met my neck.

"This spot here is where you smell the sweetest." He kissed it again.

"Is it now?" I vaguely heard myself say.

"Okay, the second sweetest." His lips ran up my neck, along my jaw, before I felt him retreating from me. "We need to get cleaned up."

Then he was lifting me and carrying me to the bathroom.

CHAPTER 35

JADE

When we got to the stables a few hours later, Philip had packed the horses and had them ready to go. I put my foot in the stirrup and swung my leg over, readjusting the saddle slightly to sit more comfortably on the mare that Philip let me borrow.

Kolton was next to me a moment later and smiled, "Ready, darling?"

With a smirk, I put my heels to the sides of the mare, and she took off underneath me. I heard Kolton behind me, laughing as he followed.

A half mile up the road, we slowed to a walk, and Kolton led us off onto one of the trails. As we made our way through the trees, I thought I heard rustling in the brush. When the mare started to get a little squirrely, I dismounted and tapped on my thigh, pulling one of my daggers free.

"Come forward and speak." I said, and when Kolton started to say something, I shushed him. There was a raised eyebrow, but I turned from him and scanned the forest. When I saw what I was looking for, I tossed the reins to Kolton, and said, "I'll be right back."

I ran straight for the shadow behind the rock, and had the wolf by the throat before it knew what I was doing.

"Shift." I commanded, using that Astral power. The wolf shuddered against the command, and I met its eye and again commanded, "SHIFT."

A moment later there was a girl no older than 12 shivering on the ground. "Yes, Astral."

"Why did you fight the command, *girl*?"

"I was scared. Alpha will be mad you caught me." She was still shivering, as Kolton came closer. I put my palm up to stop him. Any closer, and the rock we were behind wouldn't cover her. I wanted to give her that much respect.

"Jade?"

"It's fine. Stay there, please." I didn't let my eyes leave the girl.

"Why does the Alpha have you following me?"

"He just wants us new scouts to keep an eye on you."

"Why?" I felt my shoulders tense. I had already warned him about using pups, and he was still doing it.

"I don't know, Astral." Her voice shook, and she was just a scared little girl.

"I don't suppose that the Alpha has told you that the Porter Ranch is off limits, has he?" I said, crossing my arms.

"No, Astral. He said we are free to hunt on the Porter Ranch." Her eyes were wide. "Are we not supposed to be?"

"The Porter Ranch is off limits and protected by Ashstrike Sanctorum." I said, feeding my power into the words.

The girl winced, and I could feel others around me do the same. I sighed, and with a wave of my hand, and a pulling motion, there were three more young teens and a younger boy about nine standing before me.

The nine-year-old looked up at me with big brown eyes, and said, "Is that why there are so many of the Agency on the grounds?"

I looked at each of them. Gods, they were just a bunch of scared kids. I would have to talk to Carlos. Devon was inching his way to an Exorci visit. "He really has given the word that the Ranch is allowed to be hunted and traveled?"

They each nodded. "Okay. Go back to the den. I will speak to your Alpha about this. I will not report you. Again, the Porter Ranch is off limits and protected by Ashstrike Sanctorum. There is to be no trespassing or hunting on the grounds. Is that understood?"

"Yes, Astral." They said in unison before shifting and running north.

I tipped my head back and let out a heavy sigh. Kolton was there, took my hand pulling me close saying, "It's a mess, isn't it?"

"It is. Poor kids. I could have killed them today for being on this property, and I would have been in the right to do so. She was twelve. The youngest nine. He is sending children out. Puppies." I said leaning against him.

"What are you going to do?" He asked, kissing my cheek.

"Rip him apart with my bare hands." I smiled.

"Can you do that?"

"You saw what the pack did to Titus and Myka. Alphas are strong in their own right. Astral Primals are strong, too, but strong enough to rip him apart with my bare hands? Nah." I turned in his arms, and faced him. "Now, let's go and relax for a bit."

Over the next few hours we set up our little camp, made some dinner, and settled in the little clearing. We laid there for hours, just snuggled up next to each other and watching the stars. The tension had left my shoulders, and there was just... peace.

"I love when I get to go to remote places. To be able to get out of the light pollution and look at the stars." I said against his chest.

"How do you live in the city? There is so much concrete, so much noise."

"You get used to it, but I've always been happier out of the city."

"Why live there then?"

"The Bay Area has a high concentration of supernaturals. Vampires, witches, all manner of demons." I said, trying not to think about all that entails, and how it would affect us.

"Are we going to have to move back to the city?"

I froze. Did he just say *we*?

"Jade?" I felt him look down at me, and I didn't know how to answer that.

"I... I don't know." I half sat up on my elbow, and looked down at him. "Would you? You would leave the Porter Ranch to move to the Bay Area with me?"

"Darling, I told you. I'm not going anywhere. You are stuck with me now."

"I know you have said that, but do you *want* to move to the Bay Area with me? Don't you want to be here at the Ranch?"

He let out a heavy sigh and ran his hand through those long blonde waves. "I don't want to leave the ranch. It's my home. It's where I've always seen my future. The rehab project is very close to my heart, and I'd like to not have to leave."

I watched him, and his hand reached up and tucked a strand of hair behind my ear. "But, I can't not be with you. Wherever you are, that is home."

His gaze held mine for a long moment before he asked, "Would Carlos let you do your work from here?"

"I have no idea. I'd have to travel a lot, but I don't know if that is something the Agency would even allow."

"What happens when others find their bonded?" His voice was tentative and careful, almost like he didn't want to know the answer.

"They go wherever their Astral bonded go. I suspect that the Agency will expect the same of you, but..." I trailed off. I couldn't take Kolton from the Ranch. It was as much a part of him, as he is it.

"But..." He pressed.

"I don't think I can ask that of you. You and the Ranch are one in the same. You yourself have said that this place is everything you are. I can't take you from that."

"So, what if the Agency tells you to go back to the Bay Area. Do you expect me to let you leave without me?"

"No. I think I know you well enough to know you are only going to do what you want to do."

"Damn fucking straight, woman." He pulled me on top of him, and as I looked down at him, there was nothing but love and warmth in those eyes. "I'm not leaving your side except by force. If you leave without me, I *will* follow you."

"I won't make you leave the Ranch, Kolton. This is home." I fingered his shirt, and he took my hand. "It feels like home to me, too, if I'm being honest."

A small smile crossed his lips, and there was so much that I wanted to say, but I just rolled to lay next to him again and gave him a quick kiss on the cheek.

"Home." He said with a wistful sigh as if he couldn't believe it.

I woke to a high trilling sound. I waited a moment, and when I heard it again, I answered back in the same three note trill. A small flash, and Garrett was just beyond the tree line.

As carefully as I could, I separated myself from Kolton and went to meet up with Garrett. Kolton turned over to face the other direction, and mumbled something under his breath about James being a stupid fuck, and I couldn't help but smile.

Taking quick light steps, I rushed over to where Garrett was.

"What the fuck are you doing here?"

"I could ask you the same thing." His eyes flicked to Kolton. "Though, I will say thank you for not killing the pups earlier today."

"Your Alpha is a dead man with a ticking clock." I growled at him. "How fucking dare he use puppies as scouts."

Garrett had the good graces to look sheepish. "I know."

Then I heard them rushing through the trees. "You were followed."

I tried to move, but before I could get back to Kolton, white powder puffed in my face, and I instantly collapsed. My brain went foggy, and I heard rustling, and fighting. Kolton... I concentrated on the bonding mark, and I could feel him still there, feel that tether to the world, but that only meant so much.

"Damn it, Garrett. Why did you have to be here?"

"What the fuck are you doing, Darrell?" I heard Garrett say.

"Alpha sent us to collect the Astral's bonded." The one I assumed was Darrell said, "Surprised me to find you talking to her like you are old friends."

"Fuck you."

"Not into fucking traitors to the pack." The other said. "Load Garrett and the human up. Leave the Astral here. It will drive her crazy to know we have her mate and there is nothing she can do."

KOLTON! I screamed down the line. Panic enveloped me, and I tried to feel anything from him, but there was nothing but silence. Had they knocked him out? Was he alive?

He had to be alive. I was alive. We had completed the bonding. We couldn't live without each other.

I tried to move, to open my eyes, to look around to do anything, but I couldn't. Whatever it was that they used, completely left me incapacitated.

A boot kicked me over onto my back, and there was a husky voice with breath that smelled like rotted meat, say, "She's a pretty thing. Beta Darrell, can I have some fun with her before we leave?"

"Don't touch her. We are already bordering on treason and war by taking her mate. We fuck with her, the whole pack will be wiped out. Innocent and guilty alike. Even the pups."

I felt his hand on my cheek and I wanted to break his hand, but I couldn't move.

"Hands off." The beta growled. "Do you want everyone you know to be dead?"

"Like she won't kill you all for taking her bonded?" Garrett growled. I heard scuffling, and then bone break.

"That will shut you up for a while."

Then I heard Kolton. "Get away from her!"

I heard him grunt and one of the wolves say, "I can't touch him."

"Subdue him." Darrell growled, and I felt the rumbling in my chest.

"It's not getting past whatever protections are on him."

"JADE!" Then I heard another impact, and felt the ground shudder near me. Kolton! I shouted back down that connection of ours. I didn't know if he could hear me, if he could feel me.

"Let's get back to the den." Beta Darrell said. "And again, leave the Astral alone. The *Nightwhispers* won't keep her out long."

I couldn't do anything but lay there and listen to them carry Kolton and Garrett out. My heart was racing, and tears slowly rolled down the side of my face as I was helpless to stop them from taking him from me.

Thirty minutes later, Myka was leaning over me muttering. My eyes flew open, and he said, "Don't move yet. I'm still working on pulling it from your system."

He waved his hands over my body, and a few minutes later, he said, "That's about all I can do. Come on. Let's get you back to Rose. She can get you something to fully clear your head."

"Where is Kolton?" I ground out. "The wolves."

"Yeah. The wolves have him." I threw an arm around his shoulder as he helped me to the horses. He helped me up and once he knew I was okay to ride, said, "Titus was checking the line, noticed a hole, and a few minutes later they sent a ten-year-old pup to the line to hand him a note. It said that they had Kolton, gave instructions on where to find you, and what their demands were."

I grabbed the reins, turned the mare toward the trail, and saw red. "They don't get the Ranch, and if they hurt a hair on Kolton's head, their lives are forfeit. The entire pack will fall."

I put my heels to the mare, and she barreled through the tree line to the main road, and picked up speed as I muttered to the wind.

Rose was at the stable when I arrived, with tea and just said, "Carlos is waiting for you on video."

I sipped the tea, and nodded to her, as I strode for her office. I ran through every ounce of information that Garrett had given me through my time here.

I heard Carlos' voice through the speakers, and just said, "I'm fine Carlos. Calm yourself."

"Jade!" Carlos said, and when I sat down, I tipped back the last of the tea and looked at him.

"Minstrel Carlos, I hereby request authorization to wipe out the leadership of the Kiku Pack."

"Denied, for the time being."

"Asshole. They have Kolton. They are using children, *puppies* as scouts!" I said through gritted teeth.

"Jade."

"No, Carlos, they are breaking about twenty different covenants right now, and I am having none of it. The first of which is that they took my bonded."

"Astral Primal Jade." Carlos' voice came through strong and commanding. I took a deep breath, and heard about three people clear their throats.

It was then I noticed that it wasn't just Carlos on the call, but also the three primary Primals. Shit. I had just revealed way too much of what was going on, and just how personal this was. Fear overtook me, and I pulled on that thread in the world and I was finally able to take a deep breath when I felt a small pull from him.

He's alive. I rubbed the mark on my arm as I lightly folded my arms in front of me. I continued to rub it with my thumb until I was able to breathe again. Finally, after a long moment, I opened my eyes, sat up straighter and said, "Primals."

Rose's eyes widened as she looked to Myka and Titus who were standing in the door. Beyond the door were James and Fernando who looked ready to destroy the world, but were very, very confused.

"Ms. Rose, can you please ensure that your workers are apprised of the situation with your foreman, and assure their silence." I said with as much authority as I could muster.

"Yes, Astral." She said loud enough for everyone on the call to hear, then pulled Fernando and James away from the room. Myka closed the door, and nodded when the room was secure.

"It seems the situation with the pack has escalated." Primal Jacob said.

"It has." I said trying not to grit my teeth.

Primal Rebekkah's head turned as if she was studying me. "You said your Astral Bonded. The Kindrels haven't notified us of your bonding."

I didn't say a word.

"Answer me."

"I'm not sure how you wish me to respond, Primal Rebekkah. I believe the question as to why an Astral Primal's bonding hasn't been reported to the Primals, would be a question for the Kindrel. Not me."

"Jade…" Carlos whispered in reprimand.

"Carlos, what in the fuck do you expect me to say? How am I supposed to know why the Kindrels haven't reported it? Not really my Gods fucking problem."

"Astral!" Primal Kobi said, and I looked at them.

"I was addressing my cousin, not my superior in that moment, Primal. I apologize for the fact it occurred during a meeting."

Carlos shook his head and smiled, "You know they don't buy that for one minute, right?" I smiled at him and shrugged.

"Your Astral bonded was stolen by the Kiku Pack?" Primal Kobi asked.

"Yes. They used *Nightwhispers* to incapacitate me before they took him." I balled my hands into fists. "Again, I ask for permission to take out the Alpha."

"Your bonded still lives?"

"He does, Primal Kobi, or I would not be standing here before you. We completed the bonding months ago."

"Then until such time he is injured or deceased, the Alpha lives." Primal Kobi said, but smirked, one elongated fang showing, when they added, "However, if there is one drop of his blood spilt, the Alpha's life is forfeit by right of the Astral Primal bond."

The other two Primals turned their head to face Primal Kobi. "Oh, please, like you wouldn't decree the same for any other creature on this planet. An Astral Primal's bond is sacred. You would not be able to stop Astral Primal Jade if her bonded is injured, no matter what you said or how hard you tried."

"No disrespect, and while I appreciate the support, why are the Primals on this call?"

"We were already in conference when I received word that he had been taken and you were incapacitated."

"He may have flipped out a bit." Primal Rebekkah said, smiling warmly at him. They had a long history, and I smiled.

"I'm alive."

"But not okay." Carlos said carefully.

"Carlos, they have Kolton. I won't be *okay*, until he is with me and safe again." I took a deep breath.

"What is it that the Kiku Pack wants?" Primal Kobi asked.

"Territory. They want Rose Porter's wildland. We have repeatedly denied their request. Have even offered them portions north toward the border with the Kismot's, but they don't want it. They are already using Klammath, even though they aren't supposed to, and are demanding the land Rose has."

"Do they understand why they can't have it?"

"Alpha Devon knows who Rose Porter is. However, I have not explained it in detail to him, but I don't think he cares. They want to have it for their hunting grounds. You can see what the problem is that being the case right?"

"I'm sorry. Can someone explain to me why Ms. Porter isn't agreeable to the hunting use? Wouldn't it help keep other predators away from the Ranch?" Primal Jacob said.

"Primal Jacob, Rose Porter is a seer." Carlos said carefully.

The Primals' eyes glazed over and a moment later he said, now understanding the situation, "Rose Porter. The Seer of Ages. The wildland the wolves wish to take is her vision base."

"It is, Primal Jacob." I said bowing my head carefully as Rose came back into the room. "She spends each morning out there as the sun rises. The area must be free of malicious intent. She has been unable to see anything for the Agency since the wolves started hunting the grounds."

"Very well. The land must be protected. It is decreed by the Primals. An act against the land is an act against the Agency. Astral Primal Jade, you have authorization to ensure its protection by any and all means." Primal Kobi said.

"And the return of my bonded?" I asked carefully.

"You have your orders." Then the screen went black.

A moment later, Carlos called, and I answered, without a word. We just looked at each other.

"Jade. Be careful. I know that look."

"I don't know what you are talking about." I said gritting my teeth.

"Don't fuck with me." His voice was just as it was when I was sixteen and he was both furious and scared.

"They have Kolton. I will protect him. If they hurt so much as one hair on his head, the Alpha is dead. Blood spilled or not." He started to say something, "Kolton aside, the Alpha is a bully and is using puppies for things that only seasoned scouts should be doing. There is no reason to be using puppies as scouts or for any other duties. It is both pack and Agency law. Once they become soldiers, they are different. Let them be kids. They are children and have a right to be so."

He looked at me for a long moment before nodding. I asked him, looking off to the floor because I couldn't look at Carlos as I made this request. "Can you send Jesse Westbrook if I fail?"

"You want Jesse specifically?"

"He is the best Exorci on the west coast, and I also ask that Jesse make it as painful as possible."

"Jade..."

"Please, Carlos. Finish this if I fail Kolton." My voice was thick, and only after he was quiet for too long, did I look at him.

"I promise. Be safe, Jade. *Te Amo.*" And he hung up on me.

I hung my head and repeated, *Te Amo* as a tear rolled down my cheek.

Everyone waited for me to gather myself before they said, "What are your orders?"

My head rose to look at them, and more tears ran down my face. I didn't know when Rose came back into the room, but spoke to her first. "Rose, they took Kolton from me. I was right there. And they took him from me."

"Oh baby. You can feel him, right?"

"Rose, I still breathe, so yes, he is still alive." I took a deep breath, before continuing, "but that doesn't mean he isn't hurt. He fought them. I heard Kolton fight them. I can only hope that the bonding mark can protect him from the most serious of injuries."

As three sets of eyes met mine, I pulled on that thread between Kolton and I, feeding all the power I could between us. I slowly closed my eyes as it heated, and I again hoped that those Astral protections would hold tight to him.

CHAPTER 36

KOLTON

"The Astral will come for him." A tall dark-skinned man said.

"The Astral has a name." I ground out through my teeth. I had been laying here waking up for over an hour, and every time they talked about Jade it was always "The Astral."

"Oh, the dumb human can talk." That same voice said. "Like I said, the Astral will come for her mate."

I sighed, and lifted my head, but the room spun for half a moment before I winced at the pain in my jaw and slowly looked around the area they had me in. There was another man, naked with spikes through his palms. He was panting and when the dark skinned one reached over and twisted one, he bit down on a scream. "Garrett. Garrett. Garrett. Why did you feel the need to betray your pack?"

"What you are doing..." He clenched his jaw as the spike in his hand twisted again, "Is wrong. What Alpha Devon is doing is wrong."

"The Astral killed his brother." He said through ground teeth. "Is he supposed to just let that go?"

"The Astral has a name... wolf." I said, snapping my head to him. My voice echoed through the concrete room as every head turned to look at me. There wasn't much in the hollowed out concrete block. Just a couple of cell's at the back end, and the posts we were currently tied to.

His head whipped around and there was a guttural growl that ripped through the room. "Why do you keep speaking, human?"

"Because you refuse to use her name." I said through my teeth, meeting his dark eyes. They were fueled with a hatred that I couldn't understand.

I watched as his hand flung toward me and shifted into a large paw. I braced for the impact, but none came. I felt like I had been shoved, and I felt my face hit the floor. When I looked over, a large grey wolf stood over me, paw pressed against a green light just above my head.

Laughter erupted from a few feet away from me, and I looked at the man named Garrett who laughed and said, "You can't touch him."

My eyes were wide, as I looked at the wolf hovering over me. He shifted back into the human version of himself and growled, "You have a mating mark."

"What of it?" I said through my teeth meeting his eyes. I refused to show fear to these fuckers. I knew I couldn't fight them off wholly, but I did know that Jade would come, and likely not alone.

A larger pitch-black wolf came into the room and when he shifted, he said, "Enough, Darrell."

I willed myself to stay still, but then the man who was the black wolf came over and grabbed my arm. He looked at it and extracted one claw from his hand, and ran it down my bicep. A green glow covered just over my skin, where his claw would have penetrated.

"Mating protections." He thought for a long moment. "Get Marian. Tell her to bring the hemlock oil."

A small light brown wolf ran out of the room, and man looked at me and said, "I am Alpha Devon. Though, I suppose you already know who I am."

"I do." I held my head high. "I saw you in Brookings, terrorizing a family about their kids working. You realize there are child labor laws, right?"

"You know who and what I am human, yet you don't seem scared." He tipped head to the side, looked down at the bonding mark and smiled.

"I would feel more comfortable if you put some clothes on." I looked down and gave him a pitiful look.

"For someone who thinks he's all Alpha, I think you are trying to compensate for a lack in size."

His hand fully shifted into a large black paw again, but before he could touch me, an older woman with long grey hair came through the door and said, "Alpha, you summoned me with hemlock oil?"

Devon cracked his knuckles and said, "Yes Marian. Spread it over this tattoo here."

Her eyes knitted together. "You think it will break the protections?"

"It's an old legend my mother used to tell me, and it is my once chance to break through it."

The woman Marian came over, and she pulled the dropper from the vial. The woman gave me a quick apologetic look, hovered over the mark, but froze when she looked at it more carefully. "This is an Astral's bonding mark." Her hands shook as she pulled the dropper back.

"A mating mark is a mating mark. It matters not whose it is."

"Alpha, I mean no disrespect." She said her voice shaking in fear. "These markings... That is an Astral Primal's mark. Not just any Astral."

"I do not care. A mating mark is a mating mark." The Alpha growled, grabbing the vial, and dropped three drops on the mark. It burned like the fires of Hades, and then the Alpha's fist hit my jaw.

"Damn, that felt good."

I spit blood off to the side, and looked up at the Alpha. "How does it feel to hit a defenseless human?"

The alpha looked at me and smirked. "Stand up if you wish, but it will not make any difference."

I stood, and before I was fully on my feet, I swung, landing a shot square on the nose. I smirked as I felt the cartilage crumble from the pressure. "You are right. That did feel good."

He smirked and blood gushed from his nose. "You just drew Alpha blood. Your life should cease to exist. The only reason I do not end it now, is because I need your bonded alive. Your bonded will come to me, and I will get what I want, if she wants either of you to live."

Strong arms, grabbed me, and shoved me into the cell in the back of the room. I stumbled into the back, and rubbed my jaw, turning to smile at them. They were right about one thing. Jade would come, and Titus and Myka would be with her. May God help them if three Astrals showed up.

"I may not know all the ways of your world, but the fact that you drew blood on me first, may have sealed your fate, Devon."

"That is *Alpha* to you." He stood against the bars and I went to face him. When I got within arm's reach, he grabbed the front of my shirt and swung, but hit that wall of green again. I smirked.

"Looks like your little potion doesn't last long does it..." I smirked and said, "Devon."

He pushed me back, causing me to fall on my ass, but I just laid there and laughed. I heard metal creak and crack and then silence. I sat up on my elbows and looked up to where the Alpha had ripped one of the bars off a neighboring cage.

"Little wolfie got anger issues." I teased quietly, but knew everyone here would hear me.

Garrett however howled in laughter, before there was a wet crunching sound. Everyone froze, and I felt a dozen eyes on me, as the Alpha turned from where Garrett let out wet gasps for air. I stared at Garrett a moment longer, and when they stopped, I closed my eyes and took a deep breath before facing the Alpha unflinchingly.

"What was that, human?"

"I said you have anger issues and you just proved my point." I stood, brushing my hands off, and went to the bars before saying, "The Agency will come down upon the pack for all you have done."

"I will protect my pack from the Agency." Alpha Devon said before striding off out of the room.

Before he closed the door, I said just above a whisper, as I looked up at him through my eyebrows with a smile. "Honestly, at this point, it's not the Agency you should be worried about."

CHAPTER 37

JADE

"Astral." Titus said as I studied the maps on the table. Titus and Myka both had stayed up all night with me as we went over the maps, and rotated on scouting to see if they could find out where exactly they had taken Kolton. I knew these maps inside and out from the property development, but there was so much I didn't know of the terrain beyond the Porter Ranch property.

"Yes, Titus." I sighed, but said, "You don't have to call me by my title."

"You are an Astral Primal, and... anyway, this arrived for you." He handed me a small folded sheet of paper folded into a flat box. I stared and stared at it for a long moment as I pulled on that interior rope, and felt Kolton's relief wash through me. There was a twitch of pain there as well, and I rolled my shoulders. "Thank you."

Titus stood at the door, all solider-like waiting for my instructions as I opened the flat note, and read.

ASTRAL,

WE ARE EIGHT MILES DUE NORTH FROM THE SPOT NEAR THE DEER TRAIL I PUNCTURED YOUR TIRE AT. MEET ME THERE.

BRING THE PAPERWORK TO SIGN OVER THE PORTER WILDLAND OR YOU AND YOUR BONDED DIE.

-ALPHA.

PS: YOUR BONDED DREW ALPHA BLOOD.

"Dammit, Kolton." I said under my breath, and tipped my head back sighing.

"What did he do?" A voice I'd know anywhere said at the door.

I looked over at him and said, "What the fuck are you doing here?"

"What? Didn't you miss me?" Carlos said with a broad smile. I looked behind him through the glass windows that separated the office from the main room to see no less than twenty Astral trainees standing at full attention.

I raised an eyebrow and felt my anger rise to the surface. I was too worried about Kolton to hold it back so let it all out on him. "First you send me Titus and Myka because I hurt my leg, which is fully healed by the fucking way. All my weapons have been refurbed thanks to Philip, and now you show up with a mini supernatural army? What is there, twenty Astral trainees out there on top of Titus and Myka? Don't trust me to get this buttoned up on my own?"

"*Mija.—*"

"Don't you fucking, *Mija* me, mister!" I shouted at him throwing the note onto the table. "Do you trust me or not?"

His whole demeanor changed as he strode up and slammed his hands down on the table. "Of course, I fucking do. I trust that you are going to let your bond take over. You are going to have no care for your own Gods dammed well being and you will have no issue getting your bonded out alive, but at serious harm to yourself."

"So it's my ability you fail to have faith in?"

"For fuck's sake, Jade." He said, running his hand through his hair. "They are here because I want you to go in with every chance of coming out without a scratch on you. You are more than my cousin. You are a daughter to me, and I protect my own. With or without the Agency's permission."

I blinked. "So, you are using Agency resources without approval of the Primals?"

A sheepish smile crossed his face as he said, "As I said. I protect my own."

"Carlos."

"Feeling a bit guilty for yelling at me now?"

"No." I smirked at him, but he just shook his head at me.

He jerked his head to the note. "I'm assuming that he's threatening your bonded's life?"

"In a manner of speaking. Apparently, Kolton got a good swing at him. Devon said Kolton drew Alpha blood."

"Fucking idiot. Have you taught him anything, Jade?" His voice had disbelief and frustration in it, but I didn't really blame him.

"Yeah. Right in between him learning that I'm not exactly the most human of people, that every myth and legend he's ever read about is real, and that there is this overseeing governmental body that oversees all supernatural creatures, let's just add in the finite details of each creature's rules."

"At least the werewolves. He's dealing with them."

"The hope was he wouldn't be involved."

"You did warn him that your enemies would use him against you." Titus' deep voice said from the door.

"Well at least there is that." Carlos sighed dramatically.

"Are you done?" I asked, raising my eyebrows.

"I could go on." He shrugged at me, but nodded to the note again. "What else did Devon say in the note?"

"Agency talk. Just his location and that I'm supposed to meet him there with the paperwork to sign over the Porter wildland."

"And personally?"

"That Kolton drew Alpha blood." I looked back at the map to the area that Devon demanded we meet him. Carlos studied me carefully.

"Why aren't you freaking out more, *mija*?"

My eyes flicked to the bonding mark on my arm, and up to him. It took him a moment, but he looked down at my arm, and then his eyes went wide for a split second before he said, "You have the bonding mark. Please tell me Philip did it."

"Who else have I had at my disposal?"

"And you had Primal Astral protections put into it?"

"With a bit of persuasion. I did. Philip wasn't sure about doing it, but I insisted. They won't be able to hurt him." I said rolling my shoulder as a sense of unease rose within me.

Carlos nodded and then smiled. "What's the plan. Let's get him back and teach the wolves a lesson."

"You heard the Primals. I can't teach them a lesson unless they spill his blood. With the protections I have on Kolton, they won't be able to do that, so as much as I would love to destroy them, that isn't going to happen. Not to mention the mountains of paperwork that I would have to fill out for the annihilation of an entire pack."

"So it's really about the piles of paperwork involved." He huffed a laugh and shook his head. "What's the plan?"

I looked at Titus who looked at me through his eyebrows and smiled wickedly. Oh, Titus couldn't wait to get his hands on some wolves. After what they did to Myka, I knew he would be ready for some revenge. My eyes moved to the group Carlos brought with him. "Let's see if a little intimidation does any good?"

"And if that doesn't work?"

"Kolton will be in my bed tonight. Alive and well. No matter what happens. Now, Titus, please get the keys to the flatbed. The Astrals can crawl up on it and follow us into the forest."

"Yes, Astral Jade."

"Jade, we need a plan. Just going in without one is not going to set an example for the trainees out there."

"Did you bring them to help or for me to be a teacher? I won't take chances with Kolton's life."

"They need to see a Primal at work. Do what you do best, Jade."

"Carlos, you know as well as I do that I rarely plan anything out because as the saying goes, *Make the plan, execute the plan, expect the plan to go off the rails,* …"

"Kolton isn't Daniel." Carlos said carefully.

I froze. Every ounce of me went cold. "No. Kolton is a human bonded to an Astral. An Astral Primal at that. Daniel, at least, was a supernatural and had the speed and strength to protect himself. I'm not saying Kolton is weak, because he ain't. I'm just saying that we are not dealing with normal beings. The wolves have inherent strength and speed that Kolton doesn't have."

Carlos reached out and took my hand and squeezed. "I'm not saying that Kolton is weak either. That Astral bond is going to enhance his natural abilities. So, if he is strong, he'll be stronger. If he's agile, he will be more so. That's what an Astral bond to a Primal will do for a human. It will do nothing but help him, *mjia.*"

"What?" I shook my head. "I didn't know that. Why didn't I know that?"

"Believe it or not, you don't know everything." He smiled, squeezed my hand again before dropping it and saying, "So I say again, what is your plan?"

I needed Kolton back. I felt lost without him close by. I felt lost knowing he was sitting somewhere north of the meet spot, and I couldn't just go to him and crawl into his arms. Turning toward the map again, I realized I didn't know what to do. "A plan."

"A plan." He echoed.

"We don't know how many of the pack are there. We don't know where they are other than eight miles up from where he punctured Kolton's tire a few weeks ago." I pointed to a spot on the map where it had occurred and I called him from the sat phone the first time.

Carlos ran his finger up roughly eight miles from that spot, and said, "I'll have two trainee's take drones and scout the area, hopefully they can get us some numbers and a lay out. We need to have an idea of what we are walking into. "

"Carlos." My voice stuck in my throat, and I didn't realize I was on the verge of crying, until I looked up and felt the tear slip down my cheek. "I can't lose him. I can't survive that kind of loss again. I know that this is all new and we don't know what is going on, but I can't lose him."

I was pacing the office when one of the trainees came in and handed the screenshots from the drones late that afternoon. Carlos studied them carefully before laying them out and looking at the trainee to explain what they saw.

"Good news is that it's a concrete building so it will be easier to contain the damage to bystanders." The trainee said, but then looked up, and brazenly met my gaze. "The bad news is that once the drone was inside, we only got a few stills and a short video before one of the pups chomped it down thinking it was a fly."

"What did you get?"

"You are bonded to the human?" He swallowed hesitantly, but relaxed when I nodded. "Then I'm assuming the one that was impaled with a bar was your informant. Your bonded is in a cage. His back was to the drone, but he was standing. That is all I can tell you of his condition."

"What of the room?" Carlos asked.

"It's a tall concrete room, but no actual second story. I'm not sure what the room is usually used for, but there are drains, so likely a version of their prison or interrogation room." The trainee said, but just spoke to Carlos.

"You said there was another impaled with a bar?"

"Yes, Astral." He said handing me the photo. It was blurry, but I could just make out his features. I sighed, nodding. "Garrett."

Carlos looked at me again, and I just said, "Garrett was the one feeding me information on what Devon is doing. He was a good wolf. He knew Devon was overstepping the lines, but didn't know how else to stop him. Devon is out of control. Garrett really was thinking of the betterment of the pack. He said that if we couldn't stop him, he was seriously thinking of trying to petition to start a new pack in the Sierras or near Shasta." I sighed again, and set the picture down. "I would have backed him, Carlos. He deserves better than that."

Carlos turned back to the trainee and rubbed his neck. "Any pictures of Kolton, the human?"

"Like I said, just the one with his back to us." He handed it to us. "Can you feed me the video?"

He nodded and walked out the door, about the time Titus came back and said, "James and Fernando are asking questions, and not taking no for an answer."

"Handle it please, Titus." I groaned.

"They want to know why they can't help get Kolton. They say he is family, and that they want to help." Titus said carefully. "And before you ask, Boss, they have only been told he was taken for ransom. They don't know the full breath of it. Ms. Rose has been keeping them occupied. They know something bigger is going on here, and have for a while, but have let us have our space. Figured they would be brought to speed eventually, but now with Kolton, they are done waiting."

Carlos paced the office, and said, "I hate when humans get involved."

"Sorry to ruin your day." I mumbled as I sat in the chair and put my face in my hands.

"Oh, shut up Jade. I'm here to help, aren't I. It's just hard to keep them out of it."

"Minstrel Carlos. Can I make a suggestion?" Titus' voice was tentative, and I lifted my head to look at him. I'd never heard him hesitate for anything in all the years I've known him.

"Continue."

"Why not just have Ms. Rose bind their speech? She did for Kolton. Why not with them? They could then know why they can't help, and why there is so much extra security around."

I looked at Carlos, intrigued to see his response, it wasn't a bad idea. Rose could bind their mouth, and they wouldn't be able to speak to anyone about it unless they already knew of the Agency.

"I'll talk to Rose. Make sure she is okay with it first." Carlos said after thinking for a long moment. "Be ready to move out in fifteen. I'll meet you at the trucks."

When he left, I looked at Titus and he had a small smile on his face. "Yes, Astral?"

I narrowed my eyes at him, and I swore he was blushing.

"Are you... Titus, you aren't blushing, are you?"

Titus cleared his throat and made to stand up straighter. I smiled brightly at him. "Fernando."

His eyes snapped to mine. There was a small nod before he reached behind him and shut the door. "It's complicated, Astral."

"Please don't title me right now. Just tell me." I leaned against the desk, grateful for the distraction.

He took a deep breath and said, "It's complicated, because as you know, Myka and I are bonded."

"Yes."

"Myka and I aren't monogamous, we are each other's primary. We enjoy all manners of beings." He let out a long sigh. "I know it with a bonded, they are supposed to be the only person you could ever be with, but with Myka and I,... it's just different."

"Not really. I know other bonded that are more like best friends. Being bonded isn't a requirement to be romantically involved, it just happens that way more often than not."

He shifted on his feet and scratched at his arm.

"Are you more worried that I think you are cheating on Myka, or that you are in a polyamorous relationship?" He looked at me and actually tipped his head to the side as if he wasn't sure how to answer that. "I don't care. The bond is a complicated thing. I only just bonded myself, and I have no idea how it works, even though I've read all the books. As long as you and Myka are happy, everyone knows the conditions, and consent is given all around, who the fuck am I to judge?"

"Thanks for that. Most people want to lay into me about how wrong it is, or how they couldn't do that, or can't even imagine how that works."

I shrugged. "I had a relationship that involved multiple partners, so maybe I'm a bit more understanding than most. But like I said, as long as everyone consents to what is going on, then, seriously, who the hell is anyone to judge. But back to

Fernando. I'm assuming you and Myka have talked to him."

"We have, and he's just adorable, and Myka..." Titus' cheeks got very red as he said, "Once he found out how interested I was in him, he pulled Fernando aside, and went a bit dominant on him to see if he could handle us. Pushed him right up against the wall of the barn and when Fernando submitted to him, he reached out and ran his hand up Myka's cock... Myka and I may have had a bit of fun in the hay loft with him that afternoon."

I tipped my head back and laughed. "And to think that he and James were taking bets on how soon Kolton and I would be in the loft."

"Jade." Rose's voice came over the ear piece, and I reached up and clicked it.

"Yes Rose."

"Fernando and James have been advised. I've told them that Carlos is your supervisor, but they said—"

"Jade we aren't taking orders regarding Kolton's safety from anyone except for you. Are you seriously going to make us stay here and sit on our thumbs while Kolton is in danger?" James said through his earpiece.

I sighed, already making my way out to the stables where they were at, and said, "I will be there in just a moment."

Titus was right on my heels, and before we turned the corner, I stopped and faced him. "I'm glad you are happy, but I'm not letting Fernando and James go out there. Kolton wouldn't let me live if those boys got hurt."

He nodded and when we turned the corner, Myka had one hand on Fernando and James' shoulders, keeping them in place. James shook him off, surprisingly, and I saw how Myka's hand gripped Fernando's a little tighter, and his thumb moved just a bit. I nodded at him and he nodded back in understanding.

"Jade. You can't seriously —"

"I can and I will, James." I said standing tall, and bringing a dagger from my thigh. He paused. Looked at it, then at me, his eyes going wide. "I am an Astral Primal. The only one on this Ranch who outranks me is Minstrel Carlos, and it is my understanding that you won't do what he says."

"Not when it comes to Kolton. If he means as much to you as he does to us, or if what Ms. Rose said was true, and there is some kind of supernatural bond connecting you two, which we are all thrilled about by the way. You two are perfect for each other. We can't be happier."

"Your point, James?"

"My point is that, if he means as much to you as he does to us, please don't make us stay back."

"It's because he means so much to you, and you to him, that I am going to do just that."

"Jade—"

"No, James." Then I looked back at Fernando who was looking at me with pleading eyes. "No. Fernando, you both have to stay here. These aren't just mafia thugs we are going after. We are talking werewolves. They are wicked fast and smart in human form. In wolf form, you won't stand a chance. You will just end up being minced meat, and Kolton wouldn't forgive me if you guys got hurt. I'm making Philip stay, too, if that is any consolation." I added as Philip walked around the corner and leaned against the post. He nodded in understanding.

"We will just follow you." My eyes snapped back to James.

"Then I will leave three Astral's here to babysit you." I crossed my arms. "Are you really in need of a babysitter, James?"

He laughed. "That's a low blow even for you." When my hard expression didn't waiver, he let out a long breath. "This really isn't a joke."

"It's not." Philip's hard voice made Fernando and James turn to him. "I've been under the protection and owned by the Agency for a long time. They put me here to protect me from supernatural beings wanting to kill me. I'm basically in a witness protection program, but I won't tell you more on this. If Astral Jade and Minstrel Carlos are saying we need to stay here, then that is what we need to do."

James looked at Fernando and then back to Philip, his eyes wide. "These are supernatural beings. We've been dealing with supernatural beings without even knowing it?"

"It's one of Ashstrike Sanctorum's many hats. Make sure the humans stay ignorant." I smiled, "I'm willing to bet that half your high school was probably part of the Kiku Pack, honestly. You've probably dated, worked, and been friends with a lot of them. It's another reason you really shouldn't go, James."

"Probably Allyson. She was wild in bed, but had a temper and ended up cheating on me anyways." He smiled at me and finally said. "Okay. I'll stay here like a good dog."

"Bad joke James." I said chuckling.

"It was, but you giggled. Fernando, you good to stay?"

Fernando looked to Titus, then to Myka who both nodded to him, and then he met my eyes. "I'll stay, Jade, but I'll be worried sick the entire time that you are gone.

"Okay, now that we have that settled. Are the Astral Trainees ready to go?"

"Yes, Astral Primal," one of the trainee's said.

"Let's move out." I turned and jumped in the truck cab as Carlos got behind the wheel and once there was a thump on the roof, hit the gas and took off down the road.

CHAPTER 38

JADE

A mile from the meet up I saw wolves lining the road. I reached up and clicked the button at my ear and said, "Astral Teams Two and Three. Hold back at the quarter mile point."

"Yes, Astral." I heard in unison.

"They are anticipating a war." Carlos said low.

I nodded, but said, "They hurt Kolton…" My chest grew tight at the thought, and my head hurt. I ran my hands over my face, and my jaw seemed tender.

I poked at it, and Carlos noticed, saying, "Your jaw hurt?"

"Feels like it did when Daniel swung at a Chilker and missed, hitting me instead." I rubbed it again, and said, "Probably just clenching my jaw too hard."

Carlos was quiet for a long moment before saying with lethal death in his voice, "Just remember what the Primals said."

"Trust me, I'm not likely to forget." I saw the two trucks behind us slow and stop. I felt the power surge through the area, with them all going on the defensive. This many Astral in one place, was highly unheard of, and if we were not careful, we would feed each other.

We pulled up and the two Kiku Pack Betas stood at the door. The first I knew as Darrell was about six-five, very dark skinned, dark eyes, and an absolute brute. The shorter one was built a lot like Titus and Myka, light brown skinned, but white blonde hair. I got out, with Carlos, Myka and Titus standing right behind me.

However, it was the sight in the corner that caught my eye and had me seeing red. There, crumpled in a pile, were the four puppy scouts, beaten, bloody and unmoving. Each of them with a hole in their chest.

Myka and Titus were instantly over there and looking them over. When Myka turned to look at me, his eyes closed slowly, and I growled, "Jesse, as soon as we get back." Carlos gave one quick nod of his head.

Titus turned his head to look around the corner and then slowly handed off the small bodies to who we presumed were their parents.

"Betas." Carlos' voice was strained, and I couldn't think straight.

Trent's eyes flared in recognition at the sight of Carlos standing there. With a bow and fist over his chest he says, "Minstrel."

"They were puppies. They were *children*." I ground out through my teeth.

Trent's eyes fell to the ground and I saw his ragged breath. Darrell however, just looked toward where their bodies had been and said sadly, "Alpha smelled you on them. Knew that they had been caught. Said he didn't have a place in his ranks for anyone who couldn't do their job."

"They. Were. Pups." I said, and Carlos' hand took mine pulling me back. Trent and Darrell just gave a simple nod. "*This* is the Alpha you wish to serve? One who kills children because they made a mistake. *He* put them in a situation where I could have killed them for trespassing on a Seer's land. They were kids, pups, without the necessary skills to do what was asked. You want to serve *that* Alpha? Well, here's just a little bit of foreshadowing for you *Betas*. Your Alpha's life is forfeit."

They each looked to Carlos and he just said, "Your Alpha's life has a time limit. The Agency will not stand for the slaughtering of children. Pray you do not end up on their list as well."

There was a long silence before Carlos said, "Now, you know why we are here. Provide him to me unharmed and alive."

"Alpha is inside waiting for you." Darrell growled as he opened the door and followed us in.

The room was just as the trainees had described it. A large, two story open concrete warehouse. There were guards standing in front of a cage in the back room, and my heart pounded against my chest.

"Nice of you to arrive, Astral." My eyes went to the mutt who voiced his greeting.

"You can release the human now, Devon."

"The human. Is that all you are calling your bonded now? The Human?"

"Devon." My voice was deathly calm and I heard Carlos give me a warning under his breath. Carlos knew just how deadly I could get when I was this calm. *The calm before the shitshow*, he used to say.

A low growl reached me and I smirked as he said, "I am Alpha. You will address me as my rank. I give you the courtesy of yours, you *will* give me the courtesy of mine."

"I will give you the courtesy of yours when you earn it. Slaughtering children will not earn you any niceties from me. Not to mention that you refuse to work within the confines of the Agency. You are attempting to bully and blackmail for more than is rightfully yours." I said, raising my chin.

"I am trying to provide for my pack, as an Alpha does."

"You have grown too big for the area you are in. We have already talked about this. I will give you land to the north into Oregon, but I cannot and will not give you the wildland of the Porter Ranch."

"The Kismots will not allow us near their lines. You know the history there. Our pack will be eaten up." Devon said, actually sounding like someone who had given that option some thought.

"I have spoken to their King. They have agreed to call the six-mile area along the boundary there a dead zone. While that area will be technically part of their territory, they will not hunt it. This would help limit possible crossing of your paths."

"I have already declined that option. I want the Porter Ranch wildland.

"You. Will. Not. Have. It. The Primals have decreed it protected land."

"This isn't about the land anymore." Myka said behind me. "This is about the day Astral Jade was wounded by your men."

"This is personal." Titus said behind Carlos.

Devon's eyes narrowed and his features hardened. "Damn fucking straight it is. Astral Jade killed my brother that day."

"I am sorry for that. Brandon was a good man and wolf." I said, but set my shoulders and said, "You sent your pack after a lone gelding that day, to send a message to the Porter Ranch that you were going to take what you were not awarded. I fought to protect myself and the gelding. The fact your brother decided to attack me, means that I had every right to defend myself."

My eyes met his as I said, "Now. Give me my bonded back, now."

I heard a scuffle behind him and then everything happened at once. Devon shifted into his wolf form, his betas shifted into wolf form, and the room went stone still when Kolton was tossed into the middle of the room and I got the first good look at him. In the span of microseconds, I took in the eye that was swelling, the bloody nose, the bruise forming at his jaw, the broken finger, the slices that ran up and down his arms, and then the single drop of blood that I watched drop from a fresh cut on his temple and splatter on the concrete floor. There was that tug on that interior rope that told me he was okay, but as I watched another drop fall to the concrete floor, I saw red as my eyes met Devon's large black wolf eye.

"Carlos. There is no longer a need for an Exorci. His life is forfeit immediately, and it will be at my hands."

CHAPTER 39

KOLTON

Everything hurt. A few hours ago, their Alpha had come in and repeatedly put some oil over my bonding mark with Jade, and then beat me until whatever protections that were in that thing wore off, and then would start on me again. I knew my eye was going to swell and blacken, my lips were already doing so, and there was going to be a wicked bruise on my jaw from where they hit me earlier.

When they left about half an hour ago, Aaron, a guy I had known since high school, slid me some antiseptic wipes through the bars.

"I'm so sorry, man. I wish there was more I could do to help." Aaron had muttered quietly. "Make sure to wipe off your bonding mark too. He's using hemlock oil from the roots of the plant to break through the Astral's protections."

"Thanks, Aaron."

"Wish there was more I could do, but Alpha's raging pissed."

"So, you're a werewolf, huh?" I tore one of the packages he gave me, and wiped off the mark with the little cleansing pad. Hemlock root. That was supposed to be exceptionally potent. Why wasn't I dead already?

Aaron's lip lifted before saying, "Why do you think I was so good at track and field? Most of the track team was in the pack. Wipe the area just above the right side of your lip with the other one, and your left temple. Should at least keep it clean."

"Why is your Alpha so pissed?"

"He's been growing the pack. Killing other Alphas left and right and absorbing them. There are too many of us now not to be noticed, especially if we don't get more land."

"Hiding in plain sight, as they say."

Aaron nodded. "That day with the loose horse your girl rode back?" He made eye contact with me and I nodded. "I broke off when I saw you and Philip with the rifles. Tried to call off the others too, because I remember how good of a shot you were."

I grinned at him, but he continued. "Brandon was following orders. He wouldn't have hurt your Jade. He had way too much respect for her. When he leapt for the horse though, you made a clean shot."

My stomach dropped out of the bottom of me. "I killed the Alpha's brother? *That's* why this is so personal."

"Alpha is holding it against your girl, not you. You didn't know anything about us. He's holding it against her, because it was her buck knife that killed the first wolf. Here's the thing, though. We attacked an Astral. Our lives are forfeit with that act. The Agency has every right to come in and wipe us all out right now, but they aren't. I can only believe it's because of Astral Jade."

"Gods, Jade." I whispered, and opened the second pack to clean off the spots Aaron had indicated. The one at my temple burned and came back red. I wiped the area around my nose off as well, because I knew it had been bloody. Setting it after they had broken it earlier had hurt like a bitch.

Aaron's gaze went past me, he flinched, and then stood, in line in front of the cage they held me in. I felt that rope within me fill with rage, and I tried to comfort her through it. She was trying to protect me. She hadn't let me know that it was my bullet that had killed the Alpha's brother. She had been protecting me from the start.

When one of the Beta's soldiers came in, he grabbed my arm and dropped another drop of the oil on the mark. I grit my teeth, and it hurt like hell, but then there was a swipe of a paw, and I felt my right temple slice open again. When I looked at the shithead who swiped at me, he said, "You killed Brandon? It wasn't the Astral?"

"The Alpha's brother?" He nodded, and I sighed, "Apparently it was my shot that did it."

"Brandon was my mate." His paw turned back into a fist, and he punched repeatedly. I swung, landing a few hits, but then someone was pulling the soldier off me and locking the door. I heard something shatter and he growled, "That was the only bottle..."

"Alpha approaches." Someone hollered, and the entire room changed.

I pulled on my internal strength and made myself stand behind the row of people, hauling myself up by the metal bars. My usual two guards were at the door to my cage, and when I saw who walked through the door, I smiled.

"I told you assholes she would come. Oh, look, I was right... and she didn't come alone." I held back a chuckle, but let the corner of my lip lift as I tried to hear what they were talking about.

They were talking about boundaries, and a few other things I didn't fully understand or hear, but then the cage opened, and the guard reached in and grabbed me.

I swung and made contact with one of their faces, pleased with the crack I heard on impact. I grunted and shook my wrist, but he and another one of my guards grabbed my arms, and pulled me through the door. When we were close enough that Jade would have been able to hear me, they threw me forward, kicking my knees out from under me, and causing me to fall to the floor.

I looked at her smiling, and followed each curve of her in skin tight black clothing. She stood every ounce a fighter, and that look of fire in her eyes was wicked sexy and deadly all at the same time. Her eyes flicked back to the Alpha, who instantly shifted into wolf form, his beta's just behind him.

"Carlos, there is no longer a need for an Exorci. His life is forfeit immediately and it will be at my hands." Her voice was pure death.

There was a snarl from the Alpha, and then Jade's hair lifted on a non-existent wind, and she started to glow.

"*Mija.*" The Hispanic man next to her said carefully and evening. Carlos.

"Astral." Myka and Titus said, but Jade took a deep breath, and I saw their bodies shimmer slightly, before their legs shook and they bowed to one knee.

"You spilled his blood." Jade said, staring down the Alpha. The runes on her arms lit up bright enough to be seen through the black skin tight clothes she wore, but it was the bonding mark that was the brightest, and I felt my arm heat in response. I smiled brighter at her, somehow even more in love with her now. The only thought going through my head was, '*Oh, you fucked up.*'

The Alpha smirked at the challenge, and I felt more than heard him say, "Think you can take me Astral? I am Alpha of the mightiest pack on the planet."

"I am an Astral Primal, and you have signed your death warrant with those drops of blood from my Bonded." Jade said, glowing brighter. All the air in the room seemed to pull toward her, and even Carlos knelt to whatever it was that was happening.

Jade took one step toward the Alpha, throwing her hands back toward the Betas, they halted, growled, and teased, "So, your Alpha is the mightiest Alpha on the planet? I'm sure he can handle an Astral Primal, right?" Then her voice came low and commanding. "So, sit... and stay."

The Betas and all fifty or so of the pack in that room whimpered under her command and fell to their knees. Some going so far as to lay on their bellies, lay their ears back and cry.

Jade took another step toward the Alpha, who bared his teeth. The air stilled, my bonding mark glowed hotter, and I felt a trickle of energy flow up and down the redwood tree tattoo on my arm. I glanced down and saw mysterious shapes take form in the leaves and branches of the tree before I looked back toward her.

I felt my nose heal, snapping back together, then the skin tightened both above my lip, and at my temple. The vision in my eyes was getting clearer, and then it didn't feel as though my eyelids were as swollen at all. I looked down at my arms, and the cuts that were up and down my arms had healed.

I looked up to Jade and her hair lifted higher in that non-existent wind that flittered around her, before the Alpha pounced.

Jade lunged, and whimpers from the wolves could be heard throughout the warehouse as the two collided mid-air and crashed to the ground. There was a blinding light, and then the Alpha pounced backwards.

I looked to where Carlos, Myka and Titus still knelt unmoving. Their eyes and runes glowed brightly, and I swore I saw a faint light stretch between them and Jade. There was another brighter thread of light coming through the door, and I could just see where more people had knelt on one knee, with their hand in a fist over their chests, heads down.

I looked back to Jade, who grabbed onto the Alpha's back leg and twisted, sending a howling pain through the room. She was glowing so brightly, that I could only see a faint outline of her through the light.

When the Alpha turned and lunged face first, Jade swung her leg over his neck, pulling him to the ground and ... Oh... My... God.

I couldn't believe what I was seeing.

Jade had one hand on his lower jaw, the other on this snout, and was pulling them apart. His mouth opened wider than I had ever seen a dog's ever go. The screeching pain that came from the Alpha meant only one thing, she was tearing his jaw apart. Blood sprayed, and his lower jaw flew across the room and hit the wall with a thud.

The temperature in the room dropped as Jade continued by reaching down his throat and ripping pieces out. She let the Alpha's body fall to the floor, pulling skin back to expose the ribcage, shattering several ribs in the process. I blinked as she reached in and pulled his heart out.

She stared at it in her hands, and then tore it in half and threw it in two different directions, before reaching down and pulling more and more of his insides out and onto the floor.

I felt a wave of power burst through the room again.

My Jade had killed an Alpha wolf.

With. Her. Bare. Hands.

She didn't stop. Jade reached down and when she pulled each of his legs off, another wave of power burst through the room. She continued ripping him apart as Carlos finally stood and tried to get her to stop. His eyes glowed a bright purple as he commanded her to stop, but she just kept shredding.

When Carlos went to touch her, to pull her away, he pulled his hand back with a hiss. "Astral Primal Jade. I command you to freeze. Release your power. Release yourself."

Nothing. Jade just kept shredding the Alpha to pieces.

Myka and Titus stood, inhaled deeply, cutting off whatever connection they had to Jade, and reached for her, but were blown backwards.

Before I realized what I was doing, I rose and ran toward her. "Jade." I said carefully. Her eyes glowed as she continued shredding what was left of the Alpha.

I reached for her, but Carlos said, "Careful, Kolton. She's feeding on the power from all the Astrals in the area."

"Jade." I said again, when she just picked up another chunk of meat, shredding it and screaming.

When what was in her hands was gone, and before she could reach for more... well there wasn't much left of Alpha Devon, I jumped in front of her. She stopped, looked at me, and I grabbed her face between my hands feeling all that power, rage and heat feed through me.

"Darling." I said just above a whisper, and tried to grasp onto that connection between us. "Darling. Look at me."

Jade blinked and the brightness around her dimmed slightly.

I pulled her closer, and rested my forehead on hers. "Darlin', look at me. Focus on me."

Her hands rested on my hips, and I felt her fingers tighten slightly.

"That's it, Darlin'. I'm here. I'm whole. I'm alive." I breathed. I ran my thumbs along her cheekbones, wiping blood and bits from her face. That glow pulled back from her eyes, and she blinked.

"Kolton." Her voice was raspy.

"Yes, darling. I'm here." Her arms slowly wrapped around my waist and when she got to my spine, I felt her grip it tight. "It's me, darling. I'm here and I'm fine. I'm in your arms. I'm safe."

Her fingers loosened, and she said, "I'm sorry you had to see me like that." Before going limp and collapsing in my arms.

CHAPTER 40

KOLTON

I caught her before she hit the ground, and Carlos was instantly there, his fingers glowing softly as he ran his fingers over her forehead. "We need to get her back to the house. Rose can work on her and get her settled."

I turned and there was a small flash of light, as the Betas returned to human form. "Where are you taking her?"

"Back to the ranch." Carlos said carefully, but with every ounce of the authority he carried.

"Of course, Minstrel." They said in unison.

"Speak."

"You know our laws." The taller of the two said, I think he said his name was Darrell. "She defeated our Alpha. She is now our Alpha."

The look on his face said it all. The fact he said those words shocked him to his very core. I shifted her into my arms, and held her closer, as I said, "Right now she is a woman who needs to rest. I suggest..." My eyes flicked to Aaron whose smile widened as he nodded at me. "That you clean up this fucking mess and have your Council meet with her in a few days, once she has recovered. I think it's fair to say that there will be no further issue with the denial for more land?"

"Of course... I'm not exactly sure what to call you sir." The one named Trent said. "The Alpha has always been male. Therefore, their mate is always the Luna."

"Kolton is fine for now. Let Jade sort out all that shit. I'm only worried about her right now." I said, but looked to Aaron and smiled at him. "For now, Aaron can be a go between us."

"Kolton." Aaron was hesitant.

"Aaron, consider yourself promoted, temporarily. Work with these assholes and the Council. We can sort things out until Jade can tell us what to do."

"Yes, sir." Aaron and the Beta's said with a bow.

I strode out of the building, with Jade in my arms to find a hundred people on one knee with their fist over their chest. Carlos put his hand on my shoulder and said, "Astral Jade is your Alpha. Kolton her mate.

You will obey their directions. Instructions have been given to your Betas and Aaron."

All but twenty of those put their foreheads to the ground. The other twenty bowed their heads, and then Carlos said, "Astrals, load up."

Those twenty moved in unison and piled onto the back of the trucks. Myka and Titus jumped into the other truck as Carlos helped me lay Jade out in the back seat. I climbed in behind Carlos and rested Jade's head on my lap. One of the other Astrals closed my door and nodded at me.

When I looked down at Jade, some of her runes were still giving off a faint glow, but it was the redwood tree just under her elbow that held my attention. I reached down and touched it and I swear I saw the corner of her lip twitch. "I'm here, Jade. I'm here."

When we got her back to the apartment, I stripped her, and laid her on the bed. My clothes were done for, so I stripped to my boxer briefs, and went to washing her off. With each pass over her arms, she seemed to twitch more in response to my touch. The blood was drying in her hair, and while I realized there was going to be no way I could get it all out short of her taking a shower, I did the best I could.

She started muttering, and I felt my bonding mark heat. I was working on getting the blood off of her calves, when I looked up and saw her eyes burning bright.

"Sir." She whispered, and my eyes shot to her face.

Dropping the washcloth in the bowl of water next to the bed, I kneeled next to her, and said, "Darlin'."

"Sir." It was whispered, but with a heat to it that was wholly inappropriate for the moment. I reached up and moved some hair away from her cheek, and when my finger grazed her skin, her eyes met mine. They were swimming with a green glow, and I felt her desire more than anything along that bond. "Please, sir."

"Darlin', you just woke up from, well, whatever that was. You need to rest." I said, trying so hard to remain calm, because the need and heat in her gaze was making me hard.

Her hand trailed down between her legs, and I sat there transfixed by her fingers working her clit. The single finger that trailed down into the wetness I could see growing there. "Fuck, Darlin'."

"Please fuck me, Sir." Was her only plea.

I got up and positioned myself between her legs, as she never let up the circling motion on her clit. Leaning down, I ran my tongue along the length of her, flicking her clit. I slowly tasted every inch of her flesh, before slipping inside of her wet pussy. I drank up every drop that I could from her. Her moans and grip on my hair urging me on.

I wrapped both arms around her thighs to hold her in place as I tongue fucked her. When I felt her on the edge of release, I pulled back to flick her clit before clamping down, sucking and licking until she was screaming my name in release.

When she started to come down, I continued licking up and down the center of her, and repositioned the angle of her hips and ran my tongue along the rosebud of her ass. As my tongue lapped at her, she moaned, which only became louder when I slid a finger inside of her, and went back to her clit. Moments later, she was falling over the edge again.

"That's my good girl." I ground out and slid my underwear off, and tossed them aside. The hungry look she gave me was enough that, whatever hesitation I had earlier, it flew out the window. Only, as I ran the head of my cock up and down her, she moved, and the next thing I knew she was sitting above me, the head of me against her.

Rolling her hips, she moved so only the head of me was within her, and she lifted and sat in short succession. Then she slowed and met my eyes as she lowered herself onto me. The sight of her hovering over me, my cock slowly being devoured by her, had me concentrating so very hard on not cumming right there.

Reaching up, I grasped her boobs and pinched her nipples. Her head tipped back in pleasure as her pussy clenched around me. A small smile formed on my lips as I ran a hand up her throat and said, "Now, be a good girl and ride my cock."

And she did, she rolled her hips and then we were working together as I thrusted into her over and over again. When she slowed, I said, "Oh no, Darlin'. You don't get to slow down."

I grabbed her thighs, taking a portion of her weight and plowed into her over and over again. Each connection of her had her boobs bouncing with the force, and the moans of her were like a heaven song. Just as she was on the edge, I flipped her around and entered her from behind. "Please, sir, fuck me harder."

"Ask and you shall receive, Darlin'." I fucked her with everything I had. I could feel her getting right to that edge again, and slid two fingers in her ass, and the effect was immediate. I barely twitched them, and every rune on Jade's body burned bright again, as she came so hard, I didn't dare move from inside her. As the light started to dull, I twitched my fingers again, and thrusted again and again. I felt that tingling at the base of my spine, and my bonding mark burned in response. When Jade came again, with a moaned, "Kolton", it put me over the edge as I came within her.

Collapsing on the bed next to each other, the light finally faded from her runes and her eyes, as she said, "I love you, Kolton. I'll always protect you."

"I love you, Jade. Now rest. I'll watch over you." I kissed her, and her lips lingered on mine a moment longer before her eyes met mine and she smiled. "I'll get a washcloth to get us cleaned up."

"Maybe that pink one you answered the door in." Her voice fading off into unconsciousness. I chuckled, as I went to the bathroom, and got myself cleaned up. By the time I got back to the bedroom, she was fast asleep.

I cleaned her up, put a long t-shirt on her, and laid her back down. With all the power that she used today to default the wolves Alpha, I suspected she would sleep for a long time. I only hoped that when she woke, she would know what to do with the wolves.

CHAPTER 41

JADE

I blinked awake and reached for Kolton. He wasn't there and I jerked myself fully awake sitting up in bed, groaning at the sore muscles in my arms, legs, back... well everything. I looked around, and there was a book laying open on the seat of a chair that hadn't been there before next to the closet.

Looking over at the clock, it was mid-morning. I winced as I swung my legs over the edge of the bed. I stretched, and every inch of me hurt. I slowly got to my feet and trotted off to the bathroom. If it was mid-morning, Kolton was probably out and handling a few things.

When I was washing my hands though, I heard, "Yes, Ms. Rose. I have the salve ready for when she wakes, and the tea kettle ready to add the packet you made."

I dried my hands and tiptoed out of the bedroom, down the hall, and peeked around the corner into the kitchen as he said, "I know... Yes, Ma'am... I'll let you know as soon as she is up."

Leaning against the doorway, I couldn't help but stare at him as he talked to Rose. He was in a pair of loose grey sweatpants and nothing else. They were low enough on his hips, I knew there was nothing under them. I bit my lip thinking about how I had woken up and demanded he fuck me. He had done so, too, without hesitation.

I looked at the kitchen table and could almost see our endeavor there. Fuck. There wasn't anywhere in this apartment, I hadn't let Kolton take me or would let Kolton take me.

My gaze inspected every inch of him, seeking out every wound they'd inflicted on him. The image of him bent over, and those drops of blood from his temple... It was going to haunt me for a long time. There were still a few bruises along his ribs, but he was healing faster than he should have.

He tipped his head back and sighed, as he finished making his sandwich, and said, "I'm aware."

I tried to stifle a chuckle, but upon hearing me, he turned around so quickly, his sandwich went flying across the room. I outright laughed then, and he blinked, "Jade."

He was before me, kissing me. "Darling, I've been so worried." Then he blinked, and said, "Yeah, she's up. We will be down later." He reached up and threw the ear piece onto the couch behind me.

Then his arms were around me as he lifted me and kissed me again. I pushed his pants down as I wrapped my legs around him. Gods, the feel of him against me was everything. I ground against him, and I felt him moan into me. He pressed me against the wall, and pulled back just enough to say, "It's been two days. I've had to watch you sleep for two days. I finally leave your side for two fucking minutes, to make a sandwich, and *then* you wake up?"

"I've never claimed to be easy." I said, rocking my hips against the hard length of him. He growled, lifted me slightly, and then I felt him against me. He moved, and I moaned as he slid inside me. "Gods, I love the feel of you in me."

He kissed that spot at the base of my neck, and I felt him smile. "That feeling is mutual, darling."

Then he was dragging from me slowly, before re-entering me with a reverence that matched the tenderness in his kiss. While our joining wasn't long, it was slow, sweet, and that reconnection that I needed. We came together, and once I drifted back into my body, he gently set me down on my feet. Our eyes stayed locked on each other as we straightened our clothing, but then my face was in his hands and he was kissing me again.

"You are acting as though I've been away for months. What is going on, Kolton?" I rested a hand on the one he still had on my face, and he shuttered against me.

"I was kidnapped, held hostage, had hemlock root oil used on me to combat the bonding mark, beaten, had to watch Garrett being shish kebabbed by the old Alpha, dealt with more hemlock root oil, was beaten some more, watched the woman I love literally tear an Alpha apart, glow like a freaking star, and *then* when I get her back here, she practically begs me to fuck her brains out, which I enjoyed by the way, but regardless. She shone like a star when she came, and then she slept for two fucking days, hardly moving at all. Two days, Jade Cecilia Araceli Romero."

I blinked at him. He totally just full named me for sleeping. I was just about to call him out on it when he took a deep breath, "And then she casually walks out of the bedroom like it's a casual Sunday morning while I'm making something to eat and begs for a quickie."

I couldn't help but laugh. "Welcome to my life, Kolton Webster."

"Oh, if you think that is going to scare me off, think again."

"Wait... did you say hemlock oil?" I grabbed his arm and looked at the redwood tree on his arm, and it looked just as good and fresh as the day Philip had inked it. It glowed slightly as I ran my thumb over it, and the protection runes glowed brighter. "Well, at least I know they work, mostly."

I blinked and a tear fell down my cheek. Kolton had still been hurt. Someone had found a way around an Astral Primal's protection runes. How did they even think to use it? Why would they have to take that chance. What if it had killed him?

"Hey. Hey. Darling, look at me." He cradled my neck. His thumb pushed my chin up to make me look at him. "I'm fine. A little bruised, but I'm healing and feel fine."

"Hemlock oil, though. There have been long lost wives tales about it combating those protections, but the person would likely die from having it used. I didn't think anyone would be brave enough to try it. How many times?"

"A fair few. It didn't last long."

"You are just going to give me a fair few?" I raised my eyebrows at him.

"Yes. I'm here, I'm fine." He kissed me and said, "Now, go and shower. Then get comfortable on the couch. I'll bring you something to eat and drink. You need it."

He turned me toward the hall and then slapped my ass, giggling like a school boy.

"Hey, keep that up, and there will be a repeat of earlier." I said, swaying my hips a little more than was necessary. I chuckled as I looked back over my shoulder and saw him biting his fist in his mouth.

I grabbed a new towel from the closet, and when I turned the water on, I took a good look at myself in the mirror. I blinked a couple of times, because the white ink runes were much more visible on my skin. I looked down and ran my hands over my forearms and they ebbed and flowed under my touch. They hadn't been this visible since Daniel's death. "What in the world is going on?"

The mirror started to fog up, so I flipped the switch for the fan and got in the shower. I let out a heavy sigh at the feel of the hot water flowing over my sore muscles.

I tipped my head back and let the hot water run over my hair. There were clumps that still stuck together, and I realized that at some point, Kolton had tried to clean me up as much as possible, but there was only so much he could have done with my hair. I washed it quickly, and then went to scrubbing my body to get any remnants of blood off. Not to mention at least two sex sessions of sweat.

By the time I was done, Kolton had put a change of clothes on the toilet for me, and I smiled. Running a comb quickly through my hair, I wound it up into a bun to dry, got dressed, and as instructed, went and sat on the couch. I pulled the fuzzy blanket that he placed there for me, up and around my lap.

A few minutes later, he walked around the corner with a tray with a grilled turkey and cheese, French onion chips, and a coffee. "If I didn't love you already, I would fall head over heels for you all over again."

"Hey, I know there are two things you need every day, at minimum. An orgasm and your caffeine drip. I have now fulfilled both." He said, kissing my cheek.

I took a sip, and leaned my head back in bliss. "This is perfect." My eyes caught a small blinking red light in between the cushions, and I narrowed my eyes on it. "Umm, Kolton."

He raised his eyebrows in question, and when I pointed to it, his eyes widened and when he realized what it was, he slapped the front of his forehead and just said, "Shit."

Picking it up, he stuck the earpiece into his ear, and said, "Please tell me everyone changed channels." There was a long pause, where he had just let out a long breath before he froze and said, "Yes, Ms. Rose... Thank you, Ms. Rose... She just showered. She's eating now. I'll get the cream on her after... Oh, shut the fuck up, James."

Kolton was read as a tomato, and I couldn't help but giggle as I took a bite of the sandwich. It was delicious, as usual, and of course he made sure to have my favorite chips available.

His eyes narrowed, and then said, "We will be down in an hour." Making sure that he clicked off the mic this time.

"What is it? Other than the fact they have heard everything since I woke up."

"Yeah, Ms. Rose forced a close on the channel until ten minutes ago. She closely monitored it after that." He took a deep breath. "Carlos is entertaining some guests down at the office and would like your presence when you are feeling up to it."

"No mention of who?" He shook his head. "What's going on with the wolves? Have they backed down?"

"Carlos has been working with them. Myka and Titus are still here, and there is a lot that needs to be discussed, but not in this house."

I nodded, and when I went to say something, he said, "While we are within our walls, no discussions of work. Unless it's in the context of 'How was your day?' We aren't going to sit here and talk about work. Deal?"

"Deal." I said taking the last bite of my sandwich. "You've gotten real good at making those. I like yours better than the ones I make."

"I put parmesan on the outside to crisp it up. You don't. It makes it better." He shrugged. "When you are finished, I have some cream that Ms. Rose gave me to put on your sore muscles, then we need to head down to the office."

"How did she? Nevermind, it's Rose." I put a chip in my mouth, and said, "I can finish these while you work."

"You promise to behave? We don't have time for a full round, and that quickie in the kitchen, while enjoyable, was not enough." He looked me up and down, and I heated in all the right places.

"Keep looking at me like that, and we won't make that meeting downstairs. Carlos will just have to wait."

"I got the feeling Carlos might come and haul you down there if we aren't down in a timely fashion." He smiled and leaned toward me. I didn't move, and when he was only a hair from kissing me, he said, "There was a reason I said to sit on the couch darling." Before backing up and pulling the blanket back. "Now, pants off. Let me get your legs first."

"Tease."

"I'll make up for it tonight. Now, seriously, pants off."

CHAPTER 42

JADE

When we walked into Rose's office, there was a wolf I didn't recognize.

"What are you doing here, Aaron?" Kolton asked.

"I'm the highest-ranking member of the Kiku Pack, as elected by the Pack Council." The wolf Aaron said. "So, I'm temporarily Beta, until your woman names one."

"I'm sorry, what?" I said swallowing.

"There was a bit of a situation after you defeated our previous Alpha. After everyone recovered from your commands, it was determined that Beta Darrell and Beta Trent were unfit to continue as leaders since they had been a part of the capturing of your bonded." He said the words, but I didn't fully comprehend them.

"Sorry, one more time?"

"The ruling council exiled Darrell and Trent from the pack. They are being relocated to New Mexico with the assistance of Minstrel Carlos." He smiled slightly when he said, "I've known Kolton since we were kids. We used to be pretty close in high school, but pack duties and such kind of took me away. So, the council said I should help run things until you assign your Beta."

I looked to Kolton who said, "He helped me as much as he could while I was captured there. Aaron's a good man. I trust him."

"Astral Primal Alpha." Aaron smiled, then bowed almost horizontal before standing straight. "The pack is awaiting your instruction as to how to proceed."

"I'm sorry. What?"

"Ma'am, you overtook and defeated our previous Alpha." His eyes flicked to Carlos, then to Kolton, unsure how to continue.

"Darling, you shredded Devon like pulled pork. By law, you are the Kiku Pack's Alpha now." Kolton said, wrapping his arm around my waist and pulling me close.

I blinked. I hadn't really thought about what I had done. There were only small blips of images of what I had done during that fight with the Alpha. "I shouldn't have won that fight."

"Astral Primal." Carlos said. "You won that fight by law and right. The Primals have handed you the Kiku Pack. You will be stationed here at the Porter Ranch to ensure the Pack is maintained and taken care of. You will also be setting up and running the local Astral office."

"I'm sorry. *What?*"

Rose smiled and said, "Carlos has purchased the Johnson property next door. It will become an Astral training center. You will be overseeing it."

I looked at Kolton and then at Rose and Carlos. "I don't understand. *What?*"

"Just where are you lost?" Carlos said with a smile.

"Here, honey, have a cup of tea." Rose said, handing me a cup shaped like a whale. I grasped onto the tail, and tipped back a gulp.

"Thanks. Something tells me I need this." I took another sip, looked at Carlos and added, "And a margarita... hold the mix."

"So, shots?" Kolton chuckled.

"That's how we always said we needed a shot of tequila when she was growing up." Carlos said wistfully.

"I'm sorry?" Aaron's look of confusion made me smile. He apparently didn't know just how connected I was to Ashstrike Sanctorum. He was about to get one hell of a mental download.

"When she was growing up, we used to come home and say that we needed a margarita, hold the mix." Carlos said, looking to Aaron.

"When she was growing up?" He said slowly, then there was a trace of fear in his eyes as he turned to me and asked, "Is Minstrel Carlos your father, Astral Primal Alpha?"

"Not biologically, but he might as well be. He's technically a cousin by blood, but he took me in and raised me when the Iamu burned everything to ash and killed my parents." I took another sip of the tea Rose had given me. The wide eyes of the Beta... my Beta met mine and I smiled. "Didn't expect that one, did you?"

"No, ma'am."

"So, what has happened with the pack? The quick version because I have to also process everything they just said, too."

Aaron happily obliged. Most everything else was handled, and so I told him, "I'll meet with you in three days. You and the pack council should meet me at the beaver dam."

"Yes ma'am. May I head back?" He asked.

"Of course."

He looked around the room before saying, "We aren't all bad people, and after talking to the Council and learning what I have since... that day, I'm not so sure we need as much room as Devon stated, but we can discuss that in a few days with the council. I look forward to working with you, Astral Primal Alpha."

He turned and left the room and when the door shut, I muttered, "We are gonna have to come up with a new title. That is a mouth full."

I watched him stride out the main door, shift, and take off. Sighing, I looked at Carlos and Rose, "So if I recall everything you just said, I now am responsible for a wolf pack and running an Astral training center on the next-door property?"

"You heard right." Carlos said, and I felt Kolton rub comforting circles on my lower back. "Not to mention that the redevelopment project here still needs to be finished. Ben has been keeping things going, and there was next to no delay over the last couple of days. I've had to make a few calls, but we got it all sorted out."

I let out a long breath and my mind ran through all that would entail in a matter of seconds. "Will the Agency forward some additional funds to the redevelopment for the addition of a small house along the Porter Ranch and pack border? It would make things easier to keep an eye on both."

"It's already been handled. There is a million being redirected for your housing." Carlos smirked.

I blinked at him. Looked at Kolton, whose jaw dropped and said, "I'm sorry, sir. What?"

Carlos tipped his head back and laughed.

"While I realize that we can easily spend a chunk of that on the planning and construction, we don't need that much." I said firmly.

"Doesn't matter. Spend all or a portion. Build your dream home." Carlos said, leaning on his elbows on the desk.

"My dream home?" The words came out slowly and confused.

"Well, yes. You and Kolton need somewhere nice to live, have kids, and raise them. Plus, you will both have huge responsibilities on your shoulders. Kolton has to run the ranch and you'll have all your Astral Primal Alpha duties." Carlos looked at me like he was surprised at my reaction, but still was pleased with himself.

"Carlos. I've... I never thought I'd have a home." I looked at him, my voice thick.

Kolton turned me to face him, kissed me softly and whispered in my ear, "A home with you can be anywhere, but if it can be here? Why not? Would that be so bad, darling?"

Shit, the whole thing made me weak in the knees, and wanted nothing more than to go back upstairs and get on my knees before him.

I pulled back to look at him, but whispered, "No. I want a home with you, and here would be great, I'd just never thought of having a home to set roots into."

"When you were with Daniel, didn't you two ever talk about having a home in one place together?"

"We were both Agency. Setting down roots wasn't something that crossed either of our minds. We were constantly sent out all over the world, and for unknown amounts of time. So, no, I've never thought of settling down in one place. Having kids? I've done everything I can to prevent that happening, except a full extraction of the uterus. I don't live a life that is well suited for raising kids."

I looked at Carlos and he was smiling brightly. "Carlos, is the Agency really allowing me... setting me up with a life where that is possible?"

"I've cleared it with the Primals. The Johnson land will close on Friday. You have a pack and a training facility to run. You are being set up to have your own little corner of the world. Expect frequent visits from me," He said, then turned to Rose, "And a better internet system put into place."

Rose rolled her eyes. "What we have suits us fine. We have the comm system."

"Better internet *and* communication system." Carlos said, before turning back to me. "Now, I want you to go back and rest. I have movers packing up your apartment. Your things will be here next week."

"Don't forget the sex toy collection." Kolton said with a wink.

"I'm well aware of her sex toy collection. Hell, build your own sex room in the new house." Carlos told Kolton and I just shook my head.

"*Mija*. I expect more grandchildren."

"*Expect*. Carlos, Kolton and I haven't even discussed anything yet. Don't start pushing for grandkids. What if Kolton doesn't want them? What if I'm barren?"

"Oh, I want kids if you want kids, darling. If you are barren, then we will adopt all the kids you want." Kolton kissed me on the temple and smiled. "She is right, though; we haven't talked about any of that yet.

First, I have to get her to marry me, then we will discuss kids, but we sort of have our hands full right now, Minstrel."

"Please call me Carlos. You are family." Carlos said, pointing a finger at him before saying, "And I hope you love tamales because my wife and mother make the best in the state."

I stood there looking between two of the most important people in my life. "What just happened here?"

"Kolton promised me grandkids after you guys get settled and married." Carlos said, like it was nothing.

"And Carlos promised me the best tamales in the state." Kolton's stomach growled at that.

Rose chuckled, "You might want to have some overnighted, because I haven't had Maria's tamales in ages."

"I feel like my whole life just got planned out before me."

Kolton's eyes sparkled as he took my chin between two fingers, and slipped into Sir. Using that bedroom voice on me to say, "Is that a problem, Darlin'?"

My stomach tightened and my nipples instantly hardened at that tone. "Oh, for the Gods."

He bent down and kissed against my jaw before whispering in that same tone, "Is it?"

"No, Sir." I whispered. Even though I was totally being steamrolled here. I didn't hear anything I didn't agree with, just ... oh boy.

He pulled back, and then he was just Kolton again, "Good, because I don't want to have to give up tamales."

I huffed a chuckle and said, "They really are that good. I told you before, that you haven't lived until you had *mi abuela's* tamales."

"Now that we've got that all settled. Go. Rest." Carlos said, and Kolton took my hand and led me out of the room.

CHAPTER 43

KOLTON

"**I**'m not really tired since I've been resting for days." Jade said after we left the office.

"Ask Philip to get a couple horses ready. We'll go for a ride. Maybe look at a site for our new home."

"Where are you going?"

"Just upstairs quick. I forgot to grab something and I'll be right back. Need anything?" I asked kissing her quick before she shook her head, and I ran to the apartment.

I was just about to go inside when James caught me. "How's Jade doing?"

"A bit overwhelmed by all the new job duties that are being placed on her shoulders." He shifted a bit before leaning on the wall and picked at his fingers. "What's wrong?"

"Are you leaving the ranch?" His voice was careful.

"Are you looking for a promotion to Foreman?" I said it lightly, but also genuinely.

"I mean, I wouldn't say no, but I don't want you to leave. You are a great man to work for and with." He let a breath. "Look, here's the thing. You are the closest thing I have to a family anymore. You know my dad died six months ago, and he was all that I had left. You, Fernando, Philip, Ms. Rose, and now Ms. Jade... you are my family."

I smiled at him. "Well, it looks like your brother is sticking around for a long while, just to spite you."

His eyes shot up. "Really? The Agency isn't having you two move somewhere else?"

"Nope. In fact, they are setting us up pretty sweet. Building us a house on the north end of the property and everything. Jade is head of the werewolf pack and the Agency is setting up a training center on the Johnson property. She'll be overseeing that too."

"The Johnson property. I heard a rumor that there was an offer they couldn't refuse." He said looking off in that direction. "Wow."

"So, yes. You are stuck with me, James. No more bets about the hay loft, though, okay?"

"We all lost that. Who would have thought it would have been Fernando that ended up there!" He chuckled. "Well, I'll let you get back to it. Stables need to be turned over and it's my week."

He turned and strode off, a little bounce in his step. I watched as he made his way and couldn't help but smile. I turned the knob, went inside, and into my bedroom. My stomach flipped as I went to the closet and pulled down a banker box that had what I had kept of my parents belongings in it. I hadn't kept much, but when my fingers rubbed against the velvet box, I let out a shuddering breath.

"Mom. She's worthy. I promise you." I whispered, wrapping my fingers around the box, and sliding it into my pocket. Putting the banker box back on the shelf, I turned and stopped in the hall to look at the picture of my parents. I swore I saw my dad wink at me in the photo before I went down to meet up with Jade.

We opted for the truck over the horses, since Jade wanted to bring her equipment so she could look over the plans as we inspect different locations for our new home. I told her just to grab the tablet and we could tie a pack to the saddles, but she was insistent upon bringing everything. I couldn't refuse her.

Jade was standing near the ravine tapping away on her tablet, comparing something to the drawings spread out over the hood of the truck, already in full design mode. We had both looked at this spot and instantly knew that it would be the perfect place for our home. We were only half a mile from the pack territory line, an access road was easily put in without much fuss, and we would have a view of the river from the porch.

She was fascinating to watch, but when she bent over the hood of my truck again, I didn't hide the fact that I put my fist in my mouth. I saw her smirk, before she said, "Like what you see, Sir?"

Damn the way she called me sir, undid me. "Oh, very much, Darlin.'" I said looking from her boots, up those thighs, across that ass, up her waist, and finally to that face that had the most breathtaking smile I had ever seen in my life as she turned to fully face me.

"Where do you want the garage? On the entrance side to sit behind the property? Or off to the side or behind?" She asked, typing into the tablet and pulling out a pen to make some marks and adjust locations of things.

"Near the access road. I don't want to mess around too much during the winter with tracking things across the yard."

"I was thinking of putting the bedrooms on the second story, so we could have a deck to sit out and look over the river. At least for the main suite."

"Sounds good." I stood next to her, and ran my hand down her back and over her ass, giving it a squeeze. She bit that lip of hers and shit, I wanted to take her right then and there.

"How many bedrooms?" She played with the tablet pen a minute and said, "I don't want too big of a house, because we are both going to be too busy running businesses to clean. We will each need an office space on the first floor."

Her mind was going a million miles a minute. "Darling. Not every decision about the house needs to be made right here and now. Though I will ask that our office space not be in the house, so that when we are home, we are just Kolton and Jade. It will give us some separation from work."

"Good point." She started making notes, dragging and dropping boxes to quickly build out the space. I just watched her. "Any questions about what I'm doing here?"

My stomach burst into a flutter of nerves at that, because it was now or never.

"Only one." I said, bending down onto one knee, and opened the velvet box holding my parent's wedding rings in it. "Will you marry me Jade Cecilia Araceli Romero?"

She froze, and looked at me. Tears lined her eyes, and she blinked. One fell down her cheek as she said, "Yes."

"Oh, thank the Gods." I said, standing up and kissing her. When I stepped back, I pulled out my mother's wedding ring, minus the band and with a shaking hand slid it on Jade's finger. It fit perfectly. When I looked up at her she was crying freely now, and admiring the ring.

"When? How?" she asked, her eyes meeting mine.

"It's my mother's ring. The set was my parents. If you want something else, we can do it. I'll buy you whatever you want, but—"

"Shut up." She said and I looked at her in shock. "It's absolutely gorgeous. I'm honored to wear it."

I kissed her again and chuckled. "Astral Primal Alpha Jade Cecilia Araceli Romero Webster. That *is* a mouthful."

"I know names hold heritage, but Jade Webster is just fine with me." Then she smirked, and ran her hand down the length of me. "Mmm. Can I have my mouthful, Sir?"

I pushed her against the hood of the truck and just muttered, "Is that the only thing you want to be full today?"

She looked up through those lashes at me again and put her lip between her teeth.

"I love you, Jade."

"I love you, Kolton." Then with a smirk, she dropped to her knees before me.

THE END

Song Inspiration

KIMBERLY M. RINGER

THE ASHSTRIKE SANCTORUM

The Ashstrike Sanctorum
Creation Story

THE ASHSTRIKE SANCTORUM SERIES

The Ashstrike Sanctorum Series

The Astral's Bonded

The Exorci's Touch

Books Also By Kimberly M. Ringer

The Five Angels Trilogy

The Five Angels
The Ash'bani

The Helena Crystal

A Five Angels Novel

Duchess' Crown
Duchess' Throne

Other Books

Ashes and Flame

Weekend with Rylie

K imberly M. Ringer lives in Santa Cruz, California with her husband, little human, and two furballs, Wall-E (a Jack Russell mix) and Pippin (a Pomeranian Terrier mix). When she isn't writing, she is reading, playing with the dogs, playing video games or down at the beach. She's a bit geeky and nerdy, so sci-fi references and other things going on in the science world may end up in her stories.

Contact Kimberly M. Ringer:
   www.kimberlymringer.com
   Instagram: @kimberlymringer
   Facebook: https://www.facebook.com/kimberlymringer

Sign up for my newsletter and receive freebies, coupon codes, and stay up to date on all things

Kimberly M. Ringer and K.M. Ringer
Newsletter Signup

413